DARK SOLACE

The Promise Me Series, Book 9

By

Tara Fox Hall

Published by
Melange Books, LLC
White Bear Lake, MN 55110
www.melange-books.com

Cover Art by Caroline Andrus

Dark Solace
Tara Fox Hall

With Theo facing deadly odds in a fight to the death, Sar makes a pact with Lash, agreeing to give Devlin another chance in return for Theo's life. Reforging her relationship with her handsome vampiric lover mends old wounds, even as Theo moves to regain Sar just for himself. But Devlin's old enemy Ulysses appears, taking Sar prisoner and burning Devlin badly in a surprise attack. Rescued at the eleventh hour by Lash, Sar nurses Dev back to health, Theo bristling at a distance. Yet Lash's own day of reckoning is here as his long life ebbs to a finale, leaving Sar to face the decision of offering him salvation, knowing that the price is her own humanity.

Chapter One

On August thirty-first, the kettle that had been simmering for so long finally exploded.

I was spending the day with my werecougar son Devon at Danial's home, feeding and playing with him while Devon's father Theo and his faerie-demon colleague Terian were out on a job. Devon had already doubled in size since his birth, and his eyes had opened the day before. His ears were just beginning to stand up on their own. He was still drinking milk, though he also liked processed chicken.

It was so nice to sit here with him, and simply hold him. To feed him myself, to touch his tan spotted fur, to know he was mine. My body hadn't changed, so the milk I was feeding him had come from a cow and was dispensed via bottle. Both Theo and I had come to the conclusion the reason for my lack of breast milk was because I wasn't werecougar. I was less sure of that, though, wondering if all my exposure to the vampire virus in the past few years—particularly now having birthed two dhamphirs—might have made me unable to provide milk of my own. But really, here and now, it didn't matter if either was the truth. My child in my arms was the last baby I was ever going to have. I didn't want to miss a moment of it.

Holding Devon and sharing this happy moment with him brought more than its fair share of guilt, though. Devon's fraternal twin, my daughter Venus, was miles away at Hayden with her father, Devlin. I had barely seen her since her birth.

I assuaged my guilt with the knowledge that I had been told by my doctor that until my half vampire daughter came to see me as something other than food—a real enough danger with a dhamphir child—I was not to hold her or get within striking distance. Also, having seen the change in Devlin since he'd welcomed his child into the world, I had to give credit to Danial. He'd been right; Dev was going to take good care of her. I'd been wrong to think he wouldn't. I'd been wrong to think he wouldn't make a good father. Maybe I'd been wrong about him, too…

1

Stop right there, Sar. In that way lies madness, and a lot of pain. Leave it alone and remind yourself to ask Danial for a little sip of blood when he wakes up. Your longing for Dev is just an effect of the vampire virus in your system ebbing below needed levels.

Having a resistance to the vampire virus I'd been so much exposed to was a boon, as it meant I would have a much longer lifetime than a normal human, so long as I had regular infusions of vampire blood to keep me in a kind of "half-turned" state. A side effect of that was being in thrall to the donating vampire, if he gave me too much blood. That exact thing had happened last winter, when Devlin had saved my life with more than a little donating on his part. I'd fallen in love and lust, which had led to giving him an Oath, which I'd later regretted. He'd broken it, of course, just like he'd broken my heart.

Leave it alone. Focus on the positive; you're able to get blood from Danial now with no adverse effects.

Putting Dev out of my mind, I focused again on Devon, taking the bottle away from his grasping paws. "You can't eat anymore, piglet," I said affectionately, when he growled at me, extending his sharp claws to try to get the bottle one last time. "Your stomach is already round and hard. I don't want you to get sick. Go to sleep."

Devon yawned, then went to sleep, purring softly. I began to drift off, then was bluntly awakened by the front door slamming. Devon awoke immediately, and began crying. I comforted him, but stayed where I was, my arms wrapped protectively over him. If this was something bad, like an attack, I had to protect him. That meant staying where I was and keeping him quiet.

"Sar?" Theo called weakly. "Sar—"

I got up as quickly as I could, and went to the door carrying Devon. Theo was sitting on the stone bench in the mud room, swaying and holding onto the wall for support. He was hurt, covered in bruises and blood. It looked like it was all his own.

"Oh God, Theo!" I cried, going to his side. "Danial!"

Devon was screaming by this time, his claws digging into me. I held him close, trying to comfort him, not knowing what to do for Theo. He didn't seem to be healing up his injuries at all. What if he was mortally wounded?

Danial arrived, took one look at Theo and then put his arm around him. "Come on." He helped Theo into his bathroom, me following with Devon. I closed the door, then put the yowling baby werecougar down on the floor. Together Danial and I helped Theo strip off his clothes.

Danial removed his now-bloody bathrobe and handed it to me. "Sar, I'll help him wash off the blood and dirt. You get some alcohol and bandages ready, and a needle and thread. Cover the bed with an extra sheet and towels, and wait there. Some of these wounds are deep."

I did as Danial asked. Devon had calmed down some, so I laid him down gently on Danial's bed, and got moving. By the time Danial and Theo got out of the shower, I was ready.

Danial brought him out and laid him on the bed, beside Devon. I had put huge bath sheets down and they absorbed the water and some of the blood that was still leaking out of him."Why isn't he healing?" I asked worriedly.

"Probably poison-laced blades," Danial muttered. "Do you have the needle and thread?"

I had them ready, in my hands. "Right here."

"Sterilize them with the alcohol," Danial instructed. "Then sew up the wounds that are still bleeding. I'll hold him down if he wakes."

I did as he asked. I had never sewn flesh before. It was a lot like sewing leather— in a word, difficult. I had brought my newest sharpest needles. By the time I was done, they were all dull, and most of them were bent to hell. I tried to make neat stitches, doing the best I could, but the process took a long time. Theo woke up halfway through, but didn't struggle.

When I was done, I helped Danial bandage up all the wounds. Theo reached out with a grimace and held his son to him with one hand, grabbing hold of my hand with the other. "You were right to have us stay here," Theo said, tears in his eyes. "You were right, Danial."

"Never mind that," Danial said quickly. "What happened?"

"Terian and I were attacked. Just on the street, walking back to our car from the meeting. It was broad daylight. They got him in the heart at least four times."

"Is he—?" I cried.

"No, he's fine," Theo reassured. "They just wanted him out of the fighting, so they could focus on me. They were there for me." He paused, grimacing again. "When he collapsed, they overwhelmed me with numbers. There had to be at least fifteen of them."

"Who was it?" Danial said, his eyes red.

"Karl," Theo said. "And these weren't just weres. They were the Harvesters, Danial."

Danial looked apprehensive, while I was stymied. "Who are the Harvesters? It sounds like a bad rock group."

"They're a band of werehyenas and werejackals. A weretiger by the name of Satar leads them," Theo answered heavily. "I killed five of them before they brought me down."

"How did you get away?" I asked, nervously clutching his hand, as if he might disappear.

"Terian healed enough to teleport," Theo answered. "He got me here, and then went back there, to kill as many as he could—"

"I wasn't much help," Terian said, coming in the door. He was battered and bloody, his shirt with ragged gunshot holes all down the front. New unbroken skin showed through the many holes. "When I went back, they were gone."

"They'll try again," Danial said darkly. "They never give up, Theo. Not until the job is done. No matter how many people they lose."

"There's worse news," Terian said slowly. "Theo got a message on his cell right as we walked out. Robert has finally challenged him."

SHIT, could things get any worse? The day had been going so well. "When?"

"A week from now," Theo said, looking at Danial, and then at me. "One on one. I agreed to meet him. I can't back out now."

"You can't go through with it," I protested. "You're hurt."

"Robert knew you'd get attacked," Terian added. "He and Karl might be working together—"

"He's right," Danial interjected. "Terian will go with you to the fight to watch your back—"

"No," Theo said with a grunt, sitting up. "You can't interfere, none of you. I want to beat him fairly, so I can kill him and be done with this. If I have help doing it, someone else might think I needed the help, and decide I'm weak. I want this to be the last challenge for a long time."

How many other challenges had there been over the years? Ten? Fifty? A hundred? Theo had never mentioned any, but by his weary words, there had been many. *Why hadn't he told me?*

"It's your decision," Danial said seriously to Theo. "But you'd better rest up this week. You need to be in the best shape you can be. Robert is five years younger than you."

Theo nodded, then his eyes cut to me. "Sar, I want us to go home just for this week. Robert has assured me that there will be no attacks on me in that time. He wants to beat me too badly to lose his victory to someone else."

Danial opened his mouth to say something, then he closed it instead and just nodded.

I didn't trust myself to say anything, knowing the reason for Theo's sudden request. So I just nodded, too.

* * * *

That night I packed up clothes and enough food for a week, and Theo and I drove back to my house. At Danial's request, I had called Warren, and told him to come back to Danial's for the week. Though Warren was clearly curious as to why he was being recalled for guard duty when he had been given the next few days off, he just agreed.

Theo held my hand the whole way home, his eyes often glancing at Devon in the back seat, sleeping in his pet carrier.

I hadn't brought the dogs or the cats; I'd been too upset. I thought with sarcasm that we were lucky that I had remembered the house keys.

When we got there about eleven, we went straight to bed. Theo and I slept together, with Devon in the middle of us. There was only one thought in my mind that night, a thought I couldn't give voice to it: Theo thought there was a better than even chance Robert would kill him. He wanted this last week with me and Devon, to pack as much joy into his life as he could in case it ended.

* * * *

The week passed slowly. Theo and I spent much of that time just playing with Devon on the front lawn, watching him joyfully roll in the grass and chase insects. The weather was good now, every day sunny and warm. Not an hour went by that Theo didn't hug me, tell me he loved me, or kiss me. I was still recovering from my surgery, even with my accelerated healing, so we didn't do anything more. But it was enough for both of us that we were together with our baby.

I did make it a point to take long walks everyday with Theo—Devon strapped into a backpack—and to cut down on my food intake. I hadn't gained a lot of weight in my pregnancy this time, but feeling my muscles tone up put me in a positive mood. By the second to last day, I was able again to fit into my loosest pair of jeans. I was very glad to do that, even if I had to lie down on the bed and suck in my breath to get them to zip. But when I went in my pride and delight to show Theo my accomplishment, I stopped just inside the screen door, horrified at the words I was overhearing.

"You're going to be big and strong," Theo said to Devon proudly. "I hope you have a good life, Dev. I hope you can understand I love you, and that I didn't want to leave you. If I do this, you and your mom will be safe, no matter if I lose or win. But the truth is I'm hurt, and I'm probably not going to be fast enough—"

I retreated back inside, thinking frantically on what to do. *I had to do something. I* couldn't let him do this. Theo had a son. Devon needed his father. He was not growing up the way I had, with only a picture and some faint memories.

Danial wouldn't help. Neither would Terian; they were both too moral to try to sabotage Robert's challenge fight with Theo. Devlin wouldn't interfere, either; he still hated Theo. Hell, he was probably rooting for Robert to win. Titus wouldn't help, in spite of the fact he kept referring to me as his kin-daughter. That demon was far too moral, in spite of his darker tendencies. Besides, Dev would have to give permission, something that would not be

5

forthcoming. But there was one man who might help, if I could but find a way to bribe him: Lash.

I tried to teleport to Hayden over and over, willing my ability to have returned. But all my efforts did nothing but give me a headache. Finally I gave up, tears of frustration in my eyes. I'd have to drive. There was no other way. But first, I needed a cover, so Theo wouldn't suspect what I was up to and stop me.

I called Hayden immediately. When one of Devlin's werebear guards answered, I asked for Serena. She came on, a little sleepily. "Hello?"

"Serena," I said quickly. "It's Sar. I'm coming to see you now."

"What?" Serena stated, surprised. "Why—?"

"Just be ready," I instructed, and hung up.

I ran outside to see Theo, hoping that by now he'd stopped telling our son about his impending death. "Theo!" I said, not bothering to cover my upset. "Something's happened."

"What is it?" he asked anxiously.

You can do this, Sar. Now fucking do it. "Serena called. She asked me to come and see her. I think something's happened with one of the guys. I know she doesn't have any other friends—"

"Go and see her," Theo said easily. "I'll wait on dinner for you."

"It will mostly be the travel time," I said, not hiding my annoyance. *God, give me back my teleportation powers ANYTIME now, please...* "Three hours, maybe?"

"I'll just wait until you get back," Theo said permissively. "Don't worry how long it is. I know you haven't seen Venus this week." He snorted. "I'm not anxious to talk to Dev or Lash."

Good. "I'll see you later then." Giving him a quick kiss, I got in my truck, and drove to Hayden as fast as I could.

I got lost halfway, as it had been so long since I had driven there. I was also worried that Robert, or the Harvesters might try to hurt me enroute. But I had to risk it. I had a snake to wake.

When I finally got to Hayden, one of the bears let me through the gate. I parked by the side of the garage, not wanting to block anyone's door in case they needed to use their vehicle. My remote garage door opener still worked, to my relief. I walked in that way, then downstairs, trying to be both unseen and quiet. Titus was not in his lab, and neither was Lash. *Shit!*

I walked to the kitchen next, and breathed a sigh of relief. Serena was there. I hurried to her side. "Where is Lash?" I whispered.

"Why are you here—?" she asked curiously in her normal voice.

"Shh!" I grabbed her, and dragged her outside through the garage door, still in her robe. She came with me, watching me like she thought I'd lost it.

Finally, when we were far enough from the house, I asked her again where Lash was.

"Sar, why do you want to—?"

"Just tell me where he is!" I screamed.

"He's probably near the edge of the woods," she said slowly, watching me anxiously. "He spends most Saturday afternoons there, sunbathing on the large rock near the pond—"

"Thanks," I said, already turning and running across the field, swearing at the long grass that threatened to trip me.

"Sar!" she called after me, but I was already down the hill, heading fast towards the pond. But my desire was impeded by my need for air. By the time I got to the edge of the mowed part of the enormous front lawn, I'd slowed to a fast walk. My head was in constant motion, my gaze looking in all directions for Lash as I walked, yet I didn't see him.

*Maybe he was in snake form? If he was, I'd never see him in the tall grass, not until I stepped on him...*I stopped still, suddenly afraid. "Lash?" I called softly a few times, looking towards the woods. Dare I go in there looking for him? *What waited there for me, in the darkness of those trees?*

There was a rustling sound, then Lash came into view at the edge of the woods, snapping his coiled whip onto his belt as he walked in my direction through the tall grass. Relief flooded me, that I hadn't stumbled on him either in snake form or naked, as he'd likely been a few minutes before. Lash was looking down as he walked, watching the ground for some reason, and didn't see me.

I gathered my courage together, took a long breath, and then went to meet him. He heard me, his head snapping up after I'd gone a few steps. His face registered faint surprise, but didn't call out a welcome. When we were face to face, we both stopped.

"What are you out here for?" he hissed, folding his arms over his chest, his eyes and tone cold. "Dev and Venus are inside."

"Your help," I ventured. "If you'll give it to me, Lash—"

"No," he said curtly, then walked around me.

I reached out and grabbed a hold of his arm. "Wait—"

He shook me off, and kept walking.

"Please," I begged, hating the fact that I was pleading with him. "Please, Lash—"

"Sar, go home. Go to Danial. Go to Theo. Go anywhere, just leave," he hissed, still walking away

I ran after him. "I need your help, Lash."

"I won't give it to you," he hissed, still walking. "You can't afford me."

He was right about that. Being the best, he probably made 100K just to scare someone a little. I swallowed my pride, then my conscience. "I know that Lash. I'm not offering money; I'm offering you control over me. I'll do anything you ask me to."

Lash stopped, turning to look at me. Then he began walking back, eyeing me hungrily. "Anything?" he said, hissing. "Anything I ask you to do, you'll do?"

I hated him for making me crawl. "Yes," I said defiantly. "Anything."

"What do you want me to help you with?" he said, folding his arms across his chest. "My price depends on what you are asking me to do for you."

"Not me. I want you to help Theo. Robert asked him to come alone, that they would settle this one on one—"

"That's as it should be," Lash interrupted coldly. "I shouldn't interfere with a challenge."

"Don't interfere," I said. "But this wasn't done fairly. Theo is still weak from the beating he took from Karl's men. If Robert beats him, fine, just don't let him kill Theo. I don't trust that Robert won't just stab him in the back, or ambush him with more men, rather than fight him one on one—"

"Robert will kill him if he beats him, Sar," Lash hissed. "That's the way of challenges. I have always killed anyone who challenged me. You don't want them coming back for revenge later. So you're really asking me to kill Robert."

"I'm asking you to save Theo's life. Will you do it?" I pleaded desperately.

"Did you go to Dev, and he refuse your request?" Lash hissed scathingly. "I can't believe that, Sar. He still believes if something happens to Theo that you might die, too. He wouldn't refuse you, though he would make you—"

"I came to you," I said angrily. "Dev doesn't know I'm here. No one does, except Serena. Theo can't know about this—"

"You must be desperate to come to me like this," Lash hissed, his cold eyes glittering. "To put yourself in my power, knowing what I might ask of you. To trust me that I'll help you, if I say I will."

"You never hurt me. So far as I know, you haven't lied to me either. You kept our last times together a secret, just like I kept yours from everyone." I paused, meeting his cold stare. "I trust you, Lash. If you say you'll do this, I'll take you at your word, and give mine in return."

Lash looked at me, considering. "It should be doable," he hissed finally, his tone thoughtful. "Where is the location of the fight? When?"

"Tomorrow night. I'm not sure where. He's leaving around dusk—"

"I can follow Theo easily enough. I'll be waiting near your barn on a motorcycle. If you tag him with a transmitter, I can track him if he loses me. Can you put one in his vehicle?"

8

"Yes," I said without hesitation.

"I'll put it in your truck, before you go," Lash instructed. "Put it in his glove compartment within the truck manual case. He will not see it there, or think to check. Remove it after, and give it to me the next time you see me."

"Agreed." Now for the hard part. "What do you want in return?"

Lash came closer. "First kiss me, to seal our pact," he hissed.

Shit, he was going to ask me to be weresnake so he could coil with me. I shifted uneasily.

"I'm waiting," Lash hissed softly. "Unless you want to reconsider."

You can do this, Sar. You have to do it. If Theo is saved, that's all that matters.

I put my hands on Lash's arms, and slowly leaned in towards him. Lash reached up and grabbed my hair, pulling my lips forcefully to his. But the kiss was chaste, lasting only a few seconds before Lash pulled back from me. "I want you to take Dev back," he said softly.

Oh, God, no. I looked at him imploringly. "Why?"

"As much as I enjoyed you, Sar, I know you don't want to be with me now," Lash hissed bitterly. "There's no point in turning you, not when you're unwilling." He smiled crookedly. "But Dev and you still have a chance. He loves you the way I've never seen him love anyone—"

"He doesn't know the meaning of the word," I replied, more sad than bitter. "He thinks only of himself."

"I know him better than anyone else, even Danial, and I'm telling you, he loves you," Lash hissed angrily. "Give him another chance. Go to him, and tell him you forgive him. Tell him you love him, because I know you still do. Tell him you'll give him another Oath."

"How can you ask this of me?" I said angrily. "You know how I feel about what he did."

"You know how I feel about Theo," Lash replied coldly. "That didn't stop you asking me to save him."

"That's completely different!" I shouted. "Theo's decent, loving, and—"

Lash gave me a hard shove, knocking me sprawling on my behind. I looked up at him in fury from the dirt, though I wasn't bruised, except for my tattered pride.

"Stay down there," he hissed, looking down on me. "And listen."

I folded my arms across my chest, and glowered up at him.

"When I was thirty-seven, Devlin and I met. We were much alike, wanting to spend our nights partying with women, and hell-raising. After a year from hell, and some pretty bad business, we were the best of friends. But I'd been hurt bad, almost died. It took me a while to heal, even being weresnake. Devlin realized when he saw me hurt that bad that I was mortal, that if he didn't do

9

something, he was eventually going to lose me as he had all his other friends over the years."

"The potion," I supplied. "The one that extends your life."

Lash nodded. "He had Titus scour ancient texts, anything he knew of, trying to find some spell to lengthen my life. Finally he found the potion. It uses demon blood, Sar. Devlin buys some of Titus's every month, to use. It doesn't take much."

Demon blood seemed to be in everything that was transformative. But it was understandable, there was a lot of power in it. That was also likely why Lash's diet was similar to Titus's, consisting of only raw flesh and blood.

Lash crouched down, his eyes boring into mine. "It takes vampire blood too, Sar. A goodly amount. At first, Devlin just made new vampires, and took what he needed from them. It was part of the deal: he made them a vampire, and they gave him blood for a year, before leaving to live their new life. He did that for several decades, early on." Lash's tone intensified. "But when I was nearing sixty, it wasn't enough anymore. The potion began to fail. Titus said it was a problem with the vampire blood, that it didn't have enough power, as the vampires were new. I thought that was it for me then. But I'd had another few decades of relative youth, it was enough right? It was going to have to be."

Lash's tone was cutting now, sharp as a knife, heavy with emotion. "I was there when Titus told Devlin. And do you know what he did? Devlin just looked at me, and then he looked back at Titus, and told Titus to take as much blood as he needed, that he would give it to me himself from now on. However much Titus needed, to get the potion to work, to keep me alive."

I was speechless. I couldn't imagine Devlin caring that much about someone, to risk his own death, really risk it. He hadn't given Danial any of his blood in the centuries they'd lived, not one drop. He hadn't wanted to share his power, or make himself weak. But he'd put himself on the chopping block for Lash.

Lash saw my surprise and nodded. "The worst part was when Devlin was deposed as Ruler. Danial took almost all of his blood that night. Devlin was okay after, but he had none of his power. Neither did his blood. It almost killed him that first time, letting Titus take what he needed for me. The loss made him weaker than I'd ever seen him. He could barely move for days afterwards. But he said he would make it, that he wasn't done with life yet, and neither was I."

Of course. Lash has said he got the scar in Rio…it hadn't been any poison that had slowed his regeneration, but that Devlin's blood had lost much of his power…and Lash had suffered as a result, when the potion that was made from that weaker blood ceased to work. "But your scar still hasn't healed, even after Devlin regained his power at the Gathering—"

Lash talked over me. "Devlin recovered some of his power in time. But his blood was no longer strong enough to keep me healthy like I was. When I got this wound, and it didn't heal as it should, I knew that something was wrong."

Wait a minute. "Then Devlin was already planning to kill Ebediah," I said wearily. "For you. It had nothing to do with me at all. He did it in hopes his blood would become powerful enough to save you—"

"No," Lash said, hissing furiously. "Dev has no idea, not about any of this! Deposing Ebediah, and all of that was for you, Sarelle; to protect you! I went to Titus, and asked him what had happened, when the wound didn't heal. He told me that Devlin's blood wasn't powerful enough anymore. By the time Devlin got strong again, it didn't matter anyway. Years had passed since I'd had the stronger blood, and it was too late. My powers of regeneration will never come back. My life has been drawn out as long as it can be."

I sat there in the dust, and thought how awful everything was. I'd never dreamed that deposing Devlin all those years ago would have such long reaching affects. I'd doomed Lash by saving myself. Back then, I hadn't known Lash even existed. Even then, I might not have cared. But I did care about him now. He was dying now because of me. "I'm sorry."

"I never told him," Lash added sadly. "He would blame himself, and he's done enough for me. It isn't his fault that he can't make me live forever like him."

I looked up at Lash, then reached my hand up. He reached down, and hauled me to my feet. "Will you do it?" he hissed. "Or do you want to back out, Sar?"

I couldn't reconsider my path. But I could try one more time to get him to change his mind. "I can't open myself up to getting hurt, Lash," I said, tears in my eyes. "It was too painful the first time."

"I'm not asking you to turn a blind eye, or forgive him again and again," Lash hissed gently. "Give him another chance. One chance. If he fucks it up, it's on him. In fact, if he fucks up like he did before, I'm telling you now to leave him and never come back."

I was quiet, considering. "Just one chance?"

"One chance," Lash agreed. "Give Dev that, and I'll give you Theo's life. It's fair."

There wasn't another choice. And the hardest part would be explaining to Theo why I was going back to Dev. "I'll do it. Please make sure Theo doesn't see you there. I don't want to tell him until it's over—"

"You are not going to tell him at all," Lash hissed firmly. "I want Dev to think you came back to him of your own volition. I don't care what you tell Theo. Tell him you saw your child, and decided that you still loved Dev. Make something up, if you want to. But you are not to tell him the truth. And you are never, never, to breathe a word of this to Devlin."

Great, more secrets.

"That is non-negotiable," Lash hissed. "Agree to it, Sar, or walk away."

"I'll do it after you save Theo," I said softly. "I give you my word."

Lash nodded. "I know you, Sar. Your word is good enough for me."

We began to walk back towards Hayden.

"So what do I do?" I asked.

"Go home and collect yourself. Come back Saturday night, two nights from now. By then Theo will be safe, and you can concentrate on Devlin. He'll be back after ten—"

"I can't just show up unannounced," I said hopelessly. "I don't want to find any more party favors—"

"Sar, he's been with no one. You'll find him alone."

"Lash, I know Dev. He can't be alone for more than—"

"He's taken chemical help," Lash said, another crooked smile gracing his lips. "But be prepared for a marathon. It'll take a while to work out five months' worth of kinks."

"Why would he do that?" I asked in disbelief.

"Because I told him he was a loser and deserved to lose you, and that if he didn't do this, he would—"

"Why do you want me with him?" I said bluntly.

"Because he waited a long time to fall in love," Lash hissed, looking away from me. "He needs to pay attention and not fuck this up." He shot me a grin. "Besides, he needed to hear it. Dev was getting enough head from Hillary and Tiffany to get by. It was only for a couple months. I've gone longer than that, when I had to. And I'm were—"

"That's sufficient," I said quickly. "Thank you for telling me."

"I'll be there tomorrow," Lash said reassuringly. "You won't see me, but I'll call you after it's over to tell you Theo is safe."

"Okay," I said. "Be careful yourself, okay?"

"Go home," Lash said, smiling faintly. "I'm sure you have things to do. Theo is probably missing your company."

I stopped and turned to him. "Do you need some of my blood?"

Lash looked over at me. "I never turn down blood," he said casually. "But why are you offering?"

"I want you to fight your best," I answered. "Won't it help?"

Lash opened his arms, and held my eyes with his. "It won't hurt."

I went to him, and he put his arms around me, drawing me close. I smelled the scent of him—autumn leaves, musk, and earth. I felt his lips on my neck, and a moment later, his fangs sliding in. He just put them in deep enough to nick a vein, and began swallowing gently, holding me loosely. Lash took only a few swallows, and then drew his fangs out of me, pulling away.

I stopped him. "Was that enough?" I asked worriedly.

Lash kissed my wound gently. "You can't give me enough, Sar," he murmured. He stepped back, then handed me a tissue from his pocket.

I held it to my neck. At least I didn't have to worry about a wound. The bleeding would stop in a few moments. I'd probably be healed by the time I arrived home, thanks to the vampire virus levels in my blood.

Lash regarded me intently, and then he suddenly put his hand to my face, cupping my cheek gently. I looked at him in confusion. Lash dropped his hand from my face, turned from me, and walked away without looking back.

I waited until he had gotten inside Hayden, and then began treading slowly up to the house. Relieved the hardest part was over, I focused on the ton of other problems left to solve, the first being to borrow a shirt from Serena, and make sure I didn't smell like Lash.

When I went into the kitchen, Serena was there, waiting for me at the table. "Sar, what's going on?" she asked, eying me speculatively.

"Grab me a shirt, and let's go for a walk," I said tiredly, sitting down heavily in a chair.

"You can go upstairs and get one of your own," she replied kindly. "Dev and Titus are up in Canada, finishing up the last of Ebediah's affairs. Venus is sleeping, Robin is down in town, and the bears don't come over here now that Devlin's asked them to keep away from the baby. No one will hear you except Lash, who is upstairs. He must already know what this is about, since by your scent you found him."

I sagged with relief in the chair. I'd be dealing with Dev soon enough. "Thanks."

After I changed upstairs, I came back down to her. "Do I smell okay?"

She sniffed me, knowing what I was asking, then opened her robe and hugged me hard, briefly rubbing her naked body against my clothed one. "You smell like me now, Sar," she said with a smile, fastening her robe. "No snake smell. And you only smelled faintly of Lash anyway."

I went to the sink and washed my face and neck. "I'm not bleeding, am I?"

"Come on, Sarelle, tell me," Serena said, annoyed.

I couldn't tell her the truth. Lash was listening for sure. And while Lash might not harm Elle, he'd surely kill Serena to make sure Devlin never discovered our deal. "I'm thinking of seeing Dev again. Of coming here again, to stay like I used to. But I couldn't let Devlin find out until I was sure, Serena. And I was afraid of finding him with someone—"

"I understand," she said, nodding. "You should know that since you left, I have never seen him with a woman here. I can't say for when he's away, but—"

I had believed Lash. But it was good to hear it from her, too.

"—Devlin's not going to be traveling anymore," she finished. "He said he has to be here to take care of Venus. This should be the last week he's gone."

"Then all things being even, you should see me the night after tomorrow, probably," I said, giving her a smile. "Maybe we can do some gardening the next morning."

"I'd like that. I was afraid to come and see you after what happened with Cia."

"I'm sorry about that, too." Cia was still not talking to me after our words over Serena's coyote ancestry, but that was her problem.

"Never mind," Serena said, hugging me. "I'm just happy you are coming to stay again."

When I walked out, I expected to see Lash there giving me a knowing look. Instead the stairs were empty. But the tracking device was there waiting on my seat when I got into my truck. Before I went into the house, I planted it in Theo's vehicle, as Lash had instructed.

* * * *

That night over a takeout pizza by candlelight, Theo and I toasted one another. "To you and me and Devon," I said softly. "To us."

I tried not to overdo it, not wanting Theo to think that I thought he was going to die. That was a lot easier now I knew Lash would be there, watching his back.

"Sar?" Theo said reluctantly. "I need to talk about some things with you after dinner."

It had to be The Talk I Had Been Dreading. "Let's go in the living room."

After the remains of dinner had been cleaned up, we both went in on the couch, and sat down. Devon was lying on Theo's lap, purring softly. I was a bundle of nerves, my hand clenching my wine glass so hard I was surprised the stem didn't break.

"Sar, I might not come back," Theo began, reaching out and grabbing my free hand. "If I don't, I want you to go back to Danial."

I was so shocked, I swallowed some saliva, and began to cough. I got up quickly and got a drink of water, deliberately taking a while, my mind racing furiously.

Five minutes later, I sat back down. "What are you suggesting?" I asked.

"Sar, I've resigned myself to sharing you with him. I know he loves you. He'll take care of you, and Devon. For a long time, I was bitter and jealous that you went to him when I was gone. But that was selfish of me. If I was truly dead, you'd both be vulnerable. I don't want you to be alone here, trying to

14

tough it out by yourself out of some misguided sense of loyalty to me. You were happy with him, before." He looked away. "You could be again."

"You are coming back," I said firmly. "So it's easy for me to tell you that yes, I'll do that."

"If I'm coming back, I'll reach home by dawn," Theo said gruffly. "If I'm not here by then, pack a bag and go. If I'm badly injured, I'll look for you at Danial's—"

I nodded. "Okay."

"—and you should also Oath again to Devlin," Theo finished, forcing the words out. "As soon as possible."

A huge tension left me; now I had a clear way to approach Dev, Theo having given me permission. But this also seemed not only too easy, but also completely out of character for Theo. "Why now?"

"You told me once you loved Devlin, that you would never do anything to hurt him. And the truth is, Danial's not enough to keep you safe. Neither am I." He paused. "I can't say if Dev loves you. He was a jerk, to do what he did. But you are the mother of his only child. He'll protect you just for that. Once you tell him you want his protection, he'll give it to you."

"This is all rational, but you're reciting this like a movie scene," I replied. "Why? I know you don't want me to be with him again."

"Because Danial took me aside last week, and advised it," Theo growled. "Samuel has contacted him. Harriet had the baby, Sar. It was a month early and stillborn."

I closed my eyes, and sagged. Harriet had been the only other woman with blood that was kind of like mine: capable of the resistance to the virus necessary to carry a vampire's child to term. Coupled with a secret infusion of a potion with some of my blood made by Titus, Devlin had hoped to make her blood exactly like mine. But his plot hadn't worked...and now would soon be discovered. "Then they'll be coming for me to find out why."

Theo pulled me close. "Danial and Devlin are going in two weeks to meet with Samuel, Perseus, and Zane, to head them off." He paused. "Michael has expressed an interest now, too."

Theo's tone was hateful.

"They want Stephen's files on you. The bastards are going to keep trying until they succeed, or she dies—"

"Stop, please," I whispered. "I don't want to hear anymore. Please."

"Last time, I never said anything to you," Theo continued. "I didn't want to face that something might happen to me. So I stupidly thought that if I didn't talk to you about it, it wouldn't happen. I don't want you to go through what you did before." He paused. "There are documents in our safe, Sar, in an envelope marked with your name. Everything you need to access our money is in there. The account numbers, everything. Your signature and the documents will be enough, though you'll need to make sure you are signing the right names, to get to some of the stashed money."

"Okay," I whispered.

"I think that's everything," Theo concluded. "I told all of this to Danial like last time. He said he would take care of you, if anything happens tomorrow night—"

"Please," I said, putting my finger to his lips. "I understand. I'm grateful you told me this, Theo. But you are going to come back."

"Yes, I am," Theo said hugging me tightly. "Because I love you so much I'd crawl out of Hell to get to you, if I had to."

"You are not going to Hell," I said, kissing him. "You are coming to Heaven with me."

"Sar, I'm probably not going to Heaven," Theo said sadly. "I've killed too many people."

"Then wait for me, if you go first into death. Meet me by the river Styx, and I'll bribe the ferryman to take us to the same place, no matter if it's Hades or Heaven."

Theo stood up with me in his arms, and gave me a long loving look. "Come with me, you strange woman of mine. I'm ready for bed."

"Are you going to purr for me?" I said seductively, gently lifting Devon's limp sleeping form.

"Maybe later," Theo replied huskily, his arm trailing down my shoulder to lightly brush my breast. "But first you're going to purr for me."

Chapter Two

I awoke about eight, the first thought in my head that it was the day of the fight. Theo was still asleep, one arm thrown across me, his deep even breathing the only noise in the room. I kissed him softly, and got up. Devon was still asleep in his crate at the bottom of the bed.

"What time is it?" Theo asked groggily.

"About eight," I said, pulling on my blue velvet bathrobe. "Want breakfast, or you want to wait?"

"I need more sleep," Theo said seriously, rolling on his back. "This wild woman I met last night kept me up at all hours of the night—"

"I remember it was your idea," I said teasingly. "I said I was tired at one a.m., but you said—"

"I don't remember it that way," Theo said, grinning at me. "I remember—"

"Hush," I said sternly. "I'm going to go and feed Devon. But when he gets his nap late this afternoon, I'm coming back in here to refresh your memory."

"I'm looking forward to it," Theo said happily, stretching. "But first you can make me breakfast."

That day was perfect. We didn't do anything extraordinary, but we spent it together, doing things that mattered deeply to us. We had breakfast early, sharing some with Devon. Watching him gobble it down, I was tempted to tell Theo not to give him so much, but I said nothing. If Theo somehow didn't come back, I wanted him to have the memory. Devon would recover from an upset stomach.

Later, after breakfast we watched *V for Vendetta* and my favorite movie, the animated version of *The Hobbit*, with Devon sleeping on Theo's lap.

"Why do you like this, again?" Theo said curiously, as he sat through it with me.

"Because Bilbo was a hero," I answered. "He could have sat in his house and had a perfectly good life. He had a lot of chances to stay out of struggles or to run when the going got tough. He always chose instead to act, no matter what it cost him. He was the one who understood life best, because he didn't care about what people told him he had to do, or about what might happen to him. He did what he thought was right, even though he paid a heavy price for it. That's true bravery: to be afraid, to not want to do something, and to do it anyway, because it's the right thing to do."

"You get all that from watching this?" Theo said, giving me a disbelieving look. "The trilogy of movies made with real actors are much better, and go into a lot more detail."

"I've read the book many times," I replied. "The book is like the movies that were made later, and it's true, they're better. But I grew up with this. It inspires me."

"Then you feel about this like I feel about V," Theo said contentedly, giving me a kiss. "I never knew that." He kissed me again. "I'm glad I do now."

We spent our last hours in bed, just holding each other, Devon asleep in his crate. I told Theo I loved him many times. There were so many other things I wanted to say if this was the last time I saw him, but I couldn't say any of them, because I needed to be strong for him.

At nightfall, Theo dressed in dark clothes, loaded his gun, and strapped on his body armor.

I looked at him a little skeptically. "Will he have armor, too?"

"We'll probably take it off," Theo said, seeing my look. "Usually this type of fight is hand to hand, with no protection, just a knife, sword, or a whip."

I hugged him hard suddenly, and he hugged me back. "I won't be back before one, Sar. Don't start to worry until three at least. And if you don't want to wait alone, call Tears, and he'll wait here with you."

I couldn't do that. I had to wait for Lash to call my cell. Otherwise there would be a phone record Theo might someday see. "I'll be waiting with our son," I said, as confidently as I could. "Be careful."

Theo kissed me and left. I watched him back out and drive off, hoping the transmitter was working. Lash hadn't told me to flip any switches on it, not that there had been any obvious ones.

As I watched his tail lights fade, a lone headlight powered on in the gloom of my barn's long shadow. Then came the noisy growl of a Harley as a small dark figure astride a black motorcycle sped off into the night after Theo.

Lash was holding up his end. I'd better decide what to do about Devlin to hold up mine. But what to say when I showed up at Hayden tomorrow? Dev would be suspicious. It had been too long to just say I missed him, though that was true. I couldn't tell him I longed for him, that I hadn't been able to wait another day. It had to be something good. Devlin's ego would be crushed to hear his best friend had bribed me to take him back. He had to buy what I told

18

him completely. That would be easiest if I told him what he wanted to hear most. But was offering to take another Oath really what he wanted?

That line of reasoning brought me to the question that had bothered me for a while now: why had Devlin made me take an Oath that he had broken so casually? He'd gone to so much trouble to claim me as his own. Maybe it was the old reason of philandering men everywhere: he had simply thought he wasn't going to get caught.

To Hell with trying to plan, or write any kind of script to say. I'd just go tomorrow night and tell Dev I'd give him another chance. And that if he screwed up, it would be the last one.

* * * *

The hours passed by like years. I watched some movies, but couldn't keep my mind on them. I lay on the couch with Devon sleeping on my lap, dozing fitfully for minutes at a time. I'd wake, straining my ears, sure I'd heard a sound. But it was never Theo.

Finally, near one in the morning, my cell phone rang. I answered on the first ring. "Hello?"

"Theo's alive, Sar," Lash hissed.

I sank down to the couch, so relieved I let out a sob.

"He beat Robert, killed him," Lash continued. "It's over. He's taking his time now with the remains, making a mess to photograph before he incinerates it. That's good. He shouldn't be challenged again for a while."

"Thank you." I said, thinking Lash had made out like a bandit. "I'm glad you were watching—"

"I did more than watch," Lash hissed. "You were right to take our deal, Sar. Must be supernatural intuition from all that demon blood in your veins."

Ice water went down my spine. "What are you—?"

"There were others lying in wait at the old machining shop. Ten weres in all, all with full body armor, and automatic weapons. They were getting into position as Theo and Robert were stripping off their armor for their fight."

"The Harvesters?"

"Yes. Satar was there, leading them." Lash paused a half second. "It was hard killing them all quietly, but I don't think Theo noticed anything. I paid Titus to give me some of his blue fire, to take care of the remains. There are no bodies to find. Titus thought it was for another job I have coming, so he won't think anything of it."

So it was Lash who took care of Devlin's business, of at least some of the killing that needed doing. *Shudder.*

"Tasha's father had sent them," Lash continued. "I made Satar call Karl, made him tell Karl that he'd best forget his daughter, that she was dead. That it was me who killed her, not Theo. That if he was still looking for vengeance, he knew where to find me. And if he tried for me, I'd be coming back to Russia to kill him."

"You killed Tasha?" I whispered.

"Yes," Lash hissed back, his easy reply making me shiver. "It was business, Sar, just like it is sometimes for Theo. She was scared enough of me that she told me everything, without me even touching her. Her death was a quick one, quicker than she deserved, after all she had done." He paused. "My end's done now, Sar."

Not by a long shot. "What did you mean about going back to Russia to see Karl?" I asked sharply. "When were you there?"

Lash swore.

"Tell me, Lash. I gave you my word. I'll stick to it, so long as you tell me the truth."

"The truth is that Devlin sent me to look for Theo more than a year after he went missing. Danial asked me to from the first, but I refused. Devlin finally asked me to, when he saw how crazy not knowing was driving his brother. I never expected to find Theo. It had been so long since he had disappeared. But it took me only a month to follow his trail. I found him in Russia."

I couldn't speak, I was too furious.

"Sarelle, listen to me," Lash said in a dangerously soft tone. "Theo had already been bespelled. When I found him that night, he was in bed having sex with that girl. I heard him tell her he loved her, that he wanted to be with her always. When I called Devlin and reported everything to him, he told me to do nothing. To just come home, and leave Theo alone."

"Why?" I shouted, tears falling from my eyes. "How could you find him and not tell—?"

"Because I'd found Theo, and he wanted clearly not to be found," Lash answered. "There was a phone there beside the bed they were on. He could have used it to call you or Danial anytime. He didn't want to come back, or have anything to do with his old life. Devlin was worried about you. He thought that once you knew, you might be upset enough to lose your baby. You were pregnant then with Theoron. He couldn't even tell Danial, as Danial wouldn't be able to keep it from you. So it was better that no one knew, that everyone thought Theo was dead."

I rubbed my eyes. "Maybe you're right."

"Sar, Karl will not be bothering Theo again," Lash hissed. "Robert is also dead. Theo is as safe as he's going to be."

"What about the one that you made call Karl?"

"After he finished the call, I killed him," Lash hissed. "I wasn't going to leave Satar alive. He would have gotten some more weres and come back again, this time for me."

That was a relief. "Good," I whispered.

"Sar, I've kept my end of the bargain," Lash reiterated coldly. "Keep yours. I will be waiting for you at Hayden after dusk. Be there tomorrow."

"I'll be there," I said softly. "Thank you, for what you did."

Lash was quiet for a moment. "You're welcome." Then there was only a dial tone.

I hung up the phone, and got the towels ready. By Lash's description, Theo would be a mess.

Theo showed up at three. He called from outside the door and asked for the towels. When I let him in, he dropped his bloody clothes, and headed for the shower. I put his jeans, shirt, T-shirt, jacket, and underwear in a garbage bag with his shoes, then took the bundle out to the garage to have him burn it later with white fire.

After his shower, I sewed him up like before. The older wounds had mostly healed, but some of the stitches had ripped in his fight with Robert. I redid those, then saw to a few new nasty wounds, lamenting that I'd need a trip to the sewing store for new needles at the earliest opportunity.

"These will heal," he said as I sewed. "But they'll take a while. The bastard had were poison on his blade."

"Wasn't he were?" I asked, carefully sewing. "What if he cut himself on his blade by accident?"

"Werecoyote," Theo spat. "I gave him some poison, too, when I cut him. It's standard practice, Sar, in a challenge." He paused. "Robert was good, very good. He didn't make any stupid mistakes. It was close a few times."

As I applied bandages to the sewn places, Theo called Danial and left a message on his cell to say he was fine, and that we were coming back tomorrow.

"Don't you want to stay here?" I asked, surprised.

"Sar, the Harvesters are still out there," Theo answered, hanging up the phone. "I'm not going to take the chance that they might hurt you or Devon. We have to go back until I settle with them."

Since I couldn't say anything to the contrary, I nodded. "Sorry. I forgot."

"Come lie next to me?" Theo asked tenderly.

I lay down beside him, and hugged him, wondering if I should bring up Devlin.

"I love you. You make me so happy, Sar."

Probably not the time to mention Dev. "You make me happy, too. Your scent always comforts me—"

21

"What do you mean, my scent?" Theo said, pulling back and then grimacing as his fresh stitches tightened.

"I've never told you before that you smell of prairie grass, pine forest, and wide blue skies? I must have, in all our time together."

Theo gave me a peculiar smile. "You never said it, Sar. I would've remembered."

"Well, you do," I assured, snuggling into him. "And I like that. I liked it from the first time I smelled your jacket, that day after I first dreamed of you."

"I remembered how surprised I was, when I saw you had it in your bedroom," Theo said tenderly. "I remember wishing I had something of yours to smell when I thought of you."

"How do I smell to you?" I asked hesitantly.

"You smell good," Theo said, inhaling deeply. "You smell of femaleness, warmth, and softness."

"All females must smell like that," I said, rolling my eyes.

"But your scent carries something extra," Theo said. "Something like sunlight, and green things, maybe. I can't give it words. But when I smell you, I think of how good the sun feels on me when I'm walking outside on a summer day."

Danial and Devlin had always said I tasted of summer. Maybe that was why. Or maybe I smelled of summer because whatever was in my blood had that odd aspect. "Interesting to know."

"I love your scent," Theo continued. "It was hard to get used to the bit of vampire smell that's mixed in now, but I don't notice it anymore, really—"

"How do vampires smell?" I asked. "You make it sound like its bad. But they don't smell bad to me."

"Not bad, really," Theo said, backpedaling. "A little like fall, like damp earth—"

Something sounded familiar. *What?*

"—and blood, usually. Almost always, vampires smell of blood."

I didn't remember anyone smelling like blood lately. Maybe it was nothing. I kissed Theo and held him close. "Get some rest. There will be time enough tomorrow for talking."

* * * *

The next afternoon, after we had returned to Danial's, I reluctantly told Theo that I had decided to go to Devlin that night to ask for his protection. Even with what he had said to me the previous night, Theo immediately got upset.

"Why tonight?" he protested, flopping down on Danial's couch. "I know you don't really want to go. I can smell it on you, like you're fighting with yourself."

He was right. I'd have to fix that before seeing Devlin, unless I wanted to blow my deal with Lash to hell. "Because you were right last night; we need him. And I've put it off long enough."

"I don't want you to go back to him," Theo said, drawing me down into his lap. "It's been great sleeping with you every night, and not having you leave every week." He paused. "But I get that you have to. You need to be there for Venus, too."

I wanted to squirm, I was so guilty. I had to get out of here now before Danial came out from his bedroom to join our discussion. My great vampire detective/lover wouldn't be put off by a few well-told lies. "I'll be back as soon as I can—"

"Just call, if it's going to be more than overnight," Theo interrupted, picking Devon up and hugging him. "We'll worry, otherwise. Won't we?"

Calling out an affirmation, I transferred a few necessary overnight items into a bag. When I loaded it into one of Danial's SUV's, I also pocketed the transmitter from Theo's glove compartment. I'd give it back to Lash that night.

* * * *

I left early, stopping off at my old house first. Warren hadn't come back yet, but he was due any time.

I quickly went inside and got my invisible box. It no longer contained Dev's choker, only his poetry. *Did Devlin still have the choker I'd thrown at him the night I discovered he and Catherine? I'd find out shortly.*

I read the poetry quickly, hoping to feel some loving spark kindle for Devlin. But the words just sounded false to me, and I wondered how I could have ever believed them.

I'd have to get Dev to give me his blood. Once he did, I'd be in thrall to him again. If I couldn't get out of this, it was better to get it over with.

* * * *

I arrived at Hayden around three in the afternoon. Lash answered the gate intercom, and let me inside. He was waiting in the garage when I drove my truck in and parked.

I got out, and handed him the transmitter. "Do you need to search me?"

He put it in his own truck, and then faced me. "I'd say yes even if I trusted you," he hissed, baring one fang. "And I do. Assume the position."

He searched me, then my bag. "Follow me to Titus."

23

When we reached Titus in his basement lab, he turned to leave. "Wait for me," I called.

Lash stopped, turning to look at me curiously.

Titus raised his eyebrows. "She's clean," he rumbled, then cast baleful eyes to Lash. "Watch yourself, snake."

Lash hissed at him, baring fang, then started walking. "Mind your own shit. Move, Sar."

What was that about? I gave Titus a smile, then hurried after Lash.

He was waiting in the kitchen. "What do you want with me?" he hissed, leaning back against the counter. "I have things to do."

"Serena's not here, is she?" I asked. "And neither is Dev?"

"Serena's out shopping. Robin and she go every week, and have lunch in town. They are getting to be good friends."

Was I supposed to feel jealous that she had another friend besides me now? Jerk. "And Dev?"

"Dev is with Venus. Titus is heading back there shortly. He'll be home about eight or nine."

I had known I'd have hours to kill. Just not this many. "That's six hours."

"I told you not to come until dusk," Lash hissed. "You'll have to amuse yourself, I'm afraid."

"So you're just going to let me wander around by myself?" I said, folding my arms. "You've never done that before."

"You always liked to work," Lash said, tilting his head. "Your filing downstairs is just as you left it. Dev said over and over in the last few months that you would come back and finish it. Now might be a time to get started. You're safe enough down there. You don't need me."

Crazy as it sounded, I didn't want to be alone with my thoughts. I wanted to have someone to talk to. I was dreading dealing with Devlin. But at least filing would occupy me. "I'll go work on it," I answered, defeated. "You're right, there is still a lot to do—"

"Do you want to see the gardens, before you do?" Lash hissed suddenly. "You still do owe me a walk."

"That would be nice," I said with relief. "Lead the way."

The gardens were beautiful. Lash had taken my suggestions, all of them. Being so late in the summer, most of the flowers were up and blooming, though the early ones like the tulips and pansies had faded. But I'd chosen carefully to ensure there would be some flowers blooming all summer. The white and red roses were still going strong. I picked one, and stuck it in the coil of my hair, its long thorns helping to anchor it. I also picked some flocks and bee balm for the kitchen table.

"Do you like everything?" Lash hissed hesitantly. "Your notes were easy enough to follow."

"They're beautiful," I said earnestly. "You did a good job."

Lash didn't reply.

As we walked back to the house, I noticed six large trees down near the forest edge, along with many smaller ones. Some had fallen over a ditch, and broken a small stone bridge that crossed it, sending some of the stones into the depression. While two of the trees had been down some time, the other four looked new, their visible inner bark a bright orange brown color.

"What happened?" I asked. "Attack?"

"Storm," Lash hissed. "Back two weeks ago, we had close to tornado-force winds." He pointed. "See there? The side of the house is damaged also, though not badly. We are going to have to erect scaffolding out here to fix it."

"You need a spider," I said knowledgeably.

Lash gave me a strange look. "Titus could probably make a regular one huge, but I don't think—"

"I'm talking about a type of one man support," I said, trying not to laugh. "It's called a spider. You lower down a guy, and he works on the wall. It's better than a traditional scaffold, because you can lower it and raise it easily. It mounts to the roof, so it would be easy to put one up. It would save you a lot of time."

Lash stopped walking, considering me with tilted head. "How is it you know about this?" he hissed.

"I worked construction before I met Danial and retired into luxury," I teased. "I wasn't always just a pretty face."

"That may be, but you aren't physically strong enough," Lash hissed, looking me over. "Construction is a man's job. Why would anyone hire you?"

That irked me. "I didn't build anything," I said defensively. "I checked sites for violations sometimes. To do that, I had to know some of the terminology, and what was best to use for different jobs."

Lash looked at me, incredulous. "You're pulling my tail."

Now I was pissed off. "It was just an idea," I replied, then turned to go. "But don't take my advice, jerk. Go figure it out for yourself—"

Lash reached out and grabbed my arm. "Do you have pictures of this, so I can see what you're talking about?"

"No, but I could find you some on the Internet," I offered frostily. "If you are nice."

"I'm always nice," Lash hissed, grinning. "At least to you."

I didn't think so, but kept that to myself. "I'll find you some when I go inside. There must be another computer at Hayden besides Dev's laptop, right?"

Lash nodded. "Devlin has another one in his study. I'll take you there."

I hadn't even known Devlin had a study. "Okay."

Lash led me down to the basement. Only this time, instead of turning left, he turned right towards the dungeon side. The first door in that hall was huge, made of oak. He opened it. "After you."

I walked in, looking around. Devlin's study was larger than I expected. The walls were all bookshelves to the ceiling. It was surprising to know he read this much. As expected, one huge section was all poetry. The others were varied, from Samurai Tactics, U.S. military strategy, and Torture Practices of the Sudan to How to Make Friends and Influence People, 101 days of Sodom, and Justine.

"The computer is there," Lash said quietly, breaking my thoughts.

I turned it on, and booted it up. Soon, I was printing him out pictures of the scaffolding I had described to him.

"This might save us a lot of time," Lash hissed, studying the sheets. "I'll see if I can't rent one of these instead of building wooden scaffolding. It's a waste of lumber."

"You talk like you've worked construction, too," I said, looking over at him curiously.

"Like you, I wasn't always what I am now," Lash replied. "I did construction in my youth." He cracked a smile. "But unlike you, I did build things."

An ideal job if you were a snake in Florida. Lash would have been out in the sun all day, and he was certainly strong enough. "I'm glad to help out," I said, flicking off the computer. "If you need help with those trees, I can bring my chainsaw. One more blade cutting can make a huge difference."

Lash looked at me like I had to be joking. It was also obvious that he didn't think I would be much benefit. "If you want to help, we are doing it this coming Friday. It's supposed to be clear that day. The equipment is being delivered the day before."

"I'll come," I affirmed, standing up. "But now I'd better start on my filing." Heading into the records room, I began looking through the last non-white box.

Lash leaned against the door and watched me. It had been a while since he had done that, but it was familiar enough that I didn't worry about it. I was surprised, though, after his admission that watching me wasn't necessary.

When I finished the last box, I thought about starting on the white boxes, but couldn't bring myself to do it. Instead I leaned on the open drawer, running my fingers aimlessly down the files I'd marked. I didn't want to file anything else. I wanted to go curl up somewhere. I really, really didn't want to face Devlin.

There was a furtive movement behind me. I turned around fast, startled to find myself looking straight into Lash's flat eyes. To my surprise, he wasn't as tall as Danial, or Devlin, or even Theo; he was just over my own height. I'd never noticed that before.

"Sar, come have dinner," Lash offered, something close to affection in his tone. "Devlin will be home soon, and you should eat something. He will not be letting you leave the bed, once you say you want him back."

"I thought you wanted me to work," I said shortly, trying not to shudder at his words. "I thought—"

Lash reached out and hugged me, making me freeze. "You don't have to eat with me," he hissed hesitantly. "But you should eat something. Your body is still recovering from giving life."

I smelled his scent again, autumn leaves, leather, and musk. And earth, under them all. "Want to take me for sushi?" I said softly. "I haven't been, since that day with you."

"Sure," Lash hissed. He made to withdraw from me, but I held onto him.

He stopped pulling away. "What is it?" he hissed, shifting uncomfortably.

"Do you know what Annabelle looked like? I was curious."

Lash eased out of my embrace. "Come with me," he said, taking my hand. He led me back to Devlin's study, past the bookshelves to a small recessed alcove in the far wall. There hung a large portrait done in oil, illuminated with a soft spotlight. "That is Dev's Anna," he hissed. "The only portrait he keeps out. The rest are hidden away in his vault. He goes there sometimes to remember her, but he's stopped doing that so much since he met you."

I'd imagined Anna a goddess. Instead, I was surprised to see she had not been traditionally beautiful. Her hair was mousy brown, and fell around her shoulders in corkscrew curls. Her eyes were also brown, a tad small, though they shone with happiness. Her face was round, more than a little plump, which made her look friendly and comforting. Her lips were a dark pink, like mine, and not generous. At her throat was a gold choker with a small golden bear with red eyes.

"I can tell by your expression that you expected her to be prettier," Lash hissed. "Devlin speaks of her as if she was the most beautiful woman he ever saw, save you. She wasn't pretty, not by traditional human standards, at least. But he loved her, loved her more than all of the other prettier women that he might have had. The way he loves you, Sar. Though you are beautiful, without a doubt."

I didn't know what to say. Lash seemed to sense that. "Let's go," he hissed. "Or there'll be no time for sushi."

We didn't talk much as we drove to the restaurant. I was thinking a lot about Annabelle; about what her life with Dev could have been like. But once we arrived, Lash ordered us a large platter to share, accompanied by a serving for each of us of alcohol. As we were sipping, he casually mentioned that he had gotten the newest *South Park* DVD. Soon, we were lost in conversation like old friends. Which, in a way, we were.

＊ ＊ ＊ ＊

When we got back to Hayden, it was close to eight. "Go up and wait for him," Lash hissed at the stairs. "And you should change your clothes."

Good idea. I didn't want to smell like Lash for Dev, even if the hug had been innocent. "Goodnight."

"I'll see you tomorrow," Lash hissed, heading into the kitchen.

Was he hungry for dessert, or for another type of flesh? *Don't think about it...*

"Sar," Titus said in surprise, emerging from the cellar. He hugged me. "Hi."

Titus wrinkled his nose, and drew back from me. "You smell of Lash."

"I know. I'm changing my clothes," I said, irritated.

"Come below with me first," Titus rumbled, his eyes red. "I have something to discuss with you."

Sigh. I followed him downstairs to the basement. "What's up?"

Titus spoke some words. "No one can overhear us now."

"What is it?" I asked, concerned. "Is something the matter with Terian?"

"You tell me," Titus rumbled. "You asked me a while back about him, and I told you I thought he was the same. But now I'm beginning to wonder."

"I think the work that he and Theo does is affecting him," I said, after a pause. "He's more powerful, too. And he's in love. That together explains his new bold behavior."

"He's been asking about some darker spells," Titus rumbled, his eyes holding mine. "Spells that he would have shrank from when I first met him months ago."

I was tempted to tell him it was his own black influence on Terian that had done this, but I wasn't 100% sure of that. I didn't want to make Titus feel bad unless it was the truth.

"Sar, do you know why he would want to do darker magic?"

"I can only guess to protect the children or to protect Sundown. Terian was never about power for power's sake, Titus."

Titus nodded. "I agree. I just wanted to ask. You are close to him."

I wasn't really, not anymore, but I didn't say that.

"I needed to know if he was changing. Sometimes in half breeds, the demon side can overwhelm—"

"Titus, why are you telling me this?" I said suddenly. "What do you want from me?"

"I want you to watch him," Titus said sternly. "When you visit Danial, make it a point to see him. He hasn't been visiting me here much lately, and I want to know if he needs help. I can help him keep the demon part of him under control, if or when it comes to that. But it's easier to help when you catch it early."

I couldn't deal with this on top of everything else. Plus the very idea of Terian turning evil seemed like something out of a comic book. So I just nodded. "Okay."

"Thank you." Titus moved to get up. "I appreciate it."

"Titus, why do vampires smell like earth?" I asked, following him up the stairs. "They don't sleep in a coffin, or need any native soil that I know of near them."

"The legend of the earth likely came from the smell," Titus replied, his attempted chuckle more of a bass booming sound. "Or from some fanged idiot who forgot what time it was and tried to bury himself to escape the sun." He shrugged. "That does work, if the hole's deep enough."

"But why that particular smell?" I persisted.

"Most likely, the scent isn't earth at all, just some chemical mixture the human brain recognizes as earthy. I can't comment, really; vampires always smell like blood to me. I don't smell anything earthy about them, although I've heard others say that was true—"

It hit me suddenly who had smelled of earth: Lash. "It must be from Devlin's blood in the potion," I said aloud.

"What?" Titus rumbled, turning to look at me.

"Lash smells like a vampire. That earthy smell is stronger on him than it is on Danial or Dev. The Lust probably activated with him because it recognized him wrongly as a vampire instead of a weresnake."

Titus nodded thoughtfully. "You're probably right. He's been on that potion for years."

"He said it caused him pain." I bit my lip, pondering. "Why does my blood take away Lash's pain?"

"I'm not sure," Titus answered, gazing at me unblinking. "I would guess that whatever gives you the power to give a vampire child life resides in your blood. It always comes back to the blood, Sarelle. And yours is a mixture of half-demon, and powerful vampire, similar to the most important parts of the potion. Add to that your own mysterious 'summer blood' and your plasma is probably more powerful than the potion Lash takes now, even with Devlin's newfound power."

"Would it help him live longer?" I asked bluntly.

Titus pulled me into the garage, and again murmured the incantation to conceal our words.

"Lash told me about your blood," Titus rumbled as he finished. "When I told him not to take any of it, he told me you gave him permission—"

I nodded. "Yes."

"—then he told me to fuck off."

"Sounds like him," I said, smirking. "I offered him some, but he said no."

"Sar, beware of Lash," Titus cautioned. "His only loyalty is to Devlin. He cares about no one else."

My hackles went up. "You're talking about a friend."

"He's not your friend," Titus rumbled, his red eyes glowing. "And your blood might have enough power to curb his decline—"

I took a sharp intake of breath. "Then I have to tell him, make him agree to—"

"No," Titus growled. "Lash drained Tasha the night he killed her. He'd do it to you."

I got up abruptly. "Did you tell him this? You didn't, did you?"

"Of course not!" Titus retorted. "I told him he had lived as long as he was going to. And he accepted it. He has time left, though not much, respectively."

"Then I'm going to tell him." I moved to go. "Now."

Titus blocked me, heat washing over me like a bonfire. "Sar, don't tell him."

"Titus, Lash never asked for my blood. He only took it when I made him—"

And that last time, which didn't count, not really.

"—when I offered it to him to stop his pain, he refused. He's not going to hurt me."

"You tell him you can save his life, Sar, and he won't refuse," Titus rumbled. "You remember this: if you throw a drowning man a rope, sometimes you get pulled down with him."

I shot him an angry look, and then went upstairs in search of Lash. But he didn't answer his door when I knocked. Stymied, I reluctantly entered Dev's room.

The crib was missing. Worried, I checked the nursery, but there was no one there either, though the crib there was in its normal place, the covers turned down expectantly.

"Serena had said Dev and Venus were both gone yesterday," I muttered, turning off the light. "You're an idiot for panicking."

After using Devlin's shower, I got some of my clothes from Devlin's dresser, and put them on. Waiting in bed naked or even in a nightgown was too awkward after all this time.

I sat down on the bed edge and waited. Nine minutes after nine, the door opened, and Devlin came in.

Chapter Three

Devlin saw me there waiting for him and froze. My eyes traveled to his hand, still resting on the door handle. The multicolored gold band gleamed on his ring finger. We said nothing for some moments.

"Tell me you're really here," he said finally. "That I'm not dreaming this."

"I'm here," I said softly. "Was Venus with you?"

Dev nodded. "Serena is feeding her." He came closer hesitantly.

I enfolded him in my arms. He let out a soft sigh of contentment. I was immediately overcome; memories of shared passion singing through my veins, the heady aroma of his sweet scent stirring my heart.

"I've really missed you, Love," he said finally, rubbing his scratchy cheek against mine.

"I missed you, too," I admitted. "Come, sit down."

He sat on the end of the bed, beside me, then took my hand in his. "Have you come back to me?" he whispered hopefully.

What could I say? Yes, but only under duress? I'd better phrase my words carefully. "Dev, I'm here to give you a second chance. But things need to be different between us, if I do that."

He was silent, waiting.

"I understand you haven't been with anyone else—"

"How do you know that?" Devlin asked suddenly.

"Lash told me tonight, while I was waiting for you," I answered. "He said you had chemical help."

"Yes," he affirmed. "It was misery at first, but I got used to it. The drugs Titus brews even out my moods and desires, though it's still not—"

"You didn't have to do that. We were over."

"We weren't over, Sar!" Devlin said forcefully. "We were just taking a break from one another. It mattered that I show you I'd changed, that I wouldn't make the same mistake twice."

I didn't reply, averting my eyes.

"You don't believe me?" He took his hand off mine. "If you don't believe I've changed, then why are you here?" he said, looking at me searchingly.

He was suspicious. *Shit. Think fast, Sar.* "Because I missed you."

"That's not it," he said, getting to his feet. He turned to face me, golden eyes flashing. "Don't lie to me, Sarelle."

Shit! Quick, say something, anything! "Because we have a child together, even if just saying that is still a shock to me," I said, gaining surety with each word. "My father died when I was very young. I never got to know him. Theo missed out on some of Elle's formative years, when he was gone missing. I don't want that to happen with me and our daughter."

Devlin sat back down beside me, and took my right hand in both of his, caressing delicately.

"I'm here because our child should be able to have her mother and father spend time together, and not be reticent, or fighting, or not speaking." I squeezed his hand. "And because regardless of everything that's happened, I meant it when I said I loved you."

Devlin said two words, but they weren't the ones I expected to hear. "Not enough."

I looked at him in confusion. "What?"

"I was jealous, Sar. I had hoped that once I had Oathed you, and I'd gotten the other Rulers to back off, you would want to come and live with me."

Surprise showed on my face before I could mask it.

"I see your surprise. That hurts me. You have spent all this time with me, and you still act as though I only see you as some piece of ass."

Whoa. "Hey, I never said that—"

"But you thought it," Devlin retorted. "That first day with you, when I told you I loved you, you looked the same. Then months later, when we were at your house, when I told you I wanted a life with you, you looked the same again. Surprised, but not delighted. More wary, and ready to distance yourself from me the moment you could."

"Dev, it wasn't like that—"

"It is like that, Sar! It hurts me to say it out loud, but I might as well. I've got nothing left to lose." He paused. "I hoped that when we came back from the Gathering, you and I could start a new life. I understood you better then, from spending that week with you. I knew that you didn't want to leave your pets and your children, and I understood why you felt you couldn't come to me in Rio, though you wanted to. Things were falling into place almost like magic. Theo was leaving you. We were Oathed. You'd agreed to have my child."

My life had been falling apart back then. I'd never thought about Dev's perspective.

"Then suddenly, Theo loved you again. Worse, you loved him back. I knew then that you loved him far more than you loved me, that you weren't going to come and live with me here. That I'd been deluding myself thinking that you ever would."

"Devlin—"

"When I found out it was his child, I was enraged. I wanted to kill him, and just take you. But I told myself to be patient, that I could wait for you to come to me. Time would pass, and eventually, I'd only have to share you with Danial."

Once Theo died, that would be true. I looked away from him.

"I hoped in time you would reconsider living with me. Time is one thing I have plenty of."

"We both do now," I replied carefully.

"But I saw over the following months that most of what you felt for me was just because of the blood I had given you, the attraction any turn feels for their sire. I gave you a lot of my blood when I saved you. More than I had ever given anyone before, even Anna. It influenced you, made you desire me. I thought that you really loved me, as I wanted you to. But it became obvious— as more time passed and you had less of my blood in your system—that you didn't want me the way you had before. That you didn't love me, as you said you did. You loved Theo and Danial, but not me." There was utter despair in Devlin's tone now, sorrow enough to drown in. "My jealousy ate at me. Your being with Lash didn't help."

I whipped my head around to give him an angry look. "You told me what happened was okay with you."

"I know I said that," Devlin said heavily. "I trusted him with you because I knew he was loyal to me. But you tested that loyalty sorely. I can see how he looks at you now."

Remembering Lash's last look at me, I flushed. "Dev, stop—"

"You know he still hasn't been with anyone else."

I had to get the conversation off Lash. "Dev, leave him out of this. What he and I did is done and over. We need to talk about us, not The Lust, or old lovers—"

"But I am just an old lover, aren't I?" Devlin said bitterly. "Months ago, you came here after you had fought with Theo. You never even called me to tell me you were here. Why, Sar? I'll tell you why. Because you didn't want to be with me. You just needed somewhere to go to not be with him."

"You're my former Oathed One!" I shouted. "Stop making yourself out to be the victim, when it was you who broke our Oath! If all you are is an old lover of mine, that isn't my fault, it's yours!"

Devlin tilted his head up, then looked down at me. "Do you know how many women have told me they loved me? That they wanted nothing more than to spend the rest of their lives with me? Not counting the ones I had sex with, even?"

I took in his handsome face, his beautiful eyes, his sculpted body under his tight clothes. He was probably the most sexy and attractive man I'd ever known. The women who'd been attracted to him in his long life, who'd wanted him for their own, were probably every woman he'd ever met. "Probably a lot," I answered.

"I've only told you and Anna that I loved you, outside of quoting poetry and songs, of course—"

"Of course," I echoed sarcastically.

"I've only ever wanted her and you, Sar. I've never asked anyone else to Oath to me."

God, I wanted to believe him, wanted it to be true, because that made me feel like I was important, to matter so much to him. But the truth was I was not on his level.

"How can you look at me like that, when I'm trying to tell you how I feel?" Dev said, tears again forming in his eyes. "Like I can't mean a word of it."

"Because I want so badly to believe you," I replied morosely. "I wanted you to love me, to want me, from the moment I first saw you. That's why I asked you for that fantasy back last fall—"

"I told you the truth! None of it was lies, Sar!"

"I wanted so badly to mean something to you."

"I'm telling you that you do! I've been telling you now for almost a year! Why won't you believe me?"

I put out my hand, and touched the silk coverlet gently. "I didn't want to let down my guard. I was afraid of you breaking my heart if I let myself trust that you loved me." I swallowed hard, tears forming in my eyes. "I finally did though. When I came to you that night, I just wanted you to feel the baby kick—"

"Sar, I'm so sorry—"

"—and when I saw you...with her, it was just as crushing as I'd imagined. I called myself an idiot then, for knowing you were going to break my heart and letting myself love you anyway."

"I have called myself worse in these months we've been apart for doing that to you. I could give you my reasons, but they were selfish reasons, and there is no excuse—"

"Stop talking about it," I said softly, brushing my tears away. "I don't know if I can forget or forgive you for that, Devlin. But if you tell me you won't see her ever again, that can be a beginning."

"I've not spoken to or seen her since that night," he said, coming to sit again by my side. "And I won't, Love. That's a promise."

"But you're right about something." I took a deep breath, steeling myself for what I needed to say. "You asked me once if I was afraid because I wasn't enough of a woman to hold on to your love. Do you remember that?"

Anguish replaced Devlin's hopeful expression. "Sar, please—"

"Do you?" I said sharply.

"Yes, of course. I'm so sorry—"

"I was afraid," I said, wiping more tears out of my eyes. "I have always been afraid of that. I never thought Theo or Danial would grow bored with me, or that I wouldn't be enough for them." I took a deep, deep breath, and let it out. "But I doubted myself with you. I told myself repeatedly not to get too attached to you, because you weren't going to be interested in me for long. Because I know in my heart that I'm not enough to hold onto someone like you—"

Devlin laughed quietly.

I shot him an angry look. "Why are you laughing?"

"Because I was afraid that I was not enough for you," he said bitterly. "Not good enough, not kind enough, not loving enough, not decent enough." He brought my hand to his lips. "Perhaps we were both wrong."

"You're a king among men and vampires," I said in exasperation, pulling my hand out of his grasp "You're a dream come to life, Devlin."

Devlin grasped my hand and yanked me forward into his arms. "That is where you're wrong, Sarelle. I am not God, or a king, or even a dream. I'm just a man who wants to be loved." He touched his lips to mine, brushing lightly. "A man that wants your love."

I sighed. "If you truly wanted me for more than sex, Dev, why is that all we ever did?"

Dev gaped at me, blinking. "What else did you want to do? You never mentioned—"

I narrowed my eyes. "I was your guest in your home for months, Dev. When I visited, we'd have sex, we'd sometimes go out to Davy's or we'd sleep. You've never treated me as anything but a lover."

Devlin stared at me, aghast. "Why did you never tell me you felt like this?" he whispered.

"I thought that was just how things were," I answered, suddenly awkward. "That you were treating me like that because things were temporary. I felt bad about that, but I accepted it. That was one of the reasons I asked to help you, to keep busy here so I wouldn't obsess over it."

Devlin moved, reaching and pulling me roughly into his arms. "I never meant to make you feel that way," he said, smoothing my hair, kissing my tears away. "Anna never wanted to do anything but read poetry, buy new clothes, and do embroidery. I don't know how else she spent her time other than that, when she wasn't sleeping with me. I know you work hard at your home, and at Danial's. I didn't want you to have to work here."

"Dev, I'm not talking about working. Why did we never go to a movie, or even watch one together? Go out again on your motorcycle? See a play, or go out walking even—?"

Devlin squeezed me so hard he cut off my words. "I'm sorry," he said, kissing my cheek. "I didn't think you wanted to do those things with me. I know you did them with Theo and Danial, but you never mentioned any interest in doing them with me. I wanted to do them with you, but I was always hesitant to ask. That is why when Danial invited me to the movies with you, or told me that you had an appointment, I made sure to be there, even if I wasn't sure you wanted me there. I wanted to take you out again on the motorcycle, but I didn't want to risk it until it was warmer. By then, we knew you were pregnant, and it was too dangerous for you." Devlin paused. "Some of it was being busy with Ebediah's affairs in Canada. I've felt for most of this year as if all I do is work, feed, and sleep. There were many vampires and weres that were angry that needed to be dealt with or convinced to join my side. Getting that cooperation was necessary to protect against a revolt—"

"Why didn't you ever talk to me about that?" I interrupted.

"I didn't want to upset you in your pregnancy," Devlin replied. "You had enough on your mind with The Lust and everything else that was happening."

What he was saying made sense. Danial had treated me much the same when we first lived together. Perhaps women of their time had been happy doing nothing and hearing only pleasant things. As for his work...well, I had been wrapped up in other problems. Knowing Dev could be torn down from his throne might have been enough to send me over the edge.

"When you see someone once a week, you want the time to be purely enjoyable," Dev added. "I wanted to be alone with you, to have you all to myself."

I'd relaxed him enough. If I was going to make my move, now was the time. "We are alone," I said lightly, nestling my head into the hollow of his throat. "Do you really want to spend any more of this evening talking?"

Devlin tipped my head up with his fingertips, so I looked at him. "What I want is to know why you chose tonight, Love."

He wasn't as astute as Danial, but he was close enough. *Mix in some truth.* "You heard about the challenge?"

Devlin nodded. "Frankly, I'm surprised Theo won. I'm sure you were relieved—"

His sarcasm rankled me. "This isn't about him," I said angrily, grabbing his hand and pushing it away from my chin. "This is about us. Life is too short to hold grudges against people you love. I'm here because I want to be here with you." That was the truth, just not the whole truth. "I'm scared, and I need you. If you don't want me here, then just tell me to—"

"I want you here," he said quickly, hugging me tight.

I hugged him back, then kissed his neck chastely.

He caressed my arm with his fingertips lightly. "Do you believe I love you now?" he asked. "That I want you with me not just for tonight or tomorrow, but forever?"

I wasn't ready for an Oath tonight. "I believe we should take it slow," I said softly, into his skin. "We need to—"

"Do you believe me, Sarelle, when I say I love you?" Devlin said, holding my face in his hand, his golden eyes looking down into my green ones. "Do you believe me, when I say you are more than enough for me?"

"Yes," I responded. "I do."

"Do you still love me?" he asked, his eyes searching mine.

"Yes," I said softly, and kissed him passionately. "I want to lose myself in you—"

Devlin kissed me roughly, his lips devouring mine. I pushed him back abruptly, then pulled off my clothes and shoes, dumping them in a pile. Devlin did the same, discarding his suit and shirt, then moved closer to embrace me, brushing his cheek with mine.

"Where do you want me?" he said temptingly in my ear.

I was caught off guard, then realized why he was asking. "In our bed," I answered. I reached down and stroked his hardness, making him groan.

"What would you like?" he asked, easing me down to the bed beneath him. "Do you want me to sing, or—?"

I took his face in my hands. "I want you to do what you feel like doing," I said, kissing his cheeks, mouth and eyes. "Just be with me, Dev." I kissed him. "That's all I want."

* * * *

I'd forgotten how good sex could be with him. I'd wanted to, in my anger and pain.

But Devlin made me remember with every kiss, every touch, every whispered "I love you." And he remembered what I loved more than the poetry he quoted me, or the songs he sung me, or his expertise that had no equal. Devlin whispered as he made love to me, telling me everything he was feeling and how he had dreamed of me coming back to him every night, of finding me there waiting for him, of hearing my sighs as he touched me, or my cries as he gave himself to me over and over.

When we were resting, I turned to him. "Why didn't you bite me?"

He gave me a devilish smile. "I was waiting for you to ask me to."

"Then I'm asking," I replied, rolling on top of him and beginning to move.

Devlin arched his back beneath me, a lazy smile gracing his handsome features as he clasped my hips. He moved purposely, his eyes watching me as I swayed above him in rhythm, my pleasure slowly building. As my climax neared, Devlin moved faster, his eyes fixed on me lustily, his fangs bared. Our rapid breathing intensified, my heart racing as the sweat beaded on my body.

The climax hit, and I began to shudder, moaning. Devlin pulled me down, turning my head and sinking his fangs in. His body tensed suddenly, then his arms tightened around me. I begin to scream in bliss, the heady joy of orgasm suddenly escalating to white hot intensity.

Devlin moved rapidly, straining against me, his body convulsing even as his muffled moans filled my ears.

"Yes, please," I whispered, my head lolling. "I'm yours, Dev. I'm yours!"

Devlin drew back, then kissed me fiercely. Sweetness flooded my mouth, and I moaned, my tongue delving into his mouth as I pressed my lips hard against his, desperate for more.

With a groan close to pain, Devlin pushed back from me, then kissed my bites gently. "Enough, Love. I don't want to hurt you."

I nestled in his arms, my head on his chest, utterly content. Almost instantly, I dropped off to sleep.

* * * *

I yawned, then blinked, wondering where I was. Then I looked down at Devlin beside me, my face softening.

Lash had been right. I'd have to thank him. I wouldn't have given Devlin another chance, if he hadn't made me. And it was right to be here in his arms. We belonged together. We were still Oathed, no matter what the choker had or hadn't done. We had a child together. And we loved each other.

In a small corner of my mind that had somehow not been influenced by Dev's blood, I affirmed that aside from the emotional aspect, this alliance was rational. Theo and Danial were wonderful, but they didn't have the power and respect Devlin wielded...and they knew it, which was why both of them had agreed rebonding to Devlin was necessary for my safety. In the struggle to come against Perseus and Samuel, his power was going to count for a lot...

"Penny for your thoughts," Dev whispered eerily, kissing my shoulder.

I smacked him hard on his chest. "Stop being creepy," I said, giving him a dark look.

"I can't help it," he said, nibbling at my neck. "I'm very happy, Love, and I have always loved teasing you."

I didn't answer.

"What were you thinking? Something wildly inappropriate, as usual?"

I knew about Harriet from Theo, but Devlin might have more information. He was likely the one who had actually talked to Samuel. "Theo told me about Harriet," I replied hesitantly, testing the waters. "I'm wondering if they're planning on trying for me again."

Devlin hugged me. "They're demanding information. I told them of the different trials you faced in your pregnancies. So far, they've attributed their own failure with Harriet to bad luck." He paused. "There is good news; Samuel sent his condolences about your 'new barren state'—"

Hope swelled inside me. "He bought it?"

"Hook, line, and sinker," Devlin said, smiling widely. "He's stopped clamoring for me to share you with him. Once we give him your health records, we'll be free of him."

"That will be such a relief," I murmured.

"For me, too," Devlin affirmed resentfully. "I want them to fuck off, and this should make them get lost. They are never getting you, Sar. Never."

"Language," I cautioned, putting my finger to his lips. "You are a father now."

"Sar, if I loved you for nothing else, I would love you for that," Devlin said passionately. "Venus is everything to me now. I miss her if we are apart more than a few hours. I finally moved her crib to the nursery. I was waking her up by spending so much time touching her, and she needs to sleep. Serena is watching her at night. I have cut back on her other duties a little, and she is enjoying the break." He paused. "I'm sorry I didn't tell you about her and me."

I shifted uneasily.

"Truthfully, I had forgotten it happened. It wasn't for pleasure, it was business—"

"I'm good with that," I said, covering his mouth. "You can stop now."

Devlin reached up and removed my hand. "Then will you give me your Oath again?"

"Can you keep it this time?" I replied evenly. "If I should ever walk in on you again—"

"I promise you, you won't," Devlin said quickly.

"—ever again see you like that with someone else, there won't be any more chances, Dev. I mean that."

"I've learned my lesson, Sar," Devlin replied, laying his head on my chest. "It won't happen again. But I'm not demanding your Oath, if you aren't ready to give it."

That was a relief. *But why wasn't he?* "I appreciate that," I whispered finally.

"I want you to," Devlin assured quickly. "I just want you to know that I'll protect you either way, and give you my blood when you need it, though the latter I'd prefer to administer during lovemaking, to ease the pain you feel—"

That was the only reason, sure. "I appreciate that, too."

"Will you do it?" he pressed. "I have your choker here."

"Not right away," I said firmly. "But I'll come to stay with you as I did before, every week. If everything is still okay between us by the end of the year, I'll Oath to you again then."

"I can wait," Devlin said with surety. "I've waited this long. A few months won't matter."

I ran my fingers through his hair. "It will go by in a blink."

Dev sighed. "With you, yes, it will. Are you staying tonight?"

"Of course," I answered. "Go back to sleep."

* * * *

Danial was pleased that I'd made up with Devlin. He was more pleased that I would be renewing the Oath at the end of year. Still, it gave him a lot of pleasure that his was the only choker I would be wearing until then.

Theo was less happy, but he stoically accepted it as necessary. We didn't really talk about it much. Our time together was mostly taken up by caring for Devon, or discussing Elle's future, the latter being a matter of shared concern.

"She was playing with Devon all afternoon in cougar form," I said to Theo one night, after Devon went to sleep. "I'm glad they get along so well, but I'm concerned with how big she is. The patches on her face are white now."

"She's an adult," Theo replied gruffly. "She looks almost exactly like Tawny, Sar. Elle could probably have a child herself now, if she mated and stayed in lion form."

I squeezed his hand, giving him worried eyes.

"That's why she's so provocative," Theo continued. "She's getting the urge from her lion half to mate, and it's bleeding through to her human form, intensifying her desires."

"What are we going to do?" I asked.

"Take it as it comes," he said with a shrug. "There isn't anything else we can do. She's going to grow up, Sar. There's no stopping it."

"I know that," I said, annoyed. "I just wish she'd gotten a little longer to be a child. I love Devon's looks of wonder, those huge blue eyes of his taking in everything. I love his spots, the way his ears perk up at the slightest sound. I want his childhood to last a while, Theo. Elle's was too short—"

"We'll have longer with Devon. I'll help him change form in a few weeks. I want him to appear as a human child that is at least a year or two old when he first becomes human, to lessen the time he's helpless. But after he knows how to walk, we can let him remain human, so he ages a lot more slowly." He stroked my hip gently. "I'm almost fully healed."

I'd pulled out the last of Theo's stitches that day. With each one, I'd thanked Lash for saving him, then prayed for some peaceful, boring years. I wanted time with Devon as a child, time for Theo to get those experiences that he'd missed having with Elle. We'd all had enough drama and excitement lately to last us a decade or so.

* * * *

I drove to Hayden early Friday morning. After I parked my truck, I pulled on my gloves, then grabbed my gear from the truck bed. *Time to get after those fallen trees.*

I walked down by the edge of the low stone wall, carrying my chainsaw in my right hand, and the lube and gas mixture in my left hand. My tools were in the saw's case along with extra chains, in case one broke. My mind was ruminating on my conversations with Terian over the past week, prepping for a report to Titus.

Terian was gaining in power and confidence. Yet in spite of his boldness, I didn't see any traces of evil behavior to report. In fact, I preferred this new, daring Terian of action to the old reluctant Terian who'd been afraid of what he was.

There was a sudden throaty roar of heavy machinery. Excited, I hurried down the path towards it.

Lash had the bears out in force today. Several were picking up sticks and branches and mulching them, another was working on a front-end loader moving mud, and five more were standing around one crouched down, sawing one of the huge logs. I watched for a moment curiously, wondering why the scene was so quiet. Then it hit me; the dumb ass had bound his saw.

The mechanics of chainsawing wood are simple: one whole log becomes two and both obey gravity. When a long and wide chunk of wood is on the ground and that ground is uneven, the wood can shift as it is cut, closing the cut until the blade of the saw is bound between the two pieces of wood. That had happened to the werebear, imprisoning his blade. It was now buried deep in the three-foot-wide trunk.

Tugging was not going to work, even with supernatural strength. I laughed to myself, then walked over nonchalantly with a solemn face.

Lash came over to meet me. "Sar," he said, nodding once.

"I brought my saw. Where should I start?" I asked innocently.

Lash folded his arms and looked at me, clearly dubious. "You sure you want to do this?" he hissed. "You wouldn't rather be relaxing in bed?"

"Let's not have this same conversation again," I interjected. "Just tell me what you want done first."

"First, tie your shoe," he said, smirking. "I want you not to trip and fall."

"Lash!" one of the bears called. "The blade isn't coming free."

Lash hissed in irritation, then walked away scowling. "I told you to lever it up."

I put my saw down, annoyed, and crouched down in the soft mud to double knot my steel-toed boot. As I went to stand, I slipped sideways and caught myself, smearing my work shirt sleeve in muck.

I brushed it off the best I could. *No big deal.* I'd just get dirtier before the day was over. I was looking forward to that actually. I hadn't done real physical work in a long time. Besides, it was a beautiful summer day: a perfect day for working.

There was another roar from the front-end loader. The operator had made rapid progress. The fallen rock wall was quickly being fixed, water receding as the huge rocks blocking one of the drainage ditches were moved one by one.

The werebear and his pals were still trying to get the bound sawblade free. But the tree was huge, a good hundred feet long with roots and branches still attached. Even with their combined strength, all they could do was roll it over, making the saw's handle and engine go up in the air as the blade remained bound. They tried this several times, with the same result. In short, it was hilarious. Since no one had asked for my help, or told me what to do, I remained where I was, watching and smirking. It was good for men to know humility.

Another throaty roar sounded, turning my attention from the tree back to the tractor. The werebear moving fallen rocks was almost done. The last one was safely in the loader, the tractor straining under the weight, the tires almost flattened in the front. The operator dropped the rock with the others, the front tires springing back up as the load lightened. Then, to my surprise, the tractor headed back to the ditch.

Curious, I walked towards it. *What was he up to?*

As the operator parked at the very edge of the ditch and lowered the loader down into it, my eyes opened wide with horror. He was going after a boulder sunk deep into the mud of the bottom of the ditch. Not only would the loader overbalance picking up the rock, he'd be lucky if it didn't pin him under it when it fell in.

I sprinted towards the tractor, yelling. "Hey! Stop! Stop!"

Either he didn't hear me over the engine or he didn't listen. The operator reached down with the loader for the rock, scooped carefully under it, and went to lift it.

"Hey! Don't go for the last rock!" I yelled desperately.

The rock came free from the bottom of the ditch, as the operator slowly raised the dripping loader. He levered it up just enough to clear the ditch edge.

"What are you yelling for?" Lash said irritably from beside me. "He's got it."

"No, he's going to—"

The operator went to shift gears to back up. The rock rolled sideways in the loader and the wheels promptly slid forward, the front-end of the tractor slipping down into the ditch.

"—fall in," I finished.

"Christ, could anything go more wrong today?" Lash hissed loudly. "Jazz already broke one chain, and cut himself so badly he had to take off the rest of the day."

"Why do none of you know what you're doing?" I said, trying hard to make my tone nonjudgmental.

Lash narrowed his flat eyes. "I know what I'm doing, Sar. As for the bears, they're doing the best they can."

I gave him an incredulous look. "Then their best isn't good enough. They need training."

"I used to have a crack team for this kind of shit," Lash hissed, looking at me meaningfully. "They're all dead. You remember Kev and Vince, I'm sure?"

I narrowed my eyes, wondering why he was being an asshole. "Dev has enough money to hire talent outside his guards for—"

"No," Lash said coldly. "No strangers are allowed inside Hayden's grounds. What I can't make or fix with my hands, Titus does with his magic." He flicked his forked tongue at me. "Devlin doesn't hire for this type of skill. They'll learn by trial and error, just like the last bunch did years ago."

The operator in the ditch was swearing now as he tried to back the tractor up out of the ditch. But the back tires wouldn't grip, they were spinning in the mud, covering the tractor and him in sludge.

This was wasted time and wasted effort, specifically mine if I sat here and did nothing. There was a better way. "Do you want my help?" I said, folding my arms over my chest.

"You can't get that tractor out of there," Lash said, flicking his tongue at me again.

"The hell I can't," I retorted.

"This will be fun. How much you want to bet?" he hissed with a grin.

Yes, it would be fun. "What are you offering?"

44

"What do you want?"

Hmm. "I want you to tell me you are glad of my help."

"That's it?" he hissed in confusion, giving me an odd look.

"Yes," I said with fake pleasantness. "You?"

"I want you to come an extra day this week to Hayden, plus an extra day next week."

Always, it was about Dev. Oiy. "Deal," I agreed. "Now send all of them on a break. I need to concentrate without onlookers."

Lash nodded. "Guys," he said loudly. "Go inside and have an early lunch."

"But it's not even ten—" Nick said in confusion.

"Shut up and go inside," Lash hissed. "One hour."

The bears muttered and dropped their tools, then began walking up to the house. I walked over to the stuck tractor and climbed on, taking a few minutes to familiarize myself with the controls. They were similar enough to my tractor that if I went slow, I should be okay. The problem was what to do. I'd never been stuck before as bad as this. I'd always steered clear of ditches this deep.

"The clock is ticking, Sar," Lash called mirthfully. "Fifty-six minutes left."

"Shut up!" I called back sweetly.

First, I needed to get rid of the rock. I extended the loader as far as it would go, and deposited the rock on the far bank of the ditch. It was a foot back, so it shouldn't roll back in.

From here on, it was trial and error. Since going backward hadn't worked for the bear, I'd try to go forward. Putting the tractor in drive, I pressed gently on the accelerator. While the tractor went forward a foot, it wouldn't climb the far bank, even with the help of the loader. The sides of the ditch were too steep. But down about twenty feet, the ditch sides began to slope more gently. If I could get down there, I could climb out.

I turned the steering wheel, and began to work the controls. With a lot of going forward and going backward the few feet possible, I managed to turn the tractor about thirty degrees. Suddenly, the bank behind me gave way, the back tires sliding into the ditch.

Laughter and clapping sounded. Lash was laughing his ass off and giving me a round of applause. "Bravo, Sar! Now the whole tractor's in the ditch!"

My face flaming, I ignored him and put the tractor in drive. Carefully, I turned the wheel, and drove the tractor down the ditch to where the walls were sloped. As I moved, the wheels sank down deeper in the mud, the front wheels more than half buried when I stopped.

Oh, shit. A spring joined the ditch here. Instead of the foot of mud I'd been in, now I was in a foot and a half at least. I was going to be a dirt queen by the time I got out of this hole. Resigned, I began turning the tractor to face the side of the ditch. By the time I had, the place I was maneuvering in was a mud pit, and I was covered in it, my face, hair and body spattered. Angry, I pressed the accelerator too hard, and spun the tires, big chunks of mud scattering and spraying me in the process.

Lash began laughing again. I restrained my urge to curse him out, and/or find a gun and shoot him. Instead I forced myself to breathe calmly, and take it slow. Reaching out with the front-end loader, I dug the edge of the bucket into the bank in front of me, then pulled back on the lever. The loader shifted, pulling the tractor up as expected. But the front tires were smooth. They couldn't get any purchase, slipping in the mud sideways. When I reached out with the bucket again, all four tires slid back down into the ditch. Now I was partly sideways again, and the front tires were almost completely buried in mud.

"Shit!" I screamed.

Lash began laughing again.

Prick. I collected myself and tried again, with the same result. This time, I overloaded the engine, and it shut off. Tears welled in my eyes from frustration. Putting my head in my hands, I let myself cry a little. Until I did, I was going to be frantic and useless. I needed to get past this failure if I was going to have any chance of finding success.

"Sar, get off the tractor," Lash said gently from the bank. "Losing isn't worth crying over."

I raised my head and glared at him proudly. "I haven't lost!" I said angrily, wiping away my tears. "Stand back." Determined, I cranked the key, and started the tractor again. Letting it run, I dismounted and began grabbing some rocks from the far side of the bank. I inserted two rough ones under the front edge of the front wheels, then put two more in front of those. After a few minutes of searching for more, I located two final large rocks. After setting them in front of the back wheels, I got back on the tractor.

Again, I dug into the bank and levered up. This time, all four tires moved out of the muck and onto the rocks. Carefully releasing the loader from the bank, I extended the loader as far as possible, then dug in again. Slowly, I pushed the accelerator. With a roar, the tractor eased up and over the bank. Suddenly one front tire slipped off the rock. I dug in and accelerated slowly. The back tires found the front tire rocks then and held. With another throaty roar, the tractor and I were clear of the ditch.

Ecstatic, I let out a cry of pure delight. Proudly, I drove the tractor a good ten feet from the ditch and parked it, shutting off the engine. The sound of clapping filled the sudden silence.

Lash came toward me, giving applause. I went to take a bow in my triumph and smugness, and slipped in the mud. I went down hard on my side, hitting my kneecap on a rock. I cursed again, blinking back tears from the pain.

Lash took my hand, and hauled me to my feet. "You okay?" he hissed, grinning widely.

I gave him a rueful smile back, rubbing my smarting knee. "God was teaching me some humility, after helping me," I said, laughing. "I should have thanked Him for His help straight off. I'm okay."

"Good," Lash hissed gently. "Because I want you to stay. I would be glad of your help, Sar."

The respect in his tone moved me. While Lash had never treated me with disrespect—except the time he'd kissed me out of turn—this was different. There is the respect a man shows a woman because she's a woman, and he thinks she needs his protection, guidance, or help lifting something heavy. And then there is the respect a man shows a friend or a coworker when he actually values their capabilities, reasoning, or skills. It was the second kind of respect I'd heard in Lash's tone.

He believed I had something to contribute. That mattered to me a lot, maybe because it felt like years since I'd last heard that kind of respect from any man in my life.

"You sure you're okay?" Lash hissed.

I smiled quickly. "I'm fine. And I'd be glad to help—"

"Shit! She got it unstuck!" one of the bears called incredulously as the lot of them walked up.

"She did," Lash said, looking at me intently. "Just as she said she would."

And thank God it hadn't taken longer. I'd have been mortified to be crying in front of that crowd of hardened men. "So what do you want to focus on?" I asked him.

"My saw is still bound," one of the bears said grumpily. "Why don't you fix that?"

I nodded, then went over and examined the bound saw. "You're in a depression," I said. "First, is there a log roller here? It would be about four feet long. It should have a spike on one end, and a hinged hook."

"There's one in the garage," Lash hissed. "Nick, go get it now."

Nick took off at a run.

I took out my saw, and made sure that the gas and oil caps were tight. I got it started after only a few tries, then motioned the bears out of the way. I cut into the log at an angle about three inches away from the bound saw, then made another cut down, breaking out a large slice of wood.

"How is that going to help—?" one bear began sarcastically.

"Shut up, Keith," Lash hissed dangerously. "She knows what she's doing."

Trying not to feel drunk with his praise, I made another cut in the open slice spot, cutting towards the saw and the center of the log. When I was within an inch of it, the bound blade loosened.

I pulled out my saw, letting it idle. "You're free."

Keith lifted his saw out slowly. "I don't believe it," he said incredulously.

I grinned. "That is why you fail," I said in my lowest tones, then began laughing.

Lash laughed, but most of the bears looked confused, glancing at one another.

"*Star Wars?*" I said finally, rolling my eyes. "Know Yoda? The scene with the X-Wing and the Force?"

"They're too young," Lash hissed with a smile. "Start instructing, Jedi Master."

"Start with the branches first, then the tops," I said. "Work your way down the trees. If you cut in the middle again, the saw will bind just like it did before. We're in an uneven patch of ground."

Several of the bears began powering up chainsaws. Keith and I started in, quickly severing branches, then cutting pieces to length as the majority of the bears began stacking and mulching. When we reached the trunk, I showed Keith how to work down it using the logroller for support and leverage.

"I'm not cutting straight!" Keith said with irritation.

"Neither am I," I replied. "And I've been doing this for years. Just do the best you can."

By six p.m., all the trees had been taken care of, plus a load of wood had been stacked in my truck for me to take home.

"I appreciate this," I said to Lash. "It'll save Theo and me a lot of work. It's all ash and maple, good hardwood. We were behind on wood cutting anyway with me being pregnant."

Lash nodded. "Dev has no use for it anyway, other than for bonfires. He's only got the one fireplace." He turned to the bears around us. "We're done for the day, unless you're on duty."

The group of us began slowly walking towards the house. All of us were tired, and covered with sweat, including Lash. He'd pitched in with the rest; he'd been the one to load my truck with wood.

I wiped at the layer of dried mud on my face, tired and satisfied. I was a disaster to look at, but I felt absolutely wonderful. I'd done something today that mattered. My helping had made a real difference, not only in saving time and effort, but in getting to know the men guarding me. I'd learned their names today. That already made me feel more like someone who belonged here and less like a visitor.

The group of bears was now ahead of Lash and me. I'd thought we were just slow until I caught on that Lash was making sure they kept moving ahead of us, keeping eye contact with any who lagged behind until they sped up.

"Titus will teleport the rest of the wood for you tomorrow," Lash hissed. "And I thank you again, for your help. I didn't expect us to finish today."

"Why did you want me to come to Hayden an extra day?" I asked. "Dev's been swamped all this week with more Canadian loose ends. Something's always coming up he has to handle."

Lash didn't reply.

"I'm just saying that he's been busy," I added. "An extra day doesn't seem—"

Lash suddenly stopped walking and turned to me. "He likes you here. And it wasn't just for him." He looked away and began walking again. "I like to get sushi with you, Sar, and to talk about the movies we both like. There is a rock near the pond where it's good to lie and be warm in the afternoons. Summer is ending. Soon it will be fall. I'm not looking forward to winter."

Lash sounded depressed. I felt his pain. I was not looking forward to winter myself. "I'll come on Sunday," I responded. "It's supposed to be nice that day."

"You won the bet," Lash said coolly. "Why would you come anyway?"

"Because you asked me to," I said simply. "You're right, winter is coming. Lying in the sun sounds good. I need to soak up all the rays I can get."

Lash looked at me out of the corner of his eye. "I don't suppose you'd bring a swimsuit?" he asked, grinning.

"Don't press your luck," I said, making the both of us laugh.

* * * *

I did bring my swimsuit the following Sunday, but I needn't have bothered. Lash led me to the rock he'd spoken of, and then laid down in his T-shirt and jeans. The only thing he took off were his weapons, which he put within reach.

Glad to relax, I applied sunscreen to my face and hands, then laid down a few feet from him. I ended up falling asleep from the heat. It was too beautiful out here not to relax utterly, feeling the warmth of the sun on my face as it radiated through my clothes. We didn't talk at all, the only sounds from the crickets in the tall grass and the bullfrogs in the pond.

Late in the afternoon, Lash woke me with a nudge. Then he clipped his weapons back on his belt, and uttering a groan, he got to his feet.

"Are you sore?" I asked, as he helped me up.

"Just old," he said with a grin, wiping some dust off himself. "Come on. Sushi awaits. I picked some up for us yesterday."

After we walked back to the house, we ate some sushi in the kitchen. We were discussing the important properties of the devil from the movie The Ninth Gate when Devlin came downstairs in his robe.

"Hello, Sweetheart," he said, giving me a kiss.

"Hello yourself," I said, kissing him back. "Did you sleep well?"

"Yes. Is this dinner?" he said, going to the refrigerator to prepare Venus's bottle.

"Yes," Lash said, grinning. "We're talking about horror movies."

"Ah," Devlin said. "We should go to a movie tonight, the three of us."

"You two go," Lash said quickly, getting to his feet. He put his plate into the sink. "I'll stay and watch over things here."

Devlin turned to him curiously. "I thought you wanted to see—?"

"I don't think it's safe leaving Venus here alone with just the bears as guards," Lash interrupted, folding his arms across his chest. "Titus is at Leri's house in town, and he's not going to want to leave their bed to come up here on his day off."

"TMI," I said, rolling my eyes. "Why don't we just stay in and rent a pay-per-view movie?"

"Good idea," Devlin agreed. "While I'll feed Venus, you can go shower, Sar."

I shot him a curious look. Not only had I'd showered this morning, I'd done nothing but lie in the sun all day. "I'm good."

"You have leaves in your hair from lying on Lash's rock," Devlin said, pulling a few out. "There is dirt all down the back of your T-shirt, and your jeans."

"Oh," I said with embarrassment, getting to my feet. "Thanks for telling me, I didn't realize. I'll go shower."

When I was done showering and dressing, I peeked into the nursery. Devlin was feeding Venus, her bright golden eyes wide as he sang to her softly. She was going to be just as breathtaking as he was, when she got older. Giving Devlin an affectionate look, I went downstairs. Lash was waiting on the couch, his hair still wet.

I didn't think he had been dirty, either, but whatever. "What should we rent?"

Lash turned the TV up, and then turned to me. "Devlin didn't think you were dirty," he hissed softly. "Don't be offended."

"Then what—?" I whispered.

"Because I lay on that rock a lot," he hissed more softly. "It smells like me. You smelled like me, and it made Devlin remember us together. He doesn't like to think of that now."

I flushed. "Thanks for telling me. I didn't know."

"Forget it," Lash hissed, working the remote to channel surf. "I think we should watch Bloodrayne—"

"That sucked," I said, making a face. "How about Legend?"

"That's old," Devlin said, coming down with Venus. "How about that comic book hero—?"

"I thought you didn't like action movies?" I interrupted.

"I could maybe sit through it," Devlin said bravely.

"Your demon barber movie is on, Dev," Lash said, clicking on it. "I vote for that."

"How about it?" Devlin said to me. "I could watch that again."

"Sure," I said, settling back. "I'll take one for the team. Hit play.

Chapter Four

The next week passed slowly. By now, it was mid-September, and the days were getting cooler. As the seasons changed, the workload from Solutions Inc. was decreasing. I was glad of the break. Since Danial had launched the website, we'd been hammered with queries, and the backlog of cases was as long as I'd ever seen it. Also, in keeping with Theo's request for us to spend more time with Devon, Danial had cut back on accepting any new cases for the rest of the year. All this meant that I had more free time now in the afternoons to spend with Elle, Devon, and Theoron. Theo also took most afternoons off, and spent them with us, even if it was just walking, going for a picnic, or sharing a DVD and popcorn with some of the werefoxes.

Cia and I were back on speaking terms. It was all business, though: we were still sharing the cleaning duties at Danial's. She could no longer avoid me, as we needed to help each other sometimes. She still hadn't really forgiven me for being friendly with Serena, and I hadn't asked her to. In my mind, I hadn't done anything wrong that needed forgiving. For now it was enough we were working together.

The reason for our cooperation was not only dismaying, but worrisome: Mary's daughter, Jenny, was still dying from cancer. Mary had told Danial a few days ago that she thought it wouldn't be much longer. He'd reassured her he'd try to turn Jenny into a vampire, if it came to that. But he'd told Mary point blank that Jenny would have to agree to any stipulations he set forth, as well as truly want to be a vampire, before he would do it.

"Mary got quiet," Danial told me later that evening. "I'm unsure how it's going to end."

"You're going to have to turn her," I said reluctantly. "She's got no other choice, really."

"It's the age-old dilemma," he'd said, stroking my hair as we lay on his couch. "Everyone wants not to die, and no one wants that longevity to come with a price. But it always does."

52

I wondered if he'd talked more with Theo, regarding his mortality, but I didn't ask. I had enough other things to keep my mind busy.

Elle was being more social now that Danial had given her more freedom. She had been meeting Violet every weekend for a movie at the mall. Terian had been tailing her, and so far, he reported that they were just doing normal girl things, like getting fast food, trying on lipsticks, and giggling their way through teen romance movies.

As I'd promised Titus, I'd continued to keep an eye on Terian, watching for signs he was succumbing to his demon nature. So far, I'd seen nothing. He was harder and tougher than he had been, but I still ascribed that to the work he was doing now with Theo. Sundown and he still spent most of their free time together. They acted absorbed in each other, whether the activity was nighttime walks or just her helping him in his lab. Seeing them so much in love, I reassured myself that Terian was okay.

When I visited Devlin that following Friday night, I made sure to see Titus first, to report that to him. "He's acting happy and in love. There's nothing else to see, Titus."

"Keep watching him, please," Titus rumbled, his red eyes worried. "I know you don't believe anything's wrong, Sar. But it means a lot if you'll keep doing this for me."

I gave him a shrug. "Sure." Maybe Titus knew something I didn't. "See you later."

When I went upstairs to the main floor, Lash was there reclining on the sofa. Oddly, he looked dressed to go out. While his solid black clothes were the usual type he wore—jeans, heavy shirt, and turtleneck—they looked brand new.

I gave him an odd look, curious. "Do you have a hot date?"

Lash looked over at me and then switched off the TV. "I'm hoping like hell."

Who was he going out with? What he had done with Cin couldn't be called anything more than hooking up. *Did one dress up to hook up?* Devlin hadn't mentioned a new girl, nor had Lash. *Was there someone new, someone he was trying to impress?*

Lash got to his feet, then threw the remote down on the couch. "Want to go out and get dinner?" Lash hissed, eyeing me. "My treat."

I was surprised and touched to find out that I'd been the one he'd dressed up for. "So your date's with me?"

"It's probably the last sushi trip," Lash hissed awkwardly, shifting his weight from one foot to the other. "I knew you were coming, so I thought, what the hell, I'd ask."

I almost said no. I was tired, and sushi seemed a pale alternative to warm soup, toast, and possibly some cake, if there was any to be had in Hayden's kitchen. But Lash had never asked me for anything before, really. I still remembered how I'd felt years ago, before Danial had come into my life, when I'd wanted to go out and had no one to go with. Besides, I was sure to have a good time.

"Sure," I agreed. "Let me change into warmer clothes while you warm up the truck."

I quickly went upstairs, and changed into the brown top and jeans he'd picked out for me a few months earlier when he'd guarded me during a shopping trip, and then put on the tan leather duster I knew he liked. It was just warm enough outside that with it, I wouldn't have to wear a coat.

"Sushi again?" Devlin grumbled from the bed. "You're going to turn into an eel."

"Probably," I said, kissing him goodbye. "We'll be gone a few hours or so."

"Be safe," Devlin said, turning over and shutting his eyes. "I'll be ready for you when you get back. Just wake me up."

Ready for what? He must mean sex. "I will."

I hurried downstairs and out into the garage, then got into Lash's truck.

He hit the overhead door, then gave me an appreciative look. "You look nice, Mrs. O'Connor."

"You look good yourself, Mr. Lash," I teased back. "But if you don't hurry, we won't make the restaurant."

"We'll make it," Lash hissed confidently, zooming in reverse as he turned to look over his shoulder. "I rented the whole place."

* * * *

We had a good time at the restaurant. Like Lash had said, the place was empty except for us, a row of waitresses watching for every empty glass or plate. The table was crowded with plates, some of the sushi elaborate kinds I'd never before seen. It was enjoyable, but in some weird way also a little oppressive, as if this night was some kind of celebration that I wasn't privy to.

"This is very good," I said, eating some of the strange pieces. "Try some."

"I did," Lash said, downing his third sake. "You go ahead. I'm sticking to the crab tonight."

I grabbed a couple pieces. "You aren't gorging like me," I teased. "Are you feeling okay?"

"Of course," Lash hissed, giving me a funny look. "I feel fine. But winter's coming. My body is slowing down, getting ready for hibernation."

"But you don't hibernate," I said, looking at him strangely.

"I still feel the urge," Lash hissed softly. "My snake side is always present, Sar. It's not like it is with Theo, or the other weres you know. The animal inside me is always there, influencing my thoughts and actions. It's telling me to go to sleep until the weather warms."

I wasn't sure what to say, so I sipped my wine.

"We probably won't come out like this again until spring," Lash hissed softly. "So I thought it would be nice to go out one last time and get some of these delicacies I've read about online."

"Everything is wonderful," I said graciously. "It was great to try some of this stuff, even if I'm not sure what it is."

Lash smiled. "Good. I'm happy things are working out with you and Dev."

"Thank you for that," I said softly, reaching out and taking his hand. "You were right. He is trying. I'm glad that you helped us get back together, Lash."

Lash opened his mouth.

I squeezed his hand. "I'm not ever going to tell him. Don't worry about that."

Lash squeezed my hand back, then gently withdrew it. "Good. Venus needs both her mother and father."

* * * *

Lash and I were just coming in the front door of Hayden when Devlin came down the stairs dressed in his motorcycle leathers.

"Glad you're back," he said breezily. "I'm ready."

To say I was surprised was an understatement; I gaped at him.

He grinned back at me, then turned to Lash. "Do you want to come?"

"Not tonight," Lash said, settling himself on the couch under a blanket. "I'm more interested in keeping warm." He flipped on the TV and began surfing.

"Suit yourself," Devlin said with a shrug, and turned to me. "Let's go, Love."

"Where are we going?" I asked, looking at him uneasily. "On the bike?"

"For a ride," Devlin said vaguely, leading me into the garage. "I got you a set of lightweight armor. I want you to wear it. That way if anything happens, you'll be safe. Come."

Reassured, I took off my leather duster, laid it on Lash's front seat with my purse, and then began strapping on the armor. It was a simple Kevlar suit, dull black in color, the leather-like material covering everything but my feet, hands, and head. There were leather gloves with it, and also a Kevlar helmet of the same dull black color reinforced with steel and hard plastic. Devlin helped me strap it all on, and then he got on his bike, motioning for me to get on behind him.

"Does Lash have his own bike?" I asked casually, settling on behind Devlin.

"Sure," Devlin said, giving me a funny look. "It's pretty similar to mine. It's right over there."

I glanced past him. In a small alcove off to the side, another bike stood draped in a black dust cloth. It had to be the same one Lash had been riding the night he had followed Theo, saving his life. "I figured you rode together," I said, giving Devlin a smile. "It wouldn't be as fun, alone."

"He only rides in summer, when it's warm. I should now, too. I'm a father, and I have to be more careful. This will probably be our last ride until next spring, Sar."

"Then let's make it a good one," I said, clutching him around the waist.

We rode for at least two hours. The moon was almost full, and it shone down on us, illuminating everything in its glow. It reminded me very strongly of the night he and I had last ridden together, those many months ago. Everything was just as beautiful and magical, the stars just as bright. But the weather was warmer, as I had wished it to be on that long ago night. We stopped by a bridge, and drove the motorcycle into some bushes. He and I got off for a while, walking down to the edge of the river. It was rippling black and shiny in the light from the street lamps above. Devlin and I sat on a fallen tree for a while, just watching the stars, and the water passing under them. Then Devlin took me by the hand, led me under the bridge, and left me there. In a moment, he was back, his arms full. He'd carried an oversized down blanket and two small pillows in his motorcycle saddlebags, as well as a silenced explosive bullets handgun. The latter he got out and lay within reach of the makeshift bed, before helping me unstrap my armor, and taking my clothes and his off. Devlin made love to me there under the bridge by the banks of the river. Again, he didn't draw it out, using his skill so that when I came, he came with me.

We lay afterwards in each other's arms, gasping for breath. As our hearts slowed, I clutched him to me, worried suddenly that something was going to go wrong, as it usually did when things between he and I were going so well.

"Why are you anxious?" he whispered, stroking my hair back from my face. "I can scent your change in mood."

"Just worried that forever won't be long enough," I quipped, unwilling to bring heaviness to the conversation.

Devlin had no such compunction. "You don't live a long time by working hard, being careful, or even being bold, Love. It's all luck. There were several times I came close to dying, and clawed my way back. There were just as many that I couldn't stop, that Lash saved me from, or his friend."

"What friend?" I asked curiously.

"There was another guard who was a good friend to both he and I for many years," Devlin said, heavy sadness in his voice. "But let us not mention that tonight. There will be other nights to tell you of my past. This night is for us to think about the future, Sar."

His use of my name instead of an endearment got him all of my attention.

"We'll do this every year from now on," Dev continued softly. "I've ridden over this bridge many times, Sar, sometimes with Lash, and sometimes with some of the bears. It was just another bridge to cross, and it didn't matter very much—"

This wasn't about bridges at all.

"—but this is our bridge now," he said softly, touching my face gently. "Because I want you to know it means a great deal to me that you'll be here with me next year. That we'll share nights like this one again, for the rest of eternity."

There was something heartfelt in Devlin's tone which brought to mind Danial's tender words of affection. Even though his words seemed a little too smooth, I decided to give him the benefit of the doubt. "It means something to me, too. I want to be here with you, Dev. I don't want to ever be without you again."

"You won't be, Love," he said softly, kissing me.

We lay together for a while after, just holding each other, enjoying the warm breeze caressing our skin with feather touches. "We need to get going, Sar," Devlin said reluctantly. "The night is passing. In three hours or so, it will be dawn."

Quickly, we dressed, and he helped me strap the armor back on. With a last look at the river, I let him lead me back to the bike. After a careful check, Devlin and I got back on. We were less than halfway back when I felt the tire under me began to slide.

I don't know what happened. Suddenly Devlin swerved, we were leaning too far left, and all of a sudden the motorcycle was no longer beneath me, the ground rushing up to meet us. Devlin twisted in the air, trying to wrap his body around mine to protect me. As we hit the pavement with a bone-jarring crunch, I heard something snap in him. Dev let out a hiss of pain through gritted teeth as we rolled over and over, finally coming to rest on our backs near some bushes.

I lay there breathing hard, thanking God to be alive and promising fervently to never get on a motorcycle again. Devlin lay partly under me, his body still enfolding mine.

"Dev—" I whispered.

His hand covered my mouth in a flash. I went still immediately, waiting in silence, my heart hammering.

"Dalcon," a voice called. "Get up."

Our accident had been an ambush. *Who was out there? Why the hell hadn't Devlin said there was someone looking to kill him?* I would have insisted on guards if I'd known.

Devlin made no reply.

"Answer me, Dalcon, or I'll shoot your lady. When you start screaming, I'll know your vocal abilities are still there."

God. I felt frantically for my cell phone, then remembered it was in my purse on the front seat of Lash's truck.

"I'm here," Devlin said spitefully. "Who are you and what do you want with me?"

A familiar figure walked into the light. "It's him," Catherine said, rancor in each word as she stared at us with red eyes. "That's his Oathed One, Sar."

Devlin hissed, baring his fangs at her. She gave him a cold look.

A man stepped out beside Catherine. I didn't recognize his handsome features. He had brown hair to his shoulders, and green eyes like mine. His body was similar to Aran's, tall and rangy, though his shoulders were narrower, and his waist thicker. He looked to be in his twenties, but if he was vampire like Catherine, he could have been far older.

Devlin did recognize him. He hissed again, baring his fangs. "Ulysses."

"How gratifying, Dalcon," the man said. "I thought you had forgotten me."

"I had, until now," Devlin said easily.

"Get up, both of you," Ulysses said.

He had no gun or weapon. *Why wasn't Devlin kicking his ass?* We'd lost our gun, sure, but still…

Devlin got up and faced Ulysses, keeping me behind him. "You're a fool to ambush me. You've only brought yourself more misery—"

"I beg to differ," Ulysses said in a charming manner. "You owe me."

"I owe you nothing," Devlin said arrogantly.

"You owe me," Ulysses repeated with white-hot anger. "Grab them!"

Arms grabbed me from behind, pulling me away from Devlin. I screamed, kicking and pushing, but the limbs were immovable as steel bands. Devlin lunged for me, snarling, but four men grasped him, restraining him as he thrashed.

"Let us go!" I screamed. "You've signed your own death warrant—"

Ulysses strode up to Devlin, and shot him in the heart, the brief flash illuminating Devlin's explosive bullet's gun. Devlin convulsed with the impact, and went down hard.

"Dev!" I screamed, struggling hard. The man holding me laughed, then squeezed, making me choke.

"Get up," Ulysses said in contempt. "I know that leather is more than it appears."

Devlin rolled over onto his side. I sagged with relief, to see him moving. "What do you want?" he said, his words coming with effort. "I can't bring your sister back."

"You knew she was in love with you! You used her! You turned her!"

"She knew what she wanted, and I gave it to her," Devlin said contemptuously. "It's not my fault she ran afoul of some vampire hunters. If she hadn't been dumb enough to leave drained corpses lying around—"

Ulysses shot Devlin again in the back. This time, Devlin screamed.

"Stop it, Please!" I screamed. "Please!"

Ulysses shot him twice more, each bullet booming in the quiet. Devlin screamed each time, his smoking form writhing on the ground. I began sobbing, still pleading for Ulysses to stop.

Ulysses crouched down and held the gun to Devlin's head. Devlin looked up at him, his eyes red and hateful, hissing in pain.

"You think you'll heal a gunshot wound to the head, if the bullet's explosive?" Ulysses said thoughtfully. "I'm thinking not. There are all those stories about vampires being decapitated and dying. But maybe it would just paralyze you. Unless of course, I aimed for your throat, and it took your head clean off—"

This wasn't about ransom. This man wanted revenge. He was going to kill Devlin unless someone saved us. Tears flooded my eyes and ran down my cheeks. No one knew where we were. No help would come in time to save Devlin.

"—but you aren't getting off that easy," Ulysses said hatefully. "I've heard there are more than a few ways for you to die. Fire, decapitation, a stake, an explosive bullet, or pretty much anything that destroys your heart. But it's universally agreed that the most painful way is burning by sunlight." Ulysses leaned closer, his soft words ringing out in the stillness of the night. "You and I have a date with Mr. Sun at ten a.m., Dalcon. I want you to think about that tonight—"

"Fuck you, and fuck your sister!" Devlin spat with cold malice. "She was just a whore anyway—"

Ulysses shot him four more times. When the smoke and echoes cleared, Devlin was keening softly. I shuddered, knowing how badly he had to be hurt.

Ulysses got to his feet. "Bring them to the vans and let's go."

"I want my money," Catherine said to Ulysses, flashing her fangs. "I told you I could get that tracking device onto his bike—"

"You'll get it when he's dust, vampire," Ulysses said, not looking at her.

"You sold me out for money?" Devlin hissed with effort and agony, his eyes glowing faintly red. "You fucking bitch! I should've carved out your mercenary heart—"

"Why not?" she said back hatefully. "You've treated me like dirt ever since you turned me. I was fine to fuck every few decades when you were bored." She glared over at me, then back at him. "This was about me hurting you. The money's just a bonus."

Devlin and I were shoved into separate vans, the majority of men, Ulysses, and Catherine with Devlin, and two men with me. They clearly feared his power, even wounded. I'd glimpsed the bloodstained pavement where he had been lying. Even if he'd healed his wounds, Dev had to be very weak, losing that much blood. But maybe I could use their fear to my advantage.

* * * *

We drove for what seemed like a long time. The dark night was suddenly no longer magical, it was terrifying, and I couldn't think of anything except what they might be doing to Devlin. But my mind shortly moved on to thinking frantically of what they might do to me after they finished with him.

Finally, we were taken out of the vans and ushered into a large, shadowy building. As we entered the stained glass doors, I realized it was an old church. Titus wouldn't be teleporting in to save us. He couldn't walk on hallowed ground, nor could Terian. Desperately, I tried to teleport myself over and over as they dragged me inside, to no avail.

I was thrown into a room, the door locked behind me. At once I huddled and began sobbing my heart out, letting my terror and fear break free. Ten minutes later, I dried my eyes on an old sash and began getting myself together. If Lash didn't come, I'd better find some way to get out of here myself. There was no hope for Devlin unless I got help in time.

I got up and searched the room, than sat there for a long time, thinking of different scenarios and options. I was in the small, cramped room that brides had once used to get ready for their wedding. There was a phone, but it was disconnected. I couldn't use any lock picking skills, as there was most likely a guard at the door. Besides, I didn't have my tools, and there was no tool of any kind in this room. The only possible weapon was a metal cross on a stand. While helpful against demons, it wasn't heavy enough to knock a hole in the wall, especially not knowing what was on the other side. Besides, the guard would hear the noise.

I considered seduction, then bravely attempted it, calling sweetly to the guard that I was scared and lonely. There was no reply. Stymied, I sat down with my back to the wall and tried again to teleport, with no success.

Finally at about two a.m., footsteps walked up to the door, and then Ulysses came in. He shut the door behind him, then turned to me, green eyes staring into mine.

I curled myself up tight in a ball. I wanted to plead for Devlin, but I knew it wouldn't do any good. Telling him he was a bastard probably also wasn't a good idea.

"Sarelle," Ulysses said softly. "Be calm. You won't be harmed."

That was bullshit for sure. "Then let me go."

"I want no quarrel with Racklan, or O'Connor," he said, crouching down beside me.

He was going to get one with Danial shortly, for killing his brother. "Then let Dev go—"

"It's well known your lovers don't get along. O'Connor hates Dalcon. Racklan will probably thank me, as you'll revert solely to him—"

I kept my expression neutral. Enemies like Ulysses were the reason Danial and Devlin kept their kinship secret. "If you hate vampires so much, why are you partnering with one?"

"It's necessary," Ulysses replied. "When Devlin is dead, I'll call Racklan on his company line, and tell him where you are. Perhaps he'll even pay a good faith ransom for you."

That would be too late. "Please let me go," I said in the most pitiful tone I could muster.

"You are Oathed to Dalcon," Ulysses said flatly. "That's what I heard, though I don't see his symbol at your throat. You'd try to save him. You aren't going to leave here until he's dead."

This was useless. "Can you have someone take me to the bathroom then?"

He got suspicious immediately. "Don't think about escaping," he growled.

"Look," I said, holding up my hands. "This isn't a movie, and I'm not a super spy. I just want to use the ladies room and then you can lead me back here."

"You have any phones on you?"

"I don't have a phone, credit card, keys, or even any money," I said, real defeat in each word. "I'm going nowhere."

Ulysses nodded, satisfied. "Come with me," he said, gesturing to me to follow.

I got up and followed him down the hall to the bathroom. I looked in each room we passed, but there was no sign of anyone; no screams or even talking. Worse, there was nothing in any of the rooms to help me: no phones, no exits, no keys lying on tables, no tools, not even some gasoline and pack of matches conveniently within reach.

When I was finished, Ulysses put me back in the room and locked the door, then walked away.

I sat down, debating courses of action. I wanted to remove the armor, as it was stifling, and hadn't been made to sit in for long periods of time. Yet I didn't, too worried that I'd be unprepared if a chance to escape presented itself. Instead, I walked slowly back and forth for a half hour, and then rested for a half hour lying prone on the floor. I alternated between the two actions all through the rest of the night, waiting and hoping for rescue. But dawn came and went and no one appeared.

Devlin began to shriek around ten a.m. The horrible sounds of pain went on and on, undulating in volume and strength as the minutes ticked by. Unhinged, I sobbed as I listened to him scream. They were burning him, and there was nothing I could do but listen. I cursed my inability to teleport, furious at fate. A month ago we would have been safe back at Hayden the moment I'd known we were in danger. I'd forgotten everything that mattered, and relied too much on my teleportation power. *If I'd brought even one clip and my gun, I'd be free now...*

Dev's screams finally died off about eleven. I cried harder at the silence, wondering if he was dead.

The day wore on, the time passing at a crawl. No one came back to check on me, or to even offer me water, much less food. I was hungry, and desperately thirsty. In my frustration and need, I began screaming, hammering at the door with my gloved fists. But no one came.

Around three, Devlin began to shriek again. I cried out with relief that he was still alive, but despair engulfed me, knowing I couldn't do anything to stop his pain...

My head snapped up, realization dawning. *I could hear him...that meant he could hear me.* "Please, hold on," I screamed out tearfully. "I'm okay, Dev. Hold on! I love you!"

Devlin didn't reply, his screams continuing. I shouted out that I loved him and to hold on a few times more, then burst into frenzied sobbing, collapsing on the floor.

* * * *

When I came to, my watch said eight p.m. I groggily got to my feet, stretching my sore muscles.

The screaming had stopped. Whether that meant Devlin was dead, I wasn't sure. *How much burning could he withstand?* In the movies, a vampire was toast after being exposed for a minute or so. A few seconds of clouded daylight in a snowstorm had burned Devlin badly. He'd had two hours of late summer sun today. *How much pain could his mind and body endure?*

62

I hammered on the door. "Please, I have to go to the bathroom!"

Despite my hammering and pleas, no one came. Eventually, I did what I had to in the closet, crying at the shame of it. Asking God to understand, that I'd never have done this willingly if I'd had a choice, I put some old boxes of hymnals over the mess, and then closed the closet door, shutting off the stink.

Dejected and hopeless, I went back out to the middle of the room, and sat down on the floor. I was sitting there an hour later, my head on my hands, when the door opened silently, and a man wearing body armor came in.

I blinked, amazed Theo had found me. Then I took in the dull black armor.

"Sar," a familiar hissing voice said. "Come. Hurry."

I got to my feet and ran to him, stifling my cry of relief. Lash helped me put my helmet on, and then grabbed my gloved hand, leading me fast through the darkness. I followed him as fast as I could through the shadows, emerging from the church into pine trees. We ducked into the thick stand, then began running fast. When we were a hundred yards away, Lash ducked behind a tree, and took off his helmet, facing me.

"Where is Dev?" he hissed urgently, his tongue flicking the air. "Do you know?"

"I don't know," I gasped, pulling off my helmet. "I haven't seen him since they brought us here. They tortured him twice today with sunlight. I heard him screaming, Lash—" Hysteria laced my words and I clamped down hard on it, fighting for control.

Lash gave a grimace of pain. "How long?" he hissed.

"An hour each time," I replied, tears in my eyes. "Can he survive that?"

"Yes, but it's going to be bad," he said softly, rubbing his brow. "I'm telling you now, so you can prepare yourself."

"Just get him out of there, please," I said. "It doesn't matter to me. Just save him."

Lash put his hand on my shoulder and squeezed. "I'll get him. Follow this line of trees to the edge of the road. A Hummer is waiting there—"

"It's a church," I said quickly. "Titus won't be able to teleport in."

"Go, Sar," Lash ordered harshly. "We don't have time for this."

The feeling of being immersed in ice-cold water bathed me from head to toe. Lash was here all by himself. "You can't do this alone."

"I need your help," Lash hissed urgently. "Get to the Hummer. There's a rifle in the back; it's loaded and ready. Wait here and cover us when you see me coming. I'll be carrying him. With that much daylight, he'll be hurt too bad to walk."

I nodded. "I can do that."

Lash nodded once. "I know you can. Go."

I leaned in and kissed him. Lash grabbed me and kissed me back for a second, then broke away, giving me a shove towards the road.

I turned and ran for all I was worth, my legs pumping, my lungs burning. By the faint moonlight, the tree line was easy to follow. In a few minutes, I reached the road.

Breathing a sigh of relief, I opened the SUV door, grabbing the rifle sitting in the front seat. I'd expected an assault rifle, something automatic or semiautomatic, at least. This was semiautomatic, but it was a target rifle. *Why had Lash brought this?* At least the scope on top was familiar. I checked the chamber, ejecting the loaded round in the process.

When I retrieved the familiar-looking round, I understood. This rifle was loaded with a type of explosive bullets. *Had Lash converted it?* I'd never seen a rifle that took this kind of ammunition, only handguns.

Shouldering the gun, I checked the Hummer for more ammo, discovering a handgun that shot explosive bullets on the back floor and some extra clips. Grabbing them all, I loaded the gun and put it in my pocket, putting the clips in the other pocket. There was also one more clip for the rifle on the dashboard, which I put into the pocket with the handgun.

Gunshots sounded behind me suddenly. Terror and adrenaline spiking through me, I turned and began running as fast as I could back through the trees.

I got to the tree where Lash had stopped, then looked around for a gun rest with a clear view of the route from the church that offered some kind of concealment. Quickly, I headed twenty yards sideways to a nearby double trunked tree, laying the rifle through the crotch. Thank God, it was just the right height.

More gunshots sounded, then shouts. Lash had been discovered.

I began sighting in the gun, focusing the scope. This was going to be hard; they would be running and moving fast, and I'd have only a second for each shot before I'd lose the target. I was going to have to aim and shoot faster than I ever had, and make every shot count.

Lash appeared, a body swathed in cloth on his shoulder, a gun in his hand. He ducked behind a tree, shielding Devlin, then fired a few shots at his pursuers. Bullets kicked up leaves and needles all around him.

I saw glimpses of the men after him, a shoulder appearing here, then a hand with a gun there. They didn't have armor, but they were some kind of were. I'd have to get their hearts or heads to kill them.

Shaking, I took careful aim at the lead one. He was behind a tree, only his arm visible.

Lash fired again. The lead man ducked behind a tree, hiding from Lash and giving me a clear view of him. I shot him in the chest, and he fell, his heart exploding in a burst of blood.

The remaining men fired at me. I shot back a few times, making them duck their heads, trying to give Lash cover to get Devlin away. But each time he went to move they fired en mass, pinning him down.

There were too many of them. We needed something to flush them out…

Lash suddenly threw something back at them. A few seconds later, there was an explosion. Knocked off balance, I gripped the tree to steady myself, then grabbed for my gun, looking through the scope.

Lash had made it another ten yards closer to the Hummer, and killed another man with grenade shrapnel, yet they were closing in on him. But with that action, he'd given me targets aplenty.

I acted fast, picking off two more, and then another two. The last one I hit in the leg, and Lash finished him off for me, his bullet catching the man in the throat, decapitating him in a shower of gore. One raised up his head to shoot. I sighted and squeezed, the gun uselessly clicking on an empty chamber.

Swearing, I popped out the clip, pocketed it and slammed in the new one, shoving back the slide to chamber the bullet. Re-sighting, I picked off another man, hitting him in the leg, then the arm, then the heart.

There were too many left, and they were close to Lash, only fifteen feet or so. In panic, I let loose a barrage of bullets, making them duck for cover as tree trunks blew apart and toppled. Lash bolted, making it to a tree ten yards away just as my rifle clicked on empty a second time. A hail of bullets ricocheted around me as the men returned fire, blowing the double trunked tree into pieces, the large trunks crashing down in opposite directions as I huddled behind the tree stump.

The gunfire faded. I stayed down, waiting.

"He's out," an unknown voice called. "Move in."

I peered out carefully. No one shot at me. Slinging the empty rifle over my shoulders, I took out the handgun and clicked off the safety, then began moving furtively towards the Hummer. The men and Lash were in front of me now, with no clear targets. I'd have to get closer to be of any use. Hopefully, this armor worked against explosive bullets.

I moved from tree to tree, nearing the men closing in on Lash. They ignored me, focusing on him and Devlin. Just as I got close enough to shoot one, Lash made a dash for it. They shot him twice in the back, and he pitched forward from the impact, Devlin's prone form falling in the dirt.

The men came out from behind trees, walking openly towards Lash and Dev. I shot three of them down in succession, but missed the last one, who ducked behind a tree, the shot for his heart thudding harmlessly into the thick pine bark and blowing a huge chunk from the left side.

I waited carefully for him to move, my gun aimed at the remains of the trunk. Lash stayed prone, on the ground, Devlin's form still before him. One pale hand with a gold ring was visible, the skin black in places, scorched. My face twisted in anger. Bullets were too kind for these men.

"You aren't going to just walk out of here," the man shouted. "Your leader's dead. Put down your gun, and we'll let you live."

Pleased that he thought I was a professional, I almost thanked him. Biting my tongue, I sighted in on the trunk, then blew the right side into pieces. The trunk swayed, then fell, exposing the man as he made a dash towards Lash, firing three shots at me.

I ducked down, then peered around the trunk just in time to see the last man approach Lash, and ease him over with his foot. Lash made no sound as he flopped bonelessly onto his back. The man lowered his gun and shot him again in the chest. Lash's body jerked.

Fury filled me. *I didn't have a clear shot!* I broke cover, moving fast, my gun held in both hands.

The man pulled off Lash's helmet, looking down at him in contempt. "So this is the famous Lash," he said with sarcasm. "I'd heard you were the best. What a lie that was."

I almost had a shot! Just a little closer...

The man eased back the trigger, the click loud.

He was going to shoot him in the head. If Lash wasn't already dead, he'd be killed. I stopped where I was and fired, the shot hitting a tree. The man wheeled around, and shot back. I dove for the closest tree, the bullets whining past me taking the bark off inches from my side. I took a breath, then peered out, immediately catching a bullet in the arm. With a cry of fear, I fell backwards from the sudden impact.

"Argh!" the man screamed.

The bullet hadn't gone through my armor, or so I hoped. I staggered to my feet, my arm numb, grasping the tree for support.

"Arghhh!" the man screamed again. Another gunshot sounded.

I stumbled towards Lash, bathed in fear, my mind screaming at me to move faster before it was too late.

Yet another gunshot sounded.

Lash had the man fast on his knees, fangs buried in his throat. But his poison wasn't working. The man was flailing and fighting. I ran towards them just as the man put the gun to Lash's temple, and eased back the hammer. Lash glared up at the man, still biting him hard.

I took aim and fired. The side of the man's head exploded, and he sagged, the gun dropping from his hand.

Lash abruptly shoved him backwards, and looked up at me. "Thanks," he hissed.

I swayed, blinking back welling tears as I looked down at Devlin's covered form. "You wrapped him in an altar cloth."

"It was available." Lash picked up Devlin, shouldering him. As he did the cloth moved, revealing the extent of Dev's injuries on his arms: most of his naked skin scorched black, giant red blisters on the remainder weeping fluid.

I swallowed hard. "Oh God—"

"Hurry, Sar," Lash ordered. "We're not safe yet."

We hurried to the Hummer. I opened the back hatch for Lash, and he laid Dev carefully inside. "Will he be okay?" I asked.

Lash nodded. "He needs blood. I'll be back with some. Stay with him and guard him, Sar. But do it from the front seat; no closer. He'll be uncontrollable when he awakens."

I nodded.

"It'll be close to a half hour."

I put my hand on his shoulder. "You can't go back, not alone. You're hurt."

"I'm fine," Lash said with a grimace, straightening himself up. "The armor took the bullets. None got through. But I'll be feeling it tomorrow for damn sure."

I gave him an uneasy look.

"Just stay quiet here in the Hummer," he said, speed dialing his cell phone. "Lee to Jackson," he hissed into it. "Teleport now."

A moment later, Titus appeared with all of the bears, all dressed in armor and loaded up for war. I gaped in amazement. So much for Terian's decree that a being couldn't teleport more than one person at a time.

Titus and the bears clustered around Lash.

"Nick and Jazz, go to the left and create a diversion with Titus. The rest of you are with me at the front."

"How many?" Titus rumbled.

"Sar and I have killed over half," Lash replied. "There are only maybe eight or nine left, including a female vampire. Do not shoot to kill. We need all the prisoners alive, though wounds are acceptable. Meet back here in thirty minutes. Titus, stay and raze the church to the ground when we're done."

All the bears shot me a look when they heard I'd killed that many, but none said anything. Titus, Nick, and Jazz headed off through the trees, Lash and the rest going down the road a ways, then into the woods.

I locked all the doors, reloaded the pistol, and then sat there in the front seat with it in my lap, trying to muster up the strength to look back at the ruin that was Devlin.

I'd gotten another glimpse when Lash had put him in the car. His face had been unrecognizable, his eyes closed. Most of his skin was blackened, at least from what I'd seen. *How much of the damage was healable?*

I looked in the glove compartment again, this time searching for a phone, but there was none. *Danial needed to be told Devlin was safe...*

I rubbed my eyes. *Why wasn't Terian here, or Theo?* Even if they'd hated Devlin, they'd have come for me. *Hadn't anyone told them we'd been kidnapped?*

I wasn't sure how much time passed. Finally the sound of approaching bears became evident, the sounds of struggling and cursing loud in the still night air.

The werebears came into view, most of them each holding onto a male prisoner who was struggling. Last came Lash dragging Catherine, whose hands and elbows were bound.

I opened the door and got out. The scent of smoke filled my nostrils, carried by the wind.

"Let me go, you vile snake!" Catherine screamed. "I'm a state Ruler! I demand my rights—!"

"Get out of the Hummer, Sar, and stand over by the trees," Lash hissed, pulling her towards the Hummer.

"You bastard!" Catherine screeched, stumbling, trying to dig in her heels. "Let me go, Lash! He had this coming for how he treated me! He deserved it!"

Lash opened the hatch, then whirled, his knife flashing in an arc as it cut her throat. Catherine gagged, clutching at the wound. It began to close, even as her blood spilled out. Lash pushed her inside next to Devlin, then slammed the hatch, locking the doors.

There was sudden movement through the glass, and then Catherine began screaming, wailing in fear and terror. She pounded on the glass, her superhuman strength shattering it, the shards exploding outwards in a shower. She scrabbled at the ragged opening, then black hands with taloned fingers snatched her, dragging her backwards as she screeched, blackened skin falling off to reveal red angry flesh. Her screams cut off abruptly, the sound of wet crunching and sucking loud in the cool night air.

Lash suddenly walked over and grabbed another one of the prisoners. The man struggled in mortal fear, flailing and screaming. Lash decked him hard in the face, and the man went to his knees, swaying. Lash cut his throat quickly, then pushed him through the hatch opening in one fluid motion.

Again there were screams, though these cut off quickly. There was the sound of gagging, then frightened whimpering, then gurgling that became a rattling gasp.

I walked closer to the trees, sitting down with my back to a tree facing into the woods. Leaning back against the trunk, I put my helmet on, blocking out the worst of the sounds and closed my eyes.

Three more times there were screams, and each time, they died into silence. Then finally, Lash opened the back of the SUV. "Another?" he hissed softly.

"No," Devlin replied in his usual voice. "Bring the others to Hayden. I'll need to feed again in an hour or two. There is too much damage to me to heal it all at once."

"Sure," Lash hissed. "Nick," he said loudly. "Gather the prisoners and get them settled in cells. Jazz, I want a complete tally of injuries later tonight. Get moving."

There was the sound of movement.

Knowing I had to face it, I stood up and turned.

Devlin stood there with his back to me, his golden hair again shoulder length, his arms no longer black, but still an angry red, like a bad sunburn. He was naked save for the altar cloth tied around his waist. There were a few bodies lying by the open back door of the Hummer, contorted in death. Lash loaded the bodies into the SUV, then stepped back. Titus hit it with one of his fireballs. Within seconds, the Hummer was burning. The gas tank exploded soon after, making me cringe behind the nearest tree.

The smell of blood, urine, and fecal matter was pungent, laced with the sickening smell of burned rubber and oil. Titus teleported the prisoners back to Hayden and most of the men, leaving only Devlin, Lash, and I left to watch the remains of the fire as it began to die.

"I'll make a final sweep," Lash hissed to Devlin. "Ulysses was not among the men we captured or those killed. Catherine said he was to come back tonight to finish you."

"Yes," Devlin said hollowly. "He told me that, too."

"I'll be back soon," Lash hissed. "Half hour, tops." He gave Devlin a lopsided grin. "Stay here by the fire, and don't be wandering off."

"Thanks for coming for me," Devlin said softly, deep emotion in each word. "I owe you one, friend."

"You owe me nothing," Lash hissed, grinning wider. "I still owe you, Dev."

"Fuck you, Lash, I do owe you," Devlin said in broken tones, walking over to him. "I owe you everything all over again."

Lash grabbed him in a fierce hug, even though Devlin was covered with blood. Devlin held Lash to him just as tightly, as if he would never let him go.

"I'll always come for you, so long as I can still move," Lash hissed affectionately. "I'm glad you're still alive. I thought there was a good chance you wouldn't be, when Catherine said it was Ulysses who had done this."

"If you hadn't gotten here when you did, I wouldn't be," Devlin said tiredly, drawing back. "And it's my own fault, for being so fucking reckless. How did you finally find us?"

"I used the magical tracer you had Titus put on Sar months ago. You'd thought someone might try to get to Theo through her; that she might be kidnapped. We never had to use it, but the tracer was still active. The bitch of it was the signal was weak because the spell was so old. The beacon faded out miles from here, long before I got close to this spot in the Hummer. Because of that, it took a while to track you down. I had to search a lot of fucking fields and forest before I found you."

That tracing spell was what Titus had bribed Dev with to let him build his house for Leri. I'd stake my life on it...

"Where's Sar?" Devlin interrupted. "She's okay, or you would have said already—"

"She's behind you, watching us," Lash said, casting a glance at me. "And yes, she is unharmed."

Devlin didn't turn, which I thought odd. Lash moved off into the trees, making his final sweep.

I went up closer to Dev, but stayed a few feet back from him. "Are you okay?"

"No," he said softly. "I'm still badly hurt. Don't touch me or come any closer, not until I'm healed. I can smell your blood from here, and I want it desperately. Move back right now, Love."

I immediately moved back from him several yards. "I'm glad you're okay. I was so worried you were dead, Dev."

Devlin didn't reply, watching the dying embers of the incinerated Hummer.

Titus appeared. "Who's first?"

"We'll all go together," Devlin replied. "Go check on him."

Titus winked out, then reappeared with Lash.

"No sign of Ulysses," Lash hissed to Devlin. "Likely he was warned back when we attacked."

"We'll deal with him later," Devlin said hatefully. "Titus, take us home."

"One at a time," he replied. "I'm tired." Titus grabbed my hand in his and took me to Hayden, then appeared a moment later with Devlin.

Dev abruptly went to the basement door and opened it. "I'm going to go downstairs to feed. Sar, please wait for me upstairs." He went down, shutting the door after him.

"He's still badly injured, Sarelle," Titus rumbled. "His face, especially. He doesn't want you to see him until he's healed more of the injuries."

I nodded. "You'd better go back for Lash."

Titus nodded. "Go upstairs and take a long hot shower. Tell me if you discover any wounds that need healing. I'll be right back."

When I emerged from the shower, I tossed my wet hair in a clip, threw on some clothes, and then went looking for Lash. As I brought up my hand to knock on his door, Titus caught it in his grip.

"He's resting," Titus said, his red eyes glowing in the gloom. "He's been up since he realized you were both being held somewhere. He's exhausted. Let him sleep."

I nodded reluctantly, then went back to Devlin's room. After putting on some heavy pajamas, I crawled into bed, drifting off into sleep almost instantly.

* * * *

When Devlin came up sometime later, he woke me.

"Dev?" I called, suddenly scared.

"Don't turn on the light, Love," he said softly in the darkness. "I don't want you to see me like this."

I was worried for him, but also scared of what he might do in his wounded state. "Should I leave?"

"No, I won't hurt you, Love. I'll just be a moment in the shower. Stay here, please."

I nodded, knowing he could see me, and then settled back into bed. I meant to stay awake, but in my exhaustion, I drifted back to sleep.

Again he woke me when he slid into bed beside me. But instead of hugging me as he always did, he lay there on his side, not touching me.

I turned and faced him. "Will it hurt if I touch you?"

"No," Devlin said, uncomfortable. "Just don't touch my face."

I pulled him carefully into my arms, cradling his shoulders. He moved over closer to me. I reached down to help him and felt silk.

Devlin took my hand quickly, moving it into his. "I'm glad you weren't harmed. I was worried when I first heard you scream."

He had put on pajamas, to cover the remaining injuries. Don't call attention to it. "I love you," I said tenderly. "I thought I was never going to see you again, Dev."

"Me, too," he said softly, laying back on me. "I thought I'd never hold you again."

71

"I'm here," I said, biting my lips to hold back the tears. I touched him gently, sliding my hand into his hair. Instead of hair, I suddenly touched a patch of rough ridged skin. Dev instantly recoiled, moving away from me.

I felt terrible. "I'm sorry, if I hurt you."

"It's not that," he muttered brokenly. "I want to feel your arms around me more than anything, Love. But I'm still badly hurt. Worse, it will take some time to heal."

"It doesn't matter what you look like. I still love you."

"You will not say that when you see me," he said, anguished.

Time to be brave. "I'll see you tomorrow when we wake up together. You might as well show me now."

Devlin gave a deep sigh, then reached over and turned on the light. He carefully turned to face me.

I wanted to scream. Ulysses had taken one of Dev's beautiful golden eyes. There was just a ruined socket where the right eye should be. His face was red in places, and there were some small patches of new skin. But most of his face was still scorched black, bubbly and blistered.

I clamped down on my terror and pity. If Dev could take the pain of his injuries, I could handle looking at them. "You must be in agony. Can't Titus do anything?"

Devlin shook his head. "Ulysses did the worst to my face, though there was one other area he worked on with equal vigor," he said morosely. "But at least the pain is bearable now."

His arms were now completely healed, his skin luminous there. I reached out, and touched his arm, stroking gently. "Come to me, so I can hold you," I offered.

Dev came into my arms. I stroked his hair, careful not to touch his face.

"Love," Devlin said, sighing. "There's more I have to tell you. I won't be able to make love with you for a while until I completely regenerate. And even then, it…I may not be the same. I've never been burned this badly there. And burning wasn't all that he did. He cut me as well."

I froze, closing my eyes at the horror of it. But from Ulysses' point of view, what better punishment? What would be more fitting? He'd wanted to hurt Devlin as much as he could. Devlin valued his good looks and his sexual prowess above all. Ulysses had taken both from Dev with sunlight. "The pain must have been unimaginable—"

"I'll heal in time," Devlin said sadly. "But I understand if you don't want to be around me until I do. I look like a monster."

I leaned in and kissed him very gently on his partially healed lips.

"How can you kiss me?" he said, abashed. "Am I not repellent to you?"

"No, of course not," I said lovingly. "I love you, Devlin Dalcon. And I'm going to take care of you until you're better."

Devlin began crying softly. I gently kissed away his tears, wincing a little at the taste of burned flesh.

Chapter Five

That next morning, I drove to Danial's house and told Theo and Danial what had happened. Both of them were furious that Lash hadn't told them of the kidnapping.

"He told me you were in bed with Devlin," Theo growled. "That he couldn't disturb you. Now who is this Ulysses? What did Devlin do to him?"

I shrugged. "Something about turning his sister and her getting killed by vampire hunters."

"Ulysses's sister was just another casualty of Devlin's ever-present lust," Danial said with a sigh. "I'm not surprised. This is not the first time this has happened, that a male came to get revenge for one of his female relatives."

"Was Dev burned before?" I asked. "It's bad this time, Danial. Really bad."

Danial held my eyes. "Was he red, or black?"

"Black," I replied queasily. "He's taken the blood of five weres plus Catherine, and he's still not healed—"

"Who is Catherine?" Theo asked.

We both ignored him. "This sounds like it's the worst so far," Danial said with a sigh. "He never learns, Sar. He should not be going out with you alone, not unless you can teleport."

"And even then, not without guards," Theo growled. "He's supposed to be protecting you. Instead you're in more danger than you were before—"

"Lash saved us," I interjected. "And I helped him. I killed at least ten of them."

"You?" Theo said, giving me a shocked look. "With what?"

"You fought, Sar?" Danial said, looking at me as if I'd grown a third arm. "How? They were much stronger—"

"Yes, me," I said, suddenly irritated for some reason. "I'm an excellent shot, especially with a rifle." I paused. "I need to get back to Devlin. Danial, I'll be back later in the week to help you with e-mail, and hopefully see Theoron and Elle. Maybe we can see a movie here and get a pizza or something?"

Danial nodded. "That sounds like an excellent idea, Dearheart. Let's wait to make plans, though, until Devlin's healing progresses a little further. He needs you beside him, until the worst is over."

I nodded in return, relieved at his understanding. "All right," I turned from him to my werecougar husband, who was looking a lot less receptive. "I'll see you nights, Theo—"

"What?" Theo said incredulously. "You need to come home with me now. Devon needs you."

"Devlin needs me," I said angrily. "Devon has you, Theo. But I'd appreciate if you'll let him stay up to visit with me when I come later—"

"Do it, Theo," Danial interrupted. "Devlin needs to go with us to see the Rulers shortly. He needs to be recovered by then completely. You and I both know Samuel is not afraid of me."

I felt a chill.

Theo shut his mouth and nodded. "All right."

"I'll see you later, Sar," Danial said softly, giving me a hug. "Help Devlin call me later tonight, if he's well enough to. I want to hear his voice."

"I will," I affirmed, and then turned to Theo, holding out my arms for a hug.

He didn't move, his expression jealous and angry. Annoyed, I nodded to him and headed to the front door.

* * * *

All that week was more of the same. I left Devlin most nights and went to Danial's, telling Dev that I was trying to keep up with the workload. The truth was that I needed a break of a few hours daily when I did not smell burned flesh and blood. The odor lingered faithfully on Devlin, no matter that he showered each dawn.

Devlin regenerated a little more each day. By the end of the week, he had healed everything except his lost eye, and his privates. In the meantime, he had taken to wearing a black leather eye patch, something that oddly just increased his sex appeal.

"You now look as dangerous as I know you are," I teased. "It gives me a thrill."

"Good, because these will take longest," Devlin replied. "Repeated injuries heal slowly, Love. But in another few weeks, I should be fine."

"I'm glad," I said. "I saw your donors leaving at dawn."

75

"I don't usually take from five at a single session," Devlin said tentatively, as if he wasn't sure how I'd take it. "But I need a lot of blood. Luckily I have a lot of regulars, as I'm out of prisoners."

I'd known he would kill all of them, but the offhand way he referred to it took me aback. "Whatever helps you heal quicker," I said a little too brightly.

Devlin turned to me, his expression one of reluctance. "Vampires can drink from the dead," he said, "but it's not often done. The blood congeals quickly, and the taste…I'd liken it to eating rotten or overripe fruit. The sensation is unpleasant. But most of all, with the heart stopped, the blood doesn't flow, so very little can be sucked out. You can bite repeatedly in several places, but you're not going to end up with much for your trouble."

"I'm not judging you for killing people who were torturing you and would have killed me, too," I said, an edge to my tone. "Please don't feel badly about what you had to do."

"On the contrary, I'm feeling much better. I'll be well enough to meet with Samuel and Perseus," Devlin said, some of his old arrogance back in his tone. "Don't worry, Sar."

I hugged him gently. "I'm not. I'm more concerned that I still can't hold my only daughter. Serena says that Venus bites her every night without fail."

"V," Dev corrected. "I've been calling her V for short. But Serena's right. She won't let you go if she tastes your blood. It's better to wait until she's older. How is she?"

"Healthy and happy," I assured him. "Now get some rest."

"How was the doctor visit today?"

"My virus levels are still very elevated. Stephen said they may go even higher."

Devlin made a disgruntled face. "Then I'll be good until we know for sure. Is Theo still giving you the cold shoulder?"

"Pretty much," I admitted. "But he does have Devon there at Danial's every night to see me."

"How is Dev Jr.?" Devlin teased. "It's almost like having a son."

I rolled my eyes. "Devon is growing fast; he's got to be twenty pounds or so. And he always bounds up to see me, letting out a little welcoming chirp with his tail held high."

"But Theo is distant?"

Was he concerned for me, or hopeful that my marriage would breakup? "He acts standoffish. I'm hoping he works it out on his own." I turned to him. "But I am worried about Lash. I wanted to thank him for saving us. Titus always tells me he's resting and not to disturb him. The bedroom door is always locked. Was he hurt in the fight?"

Devlin shook his head. "No, his armor was intact. It's top of the line, Sar, and made to last. Lash is just in his room because it's going to be winter soon. He hates winter, he always has. He stays inside under blankets as much as possible, going out only when he absolutely has to. He gets cold easily, so I try to send him out with Titus when he has to go somewhere."

"Titus probably loves that."

"Northeastern winters are hard on weresnakes. But don't worry about him," Devlin assured, reaching up to stroke the underside of my chin. "He's going to be sleeping or in his room for most of the winter. When spring gets here, he'll emerge hungry and horny."

"TMI," I said, appalled. "Now enough talking. Get some rest."

* * * *

Finally, that Friday just before I left to go home, I found Lash sitting on the couch reading a book with a few blankets piled over him. It was an old illustrated children's work called *The Fossil Snake*, one I remembered from my youth.

"My mom used to read that to me," I said, sitting down next to him. "I always hoped I'd find a fossil snake myself, but I never did."

"Are you making reference to my age?" Lash hissed, baring fangs in a smile. "I'm not old enough to be stone quite yet."

"I don't think of you as a pet," I assured him. "Plus you aren't the length of a pencil—"

"Careful," Lash hissed meaningfully. "You'll hurt my pride, making cracks about my length."

I flushed. "I didn't mean it like that."

"I know you didn't," he laughed. "Long time no see."

In spite of his good mood, Lash looked tired. "I'm going to have lunch before I leave for Danial's," I said. "Do you want me to heat you up some liquefied steak?"

"Yes, please," Lash hissed. "But only a little, as I ate already today. But a little would do the trick."

It had gotten much colder this past week. By the reports, it was going to be an early fall. "Do you want another blanket?" I offered, getting up.

Lash shook his head. "The one below me is heated," he said, grinning happily. "It's not my rock in the sun, but it feels pretty damn good."

"Why don't you have Devlin install a sun room here, some kind of atrium, with an indoor pond?" I asked, seized with sudden inspiration. "You could sunbathe indoors in the winter."

Lash raised his eyebrows. "And give any attacker a built-in torture chamber for Dev right inside his home?" He shook his head. "I couldn't risk it, Sar. Heated blankets are enough."

I bit my lip, irritated with myself for not thinking of Devlin's weakness to the sun, especially in light of recent events. "Stay there where you're warm. I'll be right back."

I brought my soup and his concoction into the living room after heating them up in the microwave. "Tell me if it's not hot enough," I said, handing him the mug. "I don't have anyone here to taste it."

Lash sipped it. "Plenty hot," he said, wincing a little. "But better too hot than too cold." He eyed me. "So what's new?"

"Nothing," I complained, sipping my soup. "That's the trouble. Everyone is waiting for my teleportation powers to come back. The vampire virus is still spiking, according to Stephen's last test."

"No wonder Dev's not more cheerful," Lash hissed, smirking. "He needs to dip his prongs."

"You're a piece of work," I replied, rolling my eyes.

"I try," Lash hissed, taking another sip. "Some people like my efforts more than others."

I bit my lip, clutching my mug with both hands. "Thank you," I said emotionally. "For rescuing me."

Lash looked up at me, his expression unreadable. "Don't go out again with him alone," he hissed softly. "Not without at least two bears, not for any reason. He asks you to ever again, you refuse."

I nodded "I will. Tell me, why didn't you tell anyone we'd been kidnapped?"

Lash's flat eyes bored into mine. "Because Theo would have cared about getting you out, not about saving Dev."

"But Theo could've helped—"

Lash shook his head. "Ulysses is good. This isn't the first time he's tried to hurt Dev. I knew Devlin would be well guarded where you were being held. Theo's strong, but he's not quiet, at least, not compared to me. He would have got to you, and then shot his way out. If they found you missing or got wind of an attack, they would have killed Dev immediately, rather than risk him being rescued. I had to save you both."

It was hard not to feel like my safety had been last on his list. "Why not rescue Devlin and then me?"

"Because I needed your help," Lash said meaningfully, flashing another smile. "I'm sure you've been waiting to hear that."

I blushed. "You are giving me too much credit. I—"

"No, I'm not," Lash said simply, fixing me with his eyes. "You covered us. You did it well. And you saved my life."

"Not that I'm not bursting with your praise," I said, embarrassed. "But why not go in with one of the bears as your partner? They've got to have more training than me."

"Because I trust you to do what I tell you," Lash replied. "The bears do have training, and some of that would have made them act and react differently than you did." He sipped again. "I needed you, not them."

"Are you going to take me on jobs?" I quipped. "We did make a good team."

"Don't let my accolades go to your head," Lash hissed tersely, looking over the top of his mug at me. "Ulysses isn't gone for good. He wants Devlin dead. Next time, he might decide you are the best bait to lure Dev to his doom. Be careful."

"I'll be careful," I said, cowed. "And I'll make sure we don't go out alone."

"I'm glad he has you," Lash hissed softly. "I don't think he'll mess up again, Sar."

Why was he bringing this up now, of all times? "Hopefully not—"

"You're taking care of him," Lash interrupted suddenly. He paused, staring at me. "I thought you were another flavor of the month when I met you." He lifted his lip, his expression disgusted. "I'm sorry for how I acted, back at the beginning."

"I know you are," I replied. "It's okay. It's in the past."

Lash looked away. "For a long time I've had Dev, and that was enough. But now there's you, him and V. It's nice to have relations again."

"Yes, it is," I replied.

"That doesn't mean you can't kiss me," Lash added, baring one fang. "In families, it's expected."

I leaned over and kissed him on the cheek. "There you go."

"Fine, be that way," Lash hissed jokingly. "I guess we have to be in danger for me to get any—"

"You're going to be wearing my soup," I warned.

"So long as it's warm," he retorted. "And chicken or beef. I don't wear vegetables."

I gave him a confused look, he gave me a toothy grin, and then both of us burst out laughing.

* * * *

"Remember you aren't coming next week on Friday," Devlin reminded me later that evening. "That's September 30th, to be exact. Danial, Theo, and I will be in Canada giving your health data to the other Rulers. You are going to stay with the children at Danial's." He hugged me. "I'll miss you next week, after having you so much to myself this week."

I nodded. "I'll be with him that whole weekend. It'll work out well. Danial and I haven't seen much of each other since Theo and I moved back into our own place. Maybe we can carve pumpkins or something with Theoron and Elle."

"I heard that the Harvesters had dropped off the face of the earth," Devlin said pointedly. "I'm not surprised; they had more than a few enemies that were just waiting for them to show up stateside. I am surprised how fast Theo decided it was safe for you he and Devon to return home, given no actual bodies have been found yet." He handed me my hair clip. "Danial said Theo had moved your things back to your house a few days ago."

Danial had taken the news of Theo and me returning to my old home okay. But it was in his neutral tone as we said goodbye how much he was hurting. That it was going to be another week before we spent any time together just twisted the knife that was already in his heart.

"How is it, being home?" Devlin asked.

Theo had been ecstatic to be back at my old house. It should have felt good to be home, but to me our old house didn't feel like home anymore. Jessica and Cavity missed Briar, and spent most of their time hiding. Devon missed Elle and Theoron, and moped sulkily. The dogs missed Ivan and Aran, and sat looking out the windows hopefully. And me...I missed Danial terribly, after having spent the better part of six months living at his home, and sleeping beside him most every night. The winter that was in the first breath of chill winds loomed before me, my heart weighted with sorrow.

I'd cried the first night alone with Theo. He comforted me, blaming it on the blood Danial had given me. But the truth was just that I loved Danial, and I wanted to be with him. All I could think was that he must be terribly lonely, going to his bed alone. Right or wrong, I resented Theo for making me leave him.

"Sar?" Devlin prompted.

"I miss him," I said hastily. "But we'll work it out." I kissed him quickly. "I'll see you in a week."

* * * *

That following week, the last of September, dragged interminably. I bore it, reasoning that Theo was right, that Danial's blood needed time to work itself out of my system and I'd feel better soon. But that didn't make my feelings of loss any lighter. Theo knew I was hurting, and didn't push, spending most of each day playing with Devon until his night shift started. I did my e-mail work from home, knowing if I was around Danial that I wouldn't be leaving him again easily.

Instead of my feelings of withdrawal lessening through the week, they intensified. Two days before the big meeting, I was inside in the shower, sobbing out my frustration and longing. Theo and Devon were out on the lawn playing with the dogs, oblivious.

I got out, wrapped my hair in a towel, and dried off, rubbing at my red eyes. Catching a glimpse of myself in the mirror, I was mortified at how haunted I looked. Determined to bring some normalcy back, I lathered on lotion, conditioned my hair, and shrugged on some jeans.

I rummaged in my bra drawer, pulled out one that Danial had gotten me a year back, and then burst into fresh tears.

I want to be with him. I want that more than anything—!

Suddenly, pitch-black darkness replaced my sunlit bedroom. I blinked, trying to see.

"Sar?" a voice whispered hopefully.

"Danial?" I said, turning.

Cool arms enfolded me. "You have regained your power, my darling," Danial whispered.

I threw my arms around him and kissed him passionately. Danial picked me up and laid me on his bed, easing off my jeans. His deft hands ran up my bare flesh lightly, then parted my thighs as he maneuvered between them.

"Sar," he murmured hungrily, then his lips devoured mine, his firm flesh pressing insistently. I yielded instantly with a cry of delight, urging him on with my hands that stroked his body, caressing and squeezing.

Our lust was primal, our breathing ragged panting as we strove together in need, coupling hard and fast. Too soon we crested the wave, each of us crying out our joy in the other, our tremors fading.

Instead of withdrawing or rolling off me, Danial wrapped his body around mine, clutching me hard. "I don't want you to leave," he said desperately. "Please don't leave me, Sar. This last week has been misery."

"I have to," I said tearfully. "I don't want to, Danial, but I have to."

"Damn Theo!" Danial cursed. "Damn him for always wanting to keep you all to himself."

"This isn't about him," I said gently. "It's about not being in thrall to your will. The line where you begin and I end is blurring for me, Danial. If I stay, I'll just lose even more of myself. You don't want that to happen any more than I do."

"Don't stay away," Danial pleaded. "We can be together without exchanging—"

"I don't think we can," I whispered. "When I'm with you, I want all of you, Danial. And I want to give you all of myself and hold nothing back." I touched his cheek, wet with tears. "I don't trust myself to stop you, even when I know I should. The virus is still spiking, and all I want is for you to make love to me again and bite me—"

"And I want to desperately," Danial finished. He moved me beneath him, shifting so he entered me slightly. "I ache to be within you. Let me. Don't stop me."

"Yes," I sighed. "Please."

In a smooth motion Danial slipped inside and began thrusting, his lips covering mine as he stroked my sweaty flesh. Again he brought me, my loud screams ecstatic as he swallowed in time to his thrusts, his fangs embedded deep. He shuddered several times, then relaxed against me, spent. I held him to me, listening to him drinking, floating on the pleasure and happiness of his touch.

Danial withdrew, then kissed my neck gently. "Does it hurt, Love?"

I shook my head. "There's been no pain now for a while."

Danial touched my lips, then parted them with his finger. "Your teeth aren't sharp. I don't think Camlyn knows his ass from a teakettle."

I laughed aloud, and he hugged me happily, pulling the quilt over us. Almost immediately, I slept.

Danial awoke me. "It's nearly eight at night, Love. While I want you to stay, I felt it right to wake you and tell you."

And he likely had a meeting to get to. Grumble. "I should get back. I've been gone for hours—"

"Stay with me," Danial whispered silkily, his fingers slipping across my thigh, then inside to caress.

I tried to wrest back my control. "Theo needs—"

"I need you," Danial said seductively. "Stay here with me."

"Danial, I can't just leave him."

"Once Theo sees you are serious about staying here, he'll come back also," he explained. "It is safest here, Sar. Here Devon has children he can be himself with. Theo is in less danger here. And you and I can be together."

"Theo and Devon are happy there—"

"But are you?" Danial said pointedly. "Are you happy there with them, apart from me?"

No. The real plain truth was no. I wiped at my eyes angrily. "That's not fair."

"I'm not playing fair, I'm playing to win," Danial said, rolling me onto my back beneath him. "I'm not going to lose you again."

Instead of my expected arousal, an odd uneasiness filled me, snapping me completely awake. "Danial—"

Danial entered me again, and began to move. "You belong here with me."

"Wait—"

Danial pushed me to the mattress, his sudden weight cutting off my words. His cool lips kissed my neck, then there was needle sharp pain. I let out a screech, pushing back against him.

Danial bit down harder, thrusting faster.

"Stop, or you'll kill me," I pleaded raggedly. "What will you win then?"

Danial froze, and then slowly moved off me, distancing himself. I brought my knees into my arms and sat with my head down, huddled, my hand over the throbbing fresh bite on my neck.

"I just miss you," Danial said sadly, after some moments had passed. "I miss waking up with you, and hearing you singing as you work, and the way you'd always leave your hairbrush in the shower. I'm surrounded by people practically at all times and still the silence of your absence permeates everything around me, leaving the stillness of despair and loneliness to fill my empty spirit."

"That sounds like poetry," I said, reaching out and clasping his hand.

"It's not," Danial replied despondently. "It's just how I feel."

"I'm not doing this to make you suffer. I'll come see you as much as before, just like before." I managed a smile. "Now I can teleport again, that'll mean a lot less wasted time driving."

"You would not have left, if not for Theo," Danial said bitterly. "Every time you have broken with me, he was the cause."

"Danial, stop," I said firmly. "We're going to have many years together. We're Oathed, remember? Your talk of winning is ridiculous, because you've already won."

"You're right," Danial said, sighing. "I'm just jealous."

"Don't be," I said, pulling him close for a hug. "I can't sleep with you every night, or maybe see you every day. But I'll come to you when I can, and I'll think of you every night before I sleep, Danial."

"I love you," Danial said tenderly. "I could say it to you forever, and it would not be enough, to tell you what you mean to me, Sar." He drew back from me. "I have loved other women over the years. But I've never loved one so deeply as I love you."

"I know it," I said, touching his cheek. "It's the same way I feel for you, Danial. The same way I love you. Please, don't think you've lost me, because you haven't. You never could."

Danial didn't reply, he just held me in his arms tightly.

* * * *

Theo was waiting for me when I returned around midnight. Surprisingly, he didn't say anything judgmental.

"I'm glad you got your power back. Devon's already asleep in his bed. I'll be waiting for you in our bed after you shower."

That was pointed. Still, I was grateful he wasn't upset. "I'm sorry if I worried you."

"It's okay," Theo said. "You should probably go, sweetheart. It's already late."

Though the shower felt wonderful, the sensation of water on my skin delicious, more present was Danial all those miles away, and it was all I could do not to go back to him. Worried, I hurried and finished up, then climbed into bed with wet hair.

Theo turned to me. "Sar, if you need Danial again like today, go to him. I know what it's doing to you to be apart from him. It's okay with me. Just come back to me afterwards."

"Okay," I said hollowly, trying hard not to think of Danial, the desire to go back to him stronger than ever despite Theo in my arms.

"I love you," Theo said, holding me close. "Now that the virus is ebbing, hopefully Devlin and Danial can both give you blood again. I worried about you being in thrall to Dev. But now I'm just as worried about you being in thrall to Danial. I see it in your eyes, a feverishness that didn't use to be there—"

Scared, I clung to him. "I know. I feel it too."

He stroked my back. "Shh. Danial would never hurt you. But it's better this way."

Better for who? I wondered.

* * * *

The next day went by in a blur of preparation, as Theo helped Danial prepare for the meeting with the other Rulers in Canada. As much as I was nervous about it, my day was full with last minute fall chores. The highs were in the fifties now, the trees turning early this year. Soon we would need to start burning wood again and shoveling snow. I wasn't looking forward to that, but I knew better than to let winter catch me unawares.

Ghost and Darkness clustered around me, panting after their long walk with Theo. I gave them each a Cheweez, which they took politely, settling down happily to munching.

"Now you be good for Warren," I said to them. "He's going to watch you tonight. I want you to be good for him, understand?"

Both dogs wagged their tails, but their focus was all on the treat they were eating.

"I got the mail," Theo said, shutting the door behind him. "That air's cold out there."

"Any good mail?" I said, unwrapping the plate of cookies I had baked for Warren. He'd said sugar cookies were his favorite. I'd made them with Janice's fox cookie cutter from her wedding, and frosted them with orange frosting. I was hoping he would like them, and not feel like a cannibal.

"This came for you," Theo said, handing me an padded envelope. "It must be from Devlin. The return address is Hayden."

I took it from him, perplexed. What had Devlin sent me? While I was dying to rip open the package, I was conscious of Theo watching me out of the corner of his eye. Knowing Devlin, there could be almost anything in there, but odds were that whatever it was would be provocative. It was better to wait until later, when I was alone.

I put the package to the side, and left it there, unopened. "Are you ready to grill the steaks?"

Devon let out a loud purr, and began to chirp at me, looking eagerly at the countertop where the steaks were.

"Coming right up," Theo said happily. "Bring out a glass of wine and keep me company. It's a nice night." He grabbed the steaks and headed outside, Devon trotting after him.

I bit my lip to keep from smiling. He'd just said it was cold a second earlier. "Be right there."

* * * *

"We're meeting with Devlin at the airport to fly up to Canada," Theo said, shoving on his shoes. "We're going to admit everything to do with your pregnancy, including Devon. As that worked to everyone's advantage, Devlin said it didn't matter. All you have to remember is that you didn't have any surgery afterwards. You were out for the C-section, so just say you don't remember, which is factual—"

"Theo, I'm not going to be at the meeting," I said patiently. "Titus's already taken Devon and Venus to stay with Terian, Sundown, Elle and Theoron at Danial's. We should all have some fun tonight. I'm looking forward to seeing Sun, actually. Terian told me Asher likes her, so—"

"I'm just telling you what to remember for the Hallow's party," he replied. "It's coming up in another month. Samuel and the rest will be there."

I made a face. "I'll do my best not to converse with them, then. When is Titus coming for me?"

"Right after I leave at nine," Theo said, checking his watch. "And I'm late, so anytime."

"I'm surprised Lash isn't going with you," I said curiously.

85

"Devlin said he didn't trust the bears not to trash the place if they were left alone there." Theo shrugged. "It's just as well he stays behind. You know we don't get along."

"I'm aware," I said, kissing him goodbye. "Be careful."

"You be careful, too," he said softly, stroking my face. "Call Titus and tell him to come and get you. He's late."

I wasn't able to teleport to Danial's house right now, or even to the grounds of his land, but it was only temporary. Titus had put up a spell to block anyone getting in except him, just for that night, for extra security. While I felt safer knowing any attempt to attack Danial's home would be foiled, no teleporting was a pain in the ass. "I'll call right after you leave," I promised. "I just need to get some clothes on and pack some last minute things."

"I wish we both could just go back to bed," Theo said wistfully, hugging me. "That last hour with you was perfect."

"Yes, it was," I said sexily. "Now get going before I demand a repeat performance."

"You'll get one the second I get back," Theo said huskily. He gave me a last hug, and then dashed out the door.

Silently wishing him luck, I threw a few changes of clothes in a bag, my brand new sexy nightgown, an oversized T-shirt, my favorite hairbrush, and some extra conditioner. Danial had everything else I would need, especially for one night.

The new nightgown I was planning on wearing for him had come the day before in the mail. I planned to leave it there that night with a romantic note on it, saying that I'd wear it for him this weekend. For this evening, though, the T-shirt would do.

I called Terian. "Where's my demon ride, Tears?"

"Putting up some extra protective barriers around the main house. He'll be there in two minutes, he says. Sit tight."

"So much for small talk," I said, listening to the sudden dial tone. Replacing the receiver, I caught sight again of my package from Dev on the counter.

I looked it over, wondering why Dev had sent me something in the mail. He usually preferred to give me any gifts in person. Weirder, the postmark was from Georgia, from four days ago. I turned it over in my hands, foreboding filling me.

This couldn't be from Devlin. Maybe I shouldn't open it. What if it were poison? But it didn't feel like poison; there was something hard inside. Also, poison would have affected Theo when he'd carried it all the way from the mailbox to the house. *What if the poison was for me?*

Going to the sink, I grabbed my rubber gloves, put them on, and then tore open the package. Out slid a sheathed knife and one piece of paper. I set the paper aside, all my attention on the knife. It was beautiful, the hilt and sheath made of cherry wood. Eager to try it on, I opened my belt and put it through the two belt loops. Refastening my belt, I unsnapped the knife, and slid it out of its sheath. The blade was honed to a razor's edge, and engraved with acid on the top, making the steel dark and rough. The finger guard was also acid-etched. I looked closer. In the darker part of the blade—so faint as to be almost hidden—was a Japanese symbol, perhaps a word. But the lines of it were clean, freshly carved. Someone had put this symbol on the blade, most likely whomever had sent it to me. What did it mean?

Without putting down the knife, I picked up the piece of paper.

Sar, you need a good knife, so I'm giving you this one. I've sharpened it, and it should serve you well for years to come. Lash.

He'd drawn a little snake next to his name.

This was bizarre. Why was he in Georgia? He was supposed to be at Hayden. Was he on a job? Why not wait to give me the knife in person when he got back?

I was still holding the knife when Titus appeared, his blackness making me shiver.

It was always so much thicker than Terian's, so much more powerful.

"Ready to go?" Titus said gently. Then he saw me with the knife.

As I looked into his eyes, I suddenly understood he both knew what this meant, and that he was not happy about my present. My foreboding deepened. "What is this?"

"It was time, Sarelle," Titus said. "He left a week ago. Devlin thinks he went out on a job, that he's coming back later tonight."

I knew exactly what he was talking about: Lash's death. My apprehension became panic. "Why?" I asked loudly. "Lash said he had years left! Years!"

"More like months," Titus said, his red eyes holding mine. "And that was months ago."

It all came together for me at once. This was why Lash had asked me to go back to Devlin. He'd known he was dying, and he'd wanted Devlin to have someone who loved him so he wouldn't be alone, or get into too much trouble. This was why he had talked about family, and that it meant something to him. This was why he hadn't cared if he'd died saving us, because he was going to be dead soon anyway. Why he had warned me to be careful, if Dev and I went out again, because if it happened again, he wouldn't be around to save us. Why he and I had gone out for sushi that night, but he hadn't eaten much. He hadn't been feeling like hibernating, he'd been getting ready to die. And he'd asked me to come those extra days to Hayden because he'd wanted to spend some extra time with me, lying together in the sun as we had those months ago and talking to maybe the only person in his life who shared his taste in movies.

"But I saw him! I talked to him! He was fine!" I screamed hysterically.

"He got a wound on a job he did a few weeks ago," Titus rumbled. "Some were bit him. It wasn't bad, and I healed what would heal, but it turned septic anyway. His immune system is shot, and had been for a while—"

Had it been Satar who'd bit Lash? Something told me it had been. My hysteria went up another notch. "No, he was fine!" I shouted. "He saved me, saved Devlin! He carried him—!"

"He collapsed when he got back to Hayden," Titus rumbled, his red eyes smoldering. "Saving Devlin and you took everything he had left. He spent these past two weeks recovering enough strength to go wherever it is he went."

That day I'd seen Lash reading with the blankets. He hadn't moved, and his body had been mostly covered. *I'd thought he had just been cold...*

I closed my eyes, fighting tears. "But why not stay here with Dev? Why go off alone?" I shouted. "Who wants to die alone?"

"He did," Titus said, his deep voice agitated now. "And it was his choice."

Fury rapidly replaced anguish. "He only made that choice because you didn't tell him about my blood! That a massive infusion of it might work, might save him!"

"Devlin would never risk you, not even for Lash," Titus said harshly. "He'd need to take all of it, Sarelle. You'd die saving him. And there's no guarantee it would even work."

This couldn't be happening. Fate couldn't be that cruel, that Lash could save us but not himself. That he was going to die alone, without his loved ones near him, after all the good he had done. But fate was that cruel. I'd seen it firsthand, when a freak accident had left me a widow. I'd seen it later, in the years I'd spent apart from Theo, thinking he was dead. I'd seen it in the tears Danial had cried, all those times now I'd left him.

Lash had saved us. This time he needed someone else to save him. And I'd be damned if I stayed here, knowing all this, and didn't at least try.

I looked at Titus, stripped off the gloves, and resheathed the knife at my side with a sharp click. "If I did it, could you save me?" I said bluntly. "Or would he need to turn me when it was done?"

Titus completely lost it, his angry terrifying. "You are not risking your life, not for that evil snake!" he snarled, showing his many rows of teeth. He reached for me with clawed fingers, his eyes flaming, the heat coming off him making my body break out in sweat. The stench of sulfur and brimstone smothered me, his blackness engulfing me as if I'd been dropped into Hell itself.

I teleported instantly, evading him, and then I was standing holding my purse and duffel bag in the parking lot of the Eckerd's in Alan's Creek.

I flipped open my phone, and called Titus. He answered before it had rung once, snarling out his words. "Don't you dare, Sar! He'll kill you! Think of your children!"

I'd had enough of people telling me what to do, what I had to do, what was best for me. I was doing this. "Get whatever you need ready!" I snarled back. "And leave your phone on."

"You don't even know where he is—"

"I know." I hung up, and threw the phone in the nearby dumpster. It could be used to track me, and I needed not to be found, not for a while. Thankfully Titus hadn't recharged the tracer spell he'd put on me yet. He had been going to do that tonight, as soon as we got to Danial's house.

Taking out my old phone from my purse, I made sure the battery was charged. It was. I turned it off to save the battery, and then teleported again to Dr. Camlyn's office building in my usual exam room, number one. It took me a good twenty minutes to gather up everything I thought I would need. Then I teleported again, this time to the Everglades. If Lash had a home other than Hayden, this had to be it.

Arriving near the edge of the swamp, I was immediately besieged by mosquitoes. I hurriedly walked as fast as I could to the campground head office, covering my head with one of my shirts from my duffel bag. That kept most of them off me, though there were a few bites already on my forehead and hands.

The building was closed, being night, but I broke in easily, the door having only a simple key lock. After that experience with Ulysses, I'd kept my lock picking tools in my purse. Theo had taught me well, though he would not approve of me using my learned skills to save Lash. Theo was not going to like any of this. He was going to be enraged and he might even tell me it was over between us. But Lash was my friend and he was dying, and I didn't care.

I looked through the files to see who was registered at which campsite. With it being the off-season, the park was mostly empty, so there weren't that many groups here camping. Also, most of the older tourists elected to stay in the one hotel within the park, rather than at a campsite. If it had been summer, there would have been way too many people around to have a chance in hell of finding one man alone camping. But Lash would want as much privacy as possible. It made sense he would be in the most remote campsite there was.

I finally found him listed: Mr. Lash, party of one. He was staying at the very edge of the campground, nearest the swamp. He hadn't bothered to use an alias. But why would he? No one would have come looking for him except Dev, and he thought he was on a job. No one but Titus knew he wasn't coming back tonight to Hayden. Except Dev, Lash had no other friends to wonder where he was.

I grabbed a map from the office, leaving the door unlocked. Grabbing a can of bug repellent, I coated my clothes, then the shirt I'd draped over my head. Getting my bearings with the small penlight from my purse, I began to walk. The mosquitoes were bad, whining and buzzing around my head, but the spray repelled most of them. At least, I wasn't swatting them at every other step.

The ocean was calm to my left, the waves gently lapping. It was cloudy, and there was no moonlight to see by. Even the stars were concealed. The night was lighted only by the rest rooms, great concrete buildings that had clouds of mosquitoes near them, hunting for blood beneath the fluorescent lights.

Lash's campsite was a ways from the park office. I walked for more than an hour, checking my bearings every so often to make sure I hadn't wandered too far off the path in the dark. With every step my worry increased. *What if I wasn't in time?*

Finally, I reached the edge of the campgrounds, and saw his truck, the familiar black Avalanche Danial had been driving that fateful night we met. Behind in on the grass was a large tent, a light glowing inside.

I stopped, suddenly hesitant. *What if he wasn't alone?*

Screw it. I'd come too far to be shy now. Every minute counted. I ran to the door of the tent. "Lash?"

My utterance came out quiet, the sounds of crickets and other night insects loud in my ears.

The tent unzipped. Lash stood there, his face in shadow.

I was so relieved to find him alive that I hugged him, blinking back tears. He pulled me inside, and immediately zipped up the tent door behind me, before all the mosquitoes came in. Then he grabbed me roughly and kissed me hard, his forked tongue slipping between my lips, his arms going around me. My shirt that I had draped over my head fell off, dropping to the floor of the tent.

Lash tasted of hard alcohol. There was a mostly empty bottle of Laphroig sitting beside his inflatable bed. And he was stark naked. *This wasn't why I'd come here...*

As I went to push him off me, my hands clasped his arms. They were cooler than a vampire's, as cool as the night air. I took a sharp intake of air, breathing in his scent of earth, leaves, and musk. Underneath it now was the sweet scent of decay.

Lash broke the kiss, then paused, as if waiting for something. I rapidly blinked back tears, trying to get control of my voice enough to talk.

"Don't cry," he hissed softly, reaching up to wipe away my tears with his callused hand.

Tears streaming down my cheeks, I grabbed his face in my hands and kissed him. He groaned in satisfaction, then kissed me back, our tongues entwining as he guided me back beneath him down on his bed. Lash broke the kiss abruptly, his hands unfastening my jeans and stripping them off. He paused for a second when he saw the knife at my belt, then his actions became more hurried. Carefully, he lowered his body beside me on the bed. Rolling partly onto me, he kissed me again adamantly, his hands running up under my shirt to unfasten my bra. He pressed his hips to mine, his erection firm and unyielding against my lower belly. Letting out a hiss of longing, Lash kissed me again on my mouth, and then reared back to pull my sweatshirt off over my head, taking my bra with it. My hair caught in one of the straps, a few strands yanking free.

"Ouch!" I said involuntarily.

"Sorry," he hissed, aligning my hips with his. Moving my left leg back, he pushed in with a loud hiss.

I let out a soft cry, then clasped him to me as he began to move. His thrusts were hard, his hisses almost continuous, his face buried in my neck. I could hear his heartbeat as if it were my own, the beats so fast and irregular they seemed to almost run together. I felt a slight prick as his fangs slid in, then the pressure of gentle sucking.

I stroked his back carefully with my hands, not sure where his wound was, not wanting to hurt him. A few minutes later, he shuddered once as he came, then relaxed against me, breathing hard.

I kissed his cheek gently. At once, he pushed up from me.

"No," I said, holding him tightly. "Wait—"

"Sar," he hissed in a low apologetic tone. "I can't again. I wasn't sure I was strong enough even to be able to have you once." He looked down at me, his body still pressed to mine, and put his hand on my cheek. "I'd love to be able to be with you like that over and over, until I died. That's got to be the best way I could think of to go. But that would be selfish to ask. Thank you for coming to me one last time. I know what we just did can't have been very good for you. I'm too weak."

I put my hand over his. "No. It doesn't have to be like that—"

He kissed me very gently. "You know why I came here. It won't be much longer. *You feel the coolness of my skin?"*

No. It wasn't too late. It couldn't be! "Yes, but—"

The emotion in Lash's words silenced me. "You came to me when you knew, so you must care for me a little," he hissed softly. "Will you stay with me until it's done? You don't have to kiss me or anything like that. Just hold me in your arms, until I'm gone?"

I wiped at my eyes, which were too blurry to see. "I'll do better than that. You have another choice. You don't have to die—"

"Sar, I'm hurting bad, even with having taken your blood. It's time."

"No! Keep drinking my blood," I said, my hands slipping up from his shoulders to touch his face. "It can save you, renew your body, if you take enough."

Lash went still, then drew himself out of me, and sat on the edge of the mattress. I sat up as well, pulling the bed blanket around me.

"How do you know this?" he hissed, uncertain. "Titus said nothing."

"He didn't want to tell you! He didn't want me to come to you. But I had to try—"

"Why?" Lash hissed, putting his hand on my arm. "You got what you needed from me, and I liked giving it to you. Our deal is done, nothing owed. There is no love between us, Sar. I know what you did for Danial those years ago, but—"

"Because Dev's going to be devastated if you die, and so will I. You're my friend. I may not love you, but you did what I needed you to do, even when you had to risk your life to do it. I'm here to do what you need now."

"You don't owe me, Sar," Lash hissed, his flat eyes staring into mine. "I didn't do what I did for you, I did it for Devlin—"

"For a creature who loves quiet, you sure can't seem to shut the hell up!" I hissed back at him. "Take it, before you are so far gone it won't work!"

"It'll kill you to take that much all at once," Lash said softly, rubbing his eyes. "I'm not going to kill the woman my best friend loves so I can go on living."

"I brought blood replenishment packets," I said, showing him the box. "Take it slowly, and give them to me, but don't stop for long—"

"No," Lash said sadly. "Those will only work for a while until I take about half your blood. Then they won't work anymore. You'll still die."

"Titus knows I'm with you," I said, thinking quickly. "He knows what I came to do. Call him, when I don't respond, and he'll come. He said he could heal me."

"You are lying, Sar," Lash hissed gently, giving me a faint smile. "I know him, and he said no such thing. If he knew you were coming to save me, risking yourself for me, he would have stopped you. There is no love lost between he and I, no matter that we've worked together for many years."

I wanted to cry, because I'd done so much to come to him in time. I let out a breath I'd been holding.

"You can't save me," Lash hissed, pulling me into his arms. "Let me go."

There was only one more thing to dangle in front of him for temptation. Lash had only shown me one weakness, save his devotion and love for Devlin, in all the time I'd known him. I preyed on that weakness now. "Take the blood and then bite me. If you make me weresnake like you, I won't die. You'll be strong enough to save me, if it works—"

Lash started, then looked down at me in shock. "You don't want to be what I am."

"I'm asking you to try with me to save yourself. I'm not pregnant now, and Devlin can still have me the same if I'm were. He would probably enjoy it if my tongue was forked."

"It will change your blood," Lash hissed. "You'll be weresnake. There's no going back, Sar. You won't taste of summer ever again. Dev would never forgive me."

"Don't you think it's a small price to pay for your life? If you told Dev you were dying, had given him the choice, don't you think he would have tied you down and made you try with me? You know how he feels about you, what he's done to keep you alive this long." I paused. "Will you do it? Or were you lying to me when you said you wanted to make me like you, that given half a chance, you would?"

Lash stared back at me, unblinking.

I faced him. "You will never get another chance, Lash. And the clock is ticking."

"I wasn't lying," Lash hissed softly, hugging me. "I do want that, for you to be weresnake like me. I've wanted it since the second time we were together, when you raised The Lust on purpose because you saw how badly I needed you. I never expected that kindness, not from you. Not for me."

I felt a rush of feeling for him, hearing his raw disbelief mixed with affection.

He drew back and studied me. "But are you sure this is what you want? I'll have to bite you in the throat, Sar, as snake. I've turned other women, so I know what I'm doing, but you'll feel yourself dying before it's done. And when it's done, you'll have more to face. My snake form is frightening to most everyone. Yours will be, too. You've seen how I'm loathed for what I am. It can be very lonely, being outcast by most other weres, not to mention humans. I'll be with you, but you're going to lose a lot by doing this."

I drew back from him, settling myself on the bed. His face shifted, almost certain I'd reconsidered.

"I'm afraid," I said, touching his hand gently. "But I'm sure."

Lash squeezed my hand, then got out his cell phone and checked the battery. Like mine, his was charged with a strong signal. He put it within reach, and then opened all eight of the packets, placing them upwards in their plastic container.

I lay back down on the bed. Lash lay down beside me. Then he leaned over me, his upper body on mine, moving very carefully. In the dim light, there was something glistening on his left side. *Blood?*

"Don't touch my left side, if you can help it," Lash whispered. "I have a wound there, Sar."

"I won't." I turned my head away from him, bracing myself.

Lash settled back beside me, then took my hand in his. "You squeeze my hand," he said. "Keep a constant pressure, okay?"

I nodded. Lash kissed my throat, then gingerly sank his fangs back into the partially scabbed holes and began to drink.

His fangs might have been long, but they were small compared to a vampire's; I barely felt him drawing out my blood. While there was no sudden shock of blood loss, getting a substantial amount required Lash's continuous exertion. At first, it didn't hurt. But as time went on, my neck began to feel sore and then to throb in pain.

After about fifteen minutes, I felt lightheaded, my grip on his hand slackening. Lash stopped drinking and gave me one of the packets. Once I swallowed it down, he resumed drinking. We continued this way until we had gone through six packets and an hour and a half had passed. Lash improved steadily as he took my blood, warmth returning to his body when we reached the hour point, and with it, his strength.

I didn't feel like Lash had taken too much of my blood. The packets were doing their job, keeping me conscious and my heart beating. I just hoped they weren't diluting my blood or anything, because then he might need to take more. I cursed myself then for never asking Dr. Camlyn exactly how they worked, or how many I could take in a few hours without poisoning myself. But neither had seemed important then…

"Are you doing okay?" he hissed softly in my ear. "I'm being as gentle as I can, but I have to be hurting you. I can't give you anything for the pain, I have no magic—"

I tried to be brave. "I'm okay," I croaked out.

"Sar, you're not. Let me do what I can to ease it for you." He gently wiped my tears away, then moved onto his back, carefully pulling me atop him. With a shift of his hips, he pushed smoothly into me, then lowered my upper body down onto his. With one arm he steadied me, then his head nuzzled my throat, his fangs again finding their mark. He began thrusting very gently, almost imperceptibly, his free hand caressing and sliding over my bare skin, rubbing my breasts gently, stroking my hair and face. His other hand was in mine, still clasped securely.

I almost stopped him. But he was right in one thing: we might both die attempting this. And what did it matter, anyway? My tubes were tied, I couldn't get pregnant. And if this was the end, I wanted to go out being loved, not just bitten.

By the time we reached the eighth and last packet, I was clinging to consciousness and him with both hands. We'd come several times, both of our pleasures expressed in soft groans. Most important, it was working. From his increasing vigor and body heat, Lash was getting stronger. What I didn't know was if I had enough blood and will to finish the job. Lash had taken far more than Devlin or Danial had ever taken, even when they'd bitten me together the first time those years ago. I had never felt so weakened and depleted.

What would happen if I didn't give him enough? He'd still die. I had to keep going, to finish it, or none of what we'd done would mean anything.

I took the eighth packet from him with shaking fingers, swallowed it, and went limp against him. Lash took the empty package, set it with the rest, and slipped his fangs in, sucking gently, his hand holding mine firmly.

Ten minutes passed, then I felt myself starting to drift. I tried to hold on, but I didn't want to. I wanted to let go. All of my nerve endings were screaming in fear, Lash's efforts to distract me drowned out in pain.

But I didn't stop him. It was he who stopped himself.

"I can't take anymore," he said, moving back off of me. "You're getting cold, Sar. I've never had this much before from a woman and not had her die."

I squeezed his hand, unsure if he could actually feel any pressure.

Lash let go of my hand, and hugged me. "It doesn't matter to me if you gave me enough to save me. It's enough you took away my pain, and you're with me here at the end—"

I looked at him in shock, ignoring his words. Even in the weak candlelight, he'd changed. I reached up my hand weakly towards him.

Lash took my hand in his. "What is it?"

"Your scar…is gone…"

"You brought me back," he whispered, his words drawling, sounding faintly Southern. The hiss that had always been present in his words was gone. Yet his voice was somehow still him. "My fangs are gone."

He ran his hands up over his face, letting out an intake of breath when he felt that his scar was gone. His wound looked healed, too. It was no longer glistening. The blood had dried, falling off in places to reveal new skin underneath.

I had done it. I had saved him.

"I told you…it would work," I whispered, then let my eyes close. Now I could relax completely, knowing that whatever else happened, I'd done what I came here to do. And I wanted to drift more than anything.

"No! You stay here with me, you hear me Sar?" Lash said urgently, pulling me close with one hand, and speed dialing his cell with the other. "You are not dying now, not now!"

Everything began to grey around the edges.

"Titus? It worked, yes. Come to the Everglades, Campsite 89. Hurry!" Lash hung up, and hugged me.

"Stay with me," he whispered gently. "Titus is coming, Sar. If he can't heal you, I'll turn you. You aren't going to die, no matter what we need to do to save you. I swear it."

Wondering if he was trying to convince me or himself, I passed out in his arms.

Chapter Six

I awoke to find Titus on his knees next to me, supporting my back as he tried to pour some bitter liquid down my throat. I coughed, and he drew back the container from my lips.

"What is this stuff? It's awful!" I said, moving my mouth, trying to get the taste out. "Worse than drinking those blood-fixing packets!"

"Sar, you're insane," he said angrily, yet with an odd note that resembled pride. "You're insane, but you did it. And you are lucky as hell I came down here with Lash back in '74, so I knew where to teleport to."

I saw the dawn sky through the open tent door. The sun was just rising. "When did the night end?" I said in wonder.

"A few minutes ago," Titus said, worried. "Drink a little more. Your life depends on it, Sar. This should be enough to heal you, if you can get it down."

I took the container from him, and downed the rest of it. There was no point drawing it out. The concoction was awful and burned my throat, but I felt an immediate flash of warmth, then a building strength from within that both calmed and sustained me.

"Rest," Titus said, easing me back onto the bed.

While I still felt weak, I was nowhere as weak as I had felt before I passed out. I yawned hugely, looked around for Lash, and saw he was missing. "Where is—?"

Lash came in the tent door.

My mouth stayed open. "You're so young," I said, awed.

Lash had regained his youth. He looked about Theo's age now, maybe even younger. His face was unlined, and his scar was gone. Then I looked into his eyes. They were no longer flat snake eyes, though they were still a little reserved and dangerous-looking. They were human eyes, a dark, dark brown that was almost black, and they were filled with joy.

I'd not have said Lash was attractive when I'd met him for the first time, or even in the time I had known him. Some of that was because of the scar and his flat eyes, and some was his violent nature, the coldness that was always present in his actions and thoughts, that coldness he had said came from the snake side of him. But he was striking now, even dirty as he was; muddy almost to his waist, his boots covered in sludge.

"Why are you so dirty?"

"I've been gettin' breakfast for myself, catchin' some fish," Lash drawled, his accent deeply Southern. "The bott'm of the water heeya is deep mud. Even bein' careful, I steel got splashed. It's been a long time seeynce I did it, seeynce I hay-ed the strength and speed ta do it—"

He put his hand in mine and squeezed gently.

"Talk so I can understand you, snake," Titus growled, his eyes red. "Your voice has not changed along with your body. Your mind is still the twisted thing it always had been."

Lash gave him a cold look, but when he spoke again, his words were far more clipped, and his accent almost nonexistent. "I'm in your debt," he said seriously, his words only slightly accented. "I owe you big for this, Sarelle—"

"Call me Sar," I said softly, giving him a smile.

Lash leaned down and kissed me quickly, his mouth moving on mine. I was so surprised, I let him.

"Stop," Titus rumbled immediately. "She isn't yours."

Lash leaned back from me and shot him another nasty look. "I never said she was, Titus. But I'll kiss her if I want to without any shit from you about it."

"What did you give me?" I asked Titus.

"I gave you some of my blood," he replied. "You're young enough that it will help you to replace the blood you lost much quicker than any other spell. Time was of the essence."

"I would've never have guessed demon blood was the magical cure-all of the ages," I muttered.

Titus laughed, a great bass rumbling. "It wouldn't have helped, Sarelle, except that you already are part demon. It was the only thing I had to try, anyway. Otherwise Lash would have had to turn you." The anger and disgust in Titus's tone when he talked about Lash turning me was deep as the ocean behind us. I felt his blackness surge out of him momentarily before he clamped down on it and drew it back into himself.

I didn't look at Lash. He'd wanted me to be what he was, and now we would never coil together like he'd wanted us to. I couldn't say I was sorry for that. While I'd have done it to save him, I hadn't truly wanted to be weresnake. My reprieve now was that much sweeter, that I had been able to save him without losing my humanity.

"I always wanted a daughter," Titus said gently in his deep voice, startling me a little. "Now we are truly kin."

I'd never drank blood before, and was queasy now knowing that I had, even if I was also grateful. As I couldn't say I thought of him as a father, I just squeezed his hand. "Thank you."

"People are going to start walking around being touristy," Lash hissed. "You'd better get back to Danial's."

Shit. It was dawn. I was going to have a lot of explaining to do. "I should get back—"

Titus and Lash pushed me back gently to the bed. "I need to go. You need to stay here and rest," Titus said sternly. "He took over half of your blood, Sar. You are going to need at least a few days to recover."

"I can't!" I replied, frantic. "They'll already be looking for me! Theo will be—!"

"They were delayed in Canada," Titus said smoothly. "Leri staged an assassination attempt, pretending to be a rogue vampire. Theo is looking for the vampire, and until he finds him, Danial and Devlin are staying there, because they are reluctant to lead any danger to you or the children. Theo won't find anything, but he'll search at least a few days before giving up. It's taken care of."

"But they'll still call! They'll know I never showed up at Danial's!"

"Leri is being you," Titus said. "She's wearing your form, and lying in Danial's bedroom, pretending to be tired and worried. I had her do a little yelling and screaming like you usually do, and everyone's giving her a wide berth. No one suspects."

"I don't yell that much," I said, miffed.

Titus rolled his eyes.

Weird as this was….it was good news, except now I was going to have to be gracious to Leri for going over and above for me. "What if they get home before I'm well? Theo—"

"She's agreed to be you at a distance, not between the sheets," Titus said, baring his rows of teeth. "We need to get you home before they return. Leri had enough trouble just talking to Danial on the phone. He's by nature suspicious. She'll never be able to fake it well enough if he sees her in the flesh."

It was always Danial who knew when something was up. It was eerie, the way he knew me. "Why did you cover for me?" I said, curiously. "You told me not to come."

"And admit to Devlin I'd lost his Oathed One, who I was supposed to be guarding?" Titus said, laughing again. "Not a chance. He would have kicked my ass back to Hell in no time."

Hell, as in the real place. I swallowed hard.

"Lash, keep her here, and make sure she rests," Titus continued. "Sar, I'll see you in a few days." He left the tent, walking into the swamp.

I cut my eyes to Lash, who was watching me, a hungry look in his eyes. "Be right back," he said, then went after Titus.

I turned over and closed my eyes. Then they abruptly snapped open.

"Would it hurt her, if I was with her again?" Lash was asking Titus.

I sat upright and looked outside. Lash and Titus weren't even visible; they were at least a hundred feet away in the brush, yet I could hear them as if they were right in front of me.

"Lash—" Titus growled, blackness boiling out of him in an engulfing wave.

Lash hissed in response. "I care for her. You know that, demon. I want to be with her, if it's safe for her. Just give me a fucking true answer for once."

"I'd swear she was a succubus if I didn't know better," Titus said sarcastically. "Lash, so long as she wants you to, I don't see the harm. Her body is already healing from the blood loss. Besides, I know you already had her when she was risking her life to save you and couldn't stop you—"

"You motherfucking son of a bitch—" Lash snarled.

"Stop it!" I snapped aloud.

There was dead silence. They had heard me, far away as they were.

"Lash did what he could, Titus. It hurt a lot, saving him. And if you had helped me instead of trying to stop me—"

"I figured when you found Lash, you'd call me." Titus said angrily. "I didn't think you'd try to save him alone, without at least some magic to ease your pain."

"There wasn't time."

"I'll be coming back for you, Sar, two nights from tonight," Titus said. "And Lash, you had better be ready to let her go back with me to Devlin."

"I like her, it's true," Lash hissed, irritation in his cold tone. "But I'm not going to be Theo, betray my best friend for a woman, even one that saved my life. You know me Titus, even if you detest me. You know that's truth." He paused. "I'll let her leave with you. I'll come back a few days after that, in my truck. I'll tell Devlin the truth, all of it."

"I know you will," Titus growled, the unsaid warning again in his tone. Then he said some words.

A glow surrounded my body, then seemed to sink into me. Titus had reactivated the tracking spell. It was clear he didn't trust Lash not to take off with me.

"Keep her in bed," Titus said. "She shouldn't walk any distances for a while."

"You should help me get her to the hotel," Lash said. "I can get her a room there. She'd be more comfortable. The nights can be cool out here, and if it rains, the tent will take on water, where I'm camped—"

"Maybe tonight," Titus said, glancing at him. "But not until then. Don't move her out of bed, Lash. And don't keep her up all day either, no matter what she agrees to—"

"Stop being such an ass!" Lash hissed loudly, his fangs back in his anger. "I just took almost all her blood! I'm not going to try to fuck her brains out right after doing that! I just didn't want to do something that might hurt her—"

"Everything you touch gets hurt," Titus intoned, then his blackness lifted, vanishing.

"God damned rotten bastard cocksucker—" Lash hissed, and then he abruptly fell silent.

A few minutes later he came inside the tent and shut the door. "Sorry about the language," he hissed. "We should have assumed you might hear us after that demon blood." He changed, his fangs receding and his eyes becoming human again. "Sit up. You need to eat."

Lash gave me some water, an apple, and two sandwiches he'd brought from the convenience store on the pier. He cut up the apple for me first, and fed me the pieces slowly, then the sandwiches. Lash helped me drink a little more water when I was done eating.

"Do you want me to get you more food?" he said, putting the trash to the side on a bag. "Are you still hungry?"

I was, but I was also feeling better and better by the minute. There was only one thing lacking. "Chocolate?" I said hopefully.

Lash looked at me as if he didn't know what I could be talking about. After holding my eyes for a few seconds, he very slowly grinned, then produced several chocolate bars. He broke those up into chunks and fed those to me, then gave me another drink of water.

When I was done, he wrapped me up in the bed blanket, lay down beside me, and held me. "Sleep, Sar," he said softly, stroking my hair. "I'll be here. You're safe."

I noticed his hands were warm as they used to be, though the calluses he'd always had were missing. I fell asleep listening to his heartbeat. It was strong now, the beats more regular and much slower than they had been.

* * * *

When I awoke, it was midmorning, the sides of the tent bright with filtered sunlight. While I was still achy, I was a good deal stronger. Lash was beside me, propped up on one arm, looking down at me. He was under the covers with me now, but his body was not touching mine.

"Do you feel stronger?" he asked.

"Yes," I said, my voice soft and sleep-filled. "I desperately want a shower." I began to raise myself up slowly with effort.

"Lie there for a while yet," Lash said, reaching out to push me back down with his hand. "I'll get you a room later today, and you can shower. But you need to rest now, like Titus said."

I yawned, then lay back down, rolling over towards him so that my hands were against his chest. I was still naked, but I didn't care. Lash still had on his shirt, though it was open down the front.

It was on the tip of my tongue suddenly to ask him if some gnomes had gotten to him while I'd been asleep. It was coming home to me just how close I'd come to dying last night, and I wanted to be comforted, to feel his warm, familiar body against mine. But when I put my hand on his chest, instead of scales, there was only chest hair and warm skin. I recoiled, biting my lip.

Lash grabbed my hands, stopping me from moving back. He took in a deep breath, then let it out, his skin rippling as scales formed under my hands. "Better?" he hissed softly.

I looked up into his flat eyes. "Yes," I said gently, and then burrowed close with a sigh.

* * * *

I woke again at dusk wrapped in Lash's arms. His leg was thrown over me, the weight holding me immobile. He was snoring faintly.

I kissed his cheek. His eyes snapped open and he tensed, then he saw it was me.

"Mornin'," he said, stretching. Then he looked at the tent sides, which were rapidly darkening. "Or evenin'."

"Can you get me a room?" I asked hopefully. "I'd love a shower."

"Of course," he said, grabbing for his jeans. He slid them on, then handed me my clothes from last night. "Give me a moment to pack up some of my stuff."

I put on my wrinkled clothes as quick as possible, given I still felt tired and sore. *You should be happy you're moving at all, for almost being drained.*

Lash strapped on his weapons, grabbed my bag by the bed, then helped me to my feet. Although I'd felt strong when I'd been sitting, standing was something else. Lash had to walk beside me, steadying me, as I walked to the truck. Once he got me settled in the passenger seat, he walked to the other side, got in, and started the engine.

"What about your equipment? Your tent and your gear?"

He turned his head slightly to look at me. "Do you want me to stay in the room with you?" he said, holding my eyes. "I don't have to."

He wanted sex, not just HBO and a toilet without mosquitoes in it. "I need your help to walk," I said quickly. "I'll need your help to climb stairs, shower, and probably do a lot of other gross stuff."

"The demon blood will work by tomorrow," Lash answered, putting the truck in drive. "I can stay the night with you. No one will take anything here I'd miss."

I waited in the truck while he went in and got us a room. When he came out, he helped me up to the room, then laid me carefully on the king-size bed. "Stay here until I get back with the bag," he said firmly. "Don't shower until I'm back. I don't want you to faint in the water, and drown."

That was bullshit; he just wanted to shower with me. He'd gotten a room with only one bed for a reason. I kept that to myself and just nodded.

I used the bathroom while Lash was gone. It took me a while to get there and back, and I nearly fainted, but there were some things I simply could not ask him to help me with and this was one of them. I looked in the mirror afterwards, supporting myself on the sink with both hands. I was astounded at how awful my appearance was. No wonder Titus had been pissed off at Lash.

I was haggard, pale as ivory, and looked every inch of my thirty-four years, my eyes a little sunken in my face. Basically, I looked like hell. My neck was the worst; a huge purplish bruise all down the left side, and in the center of that, two ragged holes from his fangs. They were bloodless, raised, and sore to the touch. There was also blood smears on my neck, on my top, and in the snarled mess of my hair.

I touched my clumped hair, wincing. I'd been meaning to get it cut and highlighted. In fact, I'd been going to go to a walk-in hair salon today, and have it done. So much for that.

I made it back to the bed just in time to collapse on it. Lash came back in the room a few minutes later.

He quickly started the shower, and adjusted the temperature. Then, he helped me off with my clothes, and stripped his own off. Soon after, he was helping me into the shower, and steadying me as I carefully washed away the blood and sweat from my hair. The water felt wonderful, but the warmth of it made me weak and a little dizzy, so much so that I ended up hanging onto Lash's neck to support myself.

Without asking, he took the washcloth from my hand and took up where I'd stopped. He was gentle, nothing in his touch that indicated that he was doing any of this for any reason other than I needed him to. His hands didn't linger on me, and he didn't stroke my body as he soaped me up under the rapid fall of the water. After helping me rinse off the suds, he shut off the shower, quickly wrapped me in towels and threw one around his shoulders. Then he helped me back to the bed, rubbing my body dry before he covered me up.

It was so good to be clean, and the bed felt softer than anything. I was out like a light.

When I awoke in the predawn hours, Lash was under the covers with me, naked, holding me loosely. To my surprise, I was dressed in my plain nightgown.

He must have put it on me while I was sleeping. I was touched, knowing he'd done it to make me feel more relaxed. But I was anything but relaxed. The hardness of his lean body was pressed to my side, his erection flexing gently against me.

I'd seen him when he undressed before showering, and later, when he'd put me to bed. Both times, he'd been erect. *All I had to do was offer, and he'd take me up on it...*

Lash let out a faint snore, then shifted slightly, hugging me. I let myself relax back against him, falling back asleep.

* * * *

I woke up about dusk, my stomach growling with hunger. Ravenous, I turned my body in his arms, and looked up at him. "Hi."

Lash looked down at me with a faint smile. "You're warmer, Sar," he said softly, as he pushed back my hair with his hand. "Do you feel any stronger?"

I was hoping I looked better, but I didn't say that. I had other more important things to think about, like food. "I'm better, but I need to eat something," I replied. "Will you go with me? There's a restaurant here, if I remember right." Lash was younger now, but had his need for raw food changed with his appearance? "Are you hungry?"

"Of course," he drawled. "I'm starving. If you want to go in the bathroom, I can dress out here."

While I was dressing, I checked myself in the mirror. Titus's blood had taken effect. My face had lost its paleness, and my eyes were full of life again. I didn't look the picture of health, but at least I looked a little less like death warmed over. My neck wound was healed for the most part, the bruise having faded almost completely. But my hair was a mess from showering and not conditioning it, not even brushing it.

"You ready?" Lash said from outside.

I looked at the snarled mess, and grabbed the brush halfheartedly. This was going to take a half hour maybe, if not longer. "When I'm done brushing my hair."

Lash opened the door, took one look at me, and then took my brush from my hand, leading me into the other room. "Sit on the edge."

I sat down and he sat behind me, pulling my hair to my back, smoothing it a little.

"Hold still," he said softly, and began brushing.

While he was doing his best, my hair was much too long, and badly snarled. And I was hungry and impatient. "Take your knife and cut it."

"No," Lash said, not stopping his brushing. "Dev loves your hair. I'm not going to cut it."

"Do it," I said firmly. "I'm missing my hair appointment. They are expecting my hair to be shorter, Lash."

Lash ignored me, and continued brushing. I sat there, and let him, though it was tedious. What else could I do? Lash was being surprisingly gentle... "You did this before for another woman," I said suddenly.

He paused in mid-stroke. "My sister, many years ago. Am I pulling too much?"

"No," I said, wincing a little. "Mostly, no."

Lash worked on my hair for a good twenty minutes. When it was untangled, he put the very end in a four-inch braid, and tied both ends of it with rubber bands. Then he drew his knife, and with a high soft sawing sound, he cut that part off. My hair was now just above my waist, still very long, but at least manageable.

Lash put my braid aside, resheathed his knife, and held out his hand to me. "Ready?"

I checked him over. While his untucked shirt didn't hide his whip or knife completely, it hid enough that we probably wouldn't be barred from the restaurant. However, after Ulysses, that wasn't enough. "Do you have a gun?"

"Of course," Lash said, slipping one out from his back. "I don't go anywhere unarmed."

"Then yes," I told him, taking his hand.

We walked over to the restaurant from the hotel. Being midweek, it wasn't crowded, and we got a table without waiting near the windows. I admired the scenic view of the ocean as we looked over the menus. But the sky was darkening rapidly, a storm approaching with the night.

"I'm glad we got a room," I said. "That's going to be some storm."

"We'd have gotten wet," Lash agreed. "If it's bad when we go to leave, I'll come back for you in the truck after dinner."

When our waitress came, I ordered fettuccini, crab cakes, and some wine. We were both alive, and that was something pretty significant to celebrate. I was surprised but pleased when Lash ordered a steak, fries, and crab cakes, too. I was shocked when he told the waiter to forget the wine, to just bring water.

"I want some wine," I said dangerously. "It's been a trying twenty-four hours."

"No," Lash said, grinning. "It will just make your recovery take longer. You need to eat and rest. Water will do for tonight."

"Wine," I demanded. "Now."

"If you don't behave," Lash said in a warning tone, "I'll tie you up again, and not let you out of the room. Right to the bed, Sar, like last time."

"No, you won't—"

"Yes, I will," Lash hissed, his eyes suddenly flat. "I'll enjoy it too, even if you don't let me have you. There is more than one reason Dev and I are good friends. Now behave."

I decided I didn't need the wine that badly after all. "Okay."

We didn't talk much during dinner. While I wanted to ask him why he'd wanted to be alone to die, or why he hadn't at least said something to Devlin, I kept my mouth shut. That was really his business, not mine. Awkwardness in his company was returning along with my strength, because his appearance was so different. Instead of feeling like I was with a good friend, I felt like I was with someone I'd once known well, but didn't anymore.

Lash tore into his food, and finished his before I was half done with mine. Then he ordered another two steaks, and another order of crab cakes. I looked at him across from me as he sat there, surveying the restaurant alertly, and decided whatever fallout happened because of what I had done, it had been worth it. He was so much better than he had been. The pain that had been his constant companion for so long was gone.

He suddenly caught me looking at him, and looked back at me, his brow furrowing. "What is it, Sar?"

And, God, he was hot now. "I'm glad you're better," I said finally, blushing.

"Are you done eating?" he said, holding my gaze.

"No—"

"Then finish," he said, his tone gentle. "You should order more food as well. You skipped lunch."

His steaks came and his crab cakes. By the time he'd wolfed them down, I was finished.

"Do you want dessert?" he said enticingly, as the waiter took our plates. "They have cheesecake."

I grinned despite my shyness. "You already know the answer then," I said teasingly.

He smiled back at me. "Bring us two huge pieces."

I was struck again by how arresting he was now, compared to how he had been before. The scar had been some of it, true, but it mostly had been his eyes, the alien-ness of them. His dark eyes were a little aloof, but they were also beautiful in a way his snake eyes had not been. Most of that was that I could see so much emotion in them, where before there had been almost none.

We both had some cheesecake, and then I paid the bill with cash and we left. Lash was uncomfortable with me paying it, but he'd used the last of his cash to pay for the hotel room, and neither of us wanted to use a card that might be traced. Devlin, Theo, and Danial weren't dumb. Despite what Leri and Titus were doing, there was a really good chance Lash and I would be found before I went back with Titus. If that happened, there would be hell to pay.

We walked back to the hotel room. "The storm passed us by," I said, looking at the cloudy sky.

"It's still coming. Don't be fooled," Lash replied, picking up a large rough rock from the ground. He held it with one arm, and slid the other around me.

I didn't reply, leaning into him as we walked. We made it back to the room as a light rain began to fall.

"I'm exhausted again," I said, irritated. "But if you want to watch TV, go ahead. I can sleep right through it."

I expected Lash to say something, even just something funny, but he didn't.

I grabbed my bag and went into the bathroom. After sleeping in my nightgown most of the day, I didn't want to put it on again. Reluctantly, I put on the one nightgown I'd brought with me that was still clean, the one I'd meant to wear for Danial. It was black velvet, the neckline plunging with tiny glass beads sewn onto the bodice between my breasts, and on the straps, the sweeping skirt satin.

When I came out, Lash again didn't make any comments. He just turned off the light as I got into bed. There came a rustle of clothes in the darkness, and then he climbed in beside me.

"I'm putting my knife here on the nightstand," Lash hissed. There was a metallic noise. "Don't cut yourself. You didn't last night, but I didn't want you to." There was another rustle. "Same thing for my whip. It's beside the bed. If you get up, don't trip on it and fall."

"I won't," I replied, plumping the pillows.

Lash clicked on the TV and began surfing, finally settling on some show about life after people had disappeared from the Earth. It looked interesting, but I was so comfortable that I fell asleep before it had been on for more than a few minutes.

I woke up in the night to a clap of thunder that shook the room. Sitting up, I felt the bed was empty. Lash wasn't here. Fear washed over me like a bucket of ice water down my back. He would never have left without telling me. Something had happened.

"What's wrong?" his voice called softly. "Or did the storm wake you?"

"Lash?" I said, looking in vain into the darkness for his shape. "Where are you?"

"I'm over here by the window."

I let out a relieved breath. Thunder crashed again.

"What's wrong?" I said, worried. "Is there someone out there? Are we in danger?"

"No," he reassured. "No one knows we're here. Even if someone did know, no one has challenged me in a long time. My reputation makes anyone hesitate. Theo is the only one who I've even fought with in years, save of course the marks of my various jobs. And he's not really a match for me anyway. Not before, and definitely not now."

Lash's arrogant words hung in the darkness. His tone had seemed casual, but overly so, like he was trying too hard. The old hatred of Theo was back again in his voice. Apparently, his old personality had resurrected itself.

"Get some sleep," he continued. "No one's going to fuck with us."

Thunder crashed again, then came the first spattering of raindrops against the hotel window. Soon, the spatter became a pounding rain as the storm let loose.

"Full of yourself, aren't you?" I said, lying back down with a sigh.

"You seem to have had your fill of me," he said, his tone again overly casual. But this time I heard the rejection beneath it.

The silence stretched between us. The longer it went on, the more uncomfortable I became.

"Why are you over there?" I said finally. "Why did you get out of bed?"

Lash cleared his throat. "Because I can't sleep next to you anymore. When you rekindled my youth, you also rekindled my sex drive."

I bit my lip, searching for an answer that didn't sound like a rebuff.

Lash took my silence for disbelief. "You didn't know me in my youth," he said, amused. "I feel like I'm twenty again. It is all I can do to stay over here."

"I didn't notice it had ever lessened," I teased.

"I hadn't been with anyone since you, Sar," Lash replied. "Some of that was choice. But some of that was I no longer felt any desire for it." He paused. "All that's changed with everything else."

I said nothing, but thought he had to be lying. He had sure felt like sex the moment he saw me outside his tent. And now he was making it obvious that he wanted me to tell him to come back to bed. The truth I had to face was that I did want him.

Whatever had drawn me to Lash in the first place had faded when The Lust left me. But there was something about him now that called to me, and it wasn't his new, sexy appearance, either. I was surprised when I admitted it to myself, though I shouldn't have been surprised at all, not after what I'd just gone through to save him. It was that I cared about him.

I hadn't come here to save him because he'd been my lover months ago, or because I felt I owed him, or even for Dev's sake. I'd come because I liked him, and I wanted there to be more times we were together, more times we spent laying in the sun, or laughing over *South Park*. He was my friend, sure, but he was more than that, too. Wrong as it was, I felt more for him than a friend would. And I wanted to show him what I felt for him. I wanted to touch him, to kiss him, to run my hands over his body. I wanted to feel him touch me the same way. I hadn't been able to do much but lie there with him when I was giving him my blood. Now I was recovered, I wanted to be with him again, to feel his scales under my hands at least one more time.

I fought the desire down. *What the hell was I thinking?* I had enough to explain when I got home. Titus had covered this up, sure, but no secret was going to last for long against the threesome of Danial, Dev, and Theo. They were going to find out, sooner or later. Theo was going to be furious. Danial was going to be furious too, probably. Devlin, him I'd leave to Lash, but he was not going to be happy. He'd not liked me even smelling like Lash when he knew we hadn't been doing anything but lying on a rock together, not touching.

So what was the point of playing the virgin princess now? We'd already been together several times. Theo would not be any less angry about it, no one would. What was one more nail in the coffin now?

I sat there in the darkness, hating my life. The feeling was intense, and I was surprised how dissatisfied I was. I hadn't felt this way last night when I'd come to save Lash. I'd been happy then; happy to be living with Theo, happy I'd been on my way to see Danial, happy that Devlin was recovering and would soon be his old self again. Well, that last one was maybe more relieved than happy. *But I had been happy, hadn't I?*

Now, I was absolutely livid, feeling trapped again, like I had no choices. I hated that I couldn't tell Devlin that I cared for him, but I wanted a life apart from his. How long would it really be until he was fucking someone else again? His kind never changed.

I hated that I couldn't tell Theo that I was done with his jealousy, and his endless judging of me. I loved him, that hadn't changed, but I'd reached my breaking point with his wanting me to be the woman he had fallen in love with. I wasn't that woman anymore, and I was tired of him wanting me to be her, because I couldn't be her. She had died the day I'd given Devlin my Oath last December. It was time Theo faced that she was gone, and that the woman he called his wife now would never again be only his.

And I even hated Danial a little, for always putting his company first, for always acting like he needed me so much, and yet not being willing to give me his top priority. For a man who was always telling me not to leave him, where was he most of the time when I'd been living with him these last few months? Out traveling on jobs, and working in his office for hours straight.

In finally admitting all this to myself, I saw a few things with clarity. I loved them all, in varying degrees. And if something didn't change in a few months, we'd be right back where we'd been in January. They'd be fighting over me, and I'd be wanting to run; hell, I already did. But I couldn't leave Devlin or Danial without dying, and I didn't want to leave Theo and little Devon...

It was too much. It was all too fucking much. I wanted something for myself, something for myself that was just for me, that was for no other reason than I wanted it.

I swallowed hard. "Lash, come back to bed. I want you to."

My words echoed in the darkness, and the silence stretched.

Finally, he spoke, each word agonized. "No, I can't."

I hadn't seen that one coming. It took me a while to formulate a reply. "Do you not want me, now that you're so much younger than I am? Or are you worried Dev won't understand?" Those both seemed wrong, but I was at a loss.

"Neither," he hissed curtly, his fangs obviously back. "I need to shift forms. When you renewed my body, you renewed both forms of it. The snake side is calling me to change and shed my skin. But I can't leave you alone for the hours that would take, and I don't dare fall asleep with you next to me, because if I shift form in my sleep, forget where I am and can't see, I might bite you. My poison is back to what it once was: lethal."

There was something else going on here, besides what he'd said. But whatever it was, he needed my help again. "Shift, and I'll help you get it off. Once it's over your eyes, you should be okay to see me."

There was a long silence.

"Turn on the light," Lash said finally. "And grab the piece of rock I brought in with us tonight."

I reached for the light switch, and turned it on. The rock was on the nightstand, and I picked it up in my hands. I'd wondered why he'd brought this in tonight.

Something moved the covers at the bottom of the bed. Then a flat wedge shaped head slid up and over the bottom of the bed. Lash put out his tongue, and flicked it at me quickly. Then he was sliding up the bed to me, weaving back and forth.

All the weres I'd seen until now had been normal in size. Cia, Aran, and Ivan were regular foxes. Theo, Elle, and Nineva were normal-sized lions. The various grizzly bears might have been more powerful than normal bears, but they were also no larger than ordinary bears. Lash was not, unless most water moccasins were fifteen feet long and over ten inches at least in diameter.

He was dull black to my eyes at first, but as he got closer, I saw he did have a pattern on his scales: the background a tan color, with darker blotches and bands of brown and black all down his body. He had a stripe across each eye, and there was a ridge over each, too, making him look angry and dangerous. Covering all of him was a heavy filminess. His eyesight had to be impaired if not completely obstructed. He was most likely coming to me by scent alone.

As I watched him slide closer, I felt a little shiver of fear. I'd handled smaller snakes, saved them from being hurt by cars and tractors. But those snakes had been two feet long at most. None of them had ever been poisonous.

He coiled himself up on the bed, and I held out the rock to him. He flicked his tongue out at me, and then began to rub himself on it. As he rubbed, I saw the skin on his head detach here and there, then split. With a little more rubbing, he had loosened it enough that the edges of the silvery grey skin began folding back, the new skin of his snout showing through. But the thick skin was still covering his eyes.

He moved closer to me, nudging my hand. Carefully, I reached out and grabbed the skin, holding the edges in both hands. Lash strained forward. Slowly the skin peeled off him, uncovering his eyes. He turned to me and waited, flicking his tongue at me, his eyes cold and flat.

"Do you want me to hold it, so we can try to get it all off, or do you want me to let it go?" I asked. It was bad to pull a partly shed skin off of a snake before it was ready to come off. I didn't want to hurt him, in case the skin wasn't loose enough. I might rip loose a few scales, or even wound him.

He just looked at me, and flicked his tongue. I took that as a sign I should let go. I released my hands, letting go of the skin.

He shook his head, flicking his tongue at me.

Apparently, I'd been wrong. I reached out again, grabbing the edges of his skin. Again he moved forward, slowly slithering out of the skin inch by inch, his new scales lifting free one by one.

It was close to two hours before the last bit came free of his tail as he dropped off the bed to the floor. I gathered it up and put it on the table, as I wasn't sure what to do with it. Putting it in the garbage seemed wrong somehow.

As I sat back on the bed, Lash reared up on the floor, and looked up at me. Then he slithered fast up the side of the bed and over to me. Before I could react, he was twined up my waist and over my breasts, his long muscular body wrapped around mine, his head in front of mine, looking me in the eyes. He opened his mouth slowly, revealing his deadly looking hooked fangs, the white lining of his mouth shining. Seeing that, I remembered the other name for his species of snake: Cottonmouth.

I shivered, thinking how dead I'd be if he bit me just once.

Lash retracted his fangs, and then opened his mouth to close it softly on my hand. I felt his tongue tickling me, then wrapping around my little finger.

"You're beautiful," I said, stroking him with one hand. "But I need to lay back. You'd better move."

Lash again moved like lightning, leaving my body and coiling himself up on the bed beside me, his glossy new skin shining brightly in the light of the lamp. His scales had an intricate pattern of brown, black and tan. It made sense now why he had wanted to see me in those colors.

"Hold still," I said.

He moved his head under my hand, rubbing against me softly. I picked what I could of him up, and lay back with him on the bed, settling his body down on my lap. He was surprisingly heavy, so much dense muscle just beneath the warm scaly skin. He seemed content to lie there, not moving except for flicking his tongue every minute or so. I held him for a while, running my hands over him affectionately

I couldn't coil with him as he had wanted me to. This would have to do.

All at once, I felt him convulse under my hands and he began to shift back to human form. He shortened and thickened, and then his tail split, becoming legs, as his arms appeared to grow from his sides. Then his scales faded, to be replaced by his tan skin and black hair. I held him more and more loosely as he shifted, but soon I had a very human-looking Lash in my arms, lying on his side next to me.

"Thank you," he said, relieved. "I hate when I have to shed, and can't see. Devlin usually helps me with it."

"It's okay," I said softly, kissing him gently on the forehead. "It was neat, to see you as a snake. I'd always wondered how you looked, what pattern your scales would have—"

He gripped my arm hard with his hand, and whispered softly. "Is your invitation still open?"

I knew I shouldn't. That was a given. But he wanted me, I wanted him, and I didn't care about anything else.

"You know it won't be the same with me now," I said gently, touching his shoulder. "I'm a lot more reserved usually, when I'm not under the control of The Lust."

"You are still who you are," he said gently, running his hand down my arm. "I would want you just as much if you were covered with mud and sweat as you were that day at Hayden."

"I'm saying you may find me not as exciting—"

He looked up at me, rolling his eyes a little. "If I was any more excited, I'd be vibrating. You've seen my body ready for yours for the last twenty-four hours, Sar. And it's more than ready for you right now."

"So is mine," I said softly, bringing his hand to my thigh.

Lash slid his hand up my leg, then touched below my thatch, feeling my skin wet with desire. Instantly he shivered, his body contracting against mine. But instead of kissing me or making a move, he stayed where he was, his head raising to look up at me.

"Sar, tell me you want me," he said huskily, his eyes black with lust. "That it's okay, if I do this, that you want this to happen. Say the words."

"Why? Isn't it obvious—?"

"Because I know what Dev did to you last fall," Lash said reluctantly. "I know it wasn't your choice, at least at first." He clasped my hand in his. "The other times between you and me…they weren't either, not really, though you were nice about it. I know you don't have a lot of choices in your life now. I'm giving you this one. Don't say yes unless you really want to."

By the time he finished, I'd made my decision. My words were heavy with emotion as I whispered them, my eyes a little blurry with unshed tears. "Yes, I want to—"

Lash pulled me beneath him with a swift tug, and looked into my eyes. "Stop me, when it gets to be too much," he said seriously. He kissed me passionately, shoving my nightgown up and easing my legs apart, moving himself into position. With a loud cry he was in, and then he was thrusting rapidly, letting out guttural moans as I wrapped my legs around him, trying to pull him deeper into me. He buried his head in my neck, his arms winding around me to hold my body tight to his. Within seconds he came screaming my name, shoving himself deep as he let go. "Sar! Oh God, Sar!"

He collapsed on me, panting. I hugged him, then kissed his forehead. "Loud, are we?" I teased.

Lash pulled back from me, grinning happily. "Yes, we're both going to be," he said, kissing my cheeks and face. "I couldn't take loud noises before. My hearing was snake hearing, because I was half changed, and that was as far as I came back to human. I couldn't ever yell out how good you felt to me, or scream your name the way I wanted to. But I'm all the way back now, Sar. Before tonight is done, I'm going to make you scream my name until you're hoarse."

He began moving his hips, his hands cupping my face as he kissed me deeply, his tongue caressing me gently, yet with passion.

* * * *

"Lash," I moaned, throwing my head back, the delicious climax rushing through me. "Lash! Yes!"

Lash thrust up beneath me, then gripped my thighs hard, his hips pistoning. "Sar…Ahh! Oh Sar! Oh God, Sar!"

After catching my breath, I sat up on him, leisurely stretching. "Has anyone ever told you you're good?"

"In the last few hours? Oh, about ten times, I think," he replied, hugging me. "I think it was you."

I snuggled against him, and he flexed gently within me, shifting his hips the tiniest fraction.

"Aren't you tired?" I said incredulously.

"I figure my physical age right now is about twenty, twenty-one," he drawled. "Between that and being were, no." He kissed my lips. "Do you hurt?"

"Not yet," I said sexily. "But I could use some water."

"Stay there and don't move," he said, lifting me off him. He was back shortly with a glass of water for me.

I drank it greedily. "Thanks."

"Another?" he asked, taking the empty glass.

"No, I'm good."

"Another orgasm?" he offered, grinning.

I crooked my finger at him. "Come here, my winding bedfellow."

* * * *

Lash woke me. "Are you hungry for lunch?" he asked, touching my arm gently. "Do you want me to bring you some food?"

"No," I said, stretching. "I'm not sure why. But I feel a lot better. I want to get up, and maybe go for a walk, get some sunlight."

"You were afraid you might not see it again." He kissed me. "I wouldn't have let you die, Sar."

I shook my head to tell him that wasn't what I was saying. "I didn't know if it would work," I whispered. "I'm part vampire now. There is some doubt as to whether the were virus would work on me, with so much of the vampire one already in me. Danial mentioned something like that to Theo, once."

"The vampire one worked for me, with the demon blood as catalyst," Lash said thoughtfully. "It would have worked, Sar. Titus gave you his blood hoping it would save you. If it didn't wake you, I was going to bite you. The were virus from me, with the demon blood as catalyst from him would have worked, even if his blood or my bite alone didn't. I wouldn't have let you do it, if I wasn't sure I could save you, if it came to that."

I took a deep breath then, and let it out. "I'm glad it worked. That's as close as I ever want to come until it's my time." I looked at the clock. "God, its afternoon. When did we stop?"

"We didn't," Lash said with a snort. "Someone fell asleep in mid-fuck—"

I bit my lip, affronted. "Don't call it that, please."

114

"I'm sorry," Lash said contritely. "Come outside with me," he asked, taking my hand. "We'll lay together in the sun. Let me hold you like I did that day months ago."

"I'll burn," I said, making a face.

"Not this time of day," Lash answered. "Or I can get you some sunscreen."

"I thought you didn't have any cash?" I asked, furrowing my brow.

"I have my truck stash, for emergencies," Lash replied. "I'd forgotten about it."

"I should shower first," I said, running my hands through my hair.

"Please don't," he said softly, squeezing my hand. "I like smelling my scent on you. We can shower when we come back, if you want to. But let me hold you for a while, and breathe in the scent of us. Please?"

"All right," I said. "I think I have some sunscreen in my purse, actually."

"I'll take care of this, too," Lash said, folding up the snakeskin in a bundle.

"What do you usually do with it?" I asked, wondering if he'd let me keep a piece of it.

"Sorry, but I have to burn it," Lash said, catching my look. "It's part of me, Sar, and it could be used by someone to hurt me."

"Who would—?"

"Titus, for one," Lash hissed angrily. "It will only take a minute to burn. We'll pick a spot with a fire pit or a grill."

We went out into the bright sunlight. The warmth felt wonderful on my skin, and I basked in the light. We were overdressed again, but that was good, as the day was uncharacteristically cool for southern Florida. Lash found us a grassy spot, then he gathered up the snakeskin, and took it to a nearby grill. He lay it on the top, putting a stick over it to hold it down, and then he struck a match from a book he removed from his pocket. The second Lash touched the match to the skin, it caught like gasoline. In seconds, there were just ashes scattering on the wind.

Lash came back to me, sat down, and took off his shirt, baring his chest. I sat down beside him, happy that last night's rain had already dried.

Lash moved closer, putting his arm around me. "There is nothing like the Southern sun," he said happily. "Here, lay down."

"I know what you mean," I laid back on the grass and closed my eyes.

Lash leaned back next to me on his arms. "Sleep if you want to. And tell me when you're ready to eat again."

"Later," I said. "It feels too good here to move. The sun's going to set before long as it is."

"Yes, it is," he said softly. Giving me a light kiss, he settled back down on his hands, watching the ocean.

I dozed for a while, luxuriating in the sun's heat. Too soon, Lash was squeezing my hand, telling me we needed to go.

"Answer me something first," I asked softly. "What does the symbol on the knife mean?"

Lash was silent.

His silence, although it said volumes, was not an answer. "Do you not want me to know? It clearly was a mark you put there. You carved it there in the steel. What did you write?"

"Leave it," Lash answered reluctantly. "I believed I was never going to see you again, that I was dying."

I didn't pursue it, though I concluded what the symbol likely meant, given the tone in his voice.

Chapter Seven

"I'm sorry if I offended you earlier," Lash said, contrite. "I was just teasing. I didn't mean to imply any disrespect."

I had felt disrespected, but I should know his sense of humor by now, and his fondness for the word fuck. "It's fine, just don't call it that again."

"I won't," Lash hissed softly in my ear. He leaned closer. "Please tell me I don't have to call it intercourse, though—"

"Stop it!" I said, cracking up laughing. "But I do want you to tell me something. What do I smell like to you, that you like it so much?"

Lash didn't hesitate. "You smell like this day," he sighed with deep longing. "Like the best day there could be, with the sun shining down, and the warmth of it making me feel so good. I didn't smell it the first few times I met you. You were covered in Danial's, and later Devlin's scent, then. I smelled a trace of it the day I first brought you home from Hayden, though I thought it was some kind of perfume you were wearing. I only smelled it for what it was the first time we were together." He paused. "I couldn't get enough of it. I didn't need to be in the room with you all those months I guarded you, Sar. I was there because I wanted to be near you. It must be what Devlin means, when he says you taste of summer. Because you smell of it, at least to me."

I waited to hear him say he smelled the taint of vampire as Theo had, but he didn't. Maybe he couldn't smell it because he had his own similar taint. Lash smelled like autumn leaves, leather, and musk, but the earth scent under it had increased from what it had been. The scent of his sickness was gone.

* * * *

"Sar, even if you aren't hungry, I am," Lash said, waking me. He was already dressed in his shirt. "It's close to seven. I need to eat something."

"I am, too," I said, offering him my hand. "What do you feel like?"

"Let's decide after we shower," he said, slipping his arm around me.

It was obvious he was after more nookie. I thought up various rebuffs in favor of eating as we slowly walked back to the hotel room. Then to my shock, Lash offered me the shower first, telling me he'd go pack up the tent gear while I dressed.

Mystified, I showered, and then dressed. By the time he returned, I was perusing the room service menu to see if they had anything they could make fast so I could snack as I waited for him.

"I'll be fast," he promised. "I meant to be quicker, but the storm played hell with the tent. Some of the poles were bent."

"That's okay. Was all your stuff there?"

Lash nodded. "Including clean clothes. Give me ten minutes."

I watched the clock, sure it would take him longer. Instead, it took him nine minutes to emerge dressed, his weapons in place, his hair still wet.

"Do you want to go out?" he asked, leaning against the wall.

I put down the menu. "What do you want to do?"

"That depends on how you feel," he said, grinning faintly. "Are you too sore for more of me after this morning?"

It was time for the hard question. "How long do we have?" I asked, biting my lip.

"Titus is prompt. He'll be here at midnight, or at most, a few minutes later," Lash said, his grin fading. "We have about four hours, tops."

"I want to again, before he comes," I said quickly. "But the truth is I won't be able to for very long. I'm not hurt, but there comes a time—"

"It's okay, Sar," Lash said hurriedly, cutting me off. "I know I pushed it this morning with you. I wanted to take you out anyway, if you were willing to go."

I looked at him in surprise. "Was there something you wanted to try at the restaurant?"

"No more restaurants. There's only one bar here, but it'll do. I'll get us some food and you can have your wine, and we'll enjoy ourselves." He held out his hand to me. "Let's go."

As we walked to the Buttonwood, I got eaten by mosquitoes. "Why do they ignore you?" I asked, jealous.

"They are not ignoring me," Lash said winningly. "I'm just handling it more in stride."

I rolled my eyes and he laughed.

There weren't many people in the Buttonwood Lounge. We got a nice booth in the bar.

"Ready for wine?"

"Hell, yes," I said.

Lash ordered us a bottle, and two baskets of fish and chips for himself. I looked at the food offerings, but again, didn't feel that hungry. Lash looked worried, until the food came and I ended up eating the entire contents of one of his baskets.

"It smelled good," I said apologetically.

"Another basket," he said to the waiter. "And bring her some more fries, a lot more. She's in desperate fry straits."

The waiter gave him an odd look, then left with the empty baskets.

"You seem a little nervous," Lash said, after he left. "Is it me?"

"It's the way you watch me," I said breathily, meeting his dark eyes.

Just the edge of his mouth curved upward. "And what way is that?"

"With wicked glee," I said, drawing another delicious shuddering breath. "That as soon as I drop my eyes or turn, you're going to grab me and make everything I've ever fantasized real."

Lash grinned. "You want me to, here and now?"

I dropped my eyes, because he'd meant exactly what he'd said. "No, we've got an audience." I reached for his hand. "But I'll take you up on that as soon as we leave."

"Just tell me when you're ready," Lash hissed, relaxing back into his seat. "I'll behave until then."

"Good," I teased. "Because I remember what happened last time we were together in a bar."

Lash cracked up laughing. "Which time?" he said, smirking. "Not that both weren't enjoyable—"

I blushed deeply, then kicked him under the table, connecting hard. He yelped.

"Not that time," I replied loftily. "The time we were just sitting there talking and The Lust first rose in me. That first time with you."

Lash downed his glass of wine, then looked over at me. "I'm sorry for what I said to you that night. I did want you then, as you saw later on. I was trying not to give in to it."

Guilt rose up in me. "And I'm sorry for what they said to you in the parking lot, back—"

"You didn't say the words, Sar," Lash hissed softly, rubbing his face with his hands.

"It doesn't matter," I said, downing my wine. "I'm sorry for them all the same. They weren't true, and I should have said something then."

"You couldn't have, without telling them that I'd been with you again," he said quietly, pouring us each another glass. "Besides, I don't care what either of those fucks say. What matters is you kept secret about how weak I was." He paused. "He's good with a blade, Sar. I might not have won if Theo had been lucky, and cut me deeply enough. It was good you stopped us from fighting."

If Theo faced him now, Lash was sure he would win. He was right. He had the skill of a century in the body of a twenty-year old. Curiously, the old hatred was missing now from his tone. Lash talked of Theo more like a familiar colleague. Maybe he was just mellow from all the sex he'd had earlier today.

"I am a little nervous," I admitted.

Lash gave me a surprised look. "Are you sorry?" he asked seriously.

"No," I said, reaching out to take his hand. "But you look so different; it's still a shock to see you so young. And you're talking a lot more than you ever did before."

"Snakes are quiet," Lash said with a shrug. "Now I can be completely human without the snake part of me being present. I always liked talking to you, Sar."

I gave him a smile, then sipped my wine.

"You know they have a pool table here. It's just over there," he teased.

I kicked at him again. He evaded my kick and laughed.

Well, I could tease, too. "They have a juke box too," I said pointedly.

Lash gave me confused eyes. "So? You want some money to play something?"

"I want you to dance with me. I have change in my purse."

"No," Lash said, pouring us the rest of the bottle. "I don't dance."

"C'mon," I said teasingly. "One song."

"I can't," Lash protested. "I never learned. I'll step on your feet."

"Then I'll teach you," I said, offering my hand.

Lash looked at me with a wry smile that said he knew he was going to be sorry for this. He downed his glass of wine, probably for courage. "You had better keep this a secret, too," he said, getting up.

He followed me to the juke box. It was one of the newer ones, with access to thousands of songs online. "What are you going to pick? I've never used one of these newer ones before—"

Letting him pick or even give input might be a disaster. I hurriedly chose Joe Cocker's "When the Night Comes," then motioned Lash to come over to me. As the music started, I put his arms around me at my waist, and put my arms around his neck.

Lash stood there, looking unsure. So I shifted my weight from foot to foot and we shuffled together, swaying awkwardly. He was right, he couldn't dance. I was surprised that he could be so graceful as a snake and be this uncoordinated. All his grace was absent as he moved stiffly in my arms. It was funny, and also sweet that he didn't feel proficient, and was still willing to do it for me.

We'd only danced for maybe a minute when I noticed we'd garnered the attention of a bunch of jocks drinking at the bar. They looked college age, maybe Ivy League, or maybe on a research trip. They were shooting looks at one another and laughing, then pointedly staring back at Lash and me.

I didn't care. I was having fun. I hadn't been able to hear what they said anyway. But Lash heard it and his eyes went flat instantly. He hissed in anger, then shot them a nasty glance. At once, he escorted me back to the table.

"Stay here, Sar," he hissed furiously. "I'll be right back."

I sat down, watching Lash stride over to them, then downed the rest of my wine in one swallow, suddenly worried.

Lash stood in front of their table, then folded his arms across his chest. "Fucking shut your mouths," he hissed in a cold, cold voice. "Or I'll hurt you."

Most of the group saw he meant business, and went quiet immediately, looking away from him. But one decided to mouth off instead. "Get out of here, loser! You think you're Indiana Jones or something, with that whip—"

Lash uncoiled his whip in a flash with a flick of his wrist, and then he let it fly, shattering the light above them. The glass showered down on them in a rain as they covered their heads, yelling.

The bartender reached under the bar. Was he was getting a shotgun, or calling 911? Shit, we didn't need the police here. The last thing we needed was to be on the news, or end up in jail.

"Get the fuck out of here!" Lash snarled. The group of jocks ran, slipping a little in their haste to get away from him, their pitcher of beer falling to the floor to smash into pieces.

Lash lashed out with his whip again, sending the end to wrap itself around the bold kid. He yanked backwards, the kid flying through the air to land at his feet. Lash dropped his whip, then grabbed him by the neck. "You fucked with the wrong guy, dickweed—"

The bartender cocked the shotgun, pointing it at Lash from a few inches away. "Drop him!"

Lash held the kid up in front of him as a shield. "Go ahead. Blow him away, old man. You'd be doing the world a favor—"

I had to stop this. Someone was going to get hurt!

"I said, drop him!"

In a dexterous motion, Lash grabbed his whip from the floor. With a sharp crack, he jerked the gun out of the bartender's grip with his whip, and tossed it twenty feet behind him. The bartender leaned on the bar, hissing in pain. *God, was his wrist broken?*

Lash stared into the kid's terrified eyes. "You see that woman, the one you were making fun of? You look at her real good, because her being here saved your life, you fuck. I've killed younger kids than you for less."

121

He drew his knife, then held it to the kid's throat. The kid wet himself, urine streaming down his pant leg.

"You can't hold your beer," Lash hissed scornfully. "Leave, jackass, before I give you another hole to pee out of."

He dropped the kid, who flailed on the floor, crying, before he crawled for the exit, finally getting to his feet by the door. He dashed outside, leaving the screen door wide open.

Lash sheathed his knife, then walked over and grabbed the bartender hard by the front of his shirt, pulling him up and slightly over the bar. The bartender took one look at Lash's fangs, and cringed backward.

"We're leaving," Lash hissed. "Here's a hundred for a new light. You know what's good for you, you won't call the police, or anybody else. Or I'll come back and see you some night. Got it?"

The man nodded. Lash shoved him backward hard enough he fell behind the bar. After leaving some money in a pile on top of the bar, Lash sauntered over to me. "Ready to go?"

I nodded. I was more than ready to go. Not meeting his eyes, I followed him out, stepping gingerly over the broken glass and spilled beer.

"Sorry about that," Lash hissed, putting his arm around me as we walked back to the hotel room. "Young people today have no manners."

I didn't reply, too shocked at the ease with which he'd gotten violent. While Devlin had just as much violence in him, even he wouldn't have trashed a human-owned bar. At least, I didn't think he would. Lash wasn't sorry at all; he'd enjoyed making that kid piss himself. That was the type of man he was. I'd better remember that just because he'd been gentle with me didn't change that fact.

"What did he say?" I asked as we walked. "That kid in the bar?"

"Never you mind," he said, anger immediately in his tone. "He was a no-good fuck."

Okay, then. "I can't take you anywhere," I said lightly, and hesitantly leaned into him.

"I'm bad company," he said self-mockingly, with a touch of pride. "But he deserved it."

"Yes, but I wanted some more chocolate," I teased.

Lash nodded. "I'll drop you off at the room, and go get some, then—"

"Not so fast!" I teased, giving him a smile. "You owe me a dance still, Mr. Lash."

"Come with me then," Lash said, and switched direction, heading toward his truck parked a few feet away.

I leaned back against it as he rummaged inside. "Aren't you worried someone will report what happened?"

"Neither of them will," Lash replied with a sneer. "No man ever wants to admit he pissed himself, or that a man took his gun without it being at gunpoint." He cranked the engine to life. Suddenly, loud music began blaring from the trucks stereo system. I roared with laughter, holding onto the truck so I didn't fall down. He'd put on Thoroughgood's "Bad to the Bone." "Is this like your theme song or something?" I said, laughing.

I looked up to see him sauntering toward me, baring his fangs a little, his eyes flat. Abruptly I stopped laughing, and backed up a little bit. Lash kept coming, his walk purposeful, his eyes fastened on me. He reached out and grabbed me, his hands sliding down my arms to grasp my hands. He planted them on his hips, just below his knife and whip. "Move me," he said, slipping his arms upwards to hold me loosely

While the song was campy, it had a good beat. I gripped his hips in my hands, and began to move. In a few seconds, Lash and I were slowly swaying together to the beat of the song, as he followed the gentle pressure of my hands. All at once he seemed to get it, his movements in sync with mine. I slid my arms up from his waist and held him around his neck. Lash slipped his hand up from my waist to run his fingers into my hair, then cupped my face in his hand. Holding my eyes with his, he swayed to the beat with me, his hand on my cheek, caressing me slightly with the tips of his fingers.

Lash's eyes were dark, dark as the blackest night, darker than Danial's had ever been, and I wanted to lose myself in them, as I'd lost myself in his arms earlier today. I slid my hand up from his shoulder then, and put my hand on his cheek. He faltered briefly, losing the rhythm, then found it again quickly, his eyes never breaking with mine.

Lash leaned in closer, our faces just a few inches apart, as we moved to the music.

"How am I doing?" he whispered, putting his cheek alongside mine.

I didn't answer him, lost in enjoyment of his strong, lean body against mine moving to the beat of the music.

"Sar," he said, pulling back from me so his lips were an inch from mine. "Answer me."

"Good," I whispered hungrily, looking into his dark, dark eyes. "You're doing good."

Lash looked at me, then slowly opened his mouth, his hooked fangs growing before my eyes. "I can be better," he hissed softly, then kissed me consumingly, twining his tongue around mine, still swaying to the music with me.

By the time the song was over, I was panting with desire, and we were no longer dancing. Lash had me backed against the side of his truck, and we were kissing each other ravenously, his erection pushing into my groin eagerly through his straining jeans.

"I want you," I said hoarsely, breaking the kiss. I reached down into his jeans, cupping his swelled flesh.

"You're getting me," he hissed with a groan, pulling away from me. "But I'm not doing you out here, where everyone can see us." He shut off the truck, locked it, then took my hand, walking fast towards the room.

We made it to the room in record time. Lash swiped the card, then kicked the door open. Grabbing me, he undid his pants, then tackled me on the bed, pulling off my jeans as he wriggled out of his own. Then he was inside me, his lips everywhere kissing, his forked tongue tweaking and teasing as his hands caressed me. I was frenetic beneath him, moaning and writhing, his every motion within me both bliss and torturous tease. We came together screaming, clutching one another, our bodies shuddering.

"God," Lash panted, rolling onto his back. "I should've learned to dance decades ago. I had no idea it was such a turn on."

"Maybe you just needed the right instructor," I teased, stroking his still stiff penis.

He put his hand over mine, caressed the back of my hand gently, then let go. "I did."

I rolled on my side, facing him. "I have to ask; why didn't you want to, outside? You've…I mean, we've done other—"

"You mean me," Lash hissed tiredly. "You're right, I've done stuff that wasn't private at all. But that wasn't my choice, ever."

"Lash," I said sarcastically, withdrawing my hand. "You tried to raise The Lust in front of Theo in a parking lot."

"I know, I know," Lash said, holding up his hand. "What I did was bad. But I wouldn't have let you be embarrassed that day, even if you had reacted like I wanted."

I gave him a skeptical look. "There's no way I wouldn't have been."

Lash turned his head. "I'm not stupid. I knew that the window was closing, that soon you wouldn't want me anymore. I had to try, if there was even a chance. It was too good with you not to."

"That wasn't me," I said softly. "The real me."

"I didn't ask you for lunch trying to get sex," Lash hissed wearily. "I wanted to spend time with you, like I do now. But you'd practically given me permission to raise it in you. And so when our walk was done, I was going to try to raise it one last time." He squeezed my hand. "I had rented us a room earlier that day, Sar, in a hotel across from the Japanese restaurant. If things worked out, I was going to take you there. I was furious with Theo for spoiling it, when I wanted you so much and it was so close to happening. So I kissed you and hoped for the best. I knew he'd forgive you after, even if he'd want to kill me for what I'd done. And if I could raise it, he'd let me have you until it was sated, even if he waited outside the door with his gun so he could try to kill me right after." He squeezed again. "I wanted to be with you again, however I could."

"You have been," I said, hugging him. "You got your wish."

"That and more," Lash said, kissing my hand. "But you wished for chocolate. You still want some?"

"I'll eat whatever you bring back," I replied, stretching. "But chocolate would be nice."

Lash returned shortly with some hamburgers, French fries, and dessert for us. He devoured his, then fed me my fries, missing my mouth purposely, so he could kiss the ketchup away. We shared the towering quarter wedge of moist chocolate cake.

"I'm glad you can share this with me," I said, feeding him a piece.

Lash chewed, then gave me a smile that contained a little pain. "The flesh and blood diet was tedious, even if it was a normal snake diet. That's why I enjoyed the sushi so much, and the other things you made for me. Seeing and smelling food I couldn't eat was awful."

I understood at last why Serena's offerings of food hadn't been touched. "You—?"

"Yes, I'm the reason. I told all the other guards if they ate any of what you left out for us, I'd hurt them. I was dying for a taste, but I knew it would make me sick. I was already failing by then—"

I reached out and clasped his hand.

"—But I'd be damned if any of them were going to have something I wanted for myself, if I couldn't have it," Lash said, eyeing me pointedly. "Ever."

"I'll make you one as soon as we get back," I offered. "What kind is your favorite?"

"No," Lash said gently. "I meant what I said to Titus, Sar. I care for you deeply, but Devlin's my best friend. When we go back, I'm going to keep you at arm's length like I did before. We won't be like this again, unless you get pregnant again and you need me. Now that you're fixed, that's unlikely."

"It would just be a pie," I said, stroking his arm gently. "I make them for Danial's guards all the time."

"You know as well as I do that it's not the same with us as it is with his guards," Lash said gently. "I need to be just your guard again, not your lover."

"Can you do that?" I stated skeptically. "See me all the time, and know I'm with him, and not with you? That I'm with Theo?"

"It's not saying that it's going to be easy," Lash said, rolling his eyes. "I'll think about us together like this. I'll still want you as much as I do now. But its right. And you know as well as I that it's what we need to do, unless you want to give up Theo."

I looked at him, shocked.

"Devlin's not going to let you have another lover, Sar, not when he has to share you with two other men already," Lash said with something like regret. "Not even if it's me."

He was asking me to give up my marriage. I looked away from him.

"I know you love Theo. Can you leave him, Sar? Tell him that you want me instead? Devlin would probably amend your Oath to include me, if you would agree to drop Theo. Danial probably wouldn't care, so long as you kept seeing him the same days you do now."

That wasn't true. Danial was still harboring fantasies of the three of us together, and he would never consider Lash a replacement for Theo. As much as I cared for Lash, I couldn't consider that, either.

"Don't ask me to do that," I said softly, not looking at him. "Not after everything he and I went through to be together. I'm sorry, but I have to think of Devon, Lash. My son has to come first. I feel so hypocritical saying that after the last two days, but—"

Lash pulled me close. "I am not asking you, because I knew that this is what you would say. I understand, Sar. I know you don't love me. And it's okay that you don't."

Now I felt like pond scum. "I didn't mean to hurt you—"

"Shh," Lash said gently, kissing my lips. "You haven't. You saved me when no one else could have. And let's be honest, only Devlin would have. He is my only friend, next to you. If you need something done like when I helped you before, you let me know. I won't hurt Devlin, but anything else."

Being given carte blanche like this from Lash took me aback. "Thank you."

"Now kiss me," Lash said, moving aside our food wrappers. "Titus will be here soon, and there's not much time left. Don't waste it talking about what we can't have. In the little time we have left together, I want as many memories of you as we can make."

Lash abruptly stopped. "Was that enough chocolate? I could go out, and get you more—"

I looked at him and smiled, putting my finger to his lips. "I've had enough food, Lash. But I will always want more of you." I leaned in and kissed him eagerly.

Lash put his arms around me, his forked tongue delving deep. I sucked it gently into my mouth, then caressed it with my tongue. Lash groaned, squeezing me tight, then lay me back on the bed and began kissing down my chest, tickling me with his forked tongue as he slowly worked his way down my body.

"Then I'm going to give you more," Lash hissed tenderly. "As much more as you can take. You might be sore, but if I do this, you'll feel only pleasure."

"Then turn your body around, and face the other way," I said softly. "I don't want you left out."

His eyes widened. "You don't have to do that for me," Lash said quickly. "I don't expect it."

"You're getting it anyway. Come here," I ordered, reaching for him.

Lash let out a anticipatory sigh, then flopped onto his back, his penis already stiff. I moved down between his legs and caressed it, kissing his swollen shaft. He thrust up lightly, trembling. I licked up his length, then sucked the tip, tonguing the opening.

Lash let out a loud moan, his hands clenching the bed covers. "No one's done that to me in years," he hissed, blissful. "Decades. God, it's like heaven—"

"You said you wanted memories," I said sultrily. "If that's all you want of me, then you're going to get the best damn ones I can give you."

Then the only sounds were of him crying out as I took him deeply into me.

* * * *

Titus arrived at midnight, just as he said he would. Lash and I had finished having sex for what we knew would be the last time a few minutes before. We were lying in bed, softly kissing each other, our bodies entwined. Titus knocked, but we'd already known he was close by from the black feeling that permeated the room.

Lash turned to me, sadness in his dark eyes. He put his hand on my cheek as he had earlier, and touched me softly, caressing me with his fingertips. He brought me in for one last kiss, then got up from bed, and pulled on his jeans. I wrapped myself in the bed linens and got up myself, heading for the bathroom. I'd known I'd have to shower before going home, but I was damned if I was going to lose any time with Lash doing it.

Lash froze, his hand reaching for the door. I froze behind him, clutching the bedclothes to me.

"Lash," a familiar melodious voice called, hot with anger.

Dev. I shivered, wrapping the linens around myself tighter.

"This whole corridor is rife with the scent of sex and semen," Devlin said, his fury, hurt, and disappointment in each word. "I know Sar's in there with you. Open this door before I break it down."

Lash looked at me, then indicated the bathroom. I went in and shut the door most of the way, peeking through the crack.

Lash put his hand on the door, but didn't open it. "Yes, I've been with her, Dev. I'm sorry—"

"You took her from me," Devlin growled. "What's worse, she went. How long have you been plotting this behind my back?"

Lash opened the door. Devlin's words cut off suddenly

"We didn't," Lash hissed. "I hope you can forgive me when I explain."

"You…you're young—" Devlin gasped.

Lash went out of the room, closing the door behind himself with a click. Titus appeared inside the room, then quickly locked the door from the inside.

"Shit, Titus!" I swore at him. "Why didn't you warn us?"

"Devlin had a right to know," Titus retorted, his red eyes glowing. "Danial, Theo, and he got back an hour ago. They didn't call first, they just showed up. Leri hid in Danial's bedroom when she heard them, and called me. Devlin was the first to reach her. He knew Leri wasn't you the moment he kissed her. But he covered for you, making a show of taking her/you to Hayden. Theo and Danial protested, but I showed up by that time, and teleported her to the car. Devlin came storming out a few minutes later. As soon as we cleared Danial's driveway, he asked us where the hell you really were. He had called home, and he knew Lash wasn't at Hayden either, where he was supposed to be. When he asked me, I told him the truth. He ordered me to take him to you."

"He would have known tonight, anyway," I said, dismayed. "I just wish he hadn't found us like this. It makes it look like we were having an affair, that this was all just about us having sex." I shot him a furious look. "Why didn't you tell him the particulars?"

"That's Lash's job to explain," Titus rumbled softly, handing me my duffel bag. "Devlin's seen what you did for him. I doubt he'll be angry about you saving him."

Titus was making a point that Dev would be angry about the sex. Reckless as it was, I didn't give a damn. "I'm going to shower. I'll be out as soon as I'm done."

I took a nice long shower, dried off, conditioned my hair with what was left of the hotel conditioner, and put on my last change of clothes. Throwing my dirty clothes in with the others, I opened the door, and then stopped in my tracks.

Devlin was waiting there, sitting on the edge of the bed, his head in his hands.

I was suddenly afraid, worried to break the silence, worried he'd erupt in anger.

"Come to me, Love," he said brokenly, without looking up.

He'd been crying. I dropped my bag and went to sit beside him.

"I'm sorry for my accusation," he said softly. "He told me all of it, told me what you did for him. He told me that you did it for me, because you knew what he meant to me."

"Yes, that's true," I admitted. "But he also means something to me, Dev. I couldn't let him die."

"Must you save us all?" Devlin said tenderly, hugging me tightly.

"It's become habit now," I said teasingly, then kissed his tears away.

"I knew something was wrong with him," Devlin said heavily. "Especially when his scar wouldn't heal. But he told me he was fine, and when he and Titus took Ebediah, and Sola, he was not injured at all, the only one who wasn't. I told myself that was proof that he was okay. I didn't want to think that he might be failing—"

"That doesn't matter," I said softly. "He's well again. That's what matters."

"Hold still," Devlin said suddenly. He leaned over and, with a twist of his head, he nicked my neck, opening two short scratches that were little more than paper cuts. Devlin licked me, and then grabbed a tissue, grimacing and gagging.

My blood obviously no longer tasted like summer, even though I wasn't turned. *What had happened?*

Dev wiped his mouth off, and ran into the bathroom, still gagging. He emerged, still moving his mouth distastefully.

"I'm sorry," I said with a shrug. "It was the only way."

"It doesn't matter," Devlin said. He pulled me to my feet, then kissed my cheek. "I love you for you, not for the way you taste. And in time, your blood may taste of summer again."

I heard in his tone how much he wanted to believe that. I hoped for his sake it was true. "What is in my blood that tastes so bad? The demon blood?"

"Some of what made me grimace is the blood replenishing medication you took," he explained. "You must have grabbed the red packets instead of the blue ones that Stephen always prescribed for you. The red packets are made specifically for vampire assault victims, and so are bitter tasting for a reason, to discourage further attacks by making your blood bitter tasting for at least a week after taking one. How many did you take?"

"Seven or eight?" I offered. "I lost count." It wasn't surprising Devlin knew the taste. He'd probably loved playing the seductive vampire at the window through the years, and I doubted he would give up a lover unless it was his choice.

"Titus said Lash took over half of your blood," Devlin said, hugging me tighter. "I'm glad you're okay."

"Did you forgive him?" I said softly. "Do you forgive me?"

"There is nothing to forgive," Devlin said, letting out a breath. "If you had told me, I'd have prevented you from doing it, and then he would've died. He is like a brother to me, Sar, and except for the past year, I've been closer to him than I was to Danial." Devlin kissed my cheek again. "I'm grateful to you," he said gently. "Very grateful you saved him."

"Grateful enough to release me from my Oath to you?" I said teasingly.

"Hell, no!" Devlin said, grinning at me. "In fact I'm taking you back to Hayden with me tonight. Titus said you still need to rest. Lash said you hadn't gotten much sleep today, or last night."

Lash had indeed told him everything. I didn't reply. The silence stretched.

"Sar, he told me you were together, both when you were saving him and after. He also said he wouldn't be with you again like that unless it was okay with me. I took him at his word. He has never lied to me, and I don't lie to him, ever."

Devlin's tone was carefully neutral, but I was waiting for the other shoe to drop. "And?"

Devlin sighed. "And if there comes a time you want him to share our bed, tell him. If he asks me, I'll probably say yes. He told me today he would never ask if I forgave him, but that's him feeling guilty. It's obvious you both have chemistry. But you need to know that I'll make you take a new Oath to me, as the price for including him. It will have some new wording, because I would want assurances from you about certain things. But I will include him, provided you do that." He kissed my neck. "I'm not one to deny you a lover you lust for, provided you don't deny me my own special privileges."

There was no way in hell I was giving Dev an Oath with more rights than he'd already wrested from me. I didn't reply.

Devlin looked hard at me. "Tell me that you understand what I'm telling you, Love," he said harshly.

He was telling me I'd better never take liberties with Lash again without his knowledge. "I understand," I said, nodding. "I'm sorry you found us like you did. It sounds lame, but I was heading home with Titus tonight to tell you everything—"

"Titus is a demon," Dev interrupted, annoyed. "He gets pleasure in causing pain. I'm sure he took this opportunity to hurt me. But that doesn't matter." He picked me up. "Let's go home, Love."

Chapter Eight

Devlin carried me out of the room, and down the stairs to the parking lot. I wanted to protest that I could walk, but he was taking things so well I thought it unwise to rock the boat.

Instead of just Titus, both Titus and Lash were waiting for us next to Lash's truck.

"You sure you can take the whole thing?" Lash said to Titus, sneering.

"Shut up and drive," Titus spat back at him.

Lash and Titus got into the truck cab. Devlin boosted me up in the truck's backseat, and then climbed up after me. Lash drove into a secluded spot, and then suddenly, we were parked outside Hayden. Lash drove in through the gates, and parked in the garage. Then we all got out, and went into the kitchen.

Serena was there cutting up freshly baked bread. She looked at Dev, then cast me a frightened glance. Then she saw Lash and her eyes went wide.

"Go upstairs," Devlin said calmly. With a last worried look at me, Serena went.

Devlin turned to me. "Do you need anything to eat?"

"I ate already," I said with a blush, remembering the French fries and ketchup kisses.

Devlin gave a long-suffering sigh. "I should have guessed."

"Enough pissing and moaning," Lash hissed, following Titus downstairs. Devlin and I descended also into Titus's basement study. Titus settled in a chair. Devlin also sat in one, and pulled me down into his lap. Lash sat in another one of the chairs, sprawling indolently sideways.

"Well, what should we do?" Devlin said.

"About what?" I asked.

"Lash is not only not dead, Sar, he's young again," Devlin said flatly. "Your blood did it. We need to decide how best to cover it up. Or else every single aged and/or dying creature is going to want you. It will make the Rulers' desire for you seem like nothing."

131

Horror eclipsed every other waking thought. I clutched him.

Dev's arms tightened around me. "We'll keep you safe, Love," he murmured softly. "But we have to think of how."

"I have no ideas," Lash said with a shrug. "Titus said there was nothing that could have been done to save me, that he had drawn out my life as long as he could."

Devlin looked at Titus. "Is that true?" he said in a deadly tone.

Titus looked at Devlin. "No," he said bluntly.

Lash was on him in a minute, Titus was holding him back, Lash's knife point over his heart. Devlin struggled to get up, losing seconds as he got out from under me.

"You know that won't kill me!" Titus rasped, struggling to hold back Lash's knife with one hand, and Lash's fangs with the other. Venom dripped from them, black droplets falling steadily.

"It'll hurt a lot!" Lash hissed furiously. "And I want to hurt you, you fuck! You were going to let me die! I almost did die! Sar risked her life—!"

"Stop!" Devlin shouted, shoving Lash off Titus.

Lash hissed menacingly. He backed off, but he didn't put his knife away.

"I could've saved you, sure!" Titus said angrily. "But only by killing an older vampire at least Devlin's age, if not older. It was the older blood in Sar that saved you, Lash!"

"Why not tell me, you ass?" Devlin hissed, baring his fangs. "I would've given my blood gladly!"

"All of it?" Titus said, raising his eyebrows. "I'd have needed all of it, Devlin. You ready to die?"

Devlin looked at Lash then, in his gold eyes something close to Danial's soft look for me. "No," he said softly. "But I would've given all that I could, and I'd have gotten the rest from Danial, somehow."

"I'd have also needed another weresnake of Lash's type, one very young," Titus rumbled. "No older than twenty or so. The younger the better—"

"A child?" I said in horror.

Titus nodded. "Lash needed something to jump start his regenerative system. The blood of a younger weresnake, mixed with older vampire blood and some of mine would have stopped his decline, and made him well. But even that wouldn't have made him younger like this, Devlin."

"Even with more demon blood from you?" Lash hissed meaningfully. "Say, all of it?"

Titus growled low.

"Enough!" Devlin said angrily. "Fighting will get us nowhere. We are doing this for Sar. Shut up and think!"

"We can say I used some faerie blood, too," Titus said slowly. "That would account for the youth. I have some of Leri's."

Just why he had some of his lover's blood lying around in his lab I didn't want to know.

"Would that have done it?" Devlin asked.

"Yes," Titus said, looking at him with red eyes. "It should've worked. I can't say for how long, but probably for at least a decade or two."

"Then you will research it well, Titus," Devlin said, carefully enunciating the words. "And the next time Lash needs his battery jumped, he is going to tell me—"

Lash nodded once, and folded his arms across his chest.

"—and then you are going to make whatever you need to, do whatever you need to, in order to keep him alive," Devlin finished, his eyes were glowing red hot like coals. "And anything he ever asks you from now on, you are always to tell him the truth! Say you understand me, Titus."

Titus nodded.

Devlin turned to me. "Sar, I'll have to tell Danial. I'll need him to be a part of this, to account for the blood we would supposedly need. But you will say nothing of this, any of it, not to anyone else—"

"She is going to tell Theo," Titus rumbled sarcastically. "She's his wife, Devlin. I'm glad I spent so much effort duping you all."

Devlin rubbed his eyes in exasperation. "You will, won't you?" he said quietly to me. "You always tell him. Even when you know it would be easier for us all if you didn't."

I went and sat down in the chair, and closed my eyes. "Dev, give me a minute."

"Sar—" Devlin said

I held up my hand. "Leave me with Titus for a moment," I repeated.

Devlin looked at me strangely, but he motioned to Lash, and they left. Titus remained where he was. I said nothing, just looked into space.

"Sar, are you mad?" Titus rumbled gently. "I did what I did to protect you."

"Save it," I said softly. "I didn't ask you to stay here to talk about that."

"What then?" Titus asked, curious.

"Can anyone outside this room hear us?"

Titus said some familiar sounding words, and a glow surrounded us, and then faded. "Not now. What do you have to say to me that can't be overheard?"

I swallowed hard. "I want you to sever the bond between Theo and I."

"What?" Titus roared.

"You heard me," I said simply. "Sever the bond between us."

"I can't," Titus said. "It can't be broken—"

"Don't give me that shit!" I said, my green eyes full of anger. "If I've learned anything today, I've learned that there is always a way. And I'm betting you know one."

Blackness boiled out of Titus then, evil as Hell and just as rancid. "You are not giving up your husband and child for that scum—"

"I'm doing it for Theo!" I screamed at him. "He loves me so much, and I've put him through hell for the past year, Titus! But so long as he's bound to me, he'll stay. And I want him to be free of me, because I want him to be happy. And he's never going to be happy sharing me with anyone."

Titus relented, looking crestfallen. "Sar—"

"No, Titus," I said, my words rough and uneven with grief. "I've tried it now for months. Theo's tried it. And it's not working. Theo can't even share me with Danial very well, and now I'm back with Devlin, it's just going to be the same thing all over again. I can't do it anymore. And I've decided I don't want to do it anymore. I want my life back, Titus."

I raised my eyes and looked him square in his red ones. "I have to be with Danial. And I have to be with Devlin. But I was with Theo just because I loved him. I love him enough to let him go, so he can find what he needs with someone who can just be his."

Titus came to me and hugged me. Heat enveloped me, and for once I let myself be roasted, as it took away from how awful I was feeling, thinking about Theo with someone else.

"Sar, you love him. You shouldn't leave him."

"I'm not leaving him. But break the bond between us, so that if he chooses to leave me after I tell him what I've done, he can go."

"I can't break it that fast. I can break it in layers, over some months. But it was built over years, and that's the best I can offer. Breaking it is going to be hard anyway. There may be a backlash, where he ends up hating you. And with the way his temper can be—"

I closed my eyes and hugged him, willing the heat of him to ease the pain of his words.

"Please do it. I want him to be free to leave, if he decides to."

Titus drew back from me. "Sar, just because I do this doesn't mean he'll leave you. There is no bond between you and Danial like you have with Theo, but Danial loves you more than life."

"Maybe he won't anymore, after he finds out about Lash and I," I said bitterly. "It's going to be so fun 'fessing up to him."

"I forgave Leri, and her crime was much worse," Titus rumbled, hugging me again. "He'll forgive you, Sar."

I hugged him, wishing he was right. But I knew Theo all too well.

134

* * * *

Devlin had Titus teleport Lash, Danial, and I to Danial's home. We arrived in the great room about three a.m. Devlin told Lash to wait outside for a moment, and Titus disappeared instantly, teleporting back to Hayden. Venus was there with only the bears and Serena, after all, and none of us liked the idea of her being unprotected.

"Danial?" Devlin called, gripping my hand in his.

Danial came out of his study, and looked down at Devlin, but didn't see me. "Dev?" Danial said questioningly. "Why aren't you at Hayden? Is Sar okay?"

"It's me," Devlin said quickly. "Are you alone?"

"Yes," Danial said, giving him an odd look. "The kids are out with Terian—" Then he saw me and his face lit up. "Did he tell you?" Danial said excitedly, coming down the stairs with a grin. "Samuel and Perseus are pleased with the information. They said that they'll let you live out your life with us, Sar. It's so—"

Danial saw my expression and froze on the stairs. "What is it?" he said, as much fear as I've ever heard in his tone. "Your heart is racing, Sar—"

"She's worried you won't love her," Devlin said, rubbing his eyes. "When you find out what she did."

Danial came to me and hugged me. "I'll always love you, Sar. There is nothing—"

"Lash!" Devlin called loudly. "Get in here, please!"

Danial went still, and then recoiled back from me. "Sar, tell me you didn't—"

"She saved me with her blood," Lash said, striding into the room. "I was dying, and she came to me and saved me."

Danial looked at me with narrowed eyes. Then he cut his eyes to Lash and did a double take. "You are young!" Danial said, his voice strangled. "How—?"

"It was her blood, something in her blood," Devlin said quickly. "Titus said it was also because there was so much vampire in Lash, from the potion he's been taking for years with my blood. Her blood saved him."

"He must have almost drained her then," Danial growled, his eyes red. "You filth, that you would dare to—!"

"Shut up!" I said harshly.

Danial was so shocked he cut off. All three of them looked at me.

"I gave my blood to him willingly, along with my body," I said, my words echoing in the room. "And I'm tired of everyone giving him shit, like he forced me to or something. Of all my lovers, he's the only one who never demanded anything of me, or took anything from me without my consent. The only one Danial, including you! So knock it off!"

Danial looked at me, then took in a long deep breath. "I should have heeded Lash's warning to me those months ago," he said, every word filled with pain. "I didn't. None of us thought of him as more than a temporary annoyance. And we gave him just enough room in our jealousy and fighting over you that he slipped into your heart—"

"Stop it," I said, moving away from him. "It's not like that."

"Isn't it?" Danial whispered, upset. "You risked your life to save him. You know what he is, what kind of man he is. You knew what he felt for Theo, and for me, and how we felt about him. And you went anyway, leaving your children without a second thought—"

"Don't disrespect her, you fucking vampire," Lash hissed. "Or I'll knock you through that wall."

"Get out," Danial said, baring his fangs. "You are banned from this house, Snake."

I'd already had enough tonight. I wasn't going to listen to anything more from Danial. I glared at him, and then went to teleport.

Danial was suddenly in front of me, holding onto my wrist. "Is it too painful for you to face the truth?" Danial asked harshly. "You did these things, Sar. You have to pay the price for what you did. And the price you are going to pay when you tell Theo is going to be the heaviest of all."

"Don't you think I know that?" I shouted at him, yanking my arm out of his grasp. "Now let me go."

I stalked out the door, and into the cool night. By themselves my feet found the path to the cemetery. I tried not to think too much as I walked.

It hadn't been too bad with Danial. It could have been worse. Maybe.

I finally got to the cemetery, and stood for a while, leaning against the tree, looking over at Suri's grave. In the faint moonlight, there was only shapes, and shadows.

"Suri, I'm glad you didn't live to see this—"

"Why not?" a soft voice said at my shoulder.

I jumped, and then saw it was Lash. "Shit, you scared me," I said angrily. "What are you—?"

Lash's passionate kiss cut off my words as his arms went around me, crushing my body to his. He leaned into me, pressing me to the tree, his hungry mouth moving insistently. I resisted briefly, then gave in, putting my arms around him.

He kissed me for a long time against the tree. Although he obviously wanted more, he didn't make moves to take it further. Finally he drew back from me slightly, then kissed my forehead.

"Why are you here?" I asked, thinking guiltily how good it felt to be back in his arms.

His dark eyes looked into mine. "Devlin is talking to Danial, and he sent me out here to keep an eye on you. I think he did it mostly to get me out of Danial's sight, so Devlin could calm him down, tell him what to say about how I'm changed now."

"Did that include kissing me?"

Lash grinned, and then kissed me again. "I promised him I wouldn't make love with you," he whispered. "I never said anything about kissing you. I intend to kiss you every chance I get." He kissed me again to make his point.

"I thought you wanted to just be my guard," I said, slightly irritated. "That's what you extolled earlier this evening. Why the sudden change of heart?"

"Because of what you said in there," Lash said affectionately, cradling me against his chest. "I didn't expect you to stand up for me, Sar. But you did." He swallowed. "And besides that, I like to kiss you," he hissed, then he kissed me again, his forked tongue winding around mine.

I kissed him back, losing myself in him, thinking just of how good he was making me feel. Finally, needing breath, we separated again.

"I always liked kissing you," he hissed, tickling my ear with his tongue.

"Are you going to tell me about your tattoo now?" I said with a smile.

Lash started, surprise in his dark eyes. "I didn't think you saw," he said, sounding embarrassed. "I didn't want you to see it."

When he had changed in my arms in the bright motel room, I had seen something dark on his back briefly before we'd started talking. Later, when he'd been distracted by Dev, I'd gotten a good look, enough to see that it was a snake, a large one, slithering up his back in coils with the mouth just under his shoulders, the fangs bared to strike.

My surprise had been in not having noticed it before then. While Lash and I had been intimate many times, most of those had been in the dark, or with him partly clothed. When we'd been in the hotel, Lash had been very careful to always face me, when he knew I was watching him. It had been then that I'd finally realized he was trying to hide it from me.. "It's why you didn't shower with me, right?"

"Yes," he admitted grudgingly.

"It's a cottonmouth, isn't it?"

He nodded. "When I was eighteen, I had it done," he said shyly. "I thought it made me look fearsome. You know how it is, when you're eighteen."

"I do indeed."

"I wanted to be a badass," Lash said, grinning ruefully.

"You succeeded," I affirmed. "Though I think the tattoo was just window dressing."

Lash looked at me uncertainly. "You don't think it's…well, dumb?" he said hesitantly. "I mean, I'm already a snake. I should have gotten guns and a skull, or an eagle or a dragon, anything but a snake—"

"I think you should kiss me again," I said, smiling. "Right now."

"Why?" Lash said with both pleasure and surprise. "You can't like it—"

"I like it and I like you and I like you to kiss me," I said with a eager smile, looking up at him. I ran my hand up his shoulder to hold his face, caressing him gently. "Is that enough of a reason?"

"You know it is," Lash growled, and then he was kissing me again avidly, his hands going into my hair to tangle in it, his body leaning into mine, pushing against mine tightly.

When we separated again a few minutes later, Lash gave a reluctant sigh. "We need to go. But before we do, I have something for you, and something to say."

Here it comes, the love confession. "What?" I asked.

Instead, I was caught completely by surprise. "I want you to know I am really sorry about what happened, the first time we were together," he hissed, changing in his upset. "I would have done oral on you then, if I'd had any idea, Sar." He paused. "Tell me you know that…that I didn't…I didn't not care I might make you sick. I wouldn't have done that to you purposely, not ever. I thought I was okay, that you'd be safe, because I thought I was…um, clean."

"I know that," I said, hugging him and resisting the urge to tell him I found his struggle for words endearing. "I knew it when you went that night to check yourself out at Camlyn's."

"I want you to know, if the opportunity ever comes again…well, that won't ever happen again." He looked at me, and then quickly away. "Okay?"

"Okay."

"Good." Lash took my hand and put something made of smooth metal in it.

I looked at him oddly. "Another knife?"

"Sar, the first knife I gave you is more ceremonial that functional. I'm glad you liked it, but I intended you to just keep it as a memento of me. This one is more functional. And you can slip it in your pocket easily. You don't have to have on a belt to carry it." He flicked his hand, and the blade flipped out. "It's sharp, so be careful," Lash said seriously. "But you can carry it in your purse, and if you need a knife, you'll have one."

"Are you going to teach me how to fight with one, too?" I joked.

He gave me a faint smile. "No. You need to fight someone with a knife, you call me, and I'll do the fighting. This is just for emergencies, like phone cords or snarled hair—"

My face split into a wide smile. "You ass!"

I gave him a shove. Lash was laughing so hard he fell down on his ass in the dirt. He just sat there for a while and laughed, looking up at me. I laughed, too, then offered him a hand up.

We walked back to the house together. When we arrived, Devlin was still "talking" to Danial, and from the loud yelling that was going on, neither of us wanted to go in. Also, I was both tired and cold.

"Lash, can you go inside and tell Dev I'm teleporting back to Hayden? I'm exhausted, and I need to get some sleep."

"Just go ahead and go," Lash said, giving me a quick kiss on the forehead. "I need to stay here, but you go get some rest. I'll let him know where you went, when they're done."

I nodded, and teleported to Hayden, ending up in the kitchen. No one was there, though Serena's baking stuff was all put away. I took my second shower of the night, and then put on a fresh nightgown, and crawled into Devlin's bed. I fell asleep the moment my head hit the pillows.

I awoke hours later, when Devlin slid into bed beside me and took me in his arms.

"Danial agreed to stick to our story. But he said if Lash should fail again, he wasn't going to donate any blood to save him. But I'll get him to change his mind," Devlin said determinedly. "Somehow."

I awoke at dusk. Immediately, I felt a heavy weight on me, and it wasn't Devlin, though he was laying on my chest. Today I needed to go home and face Theo. If I waited too much longer, Danial would tell him about Lash and I, and I didn't want him to find out that way.

I got up reluctantly, and got dressed. There was no sense putting off the misery.

Devlin stretched happily. "You know, in a few days I won't need an eye patch anymore."

"I'm glad to hear that," I said, smiling briefly. "Though I find you a very sexy pirate."

"I'll still wear it sometimes for you," Dev promised. "Are you off to bake with Serena?"

"No, I've got to go see Theo and get the big confession over with."

"Shouldn't you shower first?" Devlin said, confused. "You smell like me, Sar. Theo will be angry with you just for that—"

"I'm done with that," I said, interrupting him. "I'm done with taking showers every other minute, so as not to offend him. It makes it seem as if I'm sneaking around with multiple lovers. You all know where I am at any given time, who I'm with, and what we do when I'm there. Anyone who doesn't like how I smell, they don't have to get close enough to me to let it bother them. And that includes you, too."

Devlin said nothing for a moment. "I understand. You found more than Lash that night you saved him, didn't you, my Sar?"

"Yes. I found myself. I have spent this whole last year trying to balance everybody else's needs. I just ended up driving myself crazy. I'm not going to do it anymore."

Devlin sat up. "If you need someplace to go later tonight, you know my home is open to you. Danial's is as well, even if he's still upset with you."

He was offering because he thought Theo might tell me it was over between us. It was a real possibility. I should prepare myself for it, and make some contingency plans.

"I know," I said, shooting him a grateful look. "Thank you for that. I may be back tonight, if things go badly."

"Good luck," Devlin said, lying back in bed, and folding his hands behind his head.

"Thanks," I said opening his bedroom door. "I'm going to need it."

* * * *

When I arrived at my house, Theo embraced me immediately. Then he caught Devlin's scent, and gave me a cold look. "Why didn't you shower?"

His attitude just made this easier. "Come in here, please," I said wearily. "I have things to tell you."

I sat him down on the couch and told him everything, condensing the time Lash and I spent together after I saved him into that when I had saved him, we'd had sex.

"Did he force you?" Theo growled. "Or did you want him?"

I wanted to lie, but I didn't. I wasn't going to lie to him, no matter how much easier it would have made things. "I wanted him."

There was silence for a full minute.

"Are you going to leave me and our baby, and go live with him and Devlin?" Theo asked, real fear in his tone that the answer would be yes.

"No."

Theo's fear immediately changed to fury, his fangs erupting, slurring his words. "Are you going to fuck him again?"

"I don't know," I whispered. "Devlin expressed an interest in him being with us—"

"Don't tell me another word about your deviant sex games," Theo growled menacingly.

I went quiet.

"Just the thought of you and him, the thought of him in you, that you wanted him there, really wanted *him*—"

"Theo—"

140

Theo roared, so much rage, misery, and despair that I shrank back from him on the couch. He leapt up and left, slamming out of the house. The noise woke Devon, who began to howl from our bedroom.

I went in and comforted him until he was purring again. "I'm sorry, Devon," I said, hugging him. "Whatever happens, I love you. I'm not leaving you. That isn't going to change, ever."

I lay there for a while with him, listening to him purr as I sniffled and felt sorry for myself. Then I dried my tears and told myself to be strong. This was the price. I'd known it before I'd left here. And if I had it to do over again, I would still go to save Lash. And when given the choice of being with him, I'd still look into his dark eyes and say yes.

Leaving Devon sleeping on the bed, I showered, then had dinner, giving Devon some wet cat food for a treat. Then we both went to bed.

Just before dawn, I felt Theo slide into bed beside Devon and I. But he stayed on his side, and didn't touch me. I didn't know what to say, so I waited in silence.

"I'm sorry I left how I did," he said finally. "I needed to get out some of the rage I was feeling. I drove to Danial's land, and killed a deer. I didn't eat it. I just ripped it to shreds."

I was horrified, even though by his tone he was ashamed of what he had done.

"I showered at Danial's. I talked to him for a while about everything. Devlin had told him, he said. He was upset, though not as much as I was, or am. Some of what he said made me feel better." He paused. "And some of what he said made me feel worse."

Danial had told him his supposition that what had happened was more than just sex. "I'm sorry I hurt you," I said finally. "Can you forgive me?"

Theo was silent a long, long time. "Sometimes there is just too much to forgive," he said finally. "Isn't that what you said, Sar?"

About Dev and Catherine. "Yes."

"That's how I feel."

I faced him, pushing away the guilt. "Do you want me to leave? If you do, I will. I don't want you to have to take our child from his home, and this is your home more than it is mine now. You are the one who's been here taking care of—"

"I don't want you to leave. But I can't forgive you either."

"Then what do you want me to do?" I said, exasperated. "Tell me, Theo."

"I want you to stay, and for us to go back to counseling," he said softly. "I meant what I said, when I gave you my word not to ever leave you. I love you. But you broke your promise to me, Sar, and I don't trust you, not anymore. And I can't be intimate with you if I can't trust you."

"Okay," I agreed. "I understand."

"It matters to me that you told me. It matters that you could have hid this from me, and you didn't, knowing that I might never find out. Dev, Lash, and Titus would never have told me. Danial would not have either, knowing how much it would hurt me. But you did, because you cared enough about me not to keep this a secret. You told me the truth, when you knew I'd probably turn from you because of it. That means something to me."

I waited.

"I know now that Devlin is not going to give you up," Theo said reluctantly. "Danial said as much, said that Devlin had asked you for another Oath, and that you were probably going to have to give him one, even if you didn't want to. I have to face that I was deluding myself, to think he was going to let you go, Sar. And I need counseling myself, because I can't deal with sharing you with him for the rest of our lives. And I have to. For your sake, and Devon's sake, I have to somehow make it work."

"We'll go see Carol," I affirmed, wondering if it was safe to reach for his hand.

"Do you love him, Sar?" Theo asked.

Would he believe me if I said no after what Danial had told him? "Theo, I don't—"

"Answer me!" Theo demanded, his tone serious as death. "The truth."

"I love him as a friend, almost a best friend. I couldn't let him die without trying to save him." That wasn't an answer, but it was all I felt safe saying.

"Did he ask you to leave me?" Theo said finally. "To be with him?"

"No." Lash had made it a point not to ask me, in fact. But he'd wanted me to leave Theo, and get Devlin to include him, so we could remain lovers. Without saying the words, he had made it a point to make sure I knew that, too.

"You're lying," Theo whispered.

"He didn't ask," I said defensively. "But yes, he made it clear he wanted me to. I told him no."

Theo was quiet so long I figured that was the end of the conversation. As I was drifting off to sleep, he asked pointedly, "Does he love you, Sar?"

"He never said the words."

Lash had been careful not to say them, or to make any kind of lasting commitment. But how he felt had been in the way he'd touched me, the way he'd loved me and wanted me to say his name, as he'd said mine to me so many times in the heat of passion. It had been in the way he'd held my cheek and kissed me that last time, loss and longing in his soulful dark eyes. Most of all it had been there in his affectionate, awkward tone when we'd been together in the cemetery.

"Does he love you, Sar?" Theo reiterated steely.

"Yes," I replied softly. "I know he does."

Chapter Nine

"Good afternoon, Sar, and Theo," Carol Clay said calmly as she entered. "I'm sorry that when you called I was on vacation." She sat down and faced us. "Please tell me why you wanted to meet with me today."

Theo and I both looked at each other.

He was my husband, but there was no love in his look, just weariness and bitterness. I admitted that was more than understandable. It wasn't a date: we were here to discuss my inadequacies as a wife and how to solve them. Our problems were serious, much more serious than they had been a year ago when we'd been sitting here on this same couch.

Theo looked away.

My eyes remained on him. His attire was the loose casual clothing he'd always favored because it hid his physique. I hadn't known that he was muscular until the first time I'd seen him with his clothes off. His sand-colored hair was still wet from the shower, and much longer than usual. Theo was most likely growing it back into the longer style he'd had when I first met him. Maybe he'd always preferred that style. It didn't matter. I wasn't going to ask him to cut it for me anymore no matter how this turned out.

His eyes were dark with sadness, not love, and there was a touch of anger in them as he glanced back at me. "You want to start?"

I nodded, though I really didn't want to. I took a breath, then let it out. "We're here, Carol, because I need some help coming to terms with my life."

"So do I," Theo added. "Our marriage is falling apart."

Carol looked like she heard this every day of the week. "Why would you say that?" she said calmly. "Back in December things were going well. What's changed?"

Theo and I looked at one another. Where to start? December seemed a lifetime ago.

Well, I could sum up easily enough. "Carol, I told you about Devlin, Danial's brother."

Theo shot me a shocked glance. I pointedly didn't look at him. Carol looked a little nervous too, but she nodded.

"You never said his name. I assume from this, you have told Theo what you told me?"

"Yes. Theo knows what happened with Devlin and I, but that's nothing. A lot has happened since then."

I took a breath, and then spent the better part of the next hour telling Carol about Devlin's saving me with his bite and his body, about his taking control of Canada from Ebediah, becoming Oathed to Danial and Devlin, about getting pregnant with Devon and Venus, the lust with Lash, Devlin's burning, and Lash's brush with death, and he and I having sex again. I left off the part about how I had saved him, just said I'd had crucial information for him, and that a potion from a friend had saved him.

I'd promised Devlin that I would stick to the story he'd come up with about Lash's return to youth and vigor. While I didn't like the role of slut that it made me play—like I'd gone to find Lash just to have some excuse for sex with him again— I didn't have much choice. Devlin was right: if other supernatural creatures knew about what I'd been able to do for Lash, I'd be in terrible danger from beings that would make the other Vampire Rulers look harmless. Lash wasn't the only one willing to go to great lengths not to die. According to Titus, Devlin's demon, there were others who took a potion similar to the one Lash had taken for decades. And they wouldn't stop themselves when I began to lose consciousness as Lash had. They would take all of my blood until I died. The thought was sobering, to say the least.

I finally finished my recanting with a shrug for Carol. "That's it."

Carol looked over at Theo. "What do you feel about all this, Theo?"

"I can't deal with it," Theo said angrily, running his hands through his hair. "I hate Lash more than anyone alive, and I hate Devlin too, for making me share my wife with him. He could have other women, scads of them! Why did he have to have her? Why couldn't he have left her alone?"

"If I understand right, Theo, if Devlin hadn't loved her as much as he did, Sar would be dead," Carol said gently. "Right?"

"Yes, that's right," Theo growled. "I could understand his wanting a child. Sar is the only one who could have one of his. But she did it, and that isn't enough for him! He wants her even more than he did before. He wants her to live with him, and that fucking Lash—!"

"Back to Lash," Carol said smoothly, interrupting Theo's tirade. "Sar, you say you love Theo."

"I do," I said wearily.

"Then how could you just leave for a few days to go to his worst enemy and have sex with him?"

Her incredulous tone was an echo of Danial's when I'd confessed to him, and it rankled me. "He was my friend. I didn't go to him for sex, I went to him because he needed me, and there was no one else who could find him."

"Couldn't you have told his location to the person who made the potion for him?" Carol asked pointedly.

I went from rankled to defensively annoyed. "I wanted to be with him. I wanted something I had a choice in! Danial asks for my input on decisions, but certain things I have no choice in if he feels that they are the right thing for me to do. Theo gives me choices, but he also tells me what to do. If I don't do as he says, he punishes me with sullenness, and—"

"I am never sullen," Theo said sullenly.

I stifled the insane urge to laugh. "Really?" I retorted. "How angry are you when you're smelling another man's scent on me, even when you know it's someone I'm Oathed to? You know what I do when I see them, Theo. It's not a secret. I'm tired of being made to feel dirty because of a promise I made to Devlin to protect my life, so I could stay your wife and be around my children."

Theo glared, but said nothing.

Carol's expression said she was glad she had booked us a two-hour session. She hadn't wanted to, but I'd been adamant. I'd known it would take an hour just to give her the background to catch her up. We'd been delayed enough waiting for her to get back from vacation. I had to try to heal our marriage before things fell apart so much with Theo that there was nothing to put back together.

"Theo, you should give an answer to Sar."

"You know I don't like to smell anyone else on you. I want you to be just mine, Sar."

"But I'm not just yours, Theo," I shot back. "You know how things have to be! Everyone knows it, even my parents now—"

Carol took a quick intake of breath. I glanced at her and gave her a nod, and then kept going.

"I'm tired of pretending for you. I'm not going to anymore. I can't do it! I can't give you everything that you want from me!"

"Sar, you sound very upset," Carol interrupted. "Your situation is not one I've dealt with before, but I'll try my best to help you come to terms with it. Let's take a break for a few minutes, and then begin again."

Theo and I both nodded.

Carol got up and left. I wondered crazily as I watched her go if she was leaving to pop a Valium because she needed one to deal with us for another hour.

"Do you really want to be here?" Theo asked when we were alone.

I looked over at him as if he were an idiot. "Of course not. I feel like I'm on trial for being a bad wife. But I want to do whatever I can to rebuild your trust in me."

"Why?" Theo asked nastily, sitting back on the couch. "It seems to me like you're blaming me for being jealous, when any man in my position would be."

"I'm not blaming you for feeling jealous," I amended. "I blame you for making me feel bad about how you feel, because I didn't want this when I married you. I wanted a life with you. And I didn't ask for any of this to happen."

"Why couldn't you have been with Danial and not had a child with him?" Theo growled. "If you had just left that well enough alone, Sar, we would have been fine—"

"Stop it!" I shouted, startling him. "I love Theoron! I wanted a child with Danial, and I wouldn't take it back for anything!"

"I'm sorry," Theo said quickly with remorse. "I didn't mean it, Sar. I love Theoron too. I just—"

He had meant it. "It wouldn't have mattered anyway," I said darkly. "Devlin knew even then that I might hold the key to something he'd wanted for centuries. He always had his plans for me, Theo, from the moment he first tasted my blood."

"How do you know this?" Theo asked, giving me a strange look.

I looked away, my memory of Devlin's confession unsettling. "I asked him one night what he'd planned if he got me away from Danial. Trying for a child was on his list."

"I'm not surprised," Theo said bitterly. "He's fucking diabolical."

Devlin was diabolical. I had never met anyone with his talent for manipulating people or events with the absolute ruthlessness to do whatever it took so his plans unfolded just as he wanted them to. Dev was gorgeous with his heart-shaped face, his sculpted body, his golden hair to his shoulders, and his beautiful golden eyes. Though he looked like a hero from a romance novel, Devlin was closer to the devil his name implied. He had a sadistic streak that I'd been on the receiving end of once or twice, until he had began taking a potion from Titus that had made him less edgy. He was also a philanderer, and I had been on the receiving end of that as well. The latter was the reason I no longer wore his choker. But scars from his bites still adorned my throat, one on each side, though the newer one had healed a good deal, so it was no longer a match for the original one on the other side. They marked me as his, more so even than the choker around my neck.

It was Devlin's brother Danial's symbol—the golden fox head with ruby eyes—that hung at my throat. I was Oathed to Danial, too, because when Devlin had taken my promise from me, he had included his brother. But Danial did not have his brother's faults; he'd never cheated on me. The mystery was that his collar had not fallen off when I'd broken my promise to him by being with Lash.

My theory was that the choker didn't see Lash as forbidden. Danial and Devlin had allowed me to be with him during my pregnancy, to help me combat The Lust. It made sense then that as neither of them had verbally rescinded that permission, the choker didn't register what I'd done as literal Oathbreaking.

Danial, however, was sure that it meant Devlin's cheating on me had broken not only his own Oath, but also affected Danial's, too. "I told you there was a grey area, Sar. We aren't truly Oathed anymore."

I'd been tempted to take the choker off and give it to him right there, but was worried that I wouldn't be able to. It had been a while since we shared blood. "That wasn't my doing, Danial."

Danial had glared at me. His rich brown eyes were red with anger, and his face, so perfect as to be more beautiful than handsome, was grim. He was taller than his brother Devlin was, and he towered over me as I sat at his desk, his shoulder-length hair slipping forward in a black fall around his face.

"I didn't say it was." He paused. "I still want you to work for me. But don't come to me, Sar. You can see Elle and Theoron whenever you want, as much as you want, of course. And if you need a place to stay, the spare bedroom above is yours."

I'd expected something like this, but hearing the words still hurt. I'd bit my lip, and nodded, pointedly looking away so he wouldn't see how upset I was.

After Danial had left, I'd cried for a while. But I'd dried my eyes when I was done, and gotten back to work.

Even though Danial had cut back on his caseload somewhat, Theo, Terian, Danial, and I were still putting in a lot of hours every week. He had done that reluctantly, because Theo had asked that he and I have more time together as a family with our son, Devon. In spite of having to reduce his scheduled meetings, Danial was very pleased that the business had expanded, and was looking forward to going into business with our son, Theoron, when he was old enough.

That day was coming much sooner than anyone might have expected. Theoron was now looking more like sixteen than the ten he had been at the end of the summer. He also looked the spitting image of Danial, with his dark hair, wide shoulders, and narrow waist. But he had my green eyes, though his were a much darker green, like the color of a spruce forest on a summer afternoon. He had even outstripped Elle in height, and she was none too happy about that.

"I'm the older sister!" she'd said in frustration yesterday, when Theoron had reminded her that she only looked about fourteen, while he could probably pass for being old enough to drive.

"Not anymore! Now you're my kid sister!" he had said with a grin, which of course had started a shoving match that I had to break up.

They were both good kids, though, and I didn't even need to raise my voice to do it. Both of them were smart too, very smart, and they knew something was wrong between Danial, Theo, and me. They hadn't asked me why I hadn't been spending my usual one night a week with Danial, but I knew they noticed. I hadn't said anything to them about it, deciding it was better if they brought it up to me.

It had been awkward that first week, getting used to the fact that Danial didn't want me to touch him anymore in any way. We hadn't been intimate for months while I had been pregnant, so that part of it wasn't that hard to get used to. But we had touched each other casually for almost a year now, and I found myself reaching out to him almost before I thought about it. Then, realizing what I'd done, I'd draw my hand back quickly, before I touched him. I knew he had noticed my actions, both unconscious and not, though he hadn't said anything. It was his silence about that which had been the hardest to bear.

Carol's return brought me back to the present. "Now then," she said, sitting down in her chair, "Tell me what you would like to achieve in your time here, Theo, and then Sar, you do the same."

"I want to be able to let Sar go to Danial and Devlin without being jealous. I know she has to, that it's not her fault, and I know that it's wrong to blame her. And I want to be able to trust her again, so we can be intimate again—"

"So you are not being intimate now?" Carol interjected.

"No. I don't trust Sar. I don't know if I believe she loves me like she used to because of what she did. And I think she still wants Lash, and I'm repulsed just thinking of the two of them together."

"Sar, do you still want to be with Lash?"

"I'm not going to be with him again. Devlin has forbidden it—"

"That's not what she asked you, Sarelle!" Theo growled low, cutting me off.

"Yes, I want him!" I spat the words back at him. "But I wanted Danial before too, back when he and I weren't Oathed, and I managed to keep my panties on, Theopolis!"

Theo growled softly, but said nothing.

"Sar, what do you want out of this time?" Carol asked.

"I want not to feel like I'm torn in three directions. I want no one to be jealous of anyone, or to make me feel like it's my fault that things are as they are. I want to feel in control of my life again, to be happy. I want my life back, so that it feels like it's mine, that it belongs to me again."

I lapsed into silence.

"Theo, how do you feel about what Sar just said?"

"I don't want to push her away," Theo sighed, running his hands through his hair. "I'm grateful she told me what happened, what she did. I know she didn't have to, she could have covered it up." Theo's tone was guttural and raw, his rage building with every word. "I know I should be glad, because she did what she promised she would by telling me the truth, but I just feel betrayed. It would have been bad enough if it was anyone else, but it had to be fucking Lash!"

Carol tried to head him off by speaking quickly. "Theo, you seem to have a lot of anger still, and it does seem to be directed at Sar—"

"She fucked my worst enemy! Damn right, I'm angry! She could have saved him and not done that! No one made her be with him!"

"I think that is what Sar is saying, Theo," Carol interjected. "She was with Lash at least in part BECAUSE no one made her do it; because she wanted something she had a choice in—"

"Well, I'm not MAKING her be with me!" Theo snarled. He pulled off his wedding band, and tossed it on the floor. He got to his feet in a smooth motion, and then glared down at me. "Teleport wherever you're going to be spending the night," he said coldly. "I'll be at home, with Devon." Without a backward look, Theo stalked out.

I put my head in my hands for a little while and wept. There was motion beside me a few minutes later, as Carol sat next to me. She said nothing; just put her hand on my shoulder. I slowly got control of myself, using some of the tissues on her table.

"Do you think we can work out things?" I said softly, not looking at her. "It's bad, Carol."

"It depends if you both want to," Carol said simply. "If you and Theo both want things to work out badly enough, Sar, you'll be able to work them out. But if he won't try with you to meet you halfway, you'll have to decide if you want to stay in the marriage with him, or if you want to separate."

"I don't want to lose him," I said, looking at the wall. "But I think it's going to come to that before it's all over."

Carol got up, and went back to her chair, settling into it. "We have another half hour or so. As Theo is gone, there are some other things we should discuss."

I looked over at her. "What things?"

"Do you love Lash?" she asked frankly. "You give all indications that you do."

"No. But he's a good friend. I like him to touch me and kiss me, even though I know it's wrong to want him that way. I enjoy spending time with him. He makes me laugh, the way Theo and I used to, before our lives became the mess they are. We talk a lot, about a lot of things, not just what's going on in our own sphere of the world. And that day I was with him, I told myself that it was mostly just that I wanted to forget for a while everything that had happened to me, to get some solace from my problems. I rationalized that was why I had given in. But really it was just that I liked him, and I knew Theo was going to be angry anyway, that it didn't matter if Lash had only made love to me to try to distract me—" I trailed off, as I'd said too much.

"What do you mean by that, Sarelle?" Carol said, watching me closely.

"I mean that part of saving Lash caused me a lot of pain," I said carefully.

"Does Theo know this?"

"Carol, he hates him," I said flatly. "Theo probably gets a warm happy feeling when he thinks that Lash was in terrible pain, and is angry at me for saving him just as much as he's angry about me having sex with him. To him it doesn't matter why, only that it happened. Which is just how I knew he would feel when he found out."

"Then you should bring in Lash, as well as Danial and Devlin, to some sessions."

My eyes bugged out of their sockets. "Are you joking? Do you know how bad that could—?"

"Not with Theo," Carol said simply. "Just them with you, one at a time."

"Why?" I asked, my tone shriller still. "That could still—"

"Because they may need to work with you to alter their behavior so that you feel better about your life," Carol said calmly. "From listening to you, the problem this time is not Theo's, it's yours. Your feelings of being trapped led you to having sex with Lash, even when you knew you shouldn't. And you'll continue to feel this way until you resolve those feelings. They need you to tell them what you told Theo and me today."

I didn't answer.

Carol looked at me. "Isn't it true, Sar, that in part you did what you did with Lash so you'd drive away some of your male attention? And it worked. You've said only Devlin has forgiven you for what you did, and you are only intimate with him right now. Danial and Theo are not being intimate with you since you were with Lash. And Lash is staying away from you, too, on Devlin's orders."

What she said was true. In a sad and awful way, I'd almost liked the last two weeks. I'd worked, played with my children, and had only one man who touched me intimately. It was nice, not having to satisfy a crowd. And I hadn't had to have sex with anyone in that time. Devlin still couldn't have sex yet. He was still not healed enough to, or so he said. His eye had healed a week ago, and I thought it strange that he hadn't at least attempted once yet to have me. But that was another whole separate issue.

"Sar?"

"Yes, it's true I wanted to get a break from everyone's demands. But some of it was that I really wanted to be with Lash, because I liked him, and I wanted to be with him; to have it be just us, when he wasn't dying, and when I wasn't a slave to The Lust."

"Would you be with him, if you could just be with one man?" she asked.

I blinked in surprise. "There would never be that choice."

Carol gave me an expectant look that said that wasn't an answer.

"Probably not," I said, after a moment's hesitation. "I don't want to alienate my children any more than I have already. If I left Theo to be with Lash, Elle, my daughter, would probably never speak to me again. My son, Theoron, he likes Lash, but I'm not sure if he knows exactly what went on between the two of us. It isn't the kind of information you ask your son if he's aware of. Plus, I know Lash can be violent, and as much as I like him, he kills people for a living."

"I know who he is very well, Sar" Carol said, and a little shudder went through her. "He's almost as much of a legend as Devlin is."

I rolled my eyes mentally as I could tell from her tone she was looking forward to meeting Devlin. *Or maybe it was her obsession with Ranked men.* I'd forgotten until this moment her interest and knowledge in the Who's Who list of killers.

"If you could choose one man to be with, would it be Theo?"

"Of course. But it's moot. There is no getting away from Devlin, Carol. And despite that Danial is angry at me, and refuses to be intimate with me, he didn't ask me for his choker back."

"So you are taking that his not asking for it back means he still wants you to be his?"

I gave Carol a partial smile. "Devlin said that Danial would forgive me, in time. I told him I didn't think so, and Devlin just said he thought I knew Danial better than that."

Carol got up. "Come back weekly, Sar. Come on alternate weeks with Theo, and the other weeks, come alone, or with one of the men we discussed. I'll call Theo as well, and set up some lone sessions with him, too. He has some rage to vent out still, and he should get that out, so we don't have an outburst like we had today from him."

I bent down and picked up Theo's wedding band, and slipped it on my thumb. "Okay," I said, standing, and gathering up my coat and purse. "Next week, same time?"

"Yes," Carol said, showing me to the door.

It was a good thing my insurance through Danial paid for therapy, I thought as I opened the door to walk outside. This was going to cost a fortune before it was over.

I decided to walk over to the back of the house where there were shrubs. I knew better than to just disappear in front of everyone, on a busy street sidewalk. But with Theo having taken off in the truck, there wasn't another option.

"Sar?"

I turned to see Theo coming over to me, a hesitant look on his face. I turned and waited for him.

He came to stand in front of me. "Do you have my ring?"

I took it off my thumb, handed it to him, and he slipped it back onto his left hand.

"I'm sorry for what I said," he said, and for a moment, he looked as if he might reach out and hold me, but he stopped himself, putting his hands back at his sides. Watching him, I wondered then if Titus, Devlin's demon sorcerer, had broken the first layer of our bond.

Theo and I were bound by a dream we had shared three times. It had made our love deeper, our desire to be together almost unstoppable. I'd always loved that I shared it with him, that we were something like soul mates, that our love was that true. But two weeks ago, when I'd asked Titus to break the bond we shared, I'd done it because I knew Theo would never leave me while it held us together. And if things didn't work out with us, I wanted Theo to be able to leave me, to find someone he could call his own. I'd had enough of not having choices. Theo didn't have a lot of choices either, but this was one I was going to give him, even at the risk of losing him. Titus had said he could do it over months. Every day since then, I'd watched carefully for some sign of Theo's love for me lessening. When it happened, I wanted to know.

"Let me give you a ride home," Theo continued. "I know you need to get to Devlin tonight, but I'd like to spend the time with you, if you want to."

"That'd be nice," I said, following him to the truck.

As Theo drove home, I related what Carol had said. "She wants them all to come?" Theo said with something like horror.

"That's what she said," I said heavily, looking out the window.

"Aren't you going to feel...I don't know, awkward?"

"Of course!" I snapped. "I'm going to feel ridiculous, especially with Devlin there, and Carol already dying to meet him—" I snorted, then looked over at Theo and smiled. "I mean, how is she going to be impartial?"

He gave me a hesitant smile back. "I'm sure she'll fall back on her training." He cleared his throat. "When you were late to a session last fall, she and I got to talking. It's clear she's very into the Ranking, from the questions she's asked me, almost to the point of fixation. But during the sessions she's been nothing but professional." He patted my hand. "It'll be fine."

I wanted to ask him to stop the truck, to ask him to take me in his arms and kiss me until I was lost in his love and devotion. Instead, I just nodded and looked away. Devlin expected me at Hayden, and he'd been more fanatical than usual lately about my visits to him. If I wasn't there by dusk, he'd send Titus to track me down.

Titus had placed a tracking spell on me back months ago when Theo had had some men after him. No matter where I was, he could find me and teleport directly to me. It was the same spell that Lash had used to find us when Ulysses had kidnapped Devlin and I. It had faded out too soon, allowing Ulysses to almost kill Devlin with sunlight. Titus hadn't refreshed it afterwards, which had allowed him to not know my location when I went to find Lash, allowing me just enough time to save his life. The moment my demon kin had found me in the Everglades, he had refreshed the spell, to make sure there wasn't a third time.

Last week, I had been running late, and Titus had accessed the tracing spell, appearing suddenly in the middle of the road in front of me. I'd swerved, but, it had scared the life out of me. Titus had then teleported me, my truck, and himself directly to Hayden, where Devlin was waiting in his robe with his arms crossed, his normally golden eyes red with annoyance. I'd asked him what was wrong, but he had only taken me upstairs with him, and asked me to take off my clothes. Mystified, I'd obeyed. Once I was naked, Devlin had settled in bed with me and gone to sleep. When he'd awoken, he had been very easygoing and loving, as if nothing was wrong.

I didn't know what had Devlin acting so weird. I'd have thought that Devlin was worried I'd taken off with Lash again, crazy as that was, but Lash had been at Hayden with Devlin the night I'd been late. He'd watched silently from the kitchen as I was led upstairs by Devlin. But while I wasn't sure what was making Devlin act erratically, I planned to confront him about it that night. Enough was enough. That confrontation was bound to be another knock down-drag out fight.

"Sar, are you okay?" Theo asked. "You're awfully quiet."

My weary eyes met Theo's concerned blue ones. *Screw it.* "Would you stop the truck?"

Theo looked confused, but he pulled over to the side of the road. "What is it?" he said gruffly.

I looked over at him in surprise. "You're angry again?"

"What is it?" he repeated angrily. "Are you going to try to tell me that you don't want to go to Dev? I know you do, Sar. I know you want him, just like you want fucking Lash."

"Never mind," I said, looking away from Theo so he wouldn't see my tears. "Just drive. That's what you're best at."

"No, you're going to tell me why you wanted me to stop the truck," Theo growled, dragging me over to him on the seat. He grabbed my face in his hand and made me look at him. "Spit it out."

I blinked my watery eyes, feeling pitiful. "I just wanted for you to hold me. That was it."

Theo looked at me with something like shock, and then with a sigh he crushed me in his arms. I put my arms around him hesitantly.

Why couldn't this be easier? Why couldn't I have met him back when he was human, some night? We could have gotten to know one another without all the vampire craziness, and blood, and tears...

I shook my head slightly. There was no point going there. I would never have met Theo without knowing Danial first. And Theo was werecougar. There was no changing that.

I tightened my arms around him, breathing in his scent of prairie grass and blue skies, and pine trees. He felt good in my arms. He felt right.

"I'm sorry I hurt you," I said. "I didn't do what I did to hurt you."

Theo said nothing, one of his hands running up my back, stroking me gently.

"I'll come back every week. As long as it takes, Theo."

Theo still said nothing, but he pulled me more into his lap. With a sigh, he brought my chin up from his chest and kissed me softly. I kissed him back at once hungrily. Theo groaned, one of his hands going down my back to pull my body close to his as the other slid up to tangle in my hair. His mouth opened on mine, and I kissed him back, sensations flooding me.

It had been weeks since we had touched like this. I had thought Theo hadn't wanted me anymore. But I'd been wrong. Very wrong.

Theo's tongue darted into my mouth, even as his hand reached down to unbutton my jeans. Startled, I pulled back from him, giving him surprised eyes.

Theo gave me a look of confusion, then suspicion. "What?"

"I know how you feel about being with me," I said, biting my lip. "I don't want—"

"Saving yourself for Lash?" Theo said sarcastically, his eyes narrowing.

I pushed myself off his lap, and got back on the other side of the truck seat. "Drive."

We didn't speak the rest of the way home.

* * * *

I arrived at Hayden at dusk. I'd driven instead of teleporting, because I needed the time to think. I'd also been delayed when I'd stopped to rescue a stunned bird. A female cardinal had been hit by the car in front of me, and I'd run back just in time to avoid her being flattened by a passing truck. I'd thought she was dead, but then I'd felt her heartbeat. I'd laid her on the side of the road, near some trees. Her mate was in the tree above, watching me, and screeching at me, trying to protect her. I waited a few moments, and before long, she was staggering to her clawed feet, and then with a flap of her wings, she flew up into the trees.

I smiled, seeing her back beside her mate. *If only things were so easy with me.*

The rest of the trip passed quickly. Nick buzzed me through Hayden's gate about five p.m. Within a few minutes, I pulled into the garage, and shut the overhead door with the garage door control. I didn't get out though; I just sat there, thinking.

Part of me was seriously considering leaving Theo, no matter how the counseling turned out. It wasn't because I no longer loved him, though I knew he believed that. And it wasn't that I didn't want a life with him, because I did. It was that I could never be his alone. Theo needed that from the woman he was with. He was the only one who was jealous. Danial and Devlin seemed more than content to share me between them; it was Theo who had always made problems. He was the one I'd tried the most to please in the years we'd been together. But no matter what I did, it wasn't ever enough. This stalemate with the guys wouldn't last forever. I had to do something, before my life became unlivable again...

"Are you going to get out of the truck, Sar?" a curious voice asked.

I looked up to see Lash, leaning in the open door frame, the light from the kitchen behind him casting a shadow on his face. He looked his usual menacing self today, with his whip and survival knife strapped to his belt. As always, his shaggy jet-black hair was wild, and he was dressed all in black: black, tight-fitting jeans, black shirt, black turtleneck, his tanned skin only showing on his face and hands. But I was guessing that was because he was feeling a chill from his cold-blooded animal side.

He'd startled me a little, but my only fear was of myself, because of how much I wanted him to touch me. Worse, I was going to have to tell him that it didn't matter if Devlin ever gave us permission to be together. I was married, and Theo was my first priority. That meant no more touching Lash in any way—not even kisses—except as a friend. The trouble was, could I actually get out the words?

I got out of the truck, and gave him a smile, shutting the door behind me. "I'm out," I said pointedly.

"Devlin's not back yet from seeing Danial," Lash said overly casually, still leaning on the door. "He's still trying to get him to reconsider about giving me his blood, if I began...if I need it. Titus is with him."

I said nothing, because I knew what he meant, and why he was uncomfortable.

"Do you need to search me?" I asked, giving him a smile.

"Up against the wall, and spread 'em," Lash said, giving me a leer.

I gave him a roll of my eyes, but complied. Lash expertly patted me down, and then pronounced me safe. I turned to him, and he stepped into me, backing me against the wall.

Swiftly, his arms snaked around me, and then he was holding me close to him. I breathed in his scent of autumn leaves, musk, earth, and leather. I'd often wondered if that last was only from his whip, or really part of his scent. It seemed to be part of him, and I thought that curious, even as I luxuriated in the fragrance.

"I like to hold you, breathe in the scent of you," Lash hissed, his face pressed to my throat, longing in his tone. "I miss being with you, but it's enough—"

"About that..." I began.

Lash pulled back from me, looking at me carefully. "What about it?" Lash hissed.

He was upset already. But I had to tell him we couldn't touch like this anymore. And the more I felt him touch me, the harder it was going to be for me to want to tell him no.

"Being like this doesn't seem fair to you. I can't give you anything more. I feel a little as if I'm teasing you, and I don't want...I don't want you to...to not...um..."

I faltered, but Lash was already nodding in understanding. "Sar, I'm an adult. I can handle this. And if it gets too much, I'll find someone to take care of my needs. Now that I can hide my were nature, I can be with someone who isn't snake without them suspecting or caring—"

The thought of him making love with anyone else brought jealousy in a drowning flood. "Okay!" I interrupted quickly. "I just wanted to make sure. That's enough info—"

Lash grabbed my hair roughly, and made me look at him, his lips inches from mine. "You asked me weeks ago if it was enough for me that you wanted me to kiss you. It is." He leaned in a little closer, so our lips almost touched as his dark eyes looked into mine. "Is it enough for you that you're the only one I want to kiss?"

He only wanted me. Relief crashed down. I nodded once.

"It's a moot point anyway, now," Lash hissed sadly, pressing his cheek to mine.

"Why?" I whispered. "I—"

He drew back from me. "Because Devlin forbade me today from kissing you anymore," Lash hissed. "He said you were his, not mine, and the only way I was getting inside you again was if you gave him another Oath. And until you did, I wasn't to touch you at all."

I was at a loss for words. He was touching me plenty right now.

"I'm going on a job tonight," Lash added in explanation. "I'll be changing my clothes after, so he won't smell you on me. Make sure you change your clothes and shower—"

I pushed him back from me. "Why are you doing this, Lash, if he said not to?"

"Because I wanted to feel your mouth against mine one more time, to feel your ripe body under my hands," Lash hissed, aroused. "I haven't seen you alone since that night we came back, since you defended me to Danial, telling him you had wanted to be with me, that I hadn't forced you to be. And I am going to have this time with you before I give you up." He embraced me again with a sigh.

Neither of us said anything for a few minutes. It was enough that we were here together, holding each other. *Besides, it was just a hug...*

He suddenly pulled back from me. "Do you want me to kiss you, Sar?" Lash said softly, giving me a smoky look.

"Yes, please," I breathed.

He covered my lips with his own, sliding his tongue into my mouth, and I gave myself up to him completely, losing myself in the warmth of his touch.

There were footsteps suddenly outside the garage door, and then the door to the garage began to open.

Chapter Ten

Nick came strolling through the widening opening to go to one of the Hummers. Lash broke the kiss, and hissed at him, his fangs elongating as his eyes went flat.

"Sorry—" Nick stammered, his widening eyes taking us in as he backed up quickly.

"Get the fuck out now!" Lash hissed, baring his fangs. "And shut the door behind you!"

Nick hurried to comply. The door slammed shut, leaving us in semidarkness.

"Must you be so disagreeable to everyone?" I said teasingly, giving his neck a gentle kiss.

"He's lucky I didn't bite him," Lash said irritably, nuzzling my neck in return. "I won't get another moment with you again, Sar, not like this. I want to make it last."

I looked up into Lash's dark eyes, and then I reached up and held his face in my hand, gently stroking. He went still under my hand, sighing softly, his dark eyes fastened on mine.

I hadn't understood why he'd first touched my face that day on the trail at Hayden or even a month later, when we were dancing that night in the Everglades. There had been so much else going on that I hadn't given it much thought. There hadn't been any thought in my mind when I reached out and caressed his face with my hand as we'd danced, either. I had just been moved by instinct and affection to want to put my hands on him. But in the past weeks I'd come to understand what the small gesture meant to him.

Lash had seen Theo and I that day in the kitchen, when I'd reached out and held his face as I now was holding Lash's. I'd told Theo with my eyes how much I'd loved him, and what he meant to me. I'd told him in that one look that I was his, and he was mine, and that was all that mattered. Lash had wanted to be there with me, standing in Theo's place. He had wanted me to touch him like

159

I had touched Theo, to tell him that he meant something to me. And every time he had held my face in his hand, he had been trying to tell me that he cared about me, that all his words about how our being lovers didn't mean anything had been lies.

I kissed his cheek gently. "I missed you."

Lash closed his eyes for a moment, and put his hand over my hand on his face, just holding it there as if to commit the feeling to memory. With a sigh, he reached out to me, taking my face in his hands, kissing me roughly, his hands caressing my face and neck, gently rubbing my warm skin with his. I opened my mouth on his, and gently licked him with my tongue. Lash groaned, and twined his long forked tongue around mine, stroking me gently, and making me whimper a little in longing.

Theo would be pissed if he ever found out, but part of me didn't care. I wanted to share this last moment with Lash, and he wanted to share it with me.

And God, could he kiss.

* * * *

Lash kissed me for a good twenty minutes, until it was all I could do to stop from asking him to take me right there. I could feel his body straining against the front of his jeans, wanting to be inside me. I was aching for him, the desire to feel him stroking me with his body undeniable. It had been so good between us. I wanted badly to run my hand across the length of him, to touch our naked bodies skin to skin, to let him make love to me again...

But he was right; that was moot. Giving in to my weakness for him was not going to fix any of my problems; it was only going to give me more problems. I told myself with a little anger that I should have remembered that weeks ago, when I had given in to temptation with him. It was past time to stop thinking with my loins and to start thinking with my brain.

"We have to stop," I said breathily, pulling back from Lash. "I want you too badly, and we can't do anything—"

"I know," Lash replied, agonized. He backed away from me with a sigh. "Go inside. I'll be gone tonight and tomorrow, but wait for me on the couch, say about six? Maybe we can watch a movie together, or get dinner. Devlin hasn't told me your plans yet, but I doubt you'll be going out. Devlin hasn't gone anywhere at night at all, except to teleport to Danial, since his burning last month. Even if you are going somewhere, it won't be without me, not after what happened last time."

I nodded, and went inside, shutting the door after me without a last look at him. Drawing it out wasn't going to make it any easier to leave.

I went upstairs to Devlin's bedroom, and ran the water for a cold shower, wondering where Titus was. Maybe after all of the events of the last weeks—

i.e., us now being "demon "kin"—he didn't need to check me anymore? In any case, it was a relief. He'd have a lecture for me after one whiff of snake scent.

I disrobed, and stuck all my clothes in my bag. I'd wash them when I got home. Then I stepped into the cool water, stifling a yelp.

Along with washing off Lash's scent, the cold shower helped cool my wanton thoughts. Sleep was probably the only thing I was going to be doing tonight in bed. I hadn't brought anything racy with me, either. There was no point trying to look sexy for a man who only wanted to sleep in my arms.

About ten minutes later, I was in bed, pajamas on, reading the newest Vampire Hunter D book. I was fully engrossed when Dev walked in and slammed the door behind him.

I looked up and met his annoyed eyes.

"Haven't I asked you not to read that series here?" Devlin said peevishly. "It's like me reading a book series based on a hero serial killer."

With sheer will, I kept in my retort that the book was fiction, that it took place in the future, and that the hunter was a good guy, a dhamphir like my son (plus if he wanted to read hero serial killer books, that was okay with me). There were bad vampires that got killed in this book series—all diabolically bad, of course—which means they had a lot in common with Dev.

I put the book aside. "Sorry," I said apologetically. "I forgot. I'll bring another book next time."

Devlin nodded, and his expression softened as he gazed at me. The seconds became a minute, then two as he continued to stare at me.

What was wrong now? "Are you going to shower first, or come to bed?"

"I need to shower," Devlin replied.

He'd always had a libido the size of Texas. Yet there was no lust in his words, no longing for me like I'd heard in Lash's tone earlier. He didn't even kiss me on his way to the bathroom.

As the door shut behind him with a soft click, I lay back and thought of how to broach the subject. *What if Dev had been hurt too badly to regenerate?* Ulysses had burned him repeatedly on his penis and his testicles, as well as cut him there. Since then, he'd been careful to keep his clothes on whenever I was around. In the beginning, I'd understood that he hadn't wanted me to see how bad the damage was. I'd tried to give him privacy and space while he healed, knowing he was mortified that he wasn't the gorgeous specimen of manhood that he had been before. But nearly a month had passed. Dev's face had completely healed, so the rest of him had to be healed by now to the extent that it could happen. If the permanent damage was bad, I needed to know so we could deal with it together. But how to ask about it so he wouldn't be hurt?

Theo had been scarred before. When we'd reunited, he'd been embarrassed about them, even though his scars weren't permanent. It hadn't mattered to me, but he'd been visibly relieved when the last scar tissue had faded. Theo's scars hadn't been on his sexual organs, just on his hip and back. How much more daunting must it be for Dev because of where he was hurt?

I understood that feeling of worry, of shame. But the issue wasn't going to solve itself if we didn't talk about it. Dev wasn't going to bring it up himself.

Devlin came back in the room, his golden hair wet from the shower. He undid his robe, revealing purple colored silk pants, tossed it neatly on a nearby armchair, then crawled into bed beside me. As I cradled him to my chest, he sighed a little, but didn't speak. I sighed inwardly, and forced the words out.

"Dev, what's wrong?"

He immediately went rigid in my arms. "What are you talking about, Sar?" he said with a cool tone. "Nothing is wrong."

Even if I hadn't already known something was wrong, here was proof. "Dev, I know you," I began as I ran my fingers through his hair, trying to calm him. "Please tell me what's got you acting so distant from me."

Devlin remained rigidly motionless and silent.

How to phrase it, so he wouldn't be either hurt or offended, or feel like I was demanding sex? Even though Dev had often demanded it of me, I didn't want to do that to him. "I care about you," I said finally. "And it follows naturally that I want to be intimate. I don't want you to feel rushed before you're comfortable. Though I desire you as much as I ever did, I'm willing to wait however long you need me to, until you are ready." I kissed his cheek. "I just wanted you to know that, Love."

Devlin sighed and looked up at me, his golden eyes shining. Oddly, the gold of his eyes seemed to me dimmed with fear and moroseness. "I'm not ready yet, Sar," he whispered.

I hugged him tighter. "It's okay if you aren't," I reassured. "Get some sleep."

As I reached over and turned off the light, Devlin snuggled against me, his head over my heart. We lay for a long time in the darkness, but we didn't sleep. We just lay together, thinking our own thoughts.

* * * *

The next morning, I prodded a grumbling Dev off me and went downstairs in search of breakfast. Serena was in the kitchen.

"Hey!" she said, giving me a hug. "I didn't know you were here."

"Today and part of tomorrow," I said, giving her a smile. "I haven't been spending time with Danial, so Dev wanted the time—"

I trailed off, realizing I'd said more than I wanted to. Flushing, I got some cereal, longingly eyeing the bagels in a bag on the counter. But my jeans didn't lie; only the loosest pair would fit me now. Until I lost some more weight, there would have to be carb sacrifices.

Sardonically, I theorized that not burning enough calories was not all my fault: if I spent more time in bed active instead of sleeping, I'd likely be back to my right weight...

"Want some coffee?"

I flushed, and put my weight out of my mind. "Yes, it smells delicious." I poured a cup and began putting in sugar and milk.

"You drink coffee?" Serena said, confused. "I didn't know that."

"Very rarely," I answered, giving her a smile. "It makes my stomach upset, usually. But it smelled good to me today, for some reason."

"I like coffee, but I have to drink decaf," she replied. "It makes me too edgy, otherwise. So don't worry about the caffeine."

"I'm glad to hear that. I don't need to be hyper today."

We sat at the kitchen table and sipped our drinks. I was disappointed; the coffee had smelled better than it tasted. This was why I didn't usually ever drink it, because nine times out of ten, I always...

"It's because of Lash, isn't it? Danial is upset because you went to bring him that potion for Titus. And something happened, didn't it?"

I didn't reply.

"No one has said anything," she added. "But I'm not blind. I see how Devlin is treating Lash—"

I shot her a beleaguered look. "Are they fighting?"

"No. But Devlin has been sending Lash out on jobs, and he never did that before this late in the fall. The jobs aren't important enough—from what I overheard them arguing about—to warrant his skills. It's just meeting with clients and making arrangements, mostly. I think he's doing it so Lash isn't around when you are."

"I thought that, too," I said quietly, and sipped my coffee. But it was too bitter suddenly for me to swallow. Grumpily, I got up and poured it out in the sink.

"Sar, why were you with Lash again?" Serena burst out, trying hard to keep revulsion out of her words. "You aren't pregnant, and you have Theo, Danial, and Dev—"

Livid suddenly, I turned to face her in a split second, and slammed my coffee cup in the sink so hard I was surprised it didn't break into ceramic shards. "What exactly is it about him that makes you revile him so much?" I hissed at her.

Serena's eyes went wide at my anger, and she immediately backed off. "Sar, I—"

"Tell me," I ordered, crossing my arms over my chest. "Is it because you smell that he's a snake, and maybe a fox's natural enemy? Because he kills people? Because he can be scary sometimes?"

"All of those things," Serena said, shuddering. "But mostly because of his eyes, and how cold he can be—"

"He was never cold to me," I said passionately.

Serena's eyes went wider still.

"And I—"

I shut up quickly, before my mouth spilled out everything I was thinking. I wasn't stupid. Devlin could hear me up above, and was probably listening to every word. Hearing me say what I'd almost said would have made him furious.

"And you what?" Serena ventured, watching me as if I might bite her.

"You shouldn't bar him from your bed," I said tiredly. "He was a good lover, Serena. I just wish you would reconsider, and let him come to you like the other weres."

"You want me to have sex with him?" Serena said incredulously. "I don't understand."

Sar, you can handle this. Get out the words! "I want him to be happy, or as happy as he can be," I said slowly, pulling the words out of me as if they were my intestines. "I care about him, Serena. I know you aren't snake. But if he shows interest, please don't deny him your favors. Don't treat him like an outcast. Let him come to you like the others."

"I'm afraid of him," Serena said with a tremor of fear.

"He won't hurt you," I said with surety. "He's not the one with the sadistic streak."

Serena got what I was making a point to say and nodded, reluctance in her eyes. "I'll mention when I see him that I spoke to you."

"Don't mention me," I said quickly.

Serena gave me a look. "Sar, he knows how I feel about him, especially about being his lover. I don't think he'll believe that I just came to my senses out of the blue. I can't just smile and say, 'By the way, it's okay if you want my services'."

Probably not. Lash was as smart as I was, if not smarter. "Fine, then," I amended. "Tell him that I told you how good he was, and you want to experience it for yourself. How's that?"

"Okay," she said with a shrug of her shoulders. "But I still don't understand why you want me to do this if it's you who care about him."

"Because I need to focus on my marriage, which is falling apart. I need to spend time with my children. My oldest son is almost an adult, and I want to spend time with him before it's too late. Elle isn't too far behind—"

Serena nodded, sipping her coffee.

"—and Venus already is no longer a baby. She's going to say her first word any day now. Devon has doubled in size, and he's getting bigger too. Theo plans on helping him change for the first time in November."

"Do you know how old he'll be when he changes?" Serena asked.

"Maybe two or three?" I offered. "I'm not sure. We want him to be old enough that he isn't so helpless like Theoron was when he was a baby."

"You should bring him with you sometimes. Venus is his twin. They have to be missing each other. They've been separated since birth."

She was right; Venus should see Devon. The question was how to arrange to bring the twins together when their two fathers hated one another. And that wasn't the only obstacle. "Has Venus stopped biting you yet?"

Serena shook her head. "Every single time, like clockwork. I think sometimes she does it just because she likes my blood, and other times just so she can hear me yelp a little—"

That was disturbing. "Take me to her," I said resolutely. "It's time I held her."

"Sar, I don't think—"

"Serena, she's going to bite me the first time anyway," I replied, getting to my feet. "You're strong enough; you can pull her off me if you have to. Besides, Theoron stopped biting me once he had a taste of my blood. Maybe that's all she needs, too."

Serena shrugged, but she got up and put her coffee cup in the sink.

When we arrived at the door to the nursery, Devlin was waiting inside, Venus in his arms. They both looked at me with their matching golden eyes, though Dev's held fear. "Are you sure, Love?" he said hesitantly. "You don't have to do this. I don't want you to be hurt."

My eyes narrowed. I'd known he was up here listening to us. "Might as well try," I said, putting a brave smile on my face. "Give her to me."

Devlin very carefully handed our daughter to me.

"Hello, V," I said softly.

She looked up at me, then bared her fangs in a hiss. Careful not to touch her with my bare skin, I sat down in the rocking chair and held her loosely. Venus calmed down at once, her liquid gold eyes large and curious in her small exquisite face.

She was enthrallingly perfect with her red lips, ivory skin, and her beautiful, beautiful eyes. "You don't know me well, but I'm your mom," I said in admiration. "I hope you don't bite me, my little goddess."

Serena and Devlin were hushed beside me, all of us waiting for something to happen. But Venus just lay there, looking up at me, not making a sound.

"She's as quiet as Theoron was," I whispered finally.

"Perhaps all dhamphirs are," Devlin said, laying his hand tenderly on my shoulder.

"Say cheese!" Serena squeaked happily.

I looked up in shock. Serene had Dev's digital camera/phone in her hands, and she snapped a few pictures before I could say anything.

"Serena, stop taking pictures!" I said grumpily as she snapped away. "I'm in my robe, and my hair's a mess—Youch!"

In my desire to get Serena to stop, I'd forgotten caution and curled a hand over the edge of the blanket. Venus had struck immediately.

Devlin grabbed hold of her, and began to pry her off me.

"Wait!" I gasped, pain radiating down my arm. "Let me see if she stops on her own."

Devlin paused for a minute, watching our daughter feed from my wrist. Venus was swallowing me down as if there were no tomorrow, almost gulping, the same happy noises that Devlin and Danial always made when feeding on me filling the air. Yet while I felt it was right to feed my daughter from my body, I also felt that it was wrong for her to be making those same noises, sounds I'd always associated with sex. The longer it went on the more uncomfortable I was, hearing them coming out of my baby daughter's mouth.

"She's not going to stop, Sar." Devlin sighed. "Serena, come and help me."

Devlin worked his finger into the side of Venus's mouth, and pried her tiny upper fangs out of my flesh, and then the lower ones as well. Then he and Serena lifted her out of my arms.

Venus fought them, snarling, and bit both of them in the process; though she let them go as soon as she tasted that they weren't human. Finally, Serena took her downstairs to get a bottle ready for her, as it was apparent she wanted human blood and was not going to be happy until she had more of it.

I trudged back into Devlin's bedroom, Devlin in tow. After washing the tiny holes in my hand, I put a bandage on them. Devlin didn't offer to heal them, as they were so small that my own accelerated healing abilities should take care of it in a short time.

"I'm sorry that didn't go better, Love," Dev said, hugging me.

"I waited longer with Theoron," I replied tersely. "It wasn't until he was almost five months old that I held him, that I even tried to. I should've waited."

"It might be the fresh blood I'm giving her, too," Devlin said musingly. "Theoron went a little wild the first time he got fresh blood from a human's vein, that night at the Gathering." He paused. "Nothing tastes as good as blood right from a vein. You are her first non-were, non-vampire, Love. While her palate isn't refined enough to savor the special flavor of yours, it likely tastes close to human, even with the vampire taint."

"Maybe."

"Will you sleep with me today?" Devlin pressed. "I would like us to spend some time cuddling before you leave tomorrow."

"Sure," I said, snuggling close to him. "But sooner or later, I do have to start work again downstairs. I still have all those files to do—"

"And you still need to pick out furnishings for the guest rooms," Devlin added quickly. "I'd like you to set up one as your own room, Sar."

I gave Devlin a look of shock, trying for words.

He roared with laughter. "Not for sleeping in," he chuckled, hugging me tightly. "I want you here beside me. This room I'm talking of would be for sewing, reading, or for just spending time by yourself."

Why was he offering this? There was some angle here. "That would be wonderful," I said curiously. "Serena does want me to teach her how to sew on a machine. I haven't done it in a long time, and my supplies have been packed away in one of my closets at home for the better part of a year." I smiled. "I'd like to start some new projects—"

"Good. I would like you to make me something."

"What?" I asked, intrigued.

"You made a quilt once for your mother. It was out of velvet pieces. Danial told me about it, about how beautiful it was. I want you to make one for me, for our bed."

"I'd love to. I'll just need to buy some more velvet—"

"I have some older clothes you can use. You can buy some if you need to, but I'd like you to use that to start with."

This was weirder yet. Why did Dev the clotheshorse suddenly want to let me cut up his clothes? Time to be me and ask bluntly. "Dev, I'll need to buy some anyway, as your bed is a king size. The back and the edging all should be one color, which will require some serious yardage. Even a cape wouldn't cut it for the back—"

"I have several capes you can use."

"Then I'll be happy to use your older clothes for the patchwork front, but are you sure you want me to cut them up? I'll need to cut up a lot of them, depending on the size and style—"

"I'm sure. I have trunks of clothes downstairs, Sar. One year last century, I remember I wore velvet almost every day, thinking it made me look more regal. Some of it may be too old, though. If the fabric tears too easily, just toss it out—"

He said last century like I said last year. "Are you cleaning house?" I asked, comprehension dawning. "You are, aren't you?"

"Yes," Devlin confirmed. "Danial might had had the right idea, only saving a few things that meant something to him. I always saved most everything, because I couldn't be bothered to go through it. But I want to now, because as much as I loved Anna, she is part of my past. You and Venus are here, and now that I've wrapped up Ebediah's business, I don't have to go out on business every week anymore—"

"Dev, do you still kill people?" I blurted, then flushed.

Devlin tilted my chin up to look at him. "You know I do, Sar. You know I killed the prisoners Lash and Titus took when I healed myself."

"I mean for money. Those jobs I always sent you, the ones that Danial used to do, the ones where people were asking for vengeance, for righting wrongs that the law couldn't give them justice for." I swallowed hard. "And the jobs for organized crime that Danial used to do. He said you and he used to share them. For the last few years, you have been doing them all."

Devlin looked nonplussed. "Sar, you know the answer," he said calmly. "Are you asking me because you think I will lie about it, or because—?"

"Because I need to hear it straight from you. That week I spent with you last spring; all those nights you went out, I knew it wasn't just for Ebediah's business. I didn't say anything, but I wondered if you were killing people."

"The answer is yes, but I think you are going to draw a distinction," Devlin answered. "I don't go out on jobs myself as Danial sometimes did before he met you. Even he only did it rarely, mostly sending Theo to do it. I subcontract out to about ten different hitmen who do what needs doing. Most are decent enough, and they only kill...I guess what you might call 'bad people.' But there are two others who will kill anyone who needs killing, any age, so long as the price is right. They are the ones who usually do the 'mob jobs', as you might call them. I don't pull the trigger, Sar. But I arrange it, so I consider the deaths on my head. I don't draw a distinction that I'm not the one there doing the actual killing."

I was silent, digesting all this.

"I met with some of those men that week. There were arrangements that needed to be made," Devlin said, stroking my hair. "It's a business, and it works out well for everybody. I only take a small cut, for being the go between, so the actual men doing the jobs can remain anonymous, as they prefer."

I found that chilling, but reminded myself that I had seen some of those cases firsthand. If my son had been the one robbed and beaten within an inch of his life by a gang, or my mother had been killed for her social security check by two drug addicts on a binge, I might have hired an assassin, too. I purposely didn't think about the jobs that the mob asked him to do. But of course, the harder I tried not to think about it, the more I thought about it.

"What do you get out of this? You must get something substantial, or you wouldn't bother to do it."

"Besides the small cut, there is no other money: it's an exchange of services. In return for the jobs I arrange for them a few times a year, the mob keeps an eye on most of my blood donors for me, to make sure they are taken care of, and that new ones are found when women no longer want to give me blood. And they do routine blood testing of the women, to make sure they are healthy enough to give me the amount of blood I require without dying."

"Like Angelica?"

Devlin nodded. "Danial used to pay the Italians in hits he did himself, or had Theo do. That's less expensive. Now he just gives them cash. They make a nice profit on us, running humans for vampires. But it's much easier to pay their fee than having to go out and seduce or hunt for blood ourselves every other night. That's fun sometimes, sure, but it can be very time consuming, and there's no point in living forever if one has to be constantly going to bars, and chatting up women for blood, or waiting in back alleys for unlucky young virgins looking for a shortcut—"

Maybe Danial did need the extra money from his business. The mob couldn't be cheap. "Do you prefer virgins? That comes as a surprise."

He ignored my taunt. "Do you feel differently for me, knowing this?" Devlin finished as he continued to stroke my hair. "That I choose to do this, instead of just pay them off? That it's so much less noble than Danial's fight against the evil corporate hackers, the savvy and slick suits with no conscience?"

His tone was calm, but underneath the calmness was a dangerous note. I disregarded it. It wasn't an issue this time.

"No," I answered. "I guessed that that was how it worked. You have enough money that you wouldn't care about the payout enough to do it yourself, or have the taste for it."

"That's a little too charitable for you," Devlin said, chuckling. "You know me too well to think that I don't have a taste for killing—"

"I'm only saying you don't care about killing with guns," I corrected. "Now ripping out someone's throat with your fangs, that I could see."

Devlin again roared with mirth. "You are so endearing, Sweet Sar," he crooned. "I never get tired of your humor."

I hadn't meant to be humorous, I was being sarcastic. "Are you trying to make me cringe?"

"Aren't you going to ask me about Lash?" Devlin purred. "That may make you cringe."

I didn't reply.

"Don't you want to know who he kills?" Devlin purred, his tone deeply malicious. "Aren't you curious to know if he likes it—?"

"No," I said flatly. "Because you're going to tell me the worst thing you can, because you want me to hate him. And it doesn't matter anyway—"

"Why doesn't it matter, Sar?" Devlin sneered, venom in his words. "It matters to you if I kill—"

"Because I'm not Lash's bedmate," I retorted icily. "Venus isn't his daughter, she's yours. Who you kill matters in terms of who might be after you because of it, and who might come after her and me, to get to you. If someone else is going to come looking for revenge, I want a heads-up right now."

Devlin blinked, clearly taken aback. "I'll protect you and her. You'll both be safe, Love. Please don't worry."

Devlin hugged me tightly, but didn't say anything further. Uneasy in his arms, I didn't either.

* * * *

Devlin and I woke up about five thirty the next afternoon. I told Dev I was showering and asked him if he wanted to join me, but he said only to go ahead, that he would be down later.

After a wonderful long, hot shower, I dressed and went downstairs to watch some TV. While I was tempted— perhaps insanely—to visit Venus again, I knew it wasn't a good idea. She clearly saw me as a source of food. Our days of mother-daughter bonding would have to wait until she was older.

Lash came in shortly after six, his face breaking into a grin when he saw me waiting. I gave him a welcoming smile, and he sank down beside me, turning at once to put his black socked feet up on the couch by my feet.

Not surprising that even his socks were black. Why didn't he get some black underwear as well?

"Want to watch the *Fantastic Four*?" he offered. "I TiVo-ed it for us."

"Sure," I hurriedly answered, pushing my illicit musing back under a rock where it belonged. "It's got those two guys from that FX—"

"I know you like those FX shows, Sar," Lash said with a smile. "It's all the sex—"

"And the intrigue," I laughed. "They're fun."

"But they're dark too," Lash said quietly, looking at me intently. "Happy people seem to be absent from all of the major roles."

Lash had a point. Late night FX was pretty devoid of shiny happy people smiling and laughing.

"I don't watch only FX," I said defensively. "I'm not wasting away in the darkness. There are some things I watch that are happy."

Lash gave me a look that said I most certainly did not watch anything happy.

"Okay, Mr. Sunshine, what do YOU watch that's happy?" I challenged.

"I watch *South Park*," Lash smirked.

I threw a couch pillow at his head, snorting back my laughter. Lash easily caught it, then put it under his head and sprawled out, stretching his legs across my lap. He began working the remote.

"Wait," I asked, flushing.

Lash paused the movie, looking at me closely.

"Would you come to therapy with me, either this week or next?"

"You want ME to come?" Lash said, shocked. "Why? Theo will shit a brick."

"Because our therapist said you should," I explained, giving him a shrug. "Theo won't be there, Lash, just me and you."

"I could probably do it next week," Lash said thoughtfully. "Dev's been booking me jobs here and there, and I need to meet with some people for him, too, but I can work around it. Let me check and I'll let you know next week."

"Okay."

"Just so you know, there are some things I'm not going to talk about with your therapist," Lash added with a hiss.

He was hissing again, which meant he was upset. *What things did he mean? How he loved me? Him dying?* "You don't have to talk about anything you don't want to," I reassured. "And you can swear, if you want."

"That's a relief," Lash replied. "I assume we have to sit on a couch and talk about our feelings? I've never been to therapy before."

"Must be because you are so well-adjusted," I quipped.

Lash reached down and grabbed my legs, pulling them down his way, and began tickling my socked feet.

"Ahh! Stop!" I yelled, laughing and writhing.

He was laughing, but he did stop.

"Are you hungry?" I asked. "I could make us something."

"Like what?" Lash said, giving me a hungry look back.

"I don't know…what would you like to eat?"

"I like to eat a lot of things," Lash said, giving me a suggestive smile. "Depending on what I have a yearning to taste—"

"Be serious," I chastised. "How about pancakes? Eggs? Pasta? I don't know how much time we have before Dev comes down, or what's in the refrigerator—"

"Let's go look." Lash got up immediately.

I followed him into the kitchen, and over to the fridge. He opened it, peering in. "Looks like we are out of eggs, and there's no bacon or sausage, either," Lash said with irritation. "Serena buys at least three packages every week, but that bastard Jerry's always eating it all himself—"

I remembered Jerry, one of the newer weres Dev had hired. He was short and dark haired, with an intense way about him. He had seemed nice enough, but I'd only seen him a few times at Hayden in passing. I still didn't know many of the werebears well, but I knew the single ones, like Jerry, better than the mated ones, as those six were the ones who visited Serena almost daily. Well, maybe it wasn't daily anymore, she was taking care of Venus now...

"—there's some fruit here," Lash said, making a face. "And it looks like some milk, and some vegetables, and oh look, someone did leave us one egg!"

There was real fury in his manner. *Why?* This was a pain, sure, but it wasn't that big of a deal. But he'd always had a short fuse with Theo. Maybe he had one with most people? Those jocks that'd made fun of us a month ago had brought the monster out with just a few digs at me.

"They're all such fucking selfish asses—!"

I went over behind him, and laid a hand on his shoulder, hoping to calm him. He went still beneath my fingers.

"I could make you some cornbread," I offered. "Do you like cornbread?"

Lash turned to me, longing and a touch of emotion in his dark eyes. "I love cornbread. I haven't had any in years."

"Then hand me our lone egg, and I'll get on it," I said with a smile.

Lash hugged me quickly, and then let me go, turning back around to grab the egg, and the milk. Given his lack of enthusiasm for cooking, I was surprised that he knew that milk was in cornbread, but chalked it up to the vast years he'd probably spent watching TV. Perhaps he had watched cooking shows on occasion.

I took both the egg and the milk from him, and went to the counter looking for cornmeal in the cupboard. "Preheat the oven to four hundred degrees," I said, flipping through my mental cookbook for a list of the other ingredients.

Lash began pushing the buttons of the stove, as I located everything else I needed. As I began pouring and measuring, Lash came up behind me, slipping his arms loosely around my waist as I worked, his head leaning on my shoulder. I waited for him to say something, make some comment, but he seemed content to stand there in silence.

"You have to let me go," I said, putting the last of the batter into the pans. "I've got to put these in the oven."

"Right," Lash said in one breath. He released me, and stepped away.

I slid the pans into the oven, set the times for an hour, and then turned to him. "Want some wine?" I asked. "The bread will be a while. I think there are some pretzels here—"

"Cornbread, wine, and pretzels?" Lash said, laughing. "That's not a balanced dinner."

"Probably not, but like you said, there isn't much else here—"

"Sorry about that," a voice said.

We turned to a thin blond woman at the door, a full grocery bag in her arms. She looked about Mary's age, early sixties maybe. But she was in very good shape, and when she moved, she had a spring in her step. She came in and handed the bag to Lash. He took it from her without a word, and set it on the counter.

"I'm Robin," she said softly.

I gave her a smile, and extended my hand. "I'm Sarelle."

She nodded. "I saw we were out of most everything this morning, so I took a drive down late this afternoon to get some supplies," Robin said cheerfully. "There are some eggs there, and some bagels, and bacon—"

"Thank you, Kitchen Goddess," Lash said, shooting her a grin.

Robin gave him a smile back.

That was odd. He'd been so against her coming here, back in the early spring. *What had changed to make him like her?*

"I've got to get to cleaning," Robin said, checking her watch. "But have a good night, Sarelle. You too, Lash."

"Thanks again," I said. Lash echoed me.

"If you're going to do baking again here at Hayden, Sarelle, please let me know," Robin said pleasantly. "Serena has been telling me of your skill, and I'd like to pass on a few recipes to you."

That was nice, but I wasn't used to Hayden's people being nice without an angle. "Oh?"

"I don't have children of my own," Robin explained. "The recipes are some of my traditional family ones, and I would like to pass them onto other cooks, so they aren't lost."

So long as it wasn't some kind of raw werewolf stew. "Sounds great. I like new recipes, if they aren't too complex. Probably a week from now, maybe? I'll let Serena know, and she can tell you."

"Sure thing," Robin said with a grin. With a last good-bye to us both, she left.

"She's nice," Lash hissed, putting away the salad, and the two extra packages of bacon.

He'd left out the eggs, bacon, sausage, and bagels. Looks like we'd be having a balanced meal after all.

I got out two large skillets, and began prepping, as Lash opened the packages for me. As the meat was cooking, he again came up behind me, and possessively put his arms at my waist, his thumbs hooking beneath the edge of my shirt to stroke my bare skin.

Chapter Eleven

Was he going to kiss me? What would I do if his hands suddenly slid upward? "How many eggs do you want?" I asked awkwardly.

"Four," Lash hissed softly. "Four would be nice." He let go of me, and reached back to grasp the egg carton on the counter. "Here."

I took out four eggs, and cracked them into the skillet. "How do you like them?"

"Over easy," Lash hissed almost inaudibly. "Or however you want to make them, Sar." He again moved up behind me, his hands again slipping under my shirt to touch my skin. Gently, he caressed my sides, his thumbs just grazing the bottoms of my breasts, his breath loud in my ears.

The closeness of Lash made it hard to concentrate. I breathed in the scent of him as we stood there together, the warmth of his body permeating my back. All I wanted to do was close my eyes and enjoy being held by him, to feel his arms holding me tenderly, yet possessively.

I told myself that I should open my mouth, and tell him to give me some space. I told myself that I knew better than this. Instead I relaxed back and leaned into him, letting myself be comforted.

"The eggs will be ready first," I said. "The bacon and sausage will take longer."

"Aren't you eating?" Lash hissed in my ear. "I thought we were eating together."

This time it wasn't angst that was causing his hissing; it was arousal. "I'm trying to watch my weight. I'll have a little bit of the bacon and sausage with you, and the cornbread, but not the eggs. I should really just have a bagel—"

Lash brushed my cheek with his gently, making me nearly drop my spatula. "You shouldn't lose any weight, Sar," he whispered in my ear. "You are the right size, just as you are. Your body is beautiful."

A shudder went through me at his words, images of him touching me, loving me. It was in his voice that he remembered, too...*Get a hold of yourself, Sar. You can handle this. Now do it.*

"I was thinner before I had Venus and Devon," I said grumpily, still very conscious of his arms around me and his cheek against mine. "You don't remember me that way, because by the time we were together, I was pregnant a few months—"

"Not the first time," Lash said hoarsely.

His hands slipped upwards, his thumbs stroking the sides of my breasts as he cupped them. I went still as a statue.

"You were only a month along, or less," Lash hissed softly in my ear, his tone longing. "I remember you well, Sar. How you looked in the moonlight that night, standing before me."

I shut my eyes. *Yes...he was right.* The first time I had been with him, so many months ago, I'd only been a few weeks pregnant. I had been more or less the right size then, at least for me. Now I was about ten pounds heavier.

Lash's hands crossed my chest, then his arms squeezed me back against him. "You were so fearless and determined, your eyes flashing as you demanded I take you—"

Focus, Sar, focus! "I'm not going to be supermodel thin," I uttered abruptly, blinking a lot to get the mental images of us together out of my mind. "I just want to fit into my tight jeans again, Lash. I appreciate your kind words, but I've made up my mind."

Lash didn't reply. The tension slowly evaporated as if it has never been.

"Your eggs are done," I said. "Get a plate."

Lash let me go, and turned to the cupboard.

"Do you want a bagel, too?" I asked. "I can put in one for you, and one for me."

"Sure," Lash said easily, handing me a plate. "But I can put them in while you dish it up."

Lash took care of the bagels as I carefully forked out his eggs, bacon, and the first batch of sausage. The bagels popped up a few seconds later. Lash handed me mine on a plate, then took his loaded plate immediately into the other room, a fork in his hand.

He came back in a second later. "You can't eat in there with me, because you're still cooking." He pulled out one of the bar stools, sat down at the kitchen island in back of me, and began eating.

Touched that he'd come back to keep me company, I tried to come up with some comment. The timer on the counter went off loudly, startling me so much I dropped my fork on the floor. Rolling my eyes at my teenage-like jitters, I picked it up and put it in the sink, then checked the cornbread.

"We're good to go," I said, lifting it out with the oven mitt.

"Would you cut me a few pieces?" Lash said eagerly. "I can't wait to taste it."

I almost told him he was as bad about waiting for food as Theo was, but the joke died in my throat. Shaking off my melancholy along with Theo, I cut Lash a few pieces, and one for myself. After dishing the rest of the cooked bacon and sausage to Lash and myself, I threw the last uncooked pieces in the skillet to brown and sat down next to Lash to eat. He had finished his first helping, and was eating with relish his last piece of cornbread.

"This is so good!" Lash said, giving me a happy smile. "This is just like my mother used to make. Every Sunday, she would make us cornbread. We would all wait in the kitchen, for it to come out of the oven—"

"All"? *How many siblings had Lash had?*

"—and finally it would, and she would divide it up between us," Lash sighed. "Thank you for making this for me, Sar."

"You're welcome," I replied, curious, but not wanting to pry. I got up, and turned the last pieces of bacon and sausage. "Do you want some more?" I offered, and then flushed immediately.

Lash saw me flush, and gave me a knowing smile. "Yes, please."

I handed him two more pieces of cornbread, which he devoured while I finished my meal. The last sausage and bacon was done by that time, and I gave them to him, too, with one more piece of cornbread for each of us.

"So you like Robin?"

Lash looked up at me and nodded. "I was worried initially," he said, his tone serious and measured. "I'd known some werewolves a few decades ago who had made a lot of trouble for Dev and me. But Robin's been fine. She seems to really just want some peace, and she does her job well. She doesn't shy away from me either, which is nice. She's made a point of keeping the kitchen stocked, or as stocked as she can, with this many weremen around. That's why I call her Kitchen Goddess."

"I'm happy that she's working out," I said, finishing my bagel.

"Me, too," Lash said, nodding. "Now that I don't need to—"

Lash cut off abruptly. I was motionless, too, suddenly ill at ease.

Lash had had to eat people before, because of the potion he'd taken for years. It contained a lot of demon blood, and it was fact that demons needed to ingest bodies as part of their required diet. Months back, Dev had made a comment about Lash eating Robin if she caused any trouble. Apparently, it hadn't been an idle one.

Lash was carefully not looking at me, silent and motionless as a statue. I reached out, and touched his hand. He looked up, apprehension in his dark eyes for what I was going to say.

"I know," I said softly. "I know what Titus has to do to live, and what you had to do before."

Lash looked at me in shock, then went dark red with embarrassment. "How long have you known?" he whispered, his words hoarse. "Did Dev tell you last night, because he's angry with me?"

He'd never looked so vulnerable and young. "No. I've known since sometime in July or so. Theo alluded to it one night when he was talking to Danial."

"And you still came to save me?" Lash hissed, unbelieving. "Even though you knew that I'd had to...that I...what I'd had to do to keep living?"

Now it was I who couldn't look at him. "Yes."

"I need some wine," Lash hissed. He got to his feet, and went over to the counter. Two seconds later, he was uncorking a bottle of the Groom Shiraz that Devlin seemed to keep on hand at all times. He poured us both a glass, and handed me one. We both sipped for a little, not saying anything. Hell, I'd needed the alcohol as much as he had.

"I didn't want you to know that," Lash hissed almost inaudibly. "Of all the things to have you not know about me, that would have been at the top of my list."

It would have been at the very top of my list of things not to know about, too, but I didn't say that. "It's okay," I said, sipping my wine. "You did what you had to do, Lash. Titus can't help what he is. You had to do it, or die. There's nothing more to say."

Lash stared at me, his dark eyes unreadable.

"I'm glad you're here with me, having dinner/breakfast with me," I said firmly. "It doesn't matter to me what you had to do to get here, Lash. It just matters that you're here."

Lash reached over and touched my face gently with his hand. I put down my glass, and did the same to him, and as before, he closed his eyes, savoring my touch.

Feeling welled up in me in a sudden encompassing wave. I hated that I couldn't touch him, that I couldn't take him in my arms, and tell him that it didn't matter what he'd had to do, or what he was before he met me. I wanted to tell him I cared about him, that I...

Stop, Sar. Don't you dare utter another word, not even in your mind, much less aloud.

I gritted my teeth and kept my mouth shut. Dev would be down soon. He wasn't stupid, and he'd be livid to walk in on us. It wouldn't matter to him that we weren't kissing. He would know this for what it was at a glance: two people who cared about each other sharing a tender moment.

"Why is Dev angry with you?" I asked.

Lash opened his eyes, and gave me a sad smile. He turned then and brushed his lips across the back of my hand in a quick kiss. "You know why," he whispered, and then got up.

"We should go watch the movie. Dev will be awake and around soon. He's likely got plans for you together."

I nodded, and got to my feet. "Can you put the ingredients away while I load the dishwasher?"

After everything was cleaned up and put away—including the remaining cornbread, which Lash labeled with his name to deter all would-be tasters—Lash poured us both some more wine, and we went into the living room.

Lash sprawled on the couch, putting one of his feet up behind me on the back of the couch, the other on my lap, and then he rested his hand on my arm. Instead of telling him to move over, I rested one of my hands on his leg,

"Do it. Go," I said.

Soon, we got to the scene where Dr. Doom was proposing to Sue Storm.

"—four words that can change our world—"

"I want oral sex," Lash said bluntly.

I gaped at him in shock. He laughed.

"You pervert," I said, appalled. "Shut up."

As the movie progressed, Lash made more comments like that on and off, with me amusedly responding for him to shut up. Soon, we were at the crux where Richards whipped out a pad excitedly, saying how he'd make a machine to recreate the cosmic storm.

It was too much, even for a comic book movie. "How fucking long is that going to take?" I said, disbelieving. "He's got to build an entire machine, power it, and he's got no plan for that but a cute color drawing of it—"

Lash writhed in unbridled laughter and fell off the couch, shaking the TV in its stand when he hit the floor. I roared with laughter.

He gave me a dark look laced with a smile. "I should pull you down here with me," he hissed, reaching for my foot.

I yanked it quickly out of his reach, still laughing. "Get back up here."

I looked over to see Devlin standing in the doorway, watching us, his expression neutral. I froze, as he seemed a hair's breath away from sliding into rage.

Lash was unconcerned. "Dev, come on in and sit down," he said, moving over away from me to make room on the couch. "We're watching *Fantastic Four*. It's nothing like the comic, so you might hate it, but—"

"I had another movie in mind," Devlin purred, going to the DVD player.

I looked over at Lash, unnerved, but he just shrugged.

The menu came on, indicating the movie was called *Swept Away*. Devlin settled down on the couch between us, his body sandwiching me between him and the end of the couch. Immediately, he pulled my upper body into his arms, so I was laying on him, my back to Lash.

"He loves this movie," Lash said, as if this was all just normal.

"I do," Devlin purred. "I find it romantic."

Dev wasn't just jealous, he was also angry. He's clearly chosen the movie to make some point. Apprehensive, I leaned back against him to watch.

I expected the movie to be off the wall in some way, and I was right. The male lead was tearing off the female lead's underwear before too long. Worse, he was also striking her. It was clear that the movie was meant to be humorous, especially via the dialogue in subtitles. The female lead had treated the male lead like shit, and some of what she got was him getting revenge. There was some kind of political statement here about the upper class and the lower class, too. But I was leery of the dark undercurrent that was Dev's reason for watching it now.

"Lash, you know, your hair looks a lot like the male lead's," Dev said after a few moments.

"Dev, you know I'm not Italian," Lash answered, surprised. "I'm not even European."

"What are you, Lash?" I said curiously, feeling slow on the uptake. Here I'd thought he just had a good tan from all the laying in the sun he did.

"I'm part Spanish, Hispanic, and part American," Lash said proudly. "My mother—"

"Hush," Devlin said flatly. "We are getting to the good part."

I turned to him a few minutes later. "Getting hit does not make sex better," I said, disgusted. "Not for the one getting hit." I took another look at the screen, and blinked in disbelief.

Enough was enough. "You call me when this scene is over," I said, getting up. "I'll be in the kitchen—"

"Stay here," Devlin commanded.

"Not unless you fast forward this," I replied.

As he began to do so, Lash got up and walked toward the door.

"Where are you going, Lash?" Devlin asked sharply. "You're going to miss the end—"

"I'm on duty at the gatehouse," Lash said bitterly. "And I've seen the ending, Dev. See you, Sar." He walked out and slammed the front door hard enough that dust rained down out of the doorframe.

I turned to Dev. "What does he know that I don't? Does the blonde woman get killed or something?"

Devlin settled back on to the couch. "No. Why don't you watch and judge for yourself?"

* * * *

When the credits were rolling about a half hour later, I turned my head up to look at him.

"Why do you find that romantic? She deserted her lover. Much as he might have treated her like dirt at the beginning, he seemed to really love her by the end."

"I find it romantic because she went back to her husband," Devlin said. His wide smile didn't reach his angry eyes.

I stared at him. "What?"

"You see, Sar, she didn't really love Gennarino," Devlin whispered, his eyes almost glowing. "Though he unquestionably loved her. She just gave in to him because she was swept away in the moment. As soon as she was back in the world she knew—with her rightful partner—she remembered where she belonged and who she belonged with—"

I struggled to my feet, livid. "You have any other cute movies you want to teach me lessons with?" I said coldly. "Or are you done for the night?"

"Why, Sar, I'm sure I don't know what you—"

"Save it," I said icily. "I'm going to leave now. I'll be at Danial's."

"You are going nowhere!" Devlin shouted, leaping to his feet, and locking his hand onto my arm. "Except maybe upstairs with me."

"I'll be glad to," I jeered. "So long as sleep's not all you want to do."

Devlin took a sharp breath, then bared his fangs at me. "How dare you—!"

Maybe I'd taunted the tiger too far this time. "Let me go," I ordered. "Now."

"I'm never letting you go," Devlin hissed back, his eyes red. "Never, Sar!"

Time to have it out, and then, maybe, I was leaving. I moved closer to him, making his eyes widen in surprise when I touched his shoulder with my hand, squeezing gently. "Devlin, let's drop the bullshit. What is it really? You told me you forgave me for being with Lash. He and I haven't been together since then. So why are you so jealous? Because of a few kisses and laughs?"

"I know," Devlin said heavily, the fire going out of him as he sat back down on the couch. "I know you've both done as I asked. Forgive me, Sar."

"So what is it, then?"

"I'm not taking the mood drugs anymore," Devlin replied. "I stopped yesterday. Titus said I'd have a period of emotional instability—"

Just fucking great. I sat down beside him. "Why? Why go off them now?"

"Because I need to be what I am, who I am." Devlin sighed. "I am usually very, very careful, Sar. I almost died when Ulysses took me, and by all rights, I should have. Lash and you saved me against all odds. And it was my fault I was ensnared. All I was thinking was how good we'd be together alone. Some of that was love, but some of that was the drug, dulling my senses, telling me that we'd be fine so long as I was armed. I can't afford to let that happen again, ever. I need to be edgy, ruthless, and ready to kill! Ulysses is still out there. I got word two days ago that he reentered the country this past week."

I hadn't known he was gone in the first place. "We knew he was still alive. That he'd attack again was a given."

"Sar, I'm a Ruler," Devlin said patiently. "No one attacks Rulers, save sometimes other Rulers. Certainly not a human, even one who knows some magic as Ulysses does. It is simply not done, and when it happens once a century or so, it is vampire law that the culprit be exterminated. Samuel, Perseus, Zane, and Michael all want Ulysses dead, and he's being hunted from place to place, not only by them, but also by all vampires in their territories. We have enough vampire hunters to worry about in the U.S.; we don't need one who doesn't fear the vampire ruling class."

This explained Devlin's abhorrence of my book. I'd thought he was just being pissy, but it was in his wary tone that there really were vampire hunters, and that they were dangerous. "You just said that Rulers aren't in danger from vampire hunters. So why do you care if a few other vampires get killed?"

"Think about it," Devlin said jadedly. "I control a territory, and the vampires in it pay me homage. But what happens to my respect if someone is hunting and killing them? I am not only supposed to protect the law and keep order, I also am responsible for the safety of those vampires in my territory. If someone is hunting them down like deer, I am supposed to find out who, and deal with it. A Ruler who can't protect his people is overthrown by his subjects sooner rather than later."

That made complete sense. Devlin had been trained from birth to protect the law, and—in spite of his father's many failings—to also be a good leader who not only led but also looked out for his men. It was natural that after his changing, he had still been that man, even if he hadn't been kind. "So what is the latest data on Ulysses? Do you know where he is?"

"Zane almost nailed him in Africa, but he slipped through somehow. Zane called me to let me know he was on a plane headed here. I need to end him this time, because he'll be coming for me again."

And for Lash and me, once he knew how we'd helped Devlin escape. "Does Danial know? Ulysses didn't know you were brothers, at least he seemed not to."

"Danial knows to be on guard," Devlin replied, nodding. "But he is not paying the kind of attention that he should be. But I made Theo aware. He and Terian will look out for Danial."

That was a welcome relief. Lash had to be aware, also, which meant Dev, the kids, and I would all be okay.

"So I'm going to be a little 'off' for a while," Devlin said with a grimace. "Until my emotions even out, or at least, go back to what is normal for me."

That would be approximately somewhere between borderline psychotic and sexual sadist.

"If you'll please have patience with me as—"

"I will," I agreed, then took his hand in mine. "But that's not the only problem we face, Dev. Tell me the real reason you are jealous of Lash."

Devlin looked away from me.

It was time to come clean. "Come upstairs with me, Dev."

As I closed the bedroom door behind us and locked it, I noticed that the lock was fixed. So much time had passed since Lash had kicked it in to come to my rescue back in the spring. How many times had Lash kicked in this door, and had to fix the lock later? Odds were it had been more than once...

"Sar—" Devlin began suddenly.

Forget about Lash. I turned to face Dev. "Show me yourself."

He blanched. "I'm not ready—"

"Show me now, Devlin," I said. "It's past time you did."

Devlin suddenly headed for the bathroom. I crossed the room in a few strides, and grabbed hold of him. "Show me!" I cried out, grabbing his face in my hands. "I need to know, Dev! It doesn't matter."

"It does," Devlin said, anguished.

I faced him, and without preamble, stripped off my clothes. Devlin watched me, fear building in his expression. Naked, I went to him and took his face in my hands gently. "Dev, I held you when you were burned. You are healed now—"

"I am not how I was," Devlin whispered, unwilling to meet my eyes with his own.

The longer this dragged out, the more afraid we were both going to be. "This is how you are now," I said firmly. "You are as healed as you are going to be, Dev. Show me."

Devlin sighed, and then slowly began unbuttoning his shirt.

"I want you," I said softly, then kissed him. "I want you, Devlin, just as you are. Don't be afraid."

At first, he didn't kiss me back, or even reply. But before long, Devlin succumbed to my kisses and with a groan, began kissing me back. Quickly, before I lost my nerve, I stripped off his T-shirt, baring his golden chest hair. As I ran my hands down to his jeans, apprehensive, waiting to feel ridged flesh, for him to flinch backwards suddenly with a gasp. Yet his cool skin was the smooth perfection it had always been.

Pushing him backwards to sit on the bed, I began unbuttoning his jeans. I could feel him easily underneath the heavy denim, the engorged length of him pushing almost through the waistband. As I slid the cloth down off his hips, I saw at once that he was hairless, his organs still looking newly healed. But all his equipment was intact, and fully working.

I wrapped my fingers around him and stroked gently. He inhaled sharply, then grasped my hand, moving it off him.

"Are you sensitive?" I asked tentatively. "Did what I do hurt?"

"No," Dev said bitterly. "But I look like a boy who has never reached puberty—"

I reached down and stroked him again gently, bringing a groan from his throat as he thrust involuntarily. "I like it. I can see all of you this way—"

"Stop!" Devlin said desperately, moving away again. "I have no staying power now, Sar. None. My body won't obey my will." He swallowed hard, closing his eyes. "I couldn't...I didn't want to start something with you I couldn't finish. I didn't want to disappoint you, Love."

Devlin had always prided himself on his sexual skill, his ability to finesse me with his staying power and seductive teasing. Now, he couldn't. As a result, his huge ego was in tatters, and he'd been keeping his distance rather than risk a failed romantic encounter with me. This was also why Devlin was so jealous suddenly of Lash; he knew Lash—being were—could easily make love for hours on end.

"Dev, you just got well," I consoled. "Give yourself time."

"I have been fully healed for over a week," Devlin replied, his tone raw with hopelessness. "Yet the problem remains." He kissed my hand. "I want so much to love you for hours, to show you what it's meant to me that you took care of me, that you're with me now. Instead, I'm practically useless to you."

"Hush," I said firmly. "Kiss me, and take it slow, Devlin. I want to try."

Devlin gave me a worried look, but pulled me hard against him. I kissed him passionately, sliding my hands up into his hair. He wrapped his arms around me and we fell back onto the bed. Devlin rubbed the tip of his penis between my legs, then held my gaze as he slowly bore down with his hips. Shifting, he moved closer, bringing a moan from me as I strained up against him, clutching his back. Suddenly, Devlin shuddered, then cried out in anguish as he unexpectedly spurted. He sagged, then swore angrily, his erection already softening inside me.

I hugged him close. "It's okay. It doesn't matter—"

"It does matter," Devlin said disgustedly. "I can't believe this is happening to me—"

"Pull out," I said gently. "Then lay back for me."

Devlin rolled onto his back with a sigh. I grabbed a nearby tissue, and wiped him off, then curled my hands about his penis. His flesh was limp in my grasp.

I tried to think of a single time I'd seen Devlin like this, and couldn't remember one. In the broiling Jacuzzi, when he'd been freezing after our January bike ride, when he'd been an emotional wreck our first day together in the motel, that time at the concession stand at the movies, in the doctor's office, Danial's kitchen, Hell, anywhere, he had always been ready for action, his flesh hard and firm. He had always been in complete control of himself, sometimes sustaining erections for hours at a stretch. Ulysses had struck the bull's-eye with his well-planned revenge. The loss of his sexual power was likely more horrible to Devlin than just dying would have been. Dev would remember it for as long as he lived, no matter if he regained his old skill and stamina, and even killed Ulysses.

Luckily, I wasn't without skill myself. And no matter how worried he was about his performance, there was one thing sure to make him forget that and get back in the mood. Leaning over him, I began kissing him gently, running my lips and tongue over his flaccid member.

Devlin groaned loudly. "Ahh, Sar...I have long waited to feel your lips on me, kissing me so intimately—"

I took the tip of him into my mouth and sucked teasingly. Looking up to face him, I stroked him with my tongue, letting him see how much I enjoyed feeling his flesh between my lips. His own lips parted as he beheld me, his golden eyes so hot with lust they were gleaming red in the darkness. His body almost came off the bed, his hands reaching down to grab my shoulders as I moved my lips over him, caressing him with my tongue, watching him watch me.

Devlin pushed me back. "Climb onto me," he urged, moving me astride him. "Please, Sar. Move quickly!"

His penis was lengthening again, filling out as his body made itself ready to love me again.

Hurriedly, I straddled him and began moving on him, wetting his hardening organ with my juices. He pivoted his hips and slipped inside me, then began to grind my body against his, stimulating me.

I was already close, my desire rampant with need for satisfaction. I moved my hips on his with abandon, throwing my head back. God, no one felt like he did. No one else gave me that feeling of being stroked all over inside, completely filled...

Devlin strained beneath me, panting, his eyes closed. "Sar, you're so warm—"

"Oh, yes, just like that," I moaned, rocking my hips on him, my tone complete need. "Harder—"

Devlin thrust in deeply, his hands sliding up to cup my breasts. He twitched suddenly beneath me, then began to shudder.

I was almost there. I was so close! God, please—!

Devlin came again with a harsh cry, spasming hard. As he jerked under me, his movements pushed me to climax, my loud scream of release breaking free. Devlin ground into me frantically, the sensation bringing cry after cry from my parted lips as he thrashed and jetted into me.

I sank down on his chest, my breaths ragged. "God, that was good—"

"It was successful," Devlin said bitterly. "But if you hadn't come as easily as you had, I'd have left you behind."

"It was wonderful," I said gently, kissing him. "You heard me orgasm, Love, and I heard you. We came together, both of us. That's what matters," I hugged him. "The rest we can work on."

"What if I can't fix it?" Devlin whispered, terrified. "What if I am always this sensitive?"

"We can fix it," I said confidently, much more confidently than I really felt. "You weren't born with the staying power you used to possess, right?"

"Some," Devlin said slowly, prideful. "Most of it was learned over time."

"You have all the know-how," I encouraged. "We just need to practice." I kissed him. "Just tell me when I have to take one for the team." I kissed him again. "I never get tired of hearing you come, Dev. I always want to feel you inside, stroking me—"

"I love you," Devlin said tearfully, embracing me. "I'm sorry for how I acted earlier tonight—"

I put my finger to his lips. "Don't apologize to me. Apologize to Lash. He's upset that you are angry with him."

"He told you that?" Dev said in surprise.

I nodded. "Don't be at odds over me."

"I know how he feels about you, Sar. It was wrong of me to keep you apart." He took my hand and kissed it. "If you want to—"

I shook my head, putting my finger to his lips again. "No. He and I are over."

"I know you want him, Sar," Devlin replied, confused. "I could see it tonight—"

"I do want him," I said brokenly, looking at the ceiling in hopes there was some answer up there. "But I need to give it my best shot with Theo. And that means staying away from Lash, Dev, no matter how I feel."

Devlin nodded. "Titus told me what he's doing for you."

I sighed. "I didn't want anyone to know." Next Danial would know, of course.

"I'm not going to tell anyone," Dev said knowingly. "Not even Danial. But I'd think Theo might want a say—"

"He doesn't get a say," I replied sharply, making Devlin move back. "I was the one who put it on him. He never asked to be bound to me or to dream with me."

"He never asked to be unbound, either," Devlin said quietly. "And I'm guessing if he knew—"

"Can you be satisfied with only taking my blood?" I said flatly, looking over at him in challenge. "Because Theo's okay sharing me with Danial, but he'll never really get used to sharing me with you, or not be jealous about it. He'll only be truly happy if I give you up as my lover, Dev. Can you let me go?"

"I am never letting you go," Devlin said lovingly, pulling me into his arms. "The more I'm with you, the more I want to be with you, and the more resolved I am that we were meant to be together, as Anna and I were. I will not lose you the way I lost her." He kissed me possessively. "Nothing is coming between us, Sar. Nothing and no one. Not even death."

I gave him a lopsided smile. "A tad creepy, but I do so love your romantic soul."

He smiled, baring his fangs. "Romantic, but also practical. Was the one enough for you, Love? You usually enjoy at least two." Devlin paused. "I can use other parts of my body to love you, if you want me to."

I gave him a coy smile. "Now why would I turn that down?"

Devlin grinned, again showing the tips of his fangs. "You have never asked me for anything else," he said simply. "If you liked oral sex better, as some women do, you would have asked me for it long before now. So naturally, I assumed it was not an act you welcomed or preferred." He ran his hand down, inserting it gently inside me, his deft fingers stroking. "But perhaps it's a night for widening your horizons?"

Knowing Dev, I was unsure of how wide he was proposing my horizons would grow, or if they involved exotics for which I wasn't ready. "I'm up for a little experimenting, sure. But are you done for the night?" I whispered, blushing. "Or will this be one-sided?"

"I don't know," Devlin said hesitantly. "I thought I was finished after the first time with you, but your touch awakened me again. We will have to wait and see. In the meantime, I'd like to show you some other skills of mine. There is more than one way to bring a woman pleasure, Love, and I would have you feel as much joy as your body could possibly withstand."

Like any sane woman could hear that offer and refuse. "Anything you'd like to do to bring me pleasure, go ahead and do," I answered, flashing a wicked smile. "Just watch the teeth, Love."

Devlin laughed. "It's true my fangs make it harder for me," he said, kissing my neck, then pricking gently with one fang. "They don't hook backward, as Lash's do. But I've had centuries to practice, Sar. And I guarantee that my skill there has not diminished. Lay back."

I did as he asked, my heart racing in anticipation. Devlin began kissing his way down my body, his cool lips teasing my flesh. Soon I was crying out for him, the gentle stroking of his hands and lips on my flesh a concert that drowned all my senses in sweet, captivating music.

* * * *

I awoke sometime in the late, late morning. Devlin was spooning me, snoring. I stretched contentedly, then beamed happily. Getting laid was extra nice when it had been a few weeks. Devlin had been fantastic, as expected. While the action had been one-sided after all, seeing my eyes glaze over with desire had done more to help our situation than any amount of orgasms could have. When I was spent, he'd been so at ease that he had sung to me.

I hadn't recognized the song. The inflection and rhythm made me think it was old, maybe an ancient poem that had been first written in a language other than English. The gist was two lovers meeting at night in a glade, the shadows and light of the moon spilling across their skin as they made love. It was sung from the man's point of view, much of it his longing for his lover to come back to him as he watched her walk away in the moonlight. There was also deep contentment in the song, as the man was confident that his lover would return, and that she loved him, too. When he had finished, the last clear note fading in the darkness, I'd turned to him expectantly, waiting for him to tell me the author as he usually did after singing a song or quoting a poem that he knew I wasn't familiar with.

"I wrote it," Devlin confessed, contented. "Many years ago."

"For Anna," I added with dawning understanding.

"Yes," Devlin replied. "After that first night she gave herself to me, and I knew I loved her, I composed it. Did you like it?"

For the first time, there wasn't pain in Devlin's voice when he talked of his lost love. While that made me happy for him, I was jealous, too, wondering why he was singing me her song. "It was beautiful," I said finally. "I'm sure she loved it very much."

Devlin hugged me gently, and began to sing again.

"You are the sun, the warmth and the light,
I am the moon in the dark of the night,
Will you warm me, my love, will you give me your kiss?
Do you desire me, want me, or is it just this,
That you feel me watching and waiting for you,
And as I longed for your touch, so you longed for me, too.
Come to me, live with me; say you'll be mine,

Leave your others behind you for they shall be fine
I need you with me; I would give you forever,
Make my world yours; promise always to never
Stop wanting my hands in your flax golden hair,
Or my body beside yours, together and bare.
For you are my loved one, my only you are,
Your eyes are my emeralds and you are my Sar."

I was shaking a little by the time he finished. Devlin gently kissed the tears away from my face. I didn't speak, not trusting my voice.

"I wrote it for you when I was in Rio. I couldn't stop thinking about you, no matter what I did. I finished it just before I came back in January, but I couldn't bring myself to sing it to you then, when I wasn't sure you wanted a life with me."

I hugged him, my eyes leaking again.

"It was easy for me to tell you I loved you after the first time I said the words," Devlin said hesitantly "It was much harder to bare my soul and sing you my creation." It was in his tone that he desperately hoped I liked it.

"It was beautiful," I said, my inflection wavering with emotion. "I loved it, Dev."

"I'm glad," he whispered in relief. "I liked writing it for you."

I looked into his molten golden eyes, thinking again how surprised I was that someone so gorgeous could love me, much less have gone to the lengths he had to take me for his own.

"I do love you," I said softly, touching his cheek gently. "I'm glad we have Venus. She's so beautiful, Dev—"

"She is," he said proudly, embracing me. "She has the best of both of us. V will break some hearts for sure when she's older, before she finds someone worthy of her love."

"Just like you," I teased.

Devlin pulled back to look me in the eyes. "I am done breaking hearts," he said seriously. "I'm in love with you. I'm not going to break your heart again, Sar."

I wanted to believe him, wanted him to be the man I knew he could be. But I wasn't sure if things would be different with him this time, especially now he was off the meds. So I had taken his heartfelt words with a sobering grain of salt.

"I know you won't. Go to sleep, Dev."

Chapter Twelve

The rest of the week passed quickly as October's last days drew near. Halloween was only a few weeks away, which meant soon I'd need to discuss preparations for Danial's annual Hallow's party for Elle and myself. Elle had mentioned that Tatiana was making her a new dress to wear. So far, she was annoyed that the cleavage was not lower. After seeing the dress on her, I thought the cleavage was already far too much for a girl of her age. But as Danial had still not mentioned the party to me at all, I had put off talking to him about it, worried he might tell me I was not invited this year. While the party was something I endured rather than looked forward to annually, the possibility of being told he didn't want me there wasn't something I wanted to face until I had no other choice.

Danial had been avoiding me since our discussion in his office, and I continued to avoid him as well, working mornings on Solutions, Inc., and making sure I was outside in the afternoons I stayed at his estate to visit with Elle, Devon, and Theoron. It was easy enough; I threw myself into yard work and had the kids help me.

Devon and Elle kept me company as I cut bushes, raked, mulched, and pulled the last weeds of summer at Danial's home. Theoron was a lot like Danial, in that he didn't really like the outdoors much, except for occasional walks. But Elle and Devon liked to be outside, and most of the time they lent a hand where I needed one. Not that I really needed more help. Danial was still attentive to what went on around him and he was still courteous; the harder jobs, like clearing trees, digging large holes, or cleaning up the garden for winter were always somehow already finished by the time they made it to the top of my list.

At home, I was also busy with work. While Theo and I had plenty of wood for winter at home—thanks to the trees I'd cut up at Hayden with Lash and the bears back in the late summer—there were the usual leaves to mulch, branches to burn, and machinery to put away. Devon alone kept me company there, playing in the leaves, and pouncing on the occasional mouse he found. He was far bigger than my cats Cavity and Jessica, but they were used to him now and they no longer feared him.

By the end of the week, I finally finished up most of the before-winter chores. That following Sunday, Theo helped me run the chain saws dry and turn off the water to the barn. Devon was being watched by Janice and Cia that afternoon, because as much as Theo assured me that Devon wouldn't come near the running chain saws, I was much too afraid to risk him being around when we were both cutting wood. He was too inquisitive, always getting into things, from unpacked grocery bags to the lower drawers of the kitchen to my sewing needles. One day last week, he had even eaten some of my vitamins. Although they hadn't hurt him, I'd been so worried about him getting sick that I'd just sat and watched him for signs of illness for hours, the cordless phone in my hand. He was my baby, and I admitted secretly—if not to anyone else—that I loved him best of all my children. He'd been the only one I could feed, touch, and hug from the moment he took his first breath.

After we locked the barn up for winter, Theo and I celebrated with a meal out at the local diner, the Country Kitchen. The food was very good, and we were worn out, our conversation easy and unstilted. It had been a good day, and we hadn't argued as we sometimes did when we worked together. Theo was used to giving orders, not following them, and he often thought his ideas were the best—if not the only possible way—to do things. I suspected that was a burden most wives suffered through with their husbands.

"Do you want to maybe see a movie later tonight?" Theo said suddenly, pointedly looking out the window.

I whipped my head around, my French fry in my hand forgotten. He hadn't asked me to spend time with him since I'd saved Lash. Most nights he just watched TV and I read in the other room, or in bed. When he crawled into bed beside me at night, we didn't talk or even touch. I'd been hesitant to approach him at all since our episode in the truck.

"What did you have in mind?" I said carefully.

"Just some popcorn, and an action or horror movie," Theo said, looking now at the table. "I don't know what's on TV, but we can rent one on Pay-Per-View, if you want—"

"That would be nice," I said quickly.

Theo looked up at me and smiled, relief in his eyes.

Had he actually been thinking I would refuse him? He had. Why? I pondered that as we had some dessert, but couldn't come up with anything that made sense.

190

After I paid the bill, Theo drove us home. Theo reached over and grabbed my hand in his as he drove. I was surprised but pleased, and squeezed his hand in mine, though neither of us said anything to the other.

By the time Theo had walked the dogs, and I had done a little housecleaning, it was dark. We had just decided on a newer Russell Crowe movie and placed the order when the phone rang.

Theo got up to answer it. "It's likely Danial."

But this time, it wasn't Danial.

"Your loverboy for you, Sar," Theo growled.

I knew who it had to be. What I couldn't fathom was why he was calling. "What—?"

Theo handed me the phone and stalked off, slamming the front door behind him.

So much for our plans. "Hi, Lash."

"You asked me about coming to therapy with you," Lash hissed angrily. "You didn't say which day, but I deduced from what you did say, it would be tomorrow or the next day—?"

He'd heard Theo's sniping. "Tuesday, October twenty-fifth, the day after tomorrow, at twelve o'clock. Carol had to change the time, she just called today. I was going to call you tomorrow, as I hadn't heard from you—"

"That's fine," Lash hissed, all business. "I'll meet you there, if you'll tell me directions."

I gave him the directions. "See you there."

"Goodnight."

I put the phone back in its cradle, sat back down on the couch, and tried to watch the movie, but my heart wasn't in it. Setting the TiVo to record it, I began making dinner. Pasta was easy enough. Popcorn would have to wait for another night, too.

I put in some time on the treadmill, and was just getting off when Theo came in, still angry.

"What did he want?" he growled. "Was he arranging a hot date for you both?"

Could he be more of an asshole? "He wanted to get directions for meeting me for therapy tomorrow," I said coolly.

"That's all?" Theo replied, disbelief heavy in his tone.

"That's all," I said flatly. "Are you hungry?"

"Yes," Theo said, remorseful. "Thanks for making some for me."

I handed him a dish and didn't reply, angry that he'd immediately suspected me of something. I hadn't done anything wrong, not this time, anyway.

We ate in silence, until Theo spoke.

"Why'd you ask him to go with you first? I mentioned to Danial about how Carol wanted Devlin, Lash, and him to come, and he said you hadn't mentioned anything to him about it yet."

Make it sound like I'm using any excuse to see him, Theo. "I haven't mentioned anything to Dev yet, either. He's still dealing with his injuries, and Danial isn't really speaking to me. The Hallows party is coming up quickly, and Danial's occupied exclusively with that. Besides, Lash will probably only go to the one session with me, where Dev and Danial will need to go to more than one. I don't know why Carol even wants him to come."

"I don't envy you," Theo said, looking out of the corner of his eye at me. "I wouldn't have wanted to go with Aspen."

I rolled my eyes at that comparison. "Maybe it will be a catastrophe. I'll keep you posted."

* * * *

Therapy with Lash was pretty much a complete disaster. Carol was afraid of him from the moment he walked into her office and looked at her with his reptilian eyes. When he took off his long coat before sitting down, putting his weapons in plain sight, her eyes got even bigger. I was thankful he wasn't wearing a visible gun, too. Likely, he'd left that in his truck.

Carol welcomed him in hesitantly. Lash and I sat down on the couch, and Carol sat down in her chair.

"Lash, do you know why I asked Sar to bring you with her today?" Carol began pleasantly.

"I haven't a fucking clue," Lash hissed sharply.

Carol recoiled, visibly at a loss for words.

"Lash, it's okay," I reassured.

Lash shot me a look that said he didn't understand. "You said I could swear, Sar. Or can I just not say fuck—?"

"I meant if you were angry," I explained. "Try not to swear unless you have to."

Lash rolled his eyes. "Sure."

"Sar has feelings for you," Carol said. "Do you have feelings for her?"

"She already knows I do," Lash hissed menacingly. "Get to the point, Carol."

I wanted to scream, this was so awkward and uncomfortable. *How was this helping anything?*

"Do you love her, Lash?" Carol said pointedly.

"Carol, either ask a pertinent question to Theo and Sar's relationship, or I'm leaving," Lash hissed angrily. "What I feel for her is irrelevant to her relationship with Theo."

Carol tried again. "Lash, do you wish that she would leave Theo for you?"

Lash glared at her, baring his fangs, and she recoiled in her chair just from his look. "Sar loves Theo, not me," he hissed. "What I want is for her to be happy, Carol. She isn't now. Some of it's that prick Theo's fault. He wants too much from her."

Carol nodded. "What do you want from Sar, Lash?"

Lash looked over at me, his eyes flat and hungry. "Whatever she wants to give me, Carol. She has enough men pushing her for sex, love, and her time. I'm not going to be another one."

Carol considered this.

"Carol, why did you ask me to bring Lash today?" I said. "I've told you all the facts. I don't see how going over what happened again will solve anything."

"Lash, Sar and Theo are trying to make their marriage work," Carol said gently, ignoring me. "They have several issues to work through. One of them is you. They need to resolve what you were to Sar, Theo's jealousy over it, how she feels about you, and how you feel about her, so as a couple they can move beyond the affair she had with you. That's why I asked you here."

Lash considered that, flicking his forked tongue at Carol. "That's simple enough," he hissed. "We are friends, good friends. We were lovers, but we aren't anymore, though that's not by choice—"

That wasn't true on my part, but I kept silent.

"—Sar and I aren't happy about not being able to be intimate, but that's how it is. I accept that. She accepts that. I want her to be happy, even if it's with that fucking cat—"

"Lash, do you think you could make Sar happier than Theo can?" Carol interjected.

Lash stopped talking. In a fluid motion, he got up and walked toward Carol, who shrank back in her chair again, her eyes wide. "What are you poking at me for, Carol?" he hissed. "People who can't leave a snake well enough alone tend to get bitten—"

"Lash, come back here and sit down," I said sternly. "Stop acting threatening. She's a therapist, not one of your marks."

"She's aiming to be one," Lash hissed at Carol. But he did come back to the couch, and sat down again. I put my hand on his arm, and he relaxed somewhat, moving my hand off him and putting his arm around my shoulders, stroking me with his fingers.

"Please answer the question, Lash—"

Anger flared within me. "Carol, enough with the remarks about rivalry," I said irritably. "I told you, there isn't—"

"Sar, I can see just by the way you two act that you are one tiny step away from becoming lovers again," Carol said flatly. "You are an adult, Sar, and you are married. If you want your marriage to survive, you need to ask yourself if what you feel for Lash is more important that what you feel for Theo. And whatever conclusion you come to, you need to tell both Theo and Lash the truth about what you feel."

Lash gently took his arm off me, and moved away from me on the couch. "She already told me," he hissed, upset. "She wants to try with Theo to make it work between them. She doesn't want to lose him over what she and I did together. I accept that."

"Then Sar needs to stop you when you try to touch her, and Lash, you need to respect that, and not touch her like you just did," Carol said gently. "She needs you to just be her friend. Can you do that for her, Lash?"

"Of course. I am grateful for all she did for me. I value her friendship."

"Lash, do you feel what you feel for Sar because of her part in saving you?"

What did that have to do with anything? More importantly, what would he answer?

"No. I'm grateful for her help, for what she did. But I cared for her long before that."

"Lash, can you be supportive of Sar and Theo's relationship? I know there is strong dislike between you—"

"Theo's an asshole, plain and simple. I'm not going to change my opinion of him," Lash said angrily. "Just why Sar loves him so much, I don't know. It must be for his body."

"Why do you hate him, Lash?" Carol asked.

"Because he's a simple jock, and a fool, and he talks too much. I don't like anyone who mouths off to me, and it pisses me off that I can't just kill him, like I would anyone else who says the shit he does to me. But Dev's asked me not to kill him from way back, for Danial, and so I just kick his ass usually when we fight, knowing he'll pull the same dumb shit the next time I see him, and I'll have to fight him again then. I do enjoy kicking his ass, it's true, but I wish it wasn't so easy to get a rise out of him. But maybe that is the reason Sar loves him." He smirked at me. "I hope he's not a one hit wonder."

Carol looked appalled. I glared at Lash.

"What?" he said easily. "Since he's a fuckup at everything else, it's natural to assume he's shit in the sack, too—"

"Stop being a jerk," I said gently. "Your digs aren't making this go any faster." I looked back at Carol. "I am tired of their fighting," I added wearily. "It's true that Lash runs his mouth at Theo, but Theo's just as guilty. And it's always Theo that starts the actual fighting. I tried to interfere a few times, but it didn't help. They still fought."

"Just stay out of the way," Lash said arrogantly. "It never takes me long to put him on the ground. He usually stays there, once he's down—"

"Still, it would be better if you didn't fight," Carol said firmly. "Especially as there is nothing to fight over. Sar, do your best this week to try to get Theo to control his temper for those times he can't just avoid Lash. And Lash, don't verbally bait Theo—"

"I'll keep my mouth shut, so long as he does," Lash hissed. "But I'm not taking his insults. I don't take insults from anyone but Dev, and sometimes Danial, as a favor to Dev—"

"You and Devlin are good friends?" Carol asked.

Lash nodded.

"Why? You're snake and he's vampire. A friendship between the two is unusual—"

Lash fixed her with a cold glare "I don't talk about Dev, and he doesn't talk about me. Dev's coming with Sar in two weeks. You want him to answer questions, he'll answer them then. But I don't talk about him, not without him here to hear me."

Lash had talked about him plenty with me, but maybe it was a personal thing.

Carol nodded. "I think we are done for today, then," she said, getting up. "Thank you for coming, Lash."

"That's a relief," Lash said, changing slowly back to human form, his eyes becoming dark as his fangs receded, and disappeared. He stood up. "So I can go, then?"

Carol looked at him, surprised. "I thought you would be older."

Lash gave her a faint smile. "I was older-looking before," he said, a faint drawl in his words. "It was an effect of the faerie blood, how I look now."

She was checking him out, clearly. I was irritated at her assassin groupie-ness, then told myself it was none of my business.

"Sar, I'll see you next week with Theo," Carol said, showing us to the door.

I nodded, and left, Lash at my side. When we reached the sidewalk, he turned to me. "I'm going to head back. Do you want a ride?"

What I wanted from him was a kiss and then a nice long ride, but I kept that to myself. "Come with me to brunch; my treat. It's the least I can do after you were nice enough to come here today."

Lash gave me a tilted head coupled with a calculating look. "Sounds uptight. Where?"

I immediately began babbling. "There's a restaurant I know near my house. You can drop me off after. Maybe we can go for a walk after with my dogs, if you aren't too cold. I've only got two hours before I've got to get home, so it won't be a long lunch, or anything. Theo's got an important meeting later today, and he can't walk them, so I need to—"

Lash looked at me, considering my words.

God, why couldn't I shut up? "—we both missed lunch, and after that debacle going out to lunch sounds good. I don't want to go alone. You'll like it." I gave him a scoping look. "Are you not hungry?"

"It's not that. We've only ever gone for sushi," Lash said quietly, his dark eyes very guarded. "I just never expected for you to invite me anywhere near your home where someone you knew might see us together."

He was nervous himself. My nervousness evaporated. "Why wouldn't I?" I said, giving him a strange look. "Why are you saying it like that?"

"Never you mind," Lash said quickly, turning and walking toward his truck. "Let's go if we're going."

* * * *

The instant we walked inside, I felt like I'd made a mistake. Theo and I had come here often in the past year, and our usual waitress was clearly curious about where he was, and who Lash was to me. It got even better when we got up to get our food from the buffet tables.

"Try the blintzes, they're excellent," I said, handing Lash the tongs. "There's bacon there—"

"Sar?" a curious and familiar voice said.

I whipped around to see my parents staring at us. Lash was already facing them, staring back.

Just act normal. "Mom, Chris, you know Lash," I said calmly. "Lash, you remember my parents, Chris and Tina."

"Hi, Lash," my parents said, the question of what I was doing here with him loud in their voices.

"Hello, Tina, Chris. I am seeing Sar safely home from Devlin's," Lash said quietly, putting the tongs back in the serving tray. "We stopped for lunch, as Sar said this place has good food."

Reassured, my parents gave me a hug, and shook Lash's hand before they left for their own table.

"They are good people," Lash said pensively. "I wish they didn't think I was so awful."

"They don't think you are awful," I amended gently as we sat down. "They think Devlin's awful, and you are guilty by association. You like single malt scotch and that immediately puts you on good terms with my stepfather, anyway."

196

"Still, they were happy to think you aren't here with me socially. And I can't say I blame them. They have every reason to think that of me, from what Theo's probably told them." Lash met my eyes. "He has, hasn't he?"

I looked down, stabbing some meat with my fork. Lash was right. Theo had said more than a few derogatory things about Lash this summer, when he, Danial, Theoron, Elle, and me had visited my parents. Danial had joined in, though the both of them had shut up when I'd given them my "dangerous" eyes.

"I noticed that they don't ever come to see V," Lash hissed softly. "It's because of me—"

"No," I replied. "It's because of Dev. They forgave Devlin frightening them, but they don't want to see him at all, ever. My mother refuses to set foot in Hayden again, especially if 'that demon-thing' comes around to 'space warp them there—'"

Lash cracked up laughing, and I smiled too, glancing up at him. "But Devlin won't let Venus leave Hayden. I'm hoping to convince him to let her go to Danial's, and have my parents meet her there."

Lash nodded. "That might work." He shifted in his seat. "Sar, I have an appointment tonight around eight. I'll be out for a few hours, if you try to reach me."

Why was he telling me? "Okay."

"I know you're going to be home alone," Lash said, finishing his chicken. "I wanted you to know I wouldn't be around, in case you needed me."

I put down my fork and stared at him. "How do you always know? You knew that day that I would be alone for lunch, too—"

"Brian tells me whatever I want to know," Lash said, sitting back in his chair. "And I make it a point to know if you are going to be alone, both to let Devlin know and to make sure Titus is around, in case you need help. Now that you can teleport again, Dev and Danial aren't worried about you being alone as much, but it pays to be extra careful."

"Thanks," I said, understanding his comment.

"I'm heading back up," he said, standing. "Be right back."

We tried a little of everything at the buffet. I indulged, telling myself I could go back on the diet tomorrow. Lash had sausage, sausage gravy, chicken and biscuits, bacon, beef tips, tilapia, and ham with a little rice.

"Having some rice with your meat?" I teased.

"To each his own," he hissed, giving me a grumpy look. "I didn't say anything about your four desserts—"

"Shush," I said curtly, making him smile again. "They were only three small ones."

We didn't talk further, preferring just to nibble leisurely and enjoy the sunlight. It was a cold day, but the sunlight was warm and bright on the frozen earth outside. We were sitting near the windows, and the sunlight was streaming in the windows to land on me, the table, and Lash.

He sighed with pleasure at the warmth, then he looked over at me knowingly. "You didn't ask me here for the food—"

I gave him a wide grin. "Not just for the food. I've often sat where you're sitting, and relished the sun warming me. I knew with the sunlight so bright today, it would be like that if we came here, and that you'd like it as much as I did."

"How long can we sit here before they kick us out?" Lash said with a yawn, closing his eyes and relishing the heat.

"Probably another hour," I answered. "If you keep eating more food, anyway."

"Not a problem," Lash said, quickly getting up and heading to the buffet.

* * * *

As we walked out to his truck, he nudged me with his shoulder. "Thanks for inviting me," Lash said happily. "Basking felt really good, Sar."

He opened the truck and got in, as I got in on the passenger side.

"I know how much you like the sun," I said, shutting the door softly.

"I like you more," Lash said hungrily, sliding me over against him on the seat.

I leaned against him the whole way, breathing in his scent. Too soon, we were pulling into the driveway.

"Drive over by the barn," I said suddenly. "Park behind the woodshed."

Lash gave me a curious look, but did as I asked.

I turned to him. "Do you have something we could sit on in the truck bed?"

"Sar, we can't have sex," Lash hissed, shifting in his seat. "I gave my word."

"I'm not asking you for that. I just thought we could cuddle a little, maybe kiss and touch," I tempted him. "I'd ask you to come inside my house, but Theo would smell your scent. We can't go to Hayden. My barn is too cold, and a hotel seems too tawdry just for cuddling—"

Lash gave me an incredulous look. "Sar, I may be snake, but I'm not cold enough to resist you if you get me worked up—"

"I am not going to seduce you," I said firmly.

"Yes, you are," Lash groaned, moving uncomfortably in his seat. "I'm already hard for you just talking about touching you, and I haven't kissed you at all. Kissing you and touching you will just make it worse."

"We don't have to do it, then," I said dismissively. "Just drop me off."

"Stay here," Lash hissed. He got out of the truck and slammed the door, then began rummaging in the back of the truck. A few seconds later, he was boosting me into the back, and then he crawled up behind me. "How's this?"

Lash had laid down a foldable foam mattress pad, and put a few blankets over it.

"Fine. I—"

He pressed me back with his body, kissing fiercely as his hips ground into me. I kissed him back, running my hands up under his shirt to caress his warm skin.

Before a minute was up, I was dying for the contact of our naked bodies. When he reached up under my shirt, sliding my bra up so he could cup my breasts in his hands, I arched my back with a cry and reached down, stroking him with my hand through his jeans. Lash rolled quickly onto his back and pulled me on top of him. Grabbing hold of my hand, he pressed it hard against his straining jeans. "Touch me, Sar," Lash panted. "Don't do anything more, just touch me with your hand, please—"

I grabbed the closure with shaking fingers and unzipped his pants, reaching inside. Lash convulsed the moment my fingers touched his swollen flesh. As I curled my fingers around him and brought him out, he quickly unbuttoned his jeans and slid them down. I stroked him, rubbing my thumb across the head, loving the feel of his penis so hot and firm. Lash began to thrust hard into my hand almost immediately. Within seconds, he came with a sharp cry, spilling semen onto my hand and the blanket we were lying on. Lash jerked in my arms as he finished. Tenderly, I held him, brushing his lips with my own.

"I'm sorry," Lash sighed.

I gave him an odd look. "What for?"

"Because this isn't fair to you. I can't give you any release without making love to you, or being inside you in some way. We can't do either of those. Goddamn it, I shouldn't have asked—"

"Hush," I said firmly, squeezing his erection in my hand. Lash went rigid, letting out a hiss. "Come for me again," I teased. "But this time inside me."

"We can't," Lash groaned, his organ instantly stiffening in my hand. "I gave my word. I won't break it even for you, Sar—"

"Devlin gave me permission," I tempted. "He's still hurt, Lash. He said it was okay for us to be together."

Lash groaned loudly.

"Be with me. I want you."

Lash rolled on top of me, kissing me frantically as he began pulling off my jeans. He threw them aside, then bore down with his hips…

"Sar!" Lash said loudly, jolting me out of my fantasy.

I flushed red, realizing we were at my house, and I couldn't even remember the trip home, any of it. Lash was on his side of the truck, where he was supposed to be, fully clothed. *God, could I be a bigger idiot? What had Carol just been telling me! What in hell was wrong with my self-control?*

"You okay?" Lash said curiously.

Not to mention that there was no way in the world that an inflatable mattress would fit in the back of an Avalanche truck. The bed was too small and Lash's truck had no cap, so we'd have been making love out in the open for everyone to see, freezing our asses off in the process. *Now if we had driven into the barn, put the mattress up in the loft, and gotten under some blankets there, maybe…*

"What were you thinking about?" Lash pressed insistently. "You are blushing like I caught you masturbating."

I flushed deeper, making Lash erupt in laughter. "I've got to go."

Lash moved fast to block me, grabbing hold of my arm. "What were you thinking about?" he hissed again, his shifting eyes agitated.

"About you," I admitted, sagging back onto the seat.

"About us together?"

I nodded.

"Sit here with me a while," he said, settling his arm around me. He let out a sigh, then asked, "Are you happy? Is this what you wanted from your life?"

Unexpected introspection to be coming from him. My eyes looked up to meet his dark intense ones. Was that sadness? "Lash, what do you mean—"

"Don't play dumb. It doesn't suit you," he said bluntly. "I know what you are going through now with Theo is my fault. It's not so much about you almost dying for him; it's about the sex we had. The other stuff has been going on for months. Sure, it might be a source of fighting, but Theo and you weren't going to break up over it. This is serious, like back last fall when Danial and you were together, and Theo couldn't handle it. He can't handle what we did. In fact he's probably more upset over you and me than he ever was about you and Danial."

How did he know about that? Devlin must have told him. I bit my lip.

"Are you sorry you saved me?" Lash continued. "That you said yes?"

I reached out and grabbed his face. "Never," I said forcefully. "And don't ever think that I am. If I had it to do over, I would still have gone to find you, knowing what would happen when I did. I may not be happy, Lash, but none of that is your fault. You gave me a choice, remember? And I'm doing what I can right now to see my way clear of this mess I'm in with Theo."

Lash took my hand off his face, and held it in his callused one. "I'm not sorry, either." He squeezed tightly. "I know Devlin offered you the option of including me, if you agree to his terms. I know you are going to give him another Oath, and that you'll do it soon, at the latest by the end of the year."

Oh shit. I went still.

"Don't do it unless you can handle what he'll ask of you," Lash said sternly. "Dev is sure you'll agree to whatever he asks, so long as he tells you we can be together, but I don't want to be with you at the expense of you being unhappy. I know Dev. With him, nothing is ever free."

Technically, Dev temporarily had already given permission, but to speak up about that would not be in my best interests. "Do you know what he's planning to ask?"

"No," Lash answered, uneasy. "I'd guess that he'd want me to give you times when you were just with him, maybe for me to not sleep with you in his bed at all, maybe for me not be with you without him there, participating. But it might be something worse, Sar, so just be careful. Don't do it because you know how much I want to be with you, out of some sense of pity or something—"

I had to alleviate the tension of the moment. "If I did it out of affection for you, would that be okay?" I said lightly.

Lash lunged, pushing me to the truck seat beneath him as he bared his fangs, hissing. I went still beneath him, fear making my stomach churn. A drop of saliva fell from his left fang onto my cheek. I recoiled, shivering. "You don't joke about this, Sarelle," he hissed angrily. "Now say you understand what I said, that you won't do it unless you are okay with his terms. Before you agree to anything, you ask him to list out those terms for you, all of them! Got it?"

I nodded, trembling.

"Say it!" he hissed angrily.

I repeated his words back to him, my tone uneven.

My sudden fear enraged him further. "I care about you!" he hissed. "Don't sell yourself for me, Sar. You sold yourself to Dev back in January for the lives of Danial and Theo, and you saw how well that worked! Don't do it again unless it's what you really want!"

"All right," I whispered. "Please let me up."

Lash leaned in closer, his grasp tightening. "Serena told me yesterday I could come to her, that I was welcome in her bed. I could see by her eyes she didn't want me, that she was still afraid of me! You put her up to it, Sar! Listen to me and listen well, because I am only going to tell you this once: don't interfere in my sex life ever again! I don't need your help to get laid!"

"I won't," I said, struggling beneath him. "Now let me go."

Lash brushed my neck with his fang tips, stopping my struggles instantly. "Just one thing more, Sar. My appointment tonight is with a woman I know by the name of Gina. She'll take care of my needs for me from now on. She's very skilled. It's been too long for me already without any sex, and I'm aching for the release of a woman's touch. And she is all woman."

My stomach really roiled then, imagining him with another woman, loving someone else. Hurt flooded me, then jealousy.

Lash moved off me abruptly. "Get out of my truck," he hissed. "Before I say something I'll regret later."

I hustled out of the truck, slammed the door, and darted for the house. If I could only get inside the house I'd be okay. I needed to not see him, to not think about what he was going to do with her, about how it was making me feel...

The door of the truck opened behind me. Lash reached me in a few strides, then spun me around to face him. "For a woman who says she cares for me, you seem awfully upset to think I might get some relief," he hissed, his dark eyes flashing. "Where do you get off being hurt and trying to make me feel guilty? Dev told me we could be together late last night. All today I waited for you to say something. You never said a word about it, not even in the truck just now, when I gave you the opportunity to come clean! You were happy to let me think you wanted me as much as I wanted you, because you didn't have the guts to tell me you just didn't want me anymore!"

"I still want you," I whispered, afraid of him and of how much I longed to touch him. "But I can't be with you! We can't—"

"Sure you can," Lash hissed eagerly, each guttural word exploding with desire. "I'll make it easy for you." He kissed me deeply, molding his body to mine.

God, he felt so good... "Stop, please," I said, breaking away from him.

"No," Lash hissed, his grip on me tightening. "I tried to be respectful of your decision to be with Theo because I thought you deserved a choice. But Dev was right and I was wrong. You need a little force, for someone else to take control from you. Your body's giving away your lie." He kissed me again forcefully, backing me up towards his truck as his hands roamed my body. "I can smell your wanting—"

"Stop it!" I shouted. I tried to push him away. Lash easily grabbed my hands in his and held them out at my sides, bracing me against his truck. Kicking my legs apart, he ground his pelvis up into mine lightly, letting out eager hisses, his forked tongue stroking my neck.

My heart raced, the sensation of his erection teasing. Quickly, the rising heat became undeniable, making me go limp in his grasp. And the lust for him was all my own. *God, he felt so good. He would feel even better inside me...*

"You've got me hard as rock for you," Lash hissed, lust heavy in his tone. "And it feels so good to you, doesn't it? You know how much better I can make it for you, Sar. Just say the word, and I'll take you to the nearest hotel. I'll make love to you, I'll go down on you, whatever you want, for as long as you want. You can have all of me, everything I have, everything I can give you. And whenever you're ready for more, all you ever have to do is ask—"

I shivered eagerly in his grasp, images of my fantasy instantly replaying. I wanted to tell him yes...

"I won't ever leave you less than satisfied."

I blinked at him, uncomprehending. "What?"

Lash pulled back from me, breathing hard. "Dev's not taking care of business," he hissed, smirking knowingly. "None of your boys are. You smell so strongly of your lust it's coming off you like waves, you're needing to be fucked so bad!" He grasped my hips, letting out a groan as he leaned into me. "When I get done with you, you'll be singing a different tune, if you've still got any voice left that is—"

I went from shock to instant rage, my eyes narrowing in fury. "Let me go, you son of a bitch! We're done here."

Lash drew back, his face a mask of rage. "Forget the hotel! How about I fuck you right here, against the truck?" he hissed sarcastically. "You wanted me to that night in the Everglades, just like you want me to now. Maybe we'll even have an audience, if I'm hearing things right—"

I reached up and slapped him across the face. Lash snarled, baring his fangs, but didn't hit me back. The front door was suddenly thrown open, crashing back against the side of the house.

Oh shit. Lash had said we had an audience. He'd meant...

"Get the fuck out of here, Lash!" Theo growled, pointing his gun at Lash. "Get your hands off my wife unless you want holes in you."

Lash looked up at him, hissed, and then pulled me in front of him, blocking his body.

"Hey!" I said, more annoyed than scared. "What the hell do you think you're doing?"

Lash ran his tongue up the side of my neck, making Theo's growl. "She still thinks about me inside her, Cat!" Lash said in a jovial tone, smirking. "How good each thrust felt going in, and how hard I made her come. But I'll bet she doesn't want to fuck you anymore!"

Theo roared, stepping off the deck and launching himself at Lash. Lash gave me a shove, pushing me out of the way as Theo barreled into him, knocking him off his feet. Then they were rolling over and over, punching each other, and snarling. Lash tried to bite Theo, but Theo grabbed him by the throat, holding his fangs out of reach of his body, as he smashed him in the face with his fist. I grabbed Theo's gun, but they were both moving too fast for me to aim accurately.

"Stop it!" I screamed. "Lash! Theo! Stop it!"

Theo—easily the stronger one—pummeled Lash, holding him down with one hand, and smashing his face repeatedly with his other fist. Lash took a few punches, and then he quickly resorted to his knife, drawing it soundlessly and sliding it between Theo's ribs to the hilt in a swift deft movement. Theo gasped and went limp when he felt it go in. Lash kneed him in the groin, and then rolled over on him, pushing the knife in deep and twisting it.

"Stop it!" I yelled, firing into the tree above them. The bullet's explosion severed a few small branches that fell beside them. Neither of them even looked up.

Lash twisted the knife again, making Theo cry out. "You should use your brain, you jackass," Lash hissed. Giving it one last twist, he pulled his knife out of Theo.

Theo grunted with pain, and lay there gasping, looking murderously at Lash, holding his bleeding chest, blood oozing steadily through his fingers. Lash cleaned off his blade in the dead grass, resheathed it with a click, and then looked up at me. His face was very bloody and bruised, but the wounds were already healing before my eyes, the bruises lightening, and disappearing.

He truly was in his prime. I'd never seen a were heal that fast, never. "Leave."

"I didn't start this. But I damn sure finished it. Keep your kitten on a leash, Sar."

The fuck he hadn't. "Go, Lash," I said again. "And don't come back unless you can promise not to fight with my husband." I held the gun in my hand, but I didn't aim it at him, because we both knew I wasn't going to shoot him, despite what he had just done to Theo. I wasn't going to provoke him, not with Theo on the ground hurt.

Lash's eyes narrowed, but he nodded. "Remember what I said, Sar," he hissed meaningfully, spitting blood out of his mouth onto the grass. "I meant it. Don't take an Oath to Dev unless you can handle the consequences." He turned, quickly walked to his truck, and then got in. Lash gunned the engine, spinning his wheels on the icy driveway once before they caught, and roared off.

Jesus. That had been close.

I went over to Theo and helped him to his feet. "Come inside, and I'll bandage you up."

"It's healing already," Theo said, obviously embarrassed that I'd seen him beaten again by Lash.

Like there was another way their fight could've ended. "All the same, it's deep. Let me sew it closed."

"Do you think about him, like he said?" Theo said pointedly. "He's young again, and handsome—"

I sighed, flushing. "Sometimes, yes," I admitted. "But that doesn't mean anything. Let's get inside."

"It does matter," Theo retorted. "It matters to me. I thought at first you wanted him. I saw you sitting together in the truck, but when you slapped him I felt like an idiot for not realizing sooner what was happening."

Theo had been watching us the whole time. I flushed, wondering if he had seen how much I was fighting myself as well as Lash.

"I went to get my gun, but it took me a second—"

Why'd he grabbed the 9mm, not the explosive bullets gun? I pushed that thought out of my mind quickly. I didn't like where it was heading. "I can guess what you might have thought. What happened is that Dev told Lash he had the green light with me. He thought that I was going to jump back in bed with him. I...well, I handled it badly. But that doesn't matter. He knows I meant what I said now."

I helped Theo to his feet, and we walked inside slowly. His wound was healing quickly, his flesh knitting together, but I still made him get onto the bed anyway. "Take off your shirt."

Theo pulled it over his head slowly, grimacing in pain. After taking it into the laundry, I returned, trying hard not to look at his muscular chest, his tight abs, or his wide shoulders. "Not that I'm not grateful, but why are you home?" I asked, cleaning the blood off his side with antiseptic. "I thought you had guard duty tonight."

"I do," Theo said, wincing. "I'm supposed to be on the way there now."

"I'll call Danial, tell him you're hurt—"

"I'm healing okay. Just lie here with me for a few minutes, and let me heal the rest. If you can teleport me in a half hour, I'll be okay. It was a clean cut. Lash doesn't usually use poison on his blades. If he had, I wouldn't be healing as well as I am."

Good to know, just in case. "I can do that," I said, cradling his body close and stroking his hair. "I'm glad you're okay—"

"You still smell like him," Theo said under his breath.

Men were all assholes. "Look, I'll go—"

Theo stopped me, wincing. "Stay here with me. It doesn't matter."

I eased back down next to him. "Since when?"

"You're here with me," Theo said softly. He stroked my arm. "You want to be here, don't you?"

"You're half naked in my arms and you have to ask me that?" I whispered, giving him a smile.

"That's not an answer," Theo said, growling slightly.

"I'll answer, if you'll tell me the truth about why Lash bothers you so much. And don't say it's because of me, because you hated him long before."

Theo was quiet for a minute. "Because he's a snake, that's some of it: his very scent bothers me. As for the rest, some of it is his association with Devlin, and the things I heard that he's done, or saw him do. There's you. There was Neoline, years ago, and another woman I...um...thought was attractive. Some of it's just the way he's rubbed my face in the dirt so many times, always saying he's better than I am. And it's true that he is—"

And here I'd thought he'd resist expounding. "You have to stop attacking him," I interrupted. "You just end up injured. And one of these days he's going to hurt you badly, even if he doesn't kill you."

"I know," Theo said ruefully. "He knows what buttons to push. I know I have a temper, and with him it's worse. I have almost no control with him. Just seeing his smirking face, hearing his hissing voice infuriates me. And every time I think of him fucking you, his naked body on yours, I want to beat him into pulp."

I beat down the quick flush of desire. "Promise me you'll stay away from him, Theo."

"I'll stop provoking him, I promise. I'll avoid him whenever I can. Good?"

"Good," I replied, relaxing back into his arms.

"Are you going to answer me or not, Sar?" Theo said, his blue-grey eyes serious and guarded

"Of course I think about you and me," I answered, giving him an incredulous look. "I've thought about us every day for weeks now. I was daydreaming about us about thirty seconds ago—"

"Do you want me?" Theo interrupted. "Here and now?"

I blinked, caught off guard. "You said that you—"

"Yes or no, Sar," Theo growled, his tone rough with base need.

"Yes," I said hoarsely. "I want you very much, Theo."

Chapter Thirteen

Theo kissed me deeply, pulling my body against his. The instant I felt him stiffen against me, my head went back and my eyes closed, savoring his arousal.

But Theo wanted far more than a little stroking. He pulled off my top and unhooked my bra, throwing it aside. A half second later, Theo was on me, suckling my breasts, drawing a sharp gasp of abandon from my parted lips. Together we slid off my jeans, our movements hurried. Instantly, his hands roamed my naked body, touching me as he hadn't touched me for weeks. I writhed, glorying in the feel of his powerful hands sliding over my hot skin. Eagerly, I reached for his jeans to free him, but Theo pushed me back on the bed. He got up and moved to the dresser. Sliding off his jeans to puddle at his feet, he began putting on a condom.

Watching him, my fiery lust fizzled. Theo obviously believed Lash had given me something. There was no other plausible reason, now that I was fixed. Uncomfortable, I stretched out on the bed, pretending I hadn't seen. I'd believed Lash when he'd told me that he hadn't been with anyone else but me. *Maybe this was a mistake...*

Theo carefully eased his body down on mine as he kissed me, his tongue darting into my mouth as he slipped his finger into me. He stroked my clit gently, making me murmur as I pushed up with my hips, eager to be filled. The sensations burst within, my breaths coming fast.

"Ah!" I cried, arching my back. "Please..."

Theo's fingers stroked my sudden slickness. "Sar, I've never felt you so wet for me," he said lustily, his blue eyes dark with desire. "Not ever—"

"Stop talking," I said in desperation, reaching down to squeeze his organ eagerly. I moved beneath him, trying to impale myself as I rubbed the slick head of him between my legs. Theo moved into position above me, and with a quick press of his hips, he slid himself inside.

"God, yes!" I moaned, pulling his lips to mine, as I pushed my body tight to his. "Please take me—"

Theo began thrusting gently. Each motion felt exquisite as paradise. I wanted only to feel each thrust and yet I had to move, desperate for the friction, the sheer joy of taking all he had to give with each plunge. This was heaven; what I had been longing for, dying for. Just coming last night hadn't been nearly enough, no matter that Devlin had been good with his mouth and hands. I'd wanted to feel a man inside me, feel him taking me for all I was worth…

"Sar, what's wrong?" Theo whispered, stopping. "You're shaking."

"I needed this so bad," I moaned. "Please don't stop."

Theo's eyes narrowed. "You've gone to Dev every week."

"He's injured, Danial's ignoring me, and I've stayed away from…anyone else," I said throatily, clasping him. "Please, Theo, please, I need you." I slid my hands down across his hard chest and around to his lower back, pressing up with my hips.

"So you missed being touched?" Theo said softly, thrusting into me very slowly, and slowly drawing himself almost all the way out. My only reply was an incoherent groan, as I arched my back, unwilling to release him. Theo paused just inside and flexed, teasing me, watching me writhe beneath him. "Or did you miss me touching you?"

"Yes, I missed you!" I cried, staring up into his eyes recklessly. "I kept hoping every night that you would reconsider, that you would reach out to me, to touch me, to hold me."

"Tell me you want me," Theo said throatily, again thrusting in very slowly and out again.

"Please, Theo," I panted. "I want you. Please, please, make love to me now."

"I want you, too," Theo groaned. He kissed me, then buried himself inside in a sharp thrust, his body pistoning on mine as his hands grasped my nipples, twisting and pulling. I let out a muffled cry, sucking on his tongue wildly, the sensations he was making me feel almost too much in their intensity.

He was close, but I was closer. I came in a few seconds, crying out loudly in release, clinging to him. My contractions around his engorged penis brought him roaring loudly, pulsating inside me as he came again and again.

The abrupt loss of tension was incredible, knocking out the foundations of my well-placed walls. Within a few moments, I was crying brokenly. Theo hugged me as I cried in his arms, venting all my pent up frustration, fear, hurt, anger, and mistrust.

When I got control, I reached up with shaking hands to touch his face. I ran my fingers lightly across his cheek, and back into his hair, giving him a tentative smile. He brought his hand up to the back of my head, and kissed my forehead lightly with his lips, then lowered his head to rest his forehead against mine, closing his eyes. I relaxed against him, closing my own. We stayed that way for a long moment, unmoving.

"Stay here," Theo said softly. He withdrew, and then got up, stripping off the condom and throwing it away. He picked up the phone, and began dialing.

I watched, surmising he was calling Danial.

"Danial, I'm going to be late," Theo said gruffly, his eyes roaming over me as he talked. "I had a run in with Lash and he knifed me. I'll be fine, but it will be a few hours. It was deep, and—"

Theo blushed and stopped talking. Then he said goodbye and hung up, grabbing another condom from the dresser.

"He knew, didn't he?" I asked.

"He said to say hi to you, and to come in when we were done," Theo said rolling his eyes. "He wants to see you tonight, Sar. He asked that you pack a bag to spend tonight with him."

That was odd. "Suddenly I'm forgiven?"

Theo ignored me. "Again?" Theo asked, kissing my neck softly. "Or are you finished?"

"Again, please," I instructed in a false commanding tone, lying back and giving him a smile.

He laughed, then slid the condom on. "That's my line," he said, kissing me thoroughly.

I gave him a seductive smile, and then rolled over, straddling him. Rubbing my hips against his, I stroked his firm shaft between my thighs. Theo let out a growl, then took my waist in his hands and lifted me, settling me very slowly down on his swollen shaft. I let out soft cries as he slowly penetrated inch by delicious inch.

"I know what you like," he growled softly. "Come here." He guided my lips to his, his mouth devouring mine, and he began stroking me deeply, moving my hips with his hands. With a sigh of bliss, I lost myself in the sensations.

* * * *

Theo made love to me for two hours straight, until we were covered in sweat and I was too sore to continue. We held each other in exhausted silence as our breathing slowed.

"I love you," I whispered. "Please tell me we can work out things between us, Theo. I don't want to lose you because of what I did."

"I love you, too," Theo said, looking down at me tenderly. "I forgive you, for what you did, Sar. I believe you, when you say you haven't been with Lash, and I trust you, when you say you won't be with him again."

Tears ran down my face. I hugged him quickly.

"Will you go get tested, so we can be together without protection?" Theo murmured. "I know you said Lash told you he hadn't been with anyone else, but I don't trust him, Sar. And he gave you that disease back in the spring—"

"I'll make an appointment tomorrow," I blurted, very ashamed. "I need to go anyway, as Stephen said he needed to make sure my body was doing okay after having had Devon and Venus. The vampire virus peaked, but I haven't been back to get myself checked."

"Do you want me to go with you?" Theo offered.

"No, though we have therapy we need to go to together next week," I reminded him.

"How did it go today?" Theo said, nuzzling me. "You said it was bad. Was Carol nervous?"

"We all were," I replied thoughtfully. "Carol told Lash that he had to be my friend, and not my lover, and he agreed that was what he needed to do. That was mostly it."

"That's all you talked about for an hour?" Theo said skeptically. "It doesn't look like it had any lasting effect on Lash, from what he tried to do to you on our front lawn."

I was disappointed in Lash about that myself. Yet maybe this was how he really was. But I was partly to blame, too. I should have told him the truth, and not made it seem as though I was pining for him, like some long lost love.

"Well, we also talked about how he hated you," I added. "Carol made me understand that I have to not be too friendly or casual with him, because it might lead to something more. I'm a touchy kind of person, and I reach out for someone to console them before thinking about if they are a man, and how they might take it—"

"That isn't your fault," Theo interjected. "You've always been that way."

"I have to not be that way with him. It's not fair to him, either. I don't want to make this harder for him than it has to be."

"What did he mean to you?" Theo asked, turning to look at me. "I know you, Sar, that for what happened to have happened, there must have been something between you."

I avoided his gaze. "He was just comfort," I lied. "Someone I turned to when I felt trapped. But that's over now." I bit my lip, then snuggled close to Theo, willing him silent.

About the Author

Tara Fox Hall's writing credits include nonfiction, horror, suspense, action-adventure, erotica, and contemporary and historical paranormal romance. She is the author of the paranormal action-adventure *Lash* series and the vampire romantic suspense *Promise Me* series. Tara divides her free time unequally between writing novels and short stories, chainsawing firewood, caring for stray animals, sewing cat and dog beds for donation to animal shelters, and target practice.

Other works by the author with Melange Books, LLC

Return To Me
Surrender to Me
The Origin of Fear in Spellbound 2011 Anthology
Night Music in Midnight Thirsts II Anthology
Partners in Midnight Thirsts II Anthology
Kink in Wicked Christmas Wishes Anthology
The Oath in Wicked Christmas Wishes Anthology
Bedtime Shadows Anthology
Make Me Behave Anthology
Latham's Landing, An Anthology

The Promise Me Series
Promise Me, Book 1
Broken Promise, Book 2
Taken in the Night, Book 3
Taken for his Own, Book 4
Promise Me Anthology, Book 4.5
Immortal Confessions, Book 5
Her Secret, Book 6
Point of No Return, Book 7
Lost Paradise, Book 8
Dark Solace, Book 9

Coming Soon

Eye of the Storm, Book 10, Promise Me Series

www.ingramcontent.com/pod-product-compliance
Lightning Source LLC
Chambersburg PA
CBHW030450250626
47154CB00003BA/1201